**THE PROUD, THE PASSIONATE, THE POSSESSORS
DRIVEN BY HONOR, BY AMBITION, BY
DANGEROUS EXTREMES OF LOVE . . . OR HATE**

JOHN COOPER BAINES—The Apaches called him THE HAWK for his cunning, swiftness, and deadly ferocity. A man who passionately loved the beautiful woman he married and the dynasty he built, he now faced an enemy who vowed to destroy them both.

DOROTÉA BAINES—Precious young wife of The Hawk, who had saved her from a cruel abduction, but could he protect her from ravaging nature's dangers and an evil man's perfidy?

GENERAL SANTA ANNA—His handsome virility hid a blackguard's heart; his smiling diplomacy masked a raging ambition and a ruthless plan to eliminate his greatest rival, The Hawk.

MADALENA—Her voluptuous beauty made her the play-thing of decadent rulers until fate brought her a man to claim her love with his passion, to save her soul with his courage.

ENRIQUE—Born a nobleman, destiny made him a slave in a house of shame, but no chains could imprison his spirit . . . or keep him from hoping The Hawk would set him free.

ADRIANA—Her fresh loveliness made her the object of more than one man's desire . . . and now her fickle heart fueled a dangerous competition between The Hawk's son and a rival for her love.

A Saga of the Southwest Series
Ask your bookseller for the books you have missed

A Saga of the Southwest
Book VIII

Shadow
of
the Hawk

Leigh Franklin James

Created by the producers of
Wagons West, White Indian, and
Children of the Lion.

Chairman of the Board: Lyle Kenyon Engel

BANTAM BOOKS
TORONTO · NEW YORK · LONDON · SYDNEY · AUCKLAND

SHADOW OF THE HAWK

*A Bantam Book / published by arrangement with
Book Creations, Inc.*

*Produced by Book Creations, Inc.
Chairman of the Board: Lyle Kenyon Engel.*

Bantam edition / October 1985

ISBN 0-553-25165-1

Published simultaneously in the United States and Canada

*Bantam Books are published by Bantam Books, Inc. Its trademark,
consisting of the words ''Bantam Books'' and the portrayal of a
rooster, is Registered in U.S. Patent and Trademark Office and in
other countries. Marca Registrada. Bantam Books, Inc., 666 Fifth
Avenue, New York, New York 10103.*

PRINTED IN THE UNITED STATES OF AMERICA

O   0 9 8 7 6 5 4 3 2 1

*To Marla, George, and Lyle Kenyon Engel,
who have sustained me throughout this series.*

The author acknowledges his indebtedness to Saundra Healy-Will, zookeeper, aviary department, Lincoln Park Zoo, Chicago, and to Joseph Milton Nance, history department, Texas A&M University, College Station, for data vital to the creation of this novel. Finally, to Fay J. Bergstrom, the author offers a well-merited accolade for her tireless and devoted transcriptions of his dictation, thus freeing him from the bondage of the typewriter.

SAGA OF THE SOUTHWEST FAMILY TREE

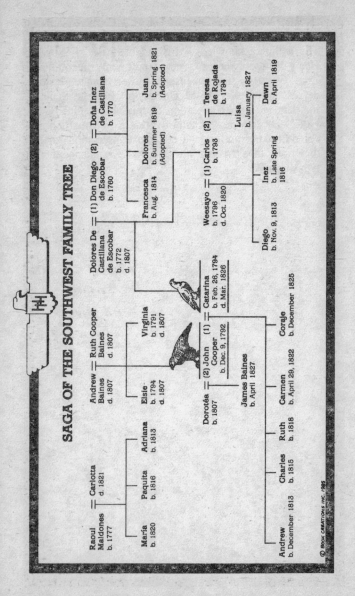

Raoul Maldones b. 1777 == Carlotta d. 1821

- Maria b. 1820
- Paquita b. 1816
- Adriana b. 1813

Andrew Baines d. 1807 == Ruth Cooper Baines d. 1807

- Elsie b. 1794 d. 1807
- Virginia b. 1791 d. 1807

Dolores De Castillana de Escobar b. 1772 d. 1807 == (1) Don Diego de Escobar b. 1760 (2) == Doña Inez de Castillana b. 1770

- Francesca b. Aug. 1814
- Dolores b. Summer 1819 (Adopted)
- Juan b. Spring 1821 (Adopted)

Dorotéa b. 1807 == (2) John Cooper b. Dec. 9, 1792 (1) == Catarina b. Feb. 26, 1794 d. Mar. 1826

- James Baines b. April 1827
- Andrew b. December 1813
- Charles b. 1815
- Ruth b. 1818
- Carmen b. April 28, 1822
- Coraje b. December 1825

Weesayo b. 1786 d. Oct. 1820 == (1) Carlos b. 1793 (2) == Teresa de Rojada b. 1794

- Diego b. Nov. 9, 1813
- Inez b. Late Spring 1816
- Luisa b. January 1827
- Dawn b. April 1819

© Book Creations Inc. 1985

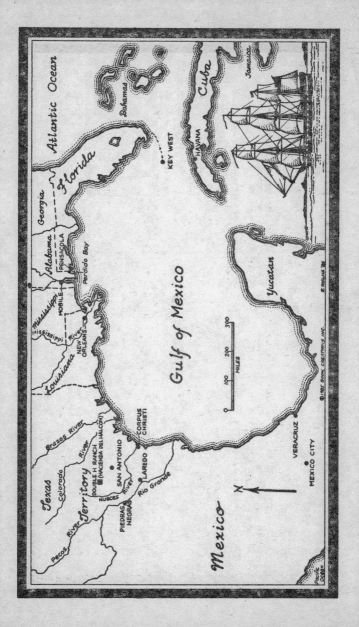

Prologue

It was Sunday, October 14, in the Year of Our Lord 1827. The weather was still and sultry as a blazing sun shone down upon the city of Veracruz. Some miles away, at his lavish estate of Mango de Clavo, General Antonio López de Santa Anna was entertaining several very special guests. Conveniently, his wife and her two maids were away in Mexico City, for she had told him that she wished to see some old friends and also replenish her wardrobe. He had generously given her a far larger sum than she had expected, and she had parted from him in a grateful and happy mood, which particularly suited his purposes.

For one thing, it meant that he could enjoy the adulation and carnal subservience of his beautiful young half-breed mistress, Martina Arrigalte, who lived some fifty miles away in a little house that he had secretly purchased for her. But more important than that, he could meet in undisturbed intimacy with several promising officers on whom he counted to advance his own overwhelmingly ambitious scheme to become ruler of all Mexico. For was he not already being hailed as *el libertador*?

Indeed, only yesterday he had addressed a group of wealthy and influential *hacendados* in the city of Veracruz on the subject of the deplorable state of the lax government. It had been a fervent, patriotic speech, proclaiming that the land of Mexico was sacred soil and must be protected not only from the Spanish rule that had once tyrannized it, but also from the ever-growing threat of the accursed *americanos* to the north. Of course it had not been necessary for him to

1

add that the government needed a man like himself at its head—that much was self-evident.

Acclaimed already for the military genius that he was, Santa Anna, still young and handsome at thirty-three, knew when to hold back and wait in the wings until the time was ripe to step forward. This was not yet the time. Still, it was well to make plans for that day, for a wise leader treated time as his ally, rather than as his enemy.

After all, had not time helped the *hacendados* to forget how he had attacked the clergy and the rich landowners, when first he had begun his tireless quest for utmost power in this new republic? Back then, his shrewdly calculated appeal had been to the impoverished *peones,* the have-nothings, to whom he had promised equality through liberation. But even as he spoke passionately and eloquently, he had been practical enough to understand that, without the backing of the rich *hacendados*—and, for that matter, even the clergy, whom he personally despised, although he himself was a devout *católico*—he could never achieve his goal. And because ultimate power, in the end, could not be grasped without force, he had also curried the support of the best military leaders, whom he needed behind him when the exact moment came for his entrance upon the stage as *el libertador*. As Santa Anna well knew, the secret was to surround oneself with ambitious men and to dominate them—for his own ambition was greater than any of theirs could ever be—while all the time leading them to believe that his own success was dependent entirely upon theirs.

Only yesterday evening he had welcomed to his villa two such ambitious men—*Comandante* Felipe Molinas from Puebla, who commanded a regiment of crack troops loyal to the current *presidente,* Guadalupe Victoria; and *Coronel* Luis Dominguez from Orizaba, a ruthless man who had risen in the ranks from corporal since the Battle of Medina in the year of 1813. The two officers had been received at Mango de Clavo in the most ostentatious way, food and wine brought to their private apartments in the huge villa, and the loveliest and youngest of his *criadas* on hand to be their tender companions through the night.

Now, as they sat at the table of the beautifully furnished

dining room this Sunday afternoon, they were being served a light repast of roasted chicken, sweet yams, ripe melons and berries, tequila, and the best vintage French wines and aged cognacs that Santa Anna had been able to import from Le Havre. The *criadas* who had attended them last night acted as serving maids and, still clad only in filmy shifts and wearing sandals, brought in boxes of fine Havana cigars and liberally filled the imported glass snifters with more cognac. Then, at Santa Anna's abrupt gesture, they left the room.

"Mis amigos," Santa Anna said, beaming, as he turned to *Comandante* Molinas at his left and then *Coronel* Dominguez at his right, "it was gracious of you to accept my invitation to spend a few hours at my humble villa."

"It was most hospitable of you to invite us, *mi general,*" Luis Dominguez, a thickly bearded, stocky man in his thirties, obsequiously retorted as he inclined his head toward his general.

"Both of you have come to my attention for your fine military records, your loyalty to our beloved country, and, above all else, your devotion to the code of military discipline and efficiency, which our young country must have if we are to make our way among the great nations of the world," Santa Anna pompously declaimed.

He smiled at them in turn, until each officer felt that the distinguished general wished nothing better than to become the most intimate of comrades with him, and was appealing to him alone. At five feet ten inches—taller by far than most Mexicans—with a broad forehead and piercing dark eyes, and clean-shaven—another rarity among the people of his country—General Santa Anna was indeed a striking figure of a man. Both the colonel and the major admired and envied him—especially his uniform, with all its medals—and each, in his turn, secretly hoped that he might do his general some outstanding service that would elevate him from a subordinate role into a rank almost equal to that of *el libertador*.

Santa Anna leaned forward and spoke in a confidential tone. *"Mis amigos,* let us for the moment forget rank and speak as I have addressed you, as friends. I know you to be loyal to me, and I know that each of you is worthy of the

highest promotion that I, as your commanding general, can
accord you.''

"You flatter us, *mi general,*" Felipe Molinas murmured
as he lowered his head in an overt gesture of servile respect to
this man whose name was already being bruited throughout
all Mexico as the coming *presidente.* In fact, in some
quarters, there were those who spoke secretly of a new
emperador—but that word had an unhappy significance to
it, ever since Augustín de Iturbide had ill-advisedly proclaimed himself emperor of Mexico and subsequently been
forced to flee the country, only to set foot again upon Mexican soil without knowing that a law had been passed ordering
his execution.

"Let us review our nation's situation at the moment,
mis amigos," Santa Anna went on in that purring voice he
used when he wished to take a man into his particular confidence. "We have a *presidente* in the good General Guadalupe Victoria. That is not his real name, of course, but one he
adopted in honor of the glorious revolution that brought
Mexico its independence from tyrannical Spain. Forgive me
if I labor with you over history, for history teaches us much,
if we know how to use its lessons."

"That remark alone shows your greatness, *mi general,*"
Molinas unctuously put in, and was rewarded with a beaming
smile from his general.

"Our good *presidente* adhered to the Plan of Iguala six
years ago," Santa Anna went on, "and two years after that
joined me in the revolt against a man whom I had loved and
supported, but who, alas, out of vanity and ruthless self-
seeking, had proclaimed himself *emperador.*" Santa Anna
shrugged and spread out his hands with a sigh. "As all of you
know, I tried my best to save Señor Iturbide, but he was not
aware of the law passed against his setting foot again upon
Mexican soil. Unfortunately, before I could intervene, he was
executed. Be that as it may, our *presidente,* Guadalupe
Victoria, was first chosen as a member of the provisional
government and then lifted to his present office. But you see,
gentlemen, there is strife between the conservatives and the
liberals, and his administration is not a total success. Vice
President Bravo will, I fear, revolt against him before much

longer. And this is why I have called you here. If there is a revolt, all the nation will know is that our government founders, and at a time when we are trying to fend off those *americanos* who settle in a province that belongs to our great country. I have done what I could to have this law of settlement revoked, to prevent more *americanos* from coming into Texas. I have even given orders to my troops to enter their settlements and to search for weapons, to determine if there are any conspirators who plot against our government. This you know already."

"Yes, *mi general*," Luis Dominguez spoke up with a smiling nod. "If it were not for leaders like you, the *gringos* would take over our entire country—may they all burn in the hottest hell *el Diablo* can heat for them!"

"I say amen to that, dear Luis," Santa Anna purred. "But bear with me a moment more. There is Vicente Guerrero to be considered, if this struggle between Bravo and Victoria grows serious. It is true that Guerrero was a fine general during the revolution, and that later he even won victories over Iturbide's troops. But then he sided with the land-owning *creoles* and the clergy and accepted the leadership of Iturbide." Again Santa Anna shrugged. "As you know, he is now a member of the provisional government. I think that he is against Bravo and would defend our *presidente*, if need be. But if that takes place, he may well succeed Victoria. Yet I will not forgive him for his adherence to the landowners and the clergy. Both of you know that I myself came from not particularly noble lineage and might even be considered a *peón*."

"Never, *mi general*!" *Comandante* Molinas loyally interrupted.

"But it's true. Let's face facts, *mis amigos*. I have always been on the side of the impoverished, of the man who toils like a slave on the land. If fate—and *el Señor Dios*, who is fate—decrees that I shall truly be a *libertador*, I swear before you that there shall be no poor in Mexico, no disinherited, no slaves. But to this end, we must have both military strength and, alas, since an army must be paid, also money."

"Sagacious of you, *mi general*," *Coronel* Dominguez vouchsafed.

"I have had a project for some little time, and I will not
bore you with the details, save to tell you that it involves an
immense fortune in pure silver, mined by *esclavos indios*
when the Spaniards ruled *Nuevo Méjico*. It so happened that
a *gringo* found the hidden mines and appropriated the silver.
My contention is that *Nuevo Méjico*, like Texas, belongs now
to Mexico, and that this *dinero*, all this silver, truly belongs
not only to the Mexican government, but to the poor, to the
peones who will no longer be slaves or impoverished, if I can
bring this treasure back into the coffers of our beloved country."

"Such a sentiment does you great credit, *mi general*,"
Molinas said with a smirk.

"I have taken some steps to retrieve the silver, and I
may tell you, *mis amigos*, that even now I wait to hear of the
success of my little plan. But if it should fail—although I
entrusted it to a man in whom I have the utmost confidence—
the three of us may put our heads together and figure out
some way of strengthening our forces so that we can achieve
what is best for the Mexican people."

He was about to continue when his majordomo, Bernardo,
suddenly entered the dining room, hurried to his side, and
bent to whisper in his ear. Santa Anna nodded, leaned to the
majordomo to whisper something back, and then, as the
servant left the dining room, addressed his guests.

"*Mis amigos*, I crave your indulgence for a few moments. An emissary of mine has come a long way to deliver a
very important message. Enjoy yourselves, and your charming maids will see that your every whim is catered to, I am
certain of it."

"It is gracious of you, *mi general*," Dominguez smilingly responded as he rose to his feet and gave Santa Anna a
formal salute.

"Oh, please, Luis, this is not a military meeting, but an
affair between me and two of my good friends. There is no
need for the observance of rank. But I thank you all the same
for your loyalty, *mi amigo*." With this, the bemedaled, black-
haired general left the room, then followed his majordomo to
a little salon just off the entrance, where his visitor awaited.

"Esteban Moravada!" Santa Anna held out both hands
with a warm smile. "I have longed to see you all this while,

Esteban! Come into my study, *amigo*, and there you will tell me what has been accomplished!''

The lean, gloomy forty-three-year-old officer hesitated, then replied, ''I am afraid I do not bring you the best of news, *mi general*.''

''I can see that you've ridden long and hard, and I know that you are devoted to me. That really is all that matters, Esteban. Come now, I'll have a *criada* bring us some refreshments. *Por Dios*, it's almost time for my *siesta*—and you could use one yourself, *hombre*.''

These cheerful words from Santa Anna greatly heartened the morose colonel. From Piedras Negras, it had been a journey of over six hundred miles to the estate of his superior, and he had accomplished it in nineteen days, changing horses in almost every town. Yet the news he bore was not good; the plot to separate the *gringo* John Cooper Baines from his silver, by means of kidnapping his beautiful young wife, had failed. All the way back, during which time he had paused only briefly to eat and drink and to catch a few hours of sleep, he had been at his wit's end trying to formulate some new plan that would bring the silver bars of the accursed *gringo* into the possession of Santa Anna. Yet the silver was in a New Orleans bank vault that was guarded around the clock, and the *gringo* Baines's *Hacienda del Halcón* was a veritable fortress; it would take an army to attack either with any hope of success.

Santa Anna jovially linked his arm with that of his subordinate, led him into the study, then clapped his hands to summon a pretty young *criada*, who entered and bowed her head in respect to her master. Santa Anna ordered her to bring hot chocolate and little cakes, then gestured his guest toward a comfortable chair opposite his desk and seated himself. He lit cigars for both of them, and they smoked in silence until the *criada* brought the tray and left. ''Now, *amigo*, your report,'' he smilingly demanded.

''As you know, *mi general*,'' Moravada began, ''I sought out my cousin Juan Cortizo, who was a leader among the Yaqui, to enlist his tribespeople. They made several raids against the settlers on the Brazos—''

''Yes.'' Santa Anna's face darkened, and his eyes narrowed. "That nest of *americano* rebels, which I myself visited not long ago and whom I compelled to kiss the sacred soil of Mexico to show their allegiance to our glorious country!" With this rhetorical interruption, Santa Anna put the palm of his right hand over his medals and struck an imperious pose.

"The very same, *excelencia*. The Yaqui were beaten off because those *gringos* were better armed than we had suspected. So then Cortizo and I contrived the idea of kidnapping the wife of this John Cooper Baines. I stationed myself in Piedras Negras, while Cortizo and some of his men went to the *gringo*'s ranch. He was to send a courier to me, telling of his success or failure. When more than a week had passed, I sent my own courier, who did not return."

"Go on, go on, *hombre*!" Santa Anna impatiently exclaimed, leaning forward across his desk, his dark eyes narrowing as he studied the face of the hesitant colonel.

"An attack was made on my life some two days after I had sent my courier to the meeting place where Cortizo was to have brought the woman, *mi general*," Moravada replied. "He was a Yaqui, apparently one of Cortizo's men. Fortunately, I was able to kill him before he could stab me to death. From this, I understood that the plan had failed. Doubtless—I do not yet know how it occurred—the *gringo* and his men were able to track his woman down and kill the Yaqui warriors, and very likely my cousin with the others. I'm very ashamed to tell you this, *mi general*—it looks as if all hope of our getting the silver by holding the woman as hostage and bargaining with the *gringo* has failed."

To the colonel's surprise, Santa Anna merely shrugged, then rose from his chair, taking his cup of chocolate with him and sipping at it daintily as he went to a map on the wall and studied it. Turning back to face Moravada, he finally replied, "I thank you all the same, Esteban. You have served me well, and it is certainly not your fault. I shall think of something else, and I'll have news for you. However, now, as your commanding officer, my orders are that you ride at once to Mexico City. I wish you to find out what is happening in the government there—it seems to be in a most unstable condition. Just yesterday morning I spoke to several wealthy landowners, and I told them that because nothing is being done in our capital, we are in a turmoil throughout the country. We have a need for strong leadership—which I hope that, before much longer, the enlightened people of Mexico will realize, and therefore choose me to bring this country the respect it merits from all other nations."

"I am at your service, as always, *excelencia*!" Colonel Moravada sprang to his feet and smartly saluted.

"Come now, I can see your dedication—but you haven't yet finished the collation that sweet little Carlotta has just brought us. Finish it, do so, by all means! Then I'll have my stable boy bring one of the finest horses I own for your journey. You will report to me as soon as you have learned what is going on at the capital."

"I shall make it my business to take notes, *excelencia*, and you will find them painstaking and exhaustive."

"But this I already know," Santa Anna chuckled. "You see, Esteban, I have the greatest confidence in you. Fear not—there will be other ways in which you can win your promotion. I shall consider this silver and think how it can be brought back to Mexico, as it will, as it *must*."

A short while later, Santa Anna himself came down the stone steps to see off his colonel, who was mounted on a magnificent black stallion from the Mango de Clavo stables. The colonel saluted again, then headed the stallion west toward the capital.

Santa Anna watched until the dust of the road hid the receding figures of rider and horse. He turned to his major-domo. "Bring me Pascal and Joaquín, Bernardo."

"At your command, *excelencia*." The majordomo bowed and hurried off.

A few moments later, two swarthy, stocky men in their thirties, wearing the uniforms of privates attached to Santa Anna's personal bodyguard, hurried to him and saluted.

"Pascal, Joaquín, a few minutes ago Colonel Esteban Moravada rode off on my black stallion toward Mexico City. He will have taken the road from Mango de Clavo to the highway. He is a traitor, and what is worse, I have just learned that he is going over to the side of Pedraza, my mortal enemy, the man who believes that only he should be *el presidente* of Mexico."

"You wish us to arrest him and bring him back, *mi general*?" Pascal demanded.

"I would not waste the time on a court-martial, Pascal. I empower you both to dispatch him before his treason can be revealed and perhaps become a scandal. If one of my own trusted officers, one on whom I have depended so often in the past, should so betray me—it is something that my enemies would make sport with, is it not?"

Pascal smiled crookedly. "We shall finish him for you, *mi general*."

"You will find me grateful. Oh, and one more thing—"

"Yes, *mi general*?" they said in unison.

"Bring back the horse, and see it is not hurt. *Gracias, amigos*."

Colonel Esteban Moravada had ridden about ten miles and slackened the stallion's gait as he neared a fruit orchard. It was truly a magnificent horse that his general had given him, a sure mark of Santa Anna's favor. This thought comforted the *coronel;* he had actually been sweating when he had had his interview with *el libertador,* and even now could hardly believe his good luck in the warm reception Santa Anna had given him. Well, his loyalty and his achievements were a matter of record, assuredly, and Santa Anna, as a commanding general, must surely recognize merit when merit was due. He promised himself to buttonhole many of the legislators in the capital and to learn all he could about the state of the government, and then he himself would bring back such lengthy and detailed reports as would show his general that Esteban Moravada had other skills besides his military abilities.

From down the road behind him he heard the sound of horses coming quickly, and he wheeled in his saddle. He frowned. He recognized the men's uniforms; they were members of Santa Anna's own bodyguard—doubtless *el libertador* had forgotten something and wished to convey a message posthaste.

He turned his horse to meet them. As he did, one of the men drew a pistol from his belt, leveled it, and pulled the trigger. Colonel Moravada had seen the swift, covert act, lifted a hand to protest, and opened his mouth—but he did not utter a sound as the ball went through his temple. He fell like a log from the black stallion, which reared and snorted wildly, until Joaquín rode up and seized the reins.

"We'd best bury him here at the edge of the orchard, *mi amigo*," he instructed Pascal, who nodded as he slipped the smoking pistol back into his belt.

Little more than an hour later, the two men were back at Mango de Clavo, and when Pascal proudly informed Santa Anna that it was he who had fired the pistol that had ended the life of this traitor, Santa Anna smiled warmly and clapped him on the back. Then, turning to Joaquín, the general said, "And I see you have brought back my fine stallion as well. You have both done an inestimable service to our country, as well as for me personally. Come downstairs—I shall reward you. I keep special gifts for just such happy occasions as this in a little room in the wine cellar."

"Your Excellency is far too kind. We did it to serve you," Joaquín speciously protested.

"I understand that. And your sentiment does you great credit, Joaquín. I promote you and Pascal to the rank of *sargento*, each of you. And, of course, the pay will be commensurate with the rank. But what I am about to give you is beyond that, and it is what your services to me are truly worth."

He led them down to a dungeonlike room, and once they were inside the door, Santa Anna drew from the pockets of his uniform two pearl-handled, one-shot derringers and calmly put a ball through both their brains.

As he closed the heavy door behind him and went to order the majordomo to dispose of the bodies discreetly, he chuckled to himself. Pascal and Joaquín would never be able to say that it was he who had ordered Moravada's death. And with Moravada out of the way, no one could now betray his plot to acquire the *gringo*'s great hoard of silver, which might well involve war with the United States, were it ever pursued to its finality.

After the majordomo had left him, he straightened his shoulders, took a deep breath, then went back to his guests, who were still in the dining room. Upon his entrance, Felipe Molinas and Luis Dominguez sprang to their feet, looking very much abashed, for the two pretty *criadas* who had waited upon them and who, last night, had shared their beds, had been seated upon their laps, exchanging passionate kisses with them.

"Oh, now, *mis amigos*"—Santa Anna laughed with an indulgent gesture—"didn't I tell you this was a private little affair, and that we must not stand upon ceremony? Go on as you were; I like to see my friends enjoy themselves. You, María, and you, Paulina, can't you see these gentlemen are languishing for your caresses? Go back upon their laps, wind your soft arms around their necks, and kiss them tenderly."

Much to the embarrassed discomfiture of the two officers, the girls promptly obeyed, and Santa Anna seated himself at the head of the table, lit a cigar, and smilingly watched the amorous byplay. Then, after a few moments, he said solemnly, "Now let me touch again on what I had been discussing with you, my dear friends, before I was summoned to receive the report of a trusted officer. I do not know what orders you will receive in the next few months, but if you should find yourselves near the Rio Grande, it is my personal wish, as your ranking general, that you harass the *gringos* in the settlements all that you possibly can. Under constant attack, they will be weakened, and I believe that because of the political situation in *los Estados Unidos*, you may have every hope of success. From the reports I have, the *americanos* are not too happy with their *presidente*, the señor John Quincy Adams, and there is much talk that next year General Andrew Jackson will replace him. Thus the attention of that country to the north of us, that land of the accursed *gringos* who seek to destroy our traditions and to take our land, will be focused upon its own affairs of state, and it will not watch too closely what is happening in this Texas province, which is part of our own Mexican territory of Coahuila. Do you follow me?"

"We are at your command, *mi general*," both officers replied.

"It will also take money to pay a strong army, if these *tejanos* have the impertinence and the gall to challenge us," Santa Anna continued. "This is no order, understand me, *mis amigos*—but if in the course of your patrols and your guarding of our sacred borders, you come across wealth that is in the hands of these *gringos*, appropriate it. After all, they live upon Mexican soil, and as such, their *dinero* rightfully belongs to this land, which is so impoverished that I shall devote my life to freeing it from that curse." He offered them his most ingratiating smile. "And now, if you will excuse me, gentlemen, I am in need of a *siesta*."

As Santa Anna left the room, the smile vanished from his face. "It is an evil star that has come upon my horizon," he murmured to himself as he walked down the tiled hallway. "I am convinced, however, that it is only temporary. I must have that treasure—I swear I will not yet give it up! But how shall I regain it, now that it has been placed in a strengthened bank and is still owned by that hated *gringo* whose *estancia* could hold out against a regiment of my best soldiers? Well, it is said that the one above, *el Señor Dios*, moves in most mysterious ways His wonders to perform—perhaps I shall learn the way before I am done with this devilishly lucky *gringo* who constantly foils my plans. If only I had that wealth, I would rule all Mexico, and there would be no one to challenge me! And, *por Dios*, I mean one day to have such power—"

And then, because he was *católico*, he crossed himself and, looking upward at the ceiling, humbly added, "Of course, it must be with Your help, *Señor Dios*! I would not have it otherwise."

One

Slightly more than three weeks had passed since John Cooper Baines and his *vaqueros* had rescued his beautiful young wife, Dorotéa, from the fierce Yaqui abductors, and life at the *Hacienda del Halcón* had begun to return to normal. By way of celebrating their happy reunion and giving thanks to God for their good fortune, the tall, blond-haired Texan proposed a fiesta at the end of the second week of October. It began with a joyous outdoor mass presided over by the young Padre Pastronaz, after which John Cooper, Dorotéa, and her father, Raoul Maldones, accompanied the priest back into the church, Dorotéa holding her infant son, James, in her arms. There, she and John Cooper knelt to take communion and then, with the priest following them in prayer, to give thanks for Dorotéa's safe deliverance.

In the evening, the sound of music and laughter filled the air, and torches and cooking fires lit up the great courtyard of the *Hacienda del Halcón* as blond-haired Bess Sandarbal and the comely young Rosa Lorcas—the chief cook for the ranch—together with several of the *vaqueros'* wives, turned sides of beef and mutton on the spits, while Miguel Sandarbal, Bess's husband and the ranch's *capataz*, carved generous portions for all the *trabajadores* who came forward with their plates. Yams and ears of sweet corn were roasted over the coals, then doused with butter churned by hand from the finest cream yielded by the prize cows of the great ranch. Several of the wives of the *vaqueros* had prepared fiery chili in true Mexican style, a great favorite among the *trabajadores*. And there were fruits and cakes and huge trays of flan, made with the eggs and milk that the ranch so liberally produced.

Several broad wooden tables had been set up in the courtyard, and at the center of the largest of them, John Cooper sat between Dorotéa and Raoul Maldones. Ramón Santoriaga, who once had served under the overwhelmingly ambitious Santa Anna and was now in charge of the military defense of the great ranch, sat across from them, next to his beautiful wife, Mercedes. Doña Inez, beloved by all and respected even more now as the bereaved widow of the gallant Don Diego de Escobar, former *intendente* of Taos, sat at the head of the table. At the opposite end sat Don Diego's son, Carlos de Escobar, with his charming wife, Teresa.

John Cooper Baines had only to look at the radiant face of his former brother-in-law and best friend to know that Carlos, like himself, had successfully begun a new life of great happiness and joy after the tragedy of losing his first wife. It had been over fifteen years ago, John Cooper recalled, that he himself had fallen in love with and married Carlos's sister, Catarina de Escobar. He had brought his bride from Taos to this fertile valley on Texas's Frio River, where Carlos had helped them found the Double H Ranch—so called because of John Cooper's Indian name: *el Halcón*—the Hawk. But after giving him five fine children, Catarina had been taken from him, murdered in cold blood by an emissary of Santa Anna's. . . .

Such gloomy thoughts quickly fled John Cooper's mind, however, as Rosa Lorcas approached the festive table with a plate of hot biscuits and a pot of honey, to be greeted by a chorus of approval. Now married to the *vaquero* Antonio Lorcas, Rosa was radiantly happy in her new life at the *Hacienda del Halcón,* and late tonight, when the feast was over, she had a secret to tell her beloved *esposo*: She was with child. John Cooper felt slightly guilty about having learned of this from Dorotéa, even before Antonio himself knew.

Setting the plate and the pot down before Doña Inez, Rosa murmured, "Señora, I baked these biscuits especially for you, knowing how you've always liked them."

"It was thoughtful of you, *querida* Rosa, *gracias*," the handsome, gray-haired woman responded with a gracious smile.

Seeing this, Carlos de Escobar rose to his feet, wineglass in hand: "A toast, *mis amigos*, to the beautiful and courageous Doña Inez de Escobar, whom the good *Señor Dios* willed should be my second mother, and who made my gallant, great-hearted father, Don Diego, happy in a strange new world after he had been unjustly banished from the Spanish court." Turning to her, he bowed as he held the wineglass out. "I salute you and thank you, and wish you long, happy years with all of us, *mi madre*."

Tears welled in Doña Inez's eyes as she rose to her feet amid the calls of *"¡Olé!"* and the sound of handclapping. "You are too kind, and I do not deserve such flattery," she said in a voice choked with emotion. "I am the one who was blessed in giving what happiness I could to Don Diego, whose memory will live forever in the hearts of everyone on this great hacienda. *Gracias*, dear Carlos. And I am blessed again to see you with your sweet *esposa*, Teresa, and your child, for Don Diego and I both prayed you would find happiness after your great loss."

She turned to regard those at the table, smiling at Ramón and his wife, Mercedes, then at Bess Sandarbal, the blond wife of the old *capataz*, and finally at John Cooper, his wife, Dorotéa, and the latter's father, Raoul Maldones. At last she said, as she straightened and lifted her own glass, "But the one who should really make a speech is John Cooper, who, perhaps more than anyone else here, brought us all such joy and prosperity, first by saving the life of *mi hijo* Carlos, and then by wedding Catarina, and finding this fertile land and establishing this great ranch where all of us live in harmony and peace. To you, my dear John Cooper, whom my Don Diego loved as if you had truly been the son of his own blood, I drink now and urge you to acknowledge our esteem for you!" With this, putting her glass to her lips, she turned to the blond Texan and saluted him.

John Cooper flushed with embarrassment as those around the table smilingly urged him to respond to Doña Inez's toast. "Thank you, it's very kind of you, dear Doña Inez," he stammered, "but truly, this is a night for all of us, and I'd only spoil it with a speech—"

"You'll please me greatly, *mi corazón*, if you'll make one all the same," Dorotéa murmured to her sinewy, yellow-bearded husband. "For my sake, then, if for no other reason?"

John Cooper's blush deepened as she put a hand to his shoulder and kissed him on the lips in front of all of them, and Raoul Maldones, with a hearty laugh, added his own encouragement: *"Por todos los santos, mi yerno,* you seem more terrified of saying a few words to those who are closest to you than you were when you boldly came back to Buenos Aires to rescue me from the firing squad! Come, *hombre,* show your mettle!"

Applause greeted this sally, and John Cooper slowly got to his feet, drawing a deep breath, and then glancing somewhat wryly down at Dorotéa, who pretended to look very stern and gave him an insistent nod. He lifted his wineglass and bowed to Doña Inez as he began, *"Mi madre,* I have been called brave by my distinguished father-in-law, Raoul Maldones, but I am the first to say you are truly the bravest of all of us. I respected you from the first moment I met you back in Taos, and I have been honored to have you as a mother-in-law and, beyond that, as a dear, loyal friend who gives inspiration and inner strength to a man's endeavors."

There was more applause, and all turned to smile at Don Diego's widow. She could not suppress her tears any longer and brushed at them with her napkin, lowering her head to acknowledge this accolade.

John Cooper waited a moment till all was still, his mood becoming solemn, for memories had begun to flood his mind now, as this night of celebration turned his thoughts back to his days as an orphan, forced to survive in what was virtually a wilderness. At last he said, "I give thanks to God, who made us all, and for the blessings we enjoy tonight—in family, friendship, and in the well-being of the *trabajadores,* who, with their families, make up this great *hacienda.* May we continue to prove the strength of our community against the dangers from enemies who are envious of our good fortune and wrongly fear we mean to take their own."

They were silent now as they listened to him. He paused

a moment to choose his words and collect his thoughts, then went on, "I don't want to change the happy feeling all of us share tonight, but I have to say what's been on my mind for some little time now. All of you know that this land of Texas technically still belongs to Mexico, and that we and the settlers on the Brazos are here because of the grants the Mexican government gave to the Austins. But you know also that we've had some trouble with Mexican soldiers and spies and the like who've tried to harass and attack us. The way I see it, that's likely to be an even greater problem for us to deal with in the future, especially if General Santa Anna seizes supreme power across the border—which, in my opinion, anyway, is what he's been trying to do all along."

He paused again, frowned, and looked out into the night, at the glow of the cooking fires, hearing the music borne on the gentle breeze that came across the Frio River. Again he took a deep breath and, squaring his shoulders, declared, "But tonight, thinking back on the adventures I had before I came to Taos and then here to Texas, remembering the kinds of people I met and lived with, I've learned this much—our great strength is our unity, our working and living together, and our belief in God and doing what's right for ourselves and our children. And I've a feeling here"—he touched his left chest—"that this strength can prevail against whatever enemies or perils we may have to face before, one day, this land we're on becomes part of a great new country of which I'm proud to be a citizen, the United States."

On the very same day that Colonel Esteban Moravada arrived at the villa of Santa Anna, a courier brought a letter to the *Hacienda del Halcón* addressed to Doña Inez de Escobar. When she saw that it was from Mother Superior Cécile of the Ursuline Convent School in New Orleans, where her precocious daughter Francesca was enrolled, her face brightened and she eagerly opened it. But a moment later, she uttered a stifled cry and put her hand to her mouth, her eyes wide with disbelief. Carlos, who was on the patio nearby, chatting with his wife, Teresa, noticed his stepmother's startled reaction and, excusing himself to Teresa, hurried up to her. "*Mi madre,* what is the matter?" he anxiously demanded.

"I cannot believe what Mother Superior has just written to me! Carlos, this is dreadful—I never dreamed—she is so young! You know how we discussed that there would be a danger in her remaining here with your son Diego, and now this. Oh, what am I to do?" Doña Inez burst into tears, clutching the letter in her hands as she stared appealingly at Carlos.

"Teresa, *querida,* come here," he called to his lovely wife. "We must help *mi madre.*"

Doña Inez drew a deep, quivering breath and shook her head. "Let us go into the house, dear Carlos, Teresa. I do not wish anyone to know of this yet. Not even John Cooper and his Dorotéa—ah, how wonderful it has been to watch them enjoy what is a kind of second honeymoon! And the dear *Señor Dios* has looked down upon them and blessed them because they are so devoted to each other! But I tell you, I was not prepared for this letter." She sighed again and retreated into the house, heading for the room that her late husband had often used as his private study.

Puzzled, Carlos and Teresa exchanged a wondering look and followed Doña Inez, who waited until they had entered, then closed the door and gestured for them to seat themselves on a comfortable couch. She clutched in her hand the letter she had just received, bit her lips, walked across the room, then uttered an anguished sigh. "It is kind of you, *mi* Carlos, Teresa, to keep me company now, when I have this weighty problem on my mind. You will recall that Francesca wrote to me a few months ago, telling of having volunteered to work at the Ursuline Hospital when the yellow-fever epidemic struck New Orleans. She obtained permission, to be sure, from the mother superior, since her grades had been excellent and she had shown great progress. In any case, there is no doubt she is a most dutiful and compassionate girl, but the trouble is she's young and impressionable—"

Carlos and Teresa both nodded sympathetically, again exchanging a wondering look. Both silently agreed that Doña Inez must be allowed to express herself exactly as her feelings directed her to do, and so they waited to hear the contents of the letter.

Doña Inez turned to them, her face distraught with anxiety, tears brimming in her beautiful dark eyes. "It appears that one evening she observed the driver of a calash bringing a young man, a Señor Jack McKinnon, stricken with the fever, to the hospital. The driver was most abusive, wanting to be rid of the sick man, so Francesca intervened and saw to it that the unfortunate soul was admitted immediately; she even went to the head doctor to arrange for it."

"That shows her kind, sweet heart," Teresa gently proffered.

"Of course, of course, there is no fault in the world that can be found with that, dear Teresa! It is what happened after this, and of which the mother superior speaks in her letter to me, that most concerns me, as you shall see. Wait a bit—I am so upset, I am telling this very badly—"

"There is no need for haste, *mi madre*," Carlos kindly broke in. "We will do all we can to help, so tell us as you wish what so greatly troubles you."

"Yes, *gracias*. Oh, *Madre de Dios*, I could not have dreamed she would be so impulsive, so foolish—and she is still so young!" Doña Inez lifted the crumpled letter in her right hand and pressed it against her heaving bosom, then uttered a choking sob and shook her head. After a moment, regaining some composure, she resumed. "According to this letter that Mother Cécile sent me, Francesca came down with a bad cold about the time the letter was written, and so the good nuns thought it wisest to isolate her from her companions and send her to the nearby hospital, for the best medical care, so that she could completely recover. As you can understand, Mother Cécile was afraid that, with the strenuous work Francesca had done during the yellow-fever epidemic, her system might be weakened and the cold could easily turn into something far more serious."

"A wise precaution, indeed," Carlos said, uneasily glancing at Teresa, for he was not yet certain what all this portended.

Again, Doña Inez shook her head and sighed, glanced down at the crumpled letter in her hand, and finally went on, "In the course of going to Francesca's room to take those articles of clothing and other effects she might need during her stay in the hospital, Mother Cécile came upon an unfinished letter in an envelope addressed to this Señor Jack McKinnon. The envelope was not yet sealed, and of course the sister recognized the name of the young man to whom Francesca had been so greatly attracted when she had helped to save his life. The mother writes here that she debated with herself whether she should read this, and finally she decided to, since the general rule is that all outgoing letters are first read by the mother superior of the school. She was not prepared for what, she read—no more than I am now, I can tell you, dear Teresa, Carlos!"

"Yes, go on, *mi madre*," urged Carlos.

Doña Inez rubbed away a tear. "The upshot of it is that Francesca, out of a clear sky, had written to this Señor McKinnon avowing her love for him and asking if she might not visit him at the plantation, so that they might talk over their plans for the future! But—it is incredible! Why, we all know that my dear Francesca is not yet fourteen, and here already she is thinking of what amounts to an elopement, and with a man nearly twice her age! I do not know what to say or to think at this moment, it so upsets me!"

"Do calm yourself, *mi madre*." Carlos went to her and put his arm around her shoulders. "I can see that this is a most delicate subject, and we must take care not to hurt Francesca, certainly not to ridicule her—and I am not even so sure that to scold or upbraid her would be wise."

"I feel the same way, Doña Inez," Teresa interposed, coming to stand beside her mother-in-law. "She has, as you know, dear Doña Inez, a keen intelligence, and perhaps it is this that makes her forget her actual age. That in itself is certainly understandable. And besides, just like Carlos, I have observed her here on the *hacienda* and seen how gracious she is, how good at heart, with a true capacity for love. Certainly, if this Señor McKinnon is at all an honorable, decent man, then he would not take advantage of her. Indeed, he would be greatly flattered that the young girl who helped save his life pays him the supreme tribute of avowing that he is her first love." She blushed a little as she turned to her husband and confided, "Don't you know, *mi querido*, that a girl or a woman never forgets the man with whom she first falls in love? He may even be an utter scoundrel—but she cannot forget that, at one time, in the first dawn of her emotions, she was drawn to him. I think that is what has happened to Francesca, pure and simple."

"You are both most kind to try to comfort me," Doña Inez told them. "You are both so dear to me, and I respect your opinions. But now, what do you think I should do? Should I go to New Orleans and talk with Francesca?"

"Yes, if you wish, surely," Teresa replied. "But I think that, were I in your place, I should first write a letter to Señor McKinnon and tell him quite frankly that because Francesca feels close to him, since she helped save his life, she has become greatly infatuated with him. I would urge him to write her a letter, gently disabusing her of this notion—to be sure, if he wishes to wait several years until she is of an age when she can properly consider marriage, that is something else again. However, I do not feel that this will happen. He is, did you not say, about twenty-six or twenty-seven years of age, Doña Inez?"

Distracted, Doña Inez could only nod and sigh again.

"Then I feel that by now he would surely have a *novia*, perhaps already someone to whom he is solemnly and formally pledged and whom he intends to marry. He could write Francesca to tell her this, to thank her for her wonderful sentiments concerning him, and to wish her well and do it in a way that would not break her heart. That is why I believe you should write him a letter, *mi madre*."

"Yes, yes, that certainly makes sense. And since the mother superior was thoughtful enough to include the address of Señor McKinnon, I can do that at once. And then I shall write a letter of maternal advice to my daughter. I should be grateful if you would read it before I send it off, dear Teresa," Doña Inez avowed.

"I should be honored, *mi madre*."

Don Diego's handsome widow seemed somewhat calmer as she lowered herself into a chair; but then, as if trying to justify her feelings, she passionately declared, "As you know, Carlos, late in my marriage to your father, when I thought I was beyond the boon of bearing him a child, the Holy Virgin to whom I constantly prayed blessed me among women by letting me bear Francesca. And because of this, and because she gave your father such wonderful happiness and pride late in his life, I am more concerned for her well-being than even for yours, Carlos, for you are already a man. And this is why I have turned to you for counsel, since we are all of one family, united by blood and by memories, by loyalty and devotion.''

Carlos, deeply touched by this declaration, came to his mother-in-law and knelt, bore her hands to his lips, and murmured, ''We, too, Teresa and I, care dearly for my half-sister Francesca. It will be well with her, you'll see, *mi madre*. Now go ahead and write your letter. And write one also to the man of whom she is so fond, and I will say my prayers, as will my wife, that he will be an honorable man and know how to keep from breaking Francesca's heart.''

After Carlos and Teresa had left, Doña Inez seated herself at her late husband's desk and began to write. The first letter was to Jack McKinnon at the sugarcane plantation upriver from New Orleans. Doña Inez chose her words with care, often looking up at the crucifix that hung on the wall opposite the door.

She wrote as if Jack McKinnon himself were present in the room, as if she had the opportunity to talk earnestly with him face to face. After explaining the contents of the unmailed letter and how she had come by it, she concluded:

> . . . Please understand, Señor McKinnon, that Francesca is of a kind, outgoing nature, and having lived here on this ranch for so many years, isolated from the opportunities to meet many different people, it was only natural that she become attracted to someone worldly yet decent like you. Indeed, the very fact that she was drawn to you presupposes that you are a kind and most honorable man; and when you expressed your gratitude for what she had done to save your life, she undoubtedly read into this far more than was intended.

You see, Señor McKinnon, my daughter is not yet fourteen. I should be infinitely grateful to you if you could write to her and discourage her—as gently as you know how, I pray you—of her infatuation. If you do feel so disposed, I beg you also to send me a copy of your letter to her.

I pray for your happiness and continued well-being, and that of my daughter.

> Sincerely,
> Doña Inez de Escobar

After folding the letter and sealing it in the envelope, she knelt to pray, crossing herself and bowing her head. Then, resuming her seat at the desk, she began her letter to Francesca:

My dearest daughter:

It is my hope that, by the time this letter reaches you, you will have recovered from the fever about which Mother Superior wrote me. I hope you will not fall back in your studies, so that when the Christmas holidays approach, you may come home to spend them with me and all your many friends here, who have asked me to send along their best wishes for your speedy recovery.

Francesca, my darling, you know that I have never been one to pry into your life, and I learned quite by accident of your letter to the Señor Jack McKinnon. I think I know how much he means to you, my dear one, and I am certain he is a fine, honorable young man, the sort of man of whom assuredly you are worthy.

But reflect a little—you are not yet fourteen, and even though first love is sweetest of all, as the poets tell us, the time is not yet right for you to say, "This is the one, the only one, whom I shall love for the rest of my life." You must first become a woman, dearest Francesca, and those years are not too far off, although you may think so now.

Do understand, my daughter, that I do not in any way reproach you for the sentiments you expressed toward Señor McKinnon. They tell me that you have a great capacity for love, and that, by the same token, you must have seen in him qualities that you admire and that you will find in the true *esposo* whom *el Señor Dios* will send to you in time. Look upon this as a happy friendship, for I am sure that he will wish you well and perhaps even tell you of his own plans for the future. You have no way of knowing, my dear one, whether or not he may already be betrothed to a woman much older than you and thus more suitable to him as a wife. Nor do you know that life on a sugarcane plantation would give you the chance to broaden your horizon and to increase your wisdom and your gifts for helping others.

When you come to me for the holidays, dear Francesca, we shall talk of this in private, and in the meantime, I hope that there will be no heartbreak for you, and that you will not be too angry with the good Mother Superior for having come upon your letter and writing me to tell me of what you had in mind. I only feared that a hasty and impulsive act might have hurt you deeply, and I never would wish you to be hurt, my darling daughter.

I enclose a locket that your dear father gave me on our first anniversary, and I wish you particularly to read the inscription on the case—it is: "May God watch over and keep you always." This is my wish for you, dearest Francesca.

Your loving mother

She carefully folded the letter and put it into the envelope with the locket. In the morning, she knew, several of the *vaqueros* would be riding to Corpus Christi to pick up a prize bull that John Cooper Baines had ordered from his factor in New Orleans. From Corpus Christi the two letters would go by ship to New Orleans. And with them would go her anxious prayers that Jack McKinnon would respond in a way that would not shatter young Francesca's first innocent dreams of love.

Two

After luncheon the next day, during which time the *vaqueros* rode off to Corpus Christi with Doña Inez's letters, Miguel Sandarbal joined John Cooper and Raoul Maldones for their weekly inspection of the western boundary of the great ranch. For the tall, blond Texan, this inevitably brought to mind that they would be retracing the route his beautiful Dorotéa had ridden with their baby when she had been abducted by Juan Cortizo and his Yaqui companions. He could not help shivering, much as if someone had walked over his grave; and yet, it was well to clear away all the shadows, since the child had not been harmed, Dorotéa had been lovingly restored to him, and their union was stronger than ever because of the courage and ingenuity she had shown during her captivity.

All the same, remembering what had once happened, John Cooper told Miguel and Raoul that it would be a good idea to have Ramón Santoriaga accompany them. Having once been an officer attached to the same regiment as Santa Anna, Ramón would know best how to strengthen this boundary and prevent any recurrence of what could well have been a tragedy. As John Cooper informed Raoul, halting his horse near the house that Ramón occupied with his wife and children, "When Ramón Santoriaga learned the true nature of Santa Anna, he came here to begin a new life, and his knowledge of military tactics has already saved us from several attacks, particularly by renegade Comanche and the Comancheros."

"You think, then, John Cooper," Dorotéa's father spoke

up, "that there will be others sent by Santa Anna against you?"

"Yes, *mi suegro*," his son-in-law responded. "I believe I now understand a good deal more of what has been happening to the settlers on the Brazos. I think it was all part of Santa Anna's plan. He's a cunning, ambitious man, a schemer, and we're going to have a lot of trouble with him before all this is over, or my name isn't John Cooper Baines."

He shook his head, as if to clear his mind of these disturbing thoughts, and Miguel and Raoul glanced at each other and nodded with understanding. Miguel remembered how the tall blond man whom the Indians called *el Halcón* had endured his own private hell when Francisco López, that other tool of Santa Anna, had killed Catarina. And just recently, again because of Santa Anna's overwhelming greed and ambition, Dorotéa's life had been endangered. Yes, the old *capataz* could easily understand why John Cooper wished to strengthen the ranch so that there would be no weak point anywhere, for one day soon there could very well be a showdown between *el Halcón* and Santa Anna himself.

Ramón came out of his house to greet the riders, and hearing John Cooper's invitation to join them, he said good-bye to Mercedes and hurried to his own stable to saddle his horse.

"You'll remember, Ramón," John Cooper said as the party set off, "how the old shepherd, Virgilio, was killed near his hut on the western boundary of our land, just before my Dorotéa was abducted. I'm afraid that from now on we'll have to anticipate what enemies may do to us, even if it requires posting permanent lookouts."

"I quite agree with you, John Cooper," Ramón answered in flawless English. "Until now, however, I have refrained from suggesting this myself, for that would mean taking some of the *trabajadores*, or even the *vaqueros*, from their daily duties."

"If that is what is necessary, then so be it," replied John Cooper, as Miguel and Raoul nodded in agreement.

"You have already decided, I know," Ramón continued as they plodded on in leisurely gait, "to keep the sheep concentrated at this end of the ranch."

"Yes, mainly because there's suitable graze for them here," John Cooper explained. "Perhaps cattle are more profitable in this climate, but when I persuaded my then father-in-law, Don Diego de Escobar, to leave Taos and come here, he brought with him a sizable flock of sheep. In any case, we make a modest profit from the wool, we have mutton for the table—both for the *trabajadores* and ourselves— and frankly, it varies the activities of the ranch, which is useful in keeping everyone happily occupied. To be sure, if we are left in peace, I have plans for raising more cattle, as well as palominos, because the profit on those superb horses is very great, and they are much in demand. I could see that when I went to Argentina." He turned to smile at Raoul Maldones, who nodded agreement. "Unfortunately, because of the unsettled situation in the government of that country, I can't depend on it as an avenue of profit. But my factor in New Orleans, Fabien Mallard, can be counted on to find new areas for the sale of not only the palominos but also some of my ranch-bred bulls, productive cows, and prime-stock heifers."

As they rode on, Ramón mused, "I recall that, close to the southern end of the western boundary, there is a hill with a view for many miles on all sides, including of the river itself. I had it in mind that we might permanently station one, or perhaps two, sharp-eyed *vaqueros* there, well armed, and perhaps with a field glass. We could build them a small shelter and a stable, and they could keep watch for intruders, and ride swiftly back to the *hacienda* at the first sign of trouble."

"An excellent idea!" John Cooper said. "And I know the exact hill you are talking about, Ramón—it indeed has a commanding view." John Cooper turned to the white-haired *capataz*. "Miguel, tomorrow let's set some of the *trabajadores* to building just such a watch house, and work with Ramón here for guidance as to how it should be constructed. It's good weather for building, crisp and clear and much cooler at night, and the men should be able to get a good deal done in short order. We'll have the first watch posted, with the swiftest horses on the ranch, before the end of the month."

"I'll see to it at once, *Halcón*," Miguel said with a nod.

Raoul now spoke up. "I only hope that the settlers on the Brazos are as well prepared. The Yaqui recently attacked them, too, did they not?"

"Yes," John Cooper replied. "And I'm sure Santa Anna was behind that as well. I shall never forget how that arrogant man who styles himself *el libertador* rode boldly into the settlement with an armed force and compelled the settlers there to kiss the ground to prove their loyalty to Mexico, whose soil he claimed it was. Legally he may have been right, but his method of trying to obtain that loyalty was damnable. And when old Henry Hornsteder refused to bow or kneel except to God—the answer that you or I or any other brave man would have tendered to that upstart—Santa Anna shot him down like a dog. They will not soon forget that cold-blooded murder, you can be sure, and I have no doubts that they are constantly strengthening themselves against future attacks from the south."

"Do you think that we shall soon have war with Mexico, *Halcón*?" Miguel anxiously asked.

John Cooper took a deep breath and pondered a moment, then solemnly responded, "I don't pretend to be a prophet, *mi compañero,* but all the news we've had from down south indicates as much. It's pretty obvious how badly Santa Anna hates us *gringos,* and should he come to supreme power in Mexico City, it will not be long, I venture, before he arrives in Texas with an army behind him."

All of the men were silent as they reflected on John Cooper's words. The bright sun, the beauty of the vegetation about them, belied the sinister shadow that the mention of the name Santa Anna evoked. Yet all who rode with John Cooper understood that this was a shadow that threatened to obscure the very freedom they and their loved ones enjoyed.

By now, the riders were approaching the far western boundary. Suddenly, Raoul pointed toward the southwest. "There's a herd of cattle—do they belong to this ranch, *mi yerno*?"

John Cooper leaned forward in his saddle, squinting, then shook his head. "No, they're wild—from across the Rio Grande, probably. At least twice a year, wild longhorns, as well as scrub animals that have left abandoned villages and mingled with them, cross the river and head this way, Raoul. Some of them are worth cutting out and taking into our own herd. But that's a chore for the *vaqueros*." He turned to Miguel. "If that herd is still in the vicinity in the morning, Miguel, you can send out a few riders with their lariats—and be sure you include Raoul's friend Felipe Mintras, or he'll be angry with you for not letting him show off his skill with the *bola*!"

"I'll see to that as well, *Halcón*," Miguel said, chuckling. "You know, *Halcón*, he's been insisting that I try my hand at that pampas *reata* of his at least twice a week, so that I can show the *vaqueros* and the *trabajadores* how it's done. He tells me that a real *capataz* should be able to do everything all his men do, and better."

"And of course, Miguel," John Cooper bantered with a boyish grin and a wink at Raoul, "he's absolutely right. When the day comes that you can't do things better than the youngest *vaquero* in our outfit, it'll be time for you to step down as *capataz*."

Miguel bristled, sat more erect in his saddle, and glared back at John Cooper. "Respectfully, *Halcón*, I may tell you that that day is not yet here. And if the good *Señor Dios* wills, it will be a long time in coming! I'll go see for myself how many *vaqueros* we'll need to round up the best animals of that wild herd!"

With this, seizing his *sombrero* and whirling it about his head, and crying out "¡*Adelante!*" he rode toward the milling herd, which numbered perhaps fifty, half of them nondescript and stunted of growth, bearing out John Cooper's explanation of their origin.

Miguel galloped on ahead, while John Cooper, frowning, urged Ramón and Raoul to follow him. "I shouldn't have said what I did," he grumbled. "He'll take it to heart and try to show off, as if he were a boy! Look—I was afraid of that—"

Suddenly, a steer with sharp, curved horns—an animal almost as large as one of John Cooper's own Texas longhorns—detached itself from the herd and, head down, charged Miguel Sandarbal's horse.

"Look out, Miguel!" John Cooper shouted. "He's been

eating locoweed—he'll try to gore you or your horse! Get away from him, *pronto*!"

But the white-haired *capataz* either did not hear, or heard and ignored John Cooper's warning, for he rode on, still waving his *sombrero* and crying out Spanish expletives intended to scare the animals into flight so that he could count them and tell with his practiced eye which ones were worthy of being rounded up and branded. He deftly skirted the charging steer, putting it at the back and left of his horse.

Unexpectedly, however, the steer turned and followed, and now Ramón and Raoul both cried out a warning, but in vain. Savagely, with a snort of fury, the maddened steer dipped its head as it charged again, goring the left haunch of Miguel's gelding. With a shrill scream of pain, the horse toppled, flinging Miguel heavily to the ground, where he lay on his side, stunned.

Grinding his teeth, John Cooper galloped on, while at the same time unsheathing "Long Girl" from the side of his saddle. He always kept his father's Lancaster rifle primed and loaded, and now, pulling to a halt and dropping the reins of his well-trained palomino, he hoisted the rifle to his shoulder and triggered a shot. The maddened steer stumbled in a cloud of dust, fell onto its side, kicked a few times, and lay still.

"You saved his life, *mi yerno*," Raoul said, catching up and crossing himself. "That was too close for comfort."

"I hope Miguel isn't seriously hurt. He took quite a fall, and he's an old man, even if he won't admit it." John Cooper replaced the rifle in the sheath and galloped toward the fallen *capataz*. Swiftly dismounting, he ran to Miguel and knelt down beside him.

Ramón Santoriaga, also dismounting, took his canteen and hurried up to the two men. He dashed a little water on Miguel's forehead and then, as the *capataz*'s eyes flickered open, held the canteen to his lips. "Drink a little, Miguel, *amigo*. How do you feel? Can you move? Have you broken anything?"

"I—I do not think so," Miguel doubtfully faltered. He winced as he slowly attempted to stretch his legs, and then gingerly he put one hand behind him to his hip. "It is sore there—and I am not so well padded as others in this company."

"That is true, Miguel—one could never accuse you of being fat from eating too much of Rosa's cooking, or Bess's, either," John Cooper said, trying to make a joke.

There was the sound of a single gunshot as Raoul Maldones mercifully killed Miguel's screaming horse.

Miguel cursed under his breath. "I—I think I am all right." His eyes fixed on the tall Texan's concerned face. "You saved my life, *Halcón*. I thought I was done for. I was a fool—I shouldn't have let that steer get behind me—and I'm sure he was eating locoweed. But it's a good herd, *Halcón*—"

"Never you mind about the herd. The men can round it up tomorrow, and they'll know what to do. Now, come along; we're going to get you back to your Bess, and she'll take care of you," John Cooper sternly said, secretly relieved that his dear friend and *compañero* had suffered no worse than a severe bruise.

The three men lifted Miguel onto John Cooper's horse, and then the Texan himself mounted. Miguel, grumbling and discomfited, and not a little embarrassed at having to be taken home like a tyro, wound his wiry arms around John Cooper's waist and muttered, "If I'd thought to look back for just a second, this wouldn't have happened—"

"Miguel, it's about time you realized that the years have caught up with you, as they're doing with all of us," John Cooper interrupted. "I didn't want this to happen, God knows. But since it has, you're not going to be able to ride horseback or move around for quite a spell."

"I'll be as good as new tomorrow, once Bess rubs some of her homemade liniment on me," Miguel protested.

"No, my old friend. I don't want to give an order, because you and I have never been on that basis before, but this time I have to, for your own good. You'll simply have to start spending more time with your lovely Bess and your children— Now wait a minute, before you start cursing me in a Spanish dialect I can't recognize. . . ." for the old *capataz* had begun to swear under his breath. "I said wait a bit! You'll still be our honorary *capataz*, and we'll come to you for advice, because there's no one on the *Hacienda del Halcón* who's had more experience than you. But physically, you won't be able to keep up with things. And that's why I want to make Raoul Maldones the active *capataz*—'' Again the old *capataz* began to swear. ''Don't you see, he has at least ten years on you, Miguel—and he's operated a huge ranch in Argentina and worked with *gauchos* who, you have to admit yourself, are the equal of our own *vaqueros*.''

''Yes, yes, *por todos los santos*,'' Miguel burst out, ''but all the same, I'm not ready to be turned out to pasture yet, *Halcón*!''

''I didn't say I was going to do that to you. But you're going to be able to take things easier now, and besides, if you want to know the truth, I'm sure Bess will be very happy that you'll be spending more time with her and the children. And you know how much you love her—''

''You don't have to say a thing like that, *Halcón*. I was the luckiest man in *Nuevo Méjico* when Don Diego—may God bless his wonderful soul!—when he bought her away from that damned *jefe indio*! All right, all right, the truth is I do feel a bit sore and a bit shaken. Maybe I should rest a little—''

''Exactly. And now let's have no more fuss and non-sense and arguments about being put out to pasture. As I say, my father-in-law will work very closely with you and get your advice, but he'll take over the active duties, and you'll be our honorary *capataz*. You won't lose face with the men, Miguel—I'll make certain of that.''

''Well, I suppose—maybe you're right, *Halcón*. The last few months or so, I've begun to feel my years, I'll admit it now, since you've brought up the matter,'' Miguel ruefully declared.

''And now you're my friend; now you're the sensible *capataz* you've always been. Let's get back to your Bess and let her rub that liniment on you.''

The next morning, after John Cooper had breakfasted with Dorotéa and his father-in-law, he went out to Miguel Sandarbal's little house to inquire about the health of the old *capataz*. As he approached the door, it opened, and golden-haired Bess Sandarbal emerged, a soft smile on her lips.

Seeing the tall Texan, she held out her hands to him and murmured, "I shall bless you in my prayers forever, Mr. Baines! You don't know how much I've wanted dear Miguel to give up this constant trial of proving himself to the younger men, showing them that he's every bit their equal and better. Now perhaps the two of us can enjoy life together the way I've hoped—and he'll be able to pay more attention to his children, who are growing up and need a father to model themselves after."

"That's exactly what I was thinking, Señora Sandarbal," John Cooper offered. "And of course Raoul Maldones will confer with Miguel from time to time and get the benefit of his experience and his opinions."

"That will please him. Thank you, Mr. Baines. And now, why don't you go in and talk to Miguel? He's been a chatterbox this morning, and I've had to scold him. I think right now he's feeling just a little pity for himself and hoping that someone like you will come along and set things right."

"I'll do just that."

As John Cooper entered the house, Bess saw a courier riding in through the archway that led to the great ranch. The man's horse was lathered with foam, and Bess quickened her footsteps to see what news he was bringing. *It must be most important,* she thought to herself.

The rider dismounted, took several deep breaths, then patted his horse and looked concernedly around.

"One of the *vaqueros* will take your horse, sir," Bess called out. "You've a letter for someone here?"

"Yes, all the way from New Orleans," the man replied. "The captain of a ship at Corpus Christi paid me five dollars on behalf of a Mr. Mallard in New Orleans to have it delivered to a Mr. John Cooper Baines of the *Hacienda del Halcón.*"

"I'll take it to him. But first, let me get one of the *vaqueros* to care for your horse, and then you can go to the kitchen there, off the main building, and Rosa Lorcas will see you're well fed and have a chance to rest."

"That's kind of you, ma'am," said the young rider, a towheaded Texan in his early twenties. He doffed his *sombrero* as he handed her the letter.

A *vaquero* came out of the bunkhouse, and Bess called to him to take care of the courier's horse, then hurried back to her own house. She found John Cooper shaking his forefinger at Miguel and pretending to be stern: "You'll stay in bed, and that's an order, Miguel!"

"Between you and Bess, I'm being treated like a baby! What's this now, Bess? Have you come back to do more scolding?"

"No, my husband." Bess shook her head. "But I'm happy to hear Mr. Baines give you an order—maybe you'll obey it, whereas you won't pay any heed to my pleadings. Mr. Baines, this letter just came for you. A courier brought it from Corpus Christi; he says a ship's captain there paid him five dollars on behalf of your factor in New Orleans to deliver it quickly."

"Thanks, Bess." John Cooper wonderingly opened the letter and quickly read it.

"It's all the way from Argentina, from the young Duvaldo brothers—sons of Señor Maldones's longtime friend Heitor Duvaldo!" John Cooper exclaimed. "They say their father was murdered by orders of the government in Buenos Aires! They've been working on their father's ranch since then, rallying the *gauchos* to defend it, and now the two of them are about to embark on a ship to bring them here. Raoul Maldones will be glad to hear this news—but saddened to learn that his good friend Heitor is dead. I must go show him this." He took another look at the letter. "Let's see, now, it's dated a little over five weeks ago—that means we might expect Duvaldo's sons before the holidays. And we'll give them a warm welcome. How terrible it must be for them to have to stand alone against the tyranny of the same people who tried to have my father-in-law shot for treason, because he wouldn't sell his land to them. Yes, in many ways what's happening in Buenos Aires reminds me of what may happen here in Texas, if Santa Anna manages to seize total power for himself!"

Three

The brig *Salamander* of Providence, Rhode Island, engaged in the South American coastal trade, had made its usual calls along the Brazilian and Argentine coast, and at one of these latter stops, the young Benito and Enrique Duvaldo had purchased passage for New Orleans. Now, several weeks later, the brig was in the placid waters of the Gulf of Mexico, within a day's journey of the Mississippi delta.

So far the weather had been pleasant, and the Duvaldo brothers, standing together on the quarterdeck, optimistically hoped that they might reach the Double H Ranch in Texas well before the holidays. There they would meet with Raoul Maldones, the good friend and former neighbor of their late father, and with John Cooper Baines, Señor Maldones's son-in-law; such had been their father's wish on his deathbed, and they would not disappoint him—although even the company and help of those two brave *hacendados* in Texas would be little consolation for having to leave the *pampas* and *estancia* where Benito and Enrique had been born and raised.

Indeed, for the past weeks aboard the *Salamander*, the two brothers had frequently spoken of what their native land meant to them, and even speculated on what they might have done if their father had not been killed as a result of the fiendish plotting of the Buenos Aires government—the hated *porteños*, as they were called.

"We could have fought shoulder to shoulder with the *gauchos*, Benito," Enrique thoughtfully declared. "And with our father beside us, we would have defied the strongest army that the *porteños* could have sent against us."

Benito, at fifteen years old the slighter and more studious of the two brothers, nodded his head in agreement. He had great respect for Enrique, who, two years his senior, was an expert horseman and handler of weapons, just as their father had once been. Enrique's cheerful and outgoing disposition had made him a great favorite among the freedom-loving *gauchos*, and Benito had no doubt that those fierce roamers of the *pampas* would indeed have stood by their side to defend their *estancia* from the land-hungry *porteños*.

"But, perhaps, in the end, the *porteños* would have prevailed," the realistic Benito said with a scowl. "After all, they have the army, the intellectuals, and even the great wealth and influence of the church on their side. Our friend Padre Camporata can attest to that—" He gestured to the other side of the quarterdeck, where there stood a plump, nearly bald, bespectacled priest, the only other paying passenger on the *Salamander*. He had boarded at a cove on the Brazilian coast, and in the past few weeks, Enrique and Benito had taken him into their confidence and, indeed, had had the priest confess them. Padre Angelo Camporata had, in turn, told the brothers his own story—that he had fled from Argentina after a corrupt official of the *porteño* government had denounced him and ordered him defrocked. Benito and Enrique had sympathetically listened to his story, for in it they perceived yet another manifestation of the tyranny perpetrated by the Buenos Aires government.

The padre's church, Madre María de Gracia, was located on the northern outskirts of the capital city, and he had been its pastor for fifteen years. His sister, who had remained in Madrid and married a wealthy *hidalgo*, had willed to him the small estate of her dead husband, as well as her own property, which included a sum of money. Some eight years ago, upon her death, Padre Camporata had received this legacy. In Argentinian money, it had amounted to some twenty thousand *pesetas*, and over the years, he had bestowed all of it upon the poor of his parish.

Initially, some of the wealthy gentry of Buenos Aires had come to the church, for Padre Camporata was known as a holy man whose sermons from the pulpit provided the most lofty of sentiments. But gradually, as more and more of the poor crowded the church, the wealthy parishioners had had to use their fans and hold scented kerchiefs to their noses. Several of them had haughtily asked that he drive away these ill-smelling, poorly clothed wretches, to which the *padre* had benignly responded, "The meek and the poor shall inherit the earth, and Heaven shall rejoice when those who have the least, yet have the strongest faith, appear before the judgment throne of *el Señor Dios*."

This had enraged the wealthy parishioners, and at last they had appealed to the bishop of Argentina himself, a pompous and extremely wealthy man, and he had issued an order to defrock the kindly little priest. When the latter had stubbornly continued to preach sermons in his church, one of the government officials had reasoned that, since the *padre* was declared defrocked, he might be treated as any traitor and either imprisoned or, better yet, assassinated. Happily for Padre Camporata, a teenaged girl who sold water overheard a conversation to the effect that this troublesome priest would soon be permanently removed from his parish and, indeed, from life itself, and she had sent word to Padre Camporata. An old fisherman had ferried him, in the dead of night, to temporary safety across the Rio La Plata, and thence, through the kindness of an elderly *hacendado*, he had been sent on to Brazil and given money enough to pay his passage away from danger.

Padre Camporata had vowed to this *hacendado* that, despite his persecution, he would continue to wear his priestly garments and, wherever he might go, would continue the good work for the poor and the oppressed. As he had told his benefactor, "Our Merciful Father in Heaven does not judge a man by the clothes on his back, nor by the lavish splendor of his living quarters or the number of *pesetas* he may have stored away for his pleasures. The poorest, even the savage *indio*, who believes devoutly in the Creator of all things and who is humble enough to pray, stands far more in His favor than even the most wealthy and powerful lords of Mother Church. To some, I know, señor, this sounds like treason, but such is what I have been taught ever since I was a boy, and it is my prayer that He will grant me more years of life that I may teach others the same."

Enrique, now gazing with pity on this pious man, was about to reply to his brother, in an effort to dispel his pessimistic mood, when the lookout in the *Salamander*'s mainmast called out that he had caught sight of a large ship closing on them from the northeast.

The captain of the *Salamander*—a bluff, stocky, ex-whaling man by the name of Davis Jasperson—bade the signalman run up flags requesting the identity of the ship and its business. Padre Camporata joined Enrique and Benito at the rail, to get a better view, and all three of them strained to see the ship in the distance. A minute later, the lookout called down that it appeared to be a three-master, and that it was not answering the signals.

The two ships were closing rapidly, and Captain Jasperson, his telescope to his eye, said to his first mate, "I can read her name now. It's the *Dos Hermanos*. Have you ever heard of her?"

The mate, a Connecticut man named Proctor, shook his head. "Maybe she doesn't understand our signals, sir."

"Maybe she doesn't want to," the captain replied ominously, then gave vent to an oath that caused even Padre Camporata—though he could not understand much English—to cross himself.

Meanwhile, on the quarterdeck of the *Dos Hermanos*, two black-bearded men in the blue uniforms of the Spanish Navy trained their own telescopes upon the *Salamander*. One of the men was tall and wiry, with a florid mustache, glittering black eyes set close together astride a hawklike beak of a nose, and the thin lips of a fanatic ascetic. The other man, some years older, was dark and stocky, with a leonine head and massive chest and shoulders. He supported himself with a cane, for years ago a spent cannonball had shattered his left leg, leaving him permanently crippled.

Like Benito and Enrique, these men were brothers—the tall one named Juan Obeira, and the stocky, crippled one Manolito. They were not, however, in the Spanish Navy, and had Captain Jasperson known their names, he would have sworn an even more violent oath and told the Duvaldo brothers and Padre Camporata that these men were truly in league with Satan himself. For both Obeiras, outlaws from Cadiz, had long had a price on their heads and would, if they were caught by the British, French, Spanish, or Americans, be summarily hanged. But for the past several years, because of the firepower and swiftness of their ship—which they repainted and renamed frequently to avoid identification—they had enjoyed virtual supremacy in the Gulf and Caribbean waters and had established, through a relative who lived near Pensacola, Florida, a secret base in a nearby cove. There they hid after their depredations along the coasts, and from there they ventured out to overpower and seize slave ships coming in from Africa. Such targets were easy pickings, for the slavers—themselves engaged in illegal trade—could hardly protest to the United States government. The slaves the Obeiras seized were then sold in Havana—where slavery was legal—at prices of up to five hundred dollars each.

Of course such a business had its dangers, but the crew that the Obeiras had assembled over the years were as unscrupulous and as expert in murder and piracy as the brothers themselves. Nor were they all Spaniards like the Obeiras, but men of many nations—outlaws, deserters, even ex-slaves—who sought an immediate profit from their war upon everyone who was weaker than they.

"Manolito, mi hermano—" The taller Obeira lowered his telescope and turned to his crippled brother. "I do not think this is a slave ship."

"Perhaps it is not, Juan." Manolito Obeira chuckled evilly. "And it is true that it bears the flag of the *Estados Unidos*. But I surmise from its course that it has come from Havana, and it is likely that it also has been to either Argentina or Brazil—therefore, it carries aboard it precious cargo that is ours for the taking. I see their flag signals—they wish to know who we are."

"That is a reasonable request, Manolito." Juan chuckled in his turn. "But there is no need to tell them until we have taken them, is it not true? With our twenty cannon and gallant crew, it will be a trifle to capture that puny brig. And do not forget how our friend Luis Marconado impressed on us the fact that he can find buyers in Havana for white slaves as well as blacks."

"All this is true, Juan—I do not argue with you. And as

procurator general of Havana, Señor Marconado will see that the authorities do ñot stick their noses into such business, because we are wise enough to contribute a small portion of our booty to his own personal fortune."

Juan Obeira again squinted through his telescope at the *Salamander*. By now, Captain Jasperson had given orders to pile on all sail and run with the wind, obviously hoping to outdistance the unknown pursuer.

"Imbeciles," Juan growled to his brother. "They think they can escape us. I count at most six cannon on that brig, and our own guns are heavier and far more accurate." He nodded meaningfully to his brother. "Tell Pablo to fire a shot across their bow, and have the signalman run up a flag ordering them to bring to for our inspection."

"Of course, *mi hermano*." The crippled Spaniard renegade barked orders, and his signalman at once ran up the appropriate flags, while the chief gunner, a burly rogue named Pablo Zaraza, who had fled Lisbon after murdering his lover's husband three years ago, trained his heaviest cannon and touched off a booming warning shot. The cannonball whistled over the brig's bow, splashing into the clear blue water beyond.

"The fools still think they can escape us," Manolito snarled when the brig continued on course. "Zaraza, have your men shoot down their masts, *pronto*, to show them that we mean business."

This time ten of the cannons of the *Dos Hermanos* roared, and both topmasts of the *Salamander* toppled and fell, dangling over the side with all their rigging. Screams could be heard in the distance as seamen were crushed beneath the falling timbers.

Indeed, back on board the *Salamander*, everything was chaos, as Benito, Enrique, and Padre Camporata helped the crew of the crippled brig free those unfortunate souls who were trapped by the falling canvas and rigging.

"Why do they attack us, *señor capitán*?" Enrique cried, as he helped the stocky Jasperson shoulder aside a heavy spar. The *Salamander*'s captain, however, was beside himself at the inexplicable and stunning attack upon his ship, and he had no time to answer. Again the cannons of the three-master roared, and this time the broadside took the lives of four seamen on the *Salamander*.

The lookout had already been killed when the first volley had toppled the mast upon which he had been perched; now the first mate, with trembling hands, adjusted his own telescope to read the flags run up on the foremast of the attacking ship, and cried out to the captain, "They call upon us to strike our colors and to stand for boarding!"

"We've no choice—the bastards!" Captain Jasperson growled in reply. "And we still don't know who or what they are—probably pirates! Very well, Mr. Proctor—strike our flag."

"We can't fight them?" Enrique demanded.

"You are a child if you think so—or a *romántico*, to use your own language," the New Englander tartly replied. "Count their guns for yourselves—they've twenty to our six, and they're used to this sort of thing. Only the most expert gunners could have felled our masts the way they did just now. No, we must surrender—I want no more bloodshed. I've already lost some of my best crewmen, devil take those murderers! But I swear there'll be an accounting, if I ever get back to New England. They can't get away with piracy like this!"

Although Captain Jasperson had resigned himself to losing his cargo and perhaps even his ship, he was not prepared for what he saw as the *Dos Hermanos* approached to within hailing distance, then lowered a boat with an armed boarding party aboard.

"Mr. Proctor!" All color seemed suddenly to drain from Captain Jasperson's face. "Do you recognize those men on the quarterdeck—the two black-bearded rogues, one of them crippled? It's the Obeira brothers! I was warned that they might be lurking in these waters! We can't be taken by them—they'll sell us for slaves, or kill the lot of us! Quickly, break out the weapons and prepare to repel boarders."

Enrique, Benito, and Padre Camporata overheard these words and stared in shock at one another as the remaining crew members of the *Salamander* hastened to the rail, armed and ready to surprise the invaders.

"Should we help them fight, Benito?" the older brother

anxiously asked. "We're not cowards, either one of us, but I fear that the odds are too great—they must outnumber us at least ten to one. And besides, if we are killed, we'll never be able to carry out our father's last wish. At all costs, we must somehow manage to stay alive and hope that we can reach the Señor Baines."

"I agree, *mi hermano*," Benito replied. "But there is little time left, and I think it would be prudent for us to arm ourselves, just in case—"

Enrique nodded in agreement, but as they turned to rush for their cabin, where they kept their pistols and swords, Padre Camporata interposed himself in their path.

"Do not be headstrong and foolish, *mis hijos*. It is best to trust in God and obey the Sixth Commandment: 'Thou shalt not kill.' I know what you are thinking—that it is your duty to your father, as well as to others, to live and take your message to the man in Texas, who is strong and brave enough to defy the evil *porteños*. But do not fear for yourselves, or for your mission. Put up no resistance, but pray steadfastly to Him, and if it is His will, I myself will find this Señor Baines and let him know what has befallen us. Let us pray now, and pray for these brave men who seek to defend the ship. I fear many will die in doing so."

Greatly comforted, Benito and Enrique nodded and said silent prayers as they watched the longboat filled with boarders draw closer. It pulled alongside, and using the damaged rigging as ladders, the bloodthirsty-looking pirates mounted toward the rail.

Captain Jasperson himself had seized a cutlass and, cocking the pistol in his left hand, signaled his men to hold back until the last second. When a swarthy rogue with a red bandanna around his forehead clambered over the side, the captain pulled the trigger. With a hideous shriek, the pirate toppled onto the deck and rolled over dead. All at once, the clash of steel and crack of pistols filled the air as the pirates swarmed aboard. Everywhere there were shouts and curses, and cries of the wounded and dying. But the boarders from the *Dos Hermanos* were far too expert in this kind of hand-to-hand combat, and in less than a minute, at least a dozen of the *Salamander*'s crew lay dead or mortally wounded on the bloodstained deck, while the captain himself was all but decapitated by a savage swing of a cutlass in the hand of the burly first mate of the *Dos Hermanos*. The rest of the American crew, seeing all was hopeless, threw down their weapons.

There were perhaps ten or eleven of them left—as well as the priest and the Duvaldo brothers, who had remained out of the fray and offered no resistance—and now the jubilant boarders prodded them with cutlasses and pistols, herding them to the rail, as another oared boat approached to transport the prisoners to the pirate ship.

But the first mate of the *Dos Hermanos*, who had killed the captain of the *Salamander*, eyed the bespectacled little black-robed priest and shouted, "Leave him aboard, *mis amigos*! Our good *capitanes* will not put a priest into slavery—it is bad luck. Let him remain adrift on this hulk and say his prayers. If they are strong enough, maybe some passing ship will save him. If not, we have not harmed him, and I call you all to witness it." And then, in a jeering tone, he addressed the priest. "You see, *mi padre*, most of us are *católico*, and so we do not sin against you. As for the rest of you—quickly, or we'll help you over the side with a prod of the dirk or the cutlass! You, too, young whelps—" He gestured toward the Duvaldo brothers. "Do as I tell you, unless you want your throats slit here and now!"

Enrique and Benito mounted the rail and were about to descend, when Enrique looked back at Padre Camporata, who was standing alone, his hands clasped in prayer. "Do not forget, *mi padre*," the older Duvaldo called out. "Do not forget us in your prayers."

"I shall not forget, *mis hijos*. I will do what I have promised, and I will pray to the dear Lord that He will grant my prayer for you. *Vaya con Dios, mis hijos*."

Shuddering with rancor, but aware that passive acceptance of their fate was the only sensible means of survival against the cutthroats who had boarded the *Salamander*, Benito and Enrique Duvaldo were taken aboard the *Dos Hermanos*, where they were ushered into the cabin of the two Obeira brothers. The pirate chiefs had already examined the surviving American sailors—whom they had ordered chained and thrown into the hold—and now it was Benito's and Enrique's turn.

Juan Obeira chuckled as he eyed the young men and, without removing his appraising gaze from them, said to Manolito, "These two strong young *niños* will bring a high price in Havana. Señor Marconado will be pleased we have brought him goods of such obvious quality."

"You are right, *mi hermano*." Manolito Obeira made a brusque gesture with his long ivory cane, the tip of which was capped with oakum so as to provide a surer grip upon the deck of a ship or the rough surface of a wharf. "You are quite right. They should bring at least a thousand *pesetas* apiece, perhaps more, if the auctioneer chooses his words and attracts the attention of the wealthiest bidders."

Enrique Duvaldo uttered an astonished cry. "You are talking of selling us, señor? But that can't be! My brother and I are Argentine citizens, not *mulatos* or *mestizos*. You cannot enslave us!"

Juan burst into raucous laughter, tilting back his head and slapping his thigh. With a cynical smirk, he informed Enrique, "Once we have taken you, young señor, you forfeit everything, including your body—and that body can be branded, whipped, or even put to death whenever we wish—until we sell you to another master, who will enjoy the same rights. Now, enough of this high-minded speech of yours. You are both captives, destined for the slave market in Havana, and you might as well make up your minds to it, if you wish to save yourselves a good deal of discomfort."

Turning to his boatswain, a Cuban *mestizo* who was the bastard of a Spanish father from an Indian house slave, he ordered, "Pedro, see if these young 'Argentine citizens,' as we are told they are, have any personal possessions of value to us."

"I've already taken that liberty, *señor capitán*," the heavyset, swarthy seaman said, grinning and nodding. "In their cabin I found a bag of gold and, in it, a little velvet case containing these, *mi jefe!*" So saying, he set down the small sack of gold coins, and then, taking the velvet case out of the pocket of his breeches, opened it with his callused thumb and showed the Obeira brothers the contents—a pair of brilliant ruby earrings.

Enrique, until now restraining himself with difficulty, suddenly cried out, "You have no right to steal that! I don't care about the gold, but those earrings belonged to our dead mother. Our father made us a gift of them—"

"And now you make a gift of them to me, señor!" Juan calmly interrupted. "If you continue to bray like the jackass you seem to prefer to be, rather than behave like a discreet and silent slave, I shall accommodate you—yes, the both of you—by having you tied to the mast and given twenty lashes with the cat by Pedro here; and I can assure you that he can tear the skin from your tender Argentine backs after only three strokes."

Before this threat, Enrique ground his teeth and finally lowered his eyes, muttering to his younger brother that here again discretion was the better part of valor.

"Put them in irons and take them below," Juan abruptly ordered.

Manolito Obeira now intervened, addressing the boatswain. "But place them in a separate cell, Pedro, apart from the others." He turned to his brother. "Juan, I agree with you that Señor Marconado is likely to want these strong young slaves, and I am sure he will pay a very handsome price for them. But if he has it in mind to put them to work in his famous Casa de Belleza—as I suspect is the case—then he will not want them damaged in any way."

"Yes, you are right, of course. Very well, Pedro—put them away, as I told you to, but apart from the rest. And see that they have food and plenty of water to drink. Who knows? If they are docile, we may even indulge them with a little wine or rum—it appears to me that, among the cargo we took from this *Salamander*, there are several cases of excellent French wines."

"Very true, *señor capitán*." The boatswain flashed a broken-toothed grin and touched his fingers to his naval cap. This and the whistle strung around his neck constituted the insignia of his office, and in his right hand he carried a short but murderously flexible rattan cane, the traditional "starter" used to quicken the lazy to their duties.

He flourished this cane at the Duvaldo brothers and, pointing with a cocked pistol in his other hand, growled, "Come along with me, and no tricks, now."

A few minutes later, their wrists and ankles shackled securely, Benito and Enrique found themselves in a small cell in the hold, with a heavy grating overhead providing just enough air to prevent suffocation. It was cramped and dark, and there was only a single, narrow bunk set against the wall, large enough to accommodate only one of them.

"We're lost now, Enrique," Benito said with a groan as he stared mournfully at his brother and then, almost disbelievingly, at his manacles and leg irons.

"We mustn't give up hope," Enrique said. "We must pray, Benito—and trust that Padre Camporata will somehow survive and reach Texas to find our father's friend, the señor Baines. We must believe in this, Benito—it is our only hope."

"Yes, I will pray with you, Enrique. I cannot believe that *el Señor Dios* would be so cruel as to let our brave father's last wish go unfulfilled, for he was always devout and honorable in all his dealings, and we have tried to follow his example."

"If our faith is strong enough, He will hear our prayers. Let us kneel now and say them, *mi hermano*."

But the clanking of their irons sounded loud in their narrow cell as they knelt to pray, giving them little hope that they would soon be delivered from their peril.

Four

Nearly two years ago, when John Cooper Baines had gone to Argentina to sell some of his palominos and long-horned steers to Raoul Maldones, Jim Bowie, the famed Indian fighter and scout, had visited the Double H Ranch. He had been disappointed at not finding the tall Texan there, but had stayed on a few days at the invitation of Miguel Sandarbal. During his stay, Bowie had talked to the *vaqueros* and the *trabajadores* about his plan to form a strong company of well-armed men, expert horsemen familiar with the terrain of Texas, who would patrol the settlements and protect them against the attacks of Indians and harassment of Mexican troops. Miguel Sandarbal had informed the workers on the ranch that he was certain John Cooper would give them permission to join this newly organized frontier corps, and, indeed, several of them had seriously considered such a move.

It had only been recently, however, that six of the *vaqueros*—now satisfied that the Double H Ranch had a large and able enough contingent of workers to defend itself—had taken their wives and children and moved to the new settlement on the Brazos River founded by and named after a Mr. Eugene Fair. With the enlistment of the six *vaqueros*, Jim Bowie's group of Texas Rangers totaled a modest twenty-five.

A twenty-sixth volunteer had approached the famous scout the very next week. His name was Moses Wilson, and he was a freed black man in his middle twenties, who just a month before had left Missouri to come to the Brazos settlement. While still a slave, he had been apprenticed to his

50

master, a Sedalia gunsmith by the name of Samuel Calkins, who had also owned Moses's mother, long his housekeeper and cook.

Late in October, Samuel Calkins had been stricken with river fever and knew himself to be dying. He had called Moses Wilson to his bedside and there, in the presence of his brother, a Baptist minister, had had the latter write out and witness a document of manumission, which made Moses a free man.

"You're the best apprentice I've ever had, Moses," Calkins had said in a faint voice as he fought for breath, "and you've earned your freedom a hundred times. I wish to God your mother was still with us, for I'd have freed her now as well—and I ask your pardon for not having done so before she died."

"She never felt herself a slave, Mr. Calkins, sir," Moses had softly replied as he bent to the dying man. "And I didn't either, if you want the truth. You're a good, kind man, and all I've learned has been from you; and I swear before you and the reverend here that I'll make use of the skills you've taught me, so help me!"

After Samuel Calkins's death, the Reverend Jeremy Calkins informed the young black apprentice that his former master had left him a hundred dollars in gold, as well as all the tools in the smithy, and recommended that he go to the Eugene Fair settlement in Texas, where a gunsmith would be an invaluable asset. With this money, Moses Wilson had bought a gelding plus a sturdy packhorse for the tools, two saddles, and adequate provisions, and, equipped with the hand-tooled pistol and long rifle his master had given him for his devoted service, he left Sedalia.

He had ridden toward the southwest until, on the fourth day of his journey, he had heard the sounds of gunfire and Indian war whoops coming from a winding valley trail about half a mile away. Quickly checking his pistol and rifle and looping his packhorse's rein around a tree branch, he had spurred his horse toward the sounds, and as he neared a grove of birch trees, he saw a small wagon stuck in a ditch, its horses rearing in fright. A band of a half dozen Kiowa

Apache were riding around the wagon, shooting arrows and discharging old muskets into its side.

Swiftly dismounting and tethering his horse to one of the trees, Moses crawled along on his belly until he was within range of the attackers and, drawing his rifle to his shoulder, squinted down the barrel and fired, instantly killing the chief of the band, who was identified by his long war bonnet with trailing eagle feathers. Then drawing the pistol, he picked off one of the braves armed with a musket, dropping him from the saddle. Swiftly reloading both rifle and pistol, he killed two more before the other Indians, fearing that a larger force than themselves might be ambushing them, galloped off toward the west.

Mounting his horse, he rode up to the wagon and found a hysterical white woman cowering in the back, while beside her crouched a black woman of about thirty, holding a smoking musket. There were also two black children, a boy and a girl of about eight and ten.

"The Indians have gone, ma'am," Moses said to the white woman. "You'll be all right now. Where were you going to?"

"Thank God you saved us." The white woman, a thin, haggard-looking creature in her forties, strove for self-control. "I am Emma Sturtevant, and my husband died of fever three days ago. Bessie and I buried him, and then we kept on going—he was heading for Mr. Fair's settlement in Texas."

"Why, ma'am, as it happens, I'm going there myself. I'll be glad to escort you and see that nobody bothers you, if you'll allow it," Moses politely offered.

"Bessie's my slave, and these are her children, Johnnie and Tammy," the woman volunteered. "I have a cousin at the settlement, and she'll just about be my only relation—my own folks are dead, and there aren't any other living relatives on my side of the family. I was ready to die just now—I thought for sure they'd kill us, maybe torture us first—"

"Best not to think about that, ma'am. They're gone now. If you feel a little better, I'll get your horses calmed down, and I'll drive them for you. I'll just attach my horse and packhorse to the back of your wagon, if that's all right with you," Moses offered.

He had safely delivered the widow and her black slave and the two children to the Eugene Fair settlement, and once there introduced himself to Simon Brown, a young scout who seemed to be considered the leader of the community. Moses showed him his document of manumission and said that he was eager to offer his services as a gunsmith to the settlement. Brown enthusiastically welcomed him and declared that there indeed was a need for a capable gunsmith, especially in light of the recent Yaqui Indian attacks and the murder of old Henry Hornsteder.

"Mr. Brown, sir," Moses replied after hearing him out, "nothing would please me more than to settle here and join Mr. Bowie's Texas Rangers, if he'll have me. That way I could be twice as valuable when it comes to defending this place against murderers like that."

The widowed Mrs. Sturtevant was reunited with her cousin, Eleanor Fairview, married to an Ohio blacksmith. The two women had gone to the same rural school as children, and since Eleanor was childless, her affable husband cheerfully consented to the widow's living in their house until her own affairs could be put in order. With a twinkle in his eye, he had told her, "I'll bet my forge that, before the year is over, Mrs. Sturtevant, you'll be finding a fitting husband among all these good men who came out here to settle down and start a new life. And you don't have to think you're imposing on us, 'cause we're more than glad to have you."

Moses Wilson had been attracted to the young black woman, Bessie, and her two children; he had learned that her husband had run away from a Missouri farm and made his way only to the next county before a bounty hunter had spotted him and, when he had tried to resist capture, killed him.

Despite the fact that the Mexican government had decreed slavery would not be allowed on the lands granted to Moses and Stephen Austin—although, assuredly, the lot of the impoverished *peones* in many Mexican provinces was even worse than slavery—a few of those families who had come to the Brazos under the guidance of Simon Brown were slaveholders who had lied about the actual status of their slaves or indentured servants. Instead, they had declared in the affidavits they had given to Eugene Fair back in Missouri that these other members of their household were orphans or children whom they had originally adopted and brought up to adulthood. Eugene Fair had been far from satisfied with these declarations, but he had had no way of disproving them and only hoped that the Mexican government did not inquire too closely and consequently cancel the agreement under which the settlement was allowed to exist.

Hence the presence of Moses Wilson as a free black man on the Brazos had aroused the enmity of those families who had thus far been able to hide their advocacy of slavery. Jeremiah Whelks, a Virginian, had come to the Brazos settlement last year with his family, a male slave, and a mulatto girl who served as his wife's maid and looked after the children. When Moses Wilson introduced himself to the heads of the households of the settlement to inform them that he would be available to repair firearms, as well as to construct new guns to order, Whelks sneered and declared, "I'd be damned if I'd let a nigger handle my weapons. And I'll bet you're a runaway, if the truth be known."

"That's where you're wrong, sir," Moses had self-effacingly responded. "I'm sorry you feel that way, but I've got my freedom paper."

"Which anybody could have forged for you for a price, I've no doubt," was Whelks's cynical reply, and he slammed the door in Moses's face.

But apart from this and a few other similar incidents, the sturdy, pleasant-mannered black was given to understand that he was welcome at the settlement. And very likely it was his distress at being insulted and called a "runaway nigger slave" that made him all the more determined to join Jim Bowie's Texas Rangers. When the famous scout witnessed a demonstration of Wilson's marksmanship—a test required of all Rangers—he simply whistled and nodded his head.

"I'm glad you came to me before we left on our next patrol, Wilson," the scout declared. "I'll be proud to have you as a member of my company, and in fact you can sign up right now. What you know about weapons will come in mighty handy, and once these settlers find out what you can do with a pistol or a rifle, I don't think you'll hear any more slurs about the color of your skin. Certainly, leastways, never from me and my boys in the Rangers.''

Smiling, Moses shook hands with Jim Bowie and declared, ''I think I made the right decision, Mr. Bowie. You know, I believe in Texas just as much as any of the white folks here do, and I swear to you I'll do my part in making this land safe for anybody who wants to settle down and live here in peace.''

''I like your spirit, Wilson—Texas needs more men like you,'' Bowie had said in parting.

It was on the sixteenth of November, 1827, three days later, that Jim Bowie assembled his Texas Rangers at a little village some sixty miles north of the Rio Grande. ''Here's what I have in mind, men,'' he told them. ''Captain Fellows and Captain Worringer will divvy up our entire corps into two groups of thirteen. Captain Fellows's party, into which you seven new men will fall, will scout in the direction of the Rio Grande, to find out if there are any Indian raiding parties about and to check on Mexican patrols. Me and Andy Worringer and the rest of us will have a look around to the north, and maybe drop in on a few ranches to see if we can't do some more recruiting. Twenty-six men, when all is said and done, is just a handful. But on the other side of the coin—and don't you fellows ever forget it—my belief is that one Texas Ranger is worth a dozen Mexican soldiers and the same number of *indios*! That's because we're all fighting to keep our homes and families secure and safe, and we're also mighty prayerful when we go into action. Well, good luck to all of you. Captain Fellows, you may take your patrol out.''

Moses Wilson, his rifle thrust into a saddle sheath and his pistol strapped into a holster belted around his waist, rode out with the others. Captain David Fellows was a wiry man in his middle thirties, a widower whose wife and two little sons had been killed by a Comanche raiding party four years ago. Ever since then, he had dedicated himself to trying to recruit men to see to the defense of this vast frontier. Jim Bowie had met him in New Orleans, and the two had become fast friends.

That night, Moses and his companions made camp near a clump of pecan trees, not far from a branch of the Nueces

River. The sturdy young black man felt not only pride but also a sense of belonging, for without exception, the *vaqueros* and the other Rangers had treated him as one of them, with no racial allusions such as he had encountered from the slaveholding families of the Brazos settlement. When they had learned he was an experienced gunsmith, they had begun to pester him with questions about the maintenance and care of rifles and pistols, and several even went as far as to ask him to make new weapons for them, promising to pay him out of their future wages.

Moses volunteered to stand guard from midnight until dawn, and he surveyed the thickly wooded area around their camp. From what he had seen of valley land here in Texas, particularly near the settlement on the Brazos where he would henceforth make his home, he was certain that it was far more fertile and fit for cultivation than anything he had seen back in Sedalia. If men could toil on this land without the constant threat of attack and bloodshed, their labors would be rewarded and their opportunities limited only by their own abilities and determination. Yes, he loved this land of Texas already, and he was proud to wear the insignia that Jim Bowie had given him, a little silver medallion onto which was etched the figure of a man on horseback with a rifle at his pommel. Instinctively, he put his hand to his throat to feel for the medallion and smiled in the darkness, as he listened to the calls of the night birds and the distant yelp of a coyote.

When he was finally relieved at dawn from his sentry post, his mind was too full of plans for the future for him to be able to snatch some sleep. Instead, he went over to the fire one of the men was making and downed a skimpy breakfast of strong coffee and a two-day-old biscuit from a batch donated by one of the settlers' wives. This and a piece of jerky sufficed him, and now, with the warm, bright sun rising swiftly, he could once again survey the terrain and pronounce it bountiful and promising.

They mounted soon after breakfast and rode on, with Captain Fellows at their head. When they reached the Rio Grande, in midafternoon, the wiry, brown-bearded captain suddenly turned in his saddle and held up his hand to halt the troop. "Mexican soldiers—mounted and heavily armed, it looks like!" he called back to them.

What he could not know was that it was a troop of some one hundred seasoned veterans under the command of *Coronel* Luis Dominguez, who had visited Santa Anna's villa at Mango de Clavo in October and received what amounted to a general order to harass the *gringos* as much as he possibly could. Indeed, at the same time, about a hundred miles to the east, *Comandante* Felipe Molinas, as ambitious as *Coronel* Dominguez, had taken Santa Anna's expression of enmity toward the *gringos* as a specific order to be carried out, and was visiting every ranch in sight, making himself and his men as unwelcome as possible.

"They're out in full force, aren't they, Cap'n?" Jack Mornay, a lean man in his late twenties, spoke up as he watched the mounted soldiers come to a halt on the other side of the Rio Grande. Colonel Dominguez had held up his hand and now was squinting through a telescope at the small group of Texas Rangers on the other side of the river. At this point, the river was extremely shallow, knee-deep at most.

"We'll have plenty to tell Jim Bowie," Captain Fellows said, nodding agreement. "Two companies of crack cavalry troops—you can see that from their formations. And all the privates and corporals have carbines and pistols. That's a powerful force."

"I just hope they're not looking for trouble," Matt Denston muttered. He was a thirty-year-old black-haired widower who had joined the Rangers to avenge the rape and murder of his young wife by a Mexican lieutenant in a little farm settlement some fifty miles south of San Antonio. "But if they are, by all that's holy, I'll give them more than they're looking for." So saying, he drew his already primed and loaded rifle from its saddle sheath and cocked it, holding it in his right hand as if it were a pistol, while he controlled the reins of his horse with his left.

"They're sitting there watching us," Captain Fellows muttered between his teeth. "And that officer at the head of the column is squinting through that damned telescope of his. No, you bastard, we don't have anything near like the bright uniforms you're sporting—we wear our pride inside, where it counts!"

Suddenly, Colonel Dominguez shouted something to his officers, then lifted his hand, as if to give the signal to attack. At once, his horsemen split themselves into three groups, those in the center dismounting and forming a firing line, and those on the two flanks detaching themselves from the long column and heading at a gallop across the shallow river toward the Rangers.

"They're trying to trap us, men!" the captain called. "Spread out, dismount, and pull your horses down. Use them as shields to fire over!"

Several of the nearest enemy horsemen opened fire, but at too great a distance. Moses Wilson had already pulled out his rifle and cocked it; and before he dismounted, he squinted down the barrel and triggered a shot. A sergeant bearing a lance in his right hand uttered an agonized yell and toppled into the shallow river, while his horse raced on up the bank and toward the Rangers.

"Fire at will! Spread out—spread out, damn it!" Captain Fellows shouted as he leaped down from his horse and pulled it by the reins toward a clump of mesquite. Forcing it down on its side, he flung himself on his belly behind it, drew out his two holstered pistols, cocked them, and taking careful aim, shot down a private who had just lifted a rifle to his shoulder; with the other pistol he winged one of the lancers, who, in slipping from his saddle, caught one booted foot in a stirrup and was dragged along by his frightened mount.

Colonel Dominguez gave another sign, and every other man in the firing line across the river knelt down on the bank and fired a withering volley; then in unison they rose and stepped back, and the second line knelt and fired. At the first volley, two of the young *vaqueros* from the Double H Ranch died instantly, and a third was hit in the shoulder. As the second volley thundered out, four more of the Rangers rolled over and lay still. The others still had to concentrate on the charging cavalrymen, and Captain Fellows, glancing frantically about him, knew his remaining men were doomed if he hesitated any longer. "To horse and retreat—ride like hell away from here! It'll be a massacre if we don't!" he shouted as he urged his horse to its feet, leaped into the saddle, and began to gallop toward the northeast.

Moses had reloaded both his pistol and rifle and, hesitating a moment longer while his unwounded companions drew their horses to their feet and mounted, felled two more lancers before he, too, realized the hopeless odds. Already Colonel Dominguez was waving his arm to indicate an all-out attack with the rest of his force.

Leaping into the saddle, Moses crouched low as he heard the whistle of lead all around him; he rode as fast as he could and soon caught up with the captain and the three other Rangers who had survived the attack.

"For no reason at all, mark you, no damned reason at all, those bastards tried to wipe us out!" Captain Fellows panted as Moses drew abreast of him. Glancing back over his shoulder, the freed black man saw that they were outdistancing their pursuers, and now Captain Fellows wheeled his horse to the east and continued the mad gallop toward safety.

Some twenty minutes later, they halted their frothing, exhausted horses, and the captain turned to look behind him. There was no sight of any Mexican soldier, even in the farthest distance. "Thank God they're not chasing us. I've got to get back to Jim Bowie and tell him about this. We lost at least a third of our entire force." He turned to look at Moses Wilson, and a bleak smile crossed his sweating face. "Wilson, you were cool as a cucumber under fire, and you made them pay a little bit for what they did to our men. That'll go into my report. You've proved you're a true Texas Ranger today. Now, let's get the hell out of this desolate-looking country and on back to the settlement, so we can tell Jim Bowie that we almost didn't make it!"

Jim Bowie paced back and forth near the barbecue fires Simon Brown had started shortly after sunset. They were to celebrate the wedding of one of the bachelors of the community who had sent for a mail-order bride from St. Louis, she having arrived early that afternoon, along with three other new settlers.

Old Minnie Hornsteder had gone along with Bowie to

the barbecue, holding on to his arm and grinning at this mark of favor, for she admired the almost legendary scout for his courage and his defiance of the Mexican army. It was she who first saw Captain Fellows, Moses Wilson, and the three other Rangers riding through the opened stockade gates into the settlement. "Hey there, Mr. Bowie," she announced, "looks like some of your patrol came back!"

"Yes, that's Captain Fellows," Bowie remarked. "I wonder where the rest of his men are?" Cupping his hands to his mouth, he bawled, "Over here, Fellows! Bring your men, get off your horses, and set yourselves for some mighty fancy Texas eating and drinking!"

Captain Fellows gave him a smart salute as he approached, but his face was glum and his tone bitter as he said, "Thanks, Mr. Bowie, but I'm afraid we're not in much of a mood to celebrate anything."

"You ran into trouble? What happened to the others?"

"All dead or captured, Mr. Bowie. We were attacked by a troop of about a hundred Mexican cavalry led by a colonel. We were on this side of the Rio Grande, and we saw them across the river on their horses with their commanding officer peeking at us through a telescope. Next thing we knew, he gave the order to attack. We returned the fire, and we sent a few of them to hell, but we lost all the rest of our men, except those you see right here. I wish to God I had better news for you, Mr. Bowie."

Jim Bowie flung his hat to the ground and cursed under his breath. "God help me, I'm going to do something about this, Dave," he finally said, after he managed to control his anger. "I'm going to go see Stephen Austin and the heads of other Texas communities to urge that all of us band together and create an even stronger force of Texas Rangers. I'll be hog-tied if Santa Anna's not at the bottom of this. That was probably one of his boot-licking officers with the order to plague the hell out of us to see how much more we can take. Well, by the Eternal, we'll take all they've got to give us, and give back worse. We're not giving up on this land yet, not by a damn sight!"

"I'll gladly say amen to that, Mr. Bowie. I'm sorry to have brought you such bad news—"

"Hell, man, don't apologize—it wasn't your fault!" Bowie almost brutally interrupted. "And it looks like you lost some of our fine *vaqueros* from the Baines ranch—that's a damn shame. They were so bright and eager to join up with us, and they wanted to make good—and now this."

"I know. Better men you couldn't ask to have, Jim," the captain morosely muttered.

Old Minnie Hornsteder had listened all this while to the two men, and now, her eyes burning with anger, she burst out, "I knew something like this was going to happen, I just knew it! Ever since that high 'n' mighty Santy Anna rode in here with his men and killed my poor Henry, I knew we were gonna have to put those damn Mexes in their place. And mebbe it's gotta be with ball and powder 'n' bayonet, even though God forbids it. I see it comin', Mr. Bowie, plain as the nose on your face, I see it comin'."

"I know how you feel, Minnie." Jim Bowie turned to her and, with a consoling gesture, put his arm around her broad shoulders. "I think even Stephen Austin knows that sooner or later the Mexican government is going to renege on its pledges to us settlers. Santa Anna won't rest until he's head of the country, and then he figures he can raise a real army and wipe us all off the face of the earth. But the Lord God willing, we're not going to wait for that to happen. We're going to get stronger all the time, and I'm going to spend night and day riding around this territory until I sign up at least a hundred more Texas Rangers, so help me God!"

Five

Handsome young Ferdinand de Lloradier, who a year ago had ridden from Taos to tell Carlos de Escobar that the Spanish *junta* had cleared his father's illustrious name, had so enjoyed his stay at the Double H Ranch that he had directed his majordomo, Honorio, to sell his estate in Taos and, at Carlos's urging, had settled permanently on the *Hacienda del Halcón*.

Being wealthy, free of any real obligations, and with no relatives to care about his coming or going, Ferdinand had, he now realized, led a life no better than that of a wastrel. Taos had been a sleepy little town, in which tradition counted for everything. The *caballeros,* dressed in their finest regalia, seemed to live only for fiestas, an occasional bullfight, or idly to court pretty girls—anything to break the monotony of a life that had changed very little during the past half century. The central government in Mexico cared little about what happened in Taos or Santa Fe, except to levy high tariffs that hampered trade, and taxes that made even the oldest and noblest families bitterly discontent. It was, indeed, these tariffs and taxes that had led John Cooper Baines to advise his then father-in-law, Don Diego de Escobar, to follow him to Texas to begin a new life free of the unimaginative and oppressive regime that had, if anything, changed for the worse since Mexico's independence from the mother country.

Young de Lloradier felt himself welcome on the Double H Ranch, and because of his native honesty and love for the outdoors, he had quickly made friends with John Cooper Baines, Miguel Sandarbal, Ramón Santoriaga, and many of the others on the *estancia*. Most of all he loved to hunt and ride, and on many a morning he rode out with John Cooper and Carlos, followed by the wolf-dog Yankee and the latter's two offspring, Maja and Fuerte. By now, these two cubs had become nearly full-grown and proved themselves as adept as their powerful sire at hunting and flushing out game.

One brisk November morning, the three men went riding shortly after dawn, with Yankee, Maja, and Fuerte joyously loping ahead, eager for the hunt.

John Cooper had chosen a route toward the southeast, where, some four miles from the ranch, began a thickly wooded stretch especially rich in game. The sky was gray, and the air was cold, wet, and invigorating, ideal weather for hunting. Carlos rode beside Ferdinand, and John Cooper's brother-in-law turned to the *caballero* from Taos and banteringly remarked, "In the short time you have been here, *mi amigo*, you've become a fixture on this *hacienda*. Now only one thing is lacking to make that fixture permanent."

"And that is?"

"Why, an *esposa, seguramente*," Carlos said with a chuckle. "Surely by now you've had a chance to see how many lovely young *criadas* there are, as well as the daughters of our brave *vaqueros* who still haven't chosen a husband. Unless, of course, you feel yourself too far above such lowly peasant stock—"

Ferdinand de Lloradier's handsome face clouded with irritation. "Please, Carlos, that's a very bad joke. It wasn't my fault that I was born to the Spanish nobility—and even when I lived in Taos, I was very discontent with my way of life. There was nothing to do there, and such girls as there were . . . well, they were shallow creatures. After all, you rogue, you stole away the loveliest, most deserving *mujer* in all Taos, your wife, Teresa."

Carlos smiled and nodded emphatically. "Yes, what you say is certainly true, and I give thanks every day of my life that she said yes to me, *mi amigo*. Well then, if you're not worried about dowries or noble blood, I'd say there are plenty of charming young women on this ranch who would be very happy to be married to you. I probably should not tell you this, as it may go to your head, but Miguel was telling me just the other day that there are at least two young women, daughters of our *vaqueros*, who find you very handsome, very much the cavalier, and would be enchanted if you were to look their way—now, don't ask me for their names, for that isn't my purpose. You must find them for yourself, Ferdinand.''

''And so I shall. To be honest with you, I enjoy hunting and riding so much that I've had little time to think about marriage; but I do want to settle down and do my part to help defend the ranch. I owe you that, and I am grateful to you and to John Cooper for letting me stay here, where I feel so much at home.''

''This is all very well, but see how far John Cooper has galloped ahead of us, as if he wants to get all the game for himself. Come on, *amigo*, I'll race you. My palomino can outrun yours!''

Laughing happily, both men kicked their heels against their horses' bellies, shouting encouragements to their mounts, and soon caught up with the tall Texan.

John Cooper, as usual, was wearing buckskins and moccasins, as had been his custom since the days he had lived with the Indians, after coming home from a hunt to find his family murdered by renegades. Even now, the wearing of this Indian costume recalled to him the adventurous, unhampered life outdoors with his blood brothers, the Jicarilla Apache, and the untrammeled freedom that such a life offered. And even now, in his middle thirties and a responsible family man, he still loved giving up a morning to ride out and hunt, just as he had done when he was a boy back on his father's land in old Shawneetown.

Yankee and his two cubs had darted toward a thicket of manzanita, and there was a loud squawking as a covey of partridges suddenly rose in the air. Instantly, John Cooper hiked ''Long Girl'' to his shoulder and pulled the trigger, and one of the plumpest birds fell like a plummet to the earth. With a joyous bark, Yankee raced ahead to fetch it and, wagging his tail like a true retriever, returned to his master, to be rewarded by a rub of John Cooper's knuckles over his head and a ''Good boy, good boy!''

Carlos and Ferdinand, meanwhile, had also gotten off

shots, almost simultaneously. Carlos only wounded one of the birds, while the *caballero* from Taos killed his. At John Cooper's command, Yankee raced toward Carlos's still-fluttering bird and, with a snap of his powerful jaws, ended its suffering; then, at John Cooper's direction, the wolf-dog loped back to present the partridge to the delighted Carlos. Meanwhile, Fuerte, also at John Cooper's order, retrieved the other partridge and brought it to Ferdinand.

"It's amazing how well you've trained these dogs, John Cooper," Ferdinand smilingly exclaimed. "I wish we had owned dogs like these back in Taos. They would have made my expeditions much more interesting than they turned out to be."

"I'm afraid some of your neighbors might have killed wolf-dogs like these, Ferdinand. They'd be afraid of them—and after all, such animals really need the unrestricted outdoors for their best work. Moreover, someone would have to train them to get along with people and distinguish friends from enemies. That took me plenty of work, I can assure you, starting with old Lobo."

"Yes, I've thought of him often," Carlos said. "Do you ever see him?"

"No, not for several years now. He said farewell to all of us when he went off with that timberwolf. Oh, he would come nearby and bay and bark every so often, to let us know that he still remembered us, but by now he's probably reverted to the wilds entirely. I wish him well—he gave me much joy, and he was loyal, just like my faithful Lije." For a moment, John Cooper was silent, remembering the past. Then, brightening, he proposed, "Let's see if we can get something better than partridges. But these three birds will provide a tasty supper tonight, once Rosa prepares them."

The hunters had no more luck that morning, however, and promising to resume the hunt the next day, they rode back to the ranch. Ferdinand de Lloradier was walking his horse to the stables when he was hailed by Miguel Sandarbal, who informed him that a courier riding on to the settlement on the Brazos had halted his journey about an hour ago to deliver a letter addressed to him. The handsome young *caballero* thanked the white-haired *capataz* and, after leaving his horse at the stable and giving it an extra ration of oats and a lump of sugar, opened the letter and read it.

It was from his majordomo, Honorio, enclosing a bank draft that represented the final portion of the proceeds of the sale of his villa and estate, as had been agreed upon when the majordomo had first informed his former employer that the prospective buyer had requested to purchase the properties in two installments. Since Honorio had indicated that the buyer, an elderly *hidalgo* who had left Santa Fe to be near his only daughter, was extremely trustworthy and solvent, de Lloradier had agreed to this proposal.

Honorio had added a paragraph expressing his personal gratitude to his former master:

I am frank to say, esteemed *patrón,* that I deeply regret no longer being in your service. Now, however, I may freely express the admiration I always had for you, not only as a master but as a man whom I could respect without hesitation. I envy you your life on the Double H Ranch, having read what you have written to me about where you now live. As for myself, thanks to your great generosity in giving me a far too large commission for having effected this sale, I may tell you that I have married a sweet widowed woman in her late thirties with two little girls and have bought a small house on the northwestern side of Taos. It is like a dream, to have a ready-made family in this way, and my *esposa,* Ginefra, has just told me that she is to bear my own first child. I thank you, and I pray each day to *el Señor Dios* to give you a long and happy life. And, of course, if ever you should require my services again, I should be proud and honored to come to your command.

Ferdinand coughed and glanced around, fearful that some-one might see there were tears in his eyes after he had finished reading this letter. At the same time he felt a pang of loneliness, for although everyone had accepted him here on the Double H Ranch, he had neither a *novia* nor an *esposa* to look after him and to spur him on to realize all that was possible within himself. He deeply envied Miguel, Carlos, and John Cooper, for their wives were helpmates in the truest sense, and such women inspired men to do great deeds.

In this wistful mood, he left the stables and, carrying his rifle, decided to walk down toward the Frio River. The weather was still pleasantly cool, though there was a touch of winter chill in the air. The skies had cleared now, and viewing the trees and the brush and the wild flowers of this sylvan setting, he thought to himself that he had made a wise decision in giving up the empty, superficial life of the *caballero* in Taos to come here.

As Ferdinand approached the riverbank, he saw a black-haired girl, probably not more than eighteen, crouching with her back to him, observing a crippled little swallow. One of its wings had been broken, and it was fluttering the other wing, cheeping pitifully as it sought to fly away from her. She knelt down, took it up gently in her palms, and stroked its tiny head with the tip of her forefinger, cooing softly to it to allay its fears. Trustingly, it rested in her hands, its eyes fixed on her sweet, heart-shaped face.

Ferdinand had moved off to one side to contemplate this and caught his breath to perceive the exquisite beauty of her features, the soft, full red lips, the warm, dark-brown eyes, the feminine compassion that emanated from her and which had soothed the fear of the crippled little bird.

He heard an angry caw and glanced up just in time to see the blur of a falcon swooping down toward her. Instantly reacting, he leveled his rifle and fired. The falcon crumpled to the ground only a few feet away from the startled girl, who uttered a cry and whirled around to stare at him.

"Forgive me, señorita!" Ferdinand lowered his rifle and came toward her. "I did not mean to frighten you, but that is a peregrine falcon, and it was attracted by the little bird you have in your hands. It wished to make its dinner of it, and it might have clawed you or struck at you with its cruel, sharp beak. I could not let it happen—"

"*Gracias, señor.* I wouldn't have known—I didn't see—"

the girl stammered, blushing hotly as she observed that this handsome *caballero* was eyeing her with unabashed admiration. And yet there was nothing offensive in his look, for his eyes were bright, and there was a warm smile on his face.

"The little bird—perhaps I can make a splint for its wing, and you can make a pet of it, señorita," he now proffered.

"That would be most kind. I—I have seen you about the ranch, señor, though I do not know your name—"

"I am Ferdinand de Lloradier, *su servidor*." He gave her a courtly bow.

The black-haired young girl blushed to her earlobes as, shyly lowering her eyes, she said, "My name is Miranda Vasquez. *Mi padre* is a *vaquero* on this *estancia*."

"Miranda. That is a lovely name, truly worthy of you, señorita."

"You are too kind. I am only a poor girl, and the daughter of a *vaquero*—" Miranda Vasquez was clearly flustered by so much attention from this dashingly handsome young man.

"It is of no importance what your father is, señorita. The fact is, I was struck with wonder—and I swear I did not mean to spy on you, except that when I came toward the river after having gone on a hunt, I was in a thoughtful mood—and when I saw you with that crippled little bird, I could not but stand and watch and wonder, for it was one of the loveliest things I have ever seen."

Her blushes were furious now, and she turned partly away from him in her shyness. "I—I am not too well educated, Señor de Lloradier, but what you are saying is more flattery than a girl like me should have—"

"Forgive me—and do not think that I am a Don Juan who seeks to charm you. Indeed, I have come here from Taos to live a simple life, Señorita Miranda, not to chase after the women. Yet it is true I have no relatives and no *novia* or *esposa*. But I am not the kind of man who will flatter any girl and then cast her aside for another and yet another—though there were many I knew in Taos who, because they had nothing better to do, gave themselves over to that kind of amusement. Please believe that I respect you and admire you very much, Señorita Miranda."

"*Gracias*, Señor de Lloradier," Miranda said. "I think— *con su permiso*—I will take this little bird to our hut, and perhaps *mi padre* will help make a splint for its broken wing." She turned to contemplate the bird, and again, with her forefinger tip, stroked its head as it uttered a faint cheep. "*Pobrecito, pobrecito*, you are safe with Miranda."

"Permit me the honor of escorting you back to your *casa*, Señorita Miranda. I know something about animals and birds, for in Taos I had a stable, and I also had a parrot that I taught to talk back to me—because I was lonely, you see. And once it broke its wing, too, and I made a splint for it and helped it. I would be very glad to do this for your little swallow," Ferdinand pleaded.

He was bewitched by this lovely girl, who was so candid and ingenuous, with such an ethereally lovely smile and such warm, dark eyes. He had noticed that, when she smiled, there were exquisite dimples on each side of her mouth. And her body was beautifully formed, with firm, high-perched breasts that pressed against her blouse and now, because of her shy embarrassment, rose and fell with agitation, which only enhanced them to his admiring eyes.

"If you—if you wish, Señor de Lloradier," she at last quavered.

The young *caballero* sighed raptly and walked beside her toward the little cottage where she lived with her graying father, Tomás Vasquez, and his elderly sister, for Miranda's mother had died three years ago, and she had been the only child. Miguel Sandarbal had hired Tomás Vasquez about five years ago, since he and several other *vaqueros* had come from Laredo in search of employment at the Double H Ranch.

"This is where I live, Señor de Lloradier," Miranda murmured as she reached the door of the cottage.

"You do not wish me to help the little bird for you, Señorita Miranda?" There was almost pathos in his tone, for he was so smitten with her loveliness and sweetness—which aroused anew his nostalgic reflections of how lonely he was in his new life—that he was loath to leave her, as if fearful that she would never reappear, or that already she was promised to some other man.

"I—I think it would be best—" she began, then faltered as she put her hand to the door.

Unable to restrain himself any longer, Ferdinand blurted out, "Tell me this, Señorita Miranda—do you have a *novio*, or are you promised to anyone?"

"Oh, no, señor, oh, no!" she said, looking scandalized, and once again the color stained her cheeks and throat.

"Good!" he laughingly exclaimed; and when her eyes grew wide with questioning wonder—for she did not understand such exuberance over the simple statement she had just made—he reassured her. "I did not mean to startle you, dear Señorita Miranda. But I hope to see you again."

"It is as God wills, señor. And I thank you again for saving me from that bird with the cruel beak and talons—it would have killed my little swallow. And now I must say *adiós*, Señor de Lloradier. My father and *mi tía* will wonder where I have been so long—oh, I forgot to bring water from the river as I was bidden! They will be very vexed with me. They will wonder what has happened to my mind—"

"Then perhaps I should introduce myself and tell them that it was all my fault," Ferdinand eagerly proposed.

Miranda was in a quandary; her aunt had brought her up to be pious, chaste, and self-effacing until such time as perhaps the young son of some esteemed *vaquero* here at the *hacienda* would take note of her and come ask her father for her hand in marriage. But innocent as she was, the attention of so handsome a *caballero*, who had undoubtedly saved her from a serious accident, made her hesitate on the borders of propriety, for she did not wish to offend him. "Well, then, if you like, perhaps it is best that you tell my father about the falcon, Señor de Lloradier," she conceded.

The raven-haired girl opened the door and, nervously glancing back over her shoulder, entered. Her aunt, gray-haired and stout, came out of the kitchen to call, "Is that you, *querida*? I have waited for the water, and we are both thirsty." Then, catching sight of the tall, slim *caballero* in his riding breeches and dark jacket, she lifted her apron to her mouth and stared wide-eyed at him.

At the same time, Tomás Vasquez emerged from one of the two bedrooms and, seeing Ferdinand de Lloradier swiftly untie the strings of the broad-brimmed black hat that he had worn during the hunt, glanced first at his sister and then at Miranda, as he said, "Is anything wrong, *mi niña*?"

"Forgive me, Señor Vasquez," de Lloradier quickly intervened, then proceeded to recount the episode involving the swallow and the falcon.

"*¡Ayúdame!*" the gray-bearded stocky *vaquero* gasped when the story came to an end. "A falcon? It could have pecked your eyes out, heart of my life! The water means nothing! Are you well, Miranda? Were you hurt?"

"Oh, no, *mi padre*, thanks to this fine señor who saw the falcon when I did not—but you see, here is the swallow. Its wing is broken, and I said that you would know how to make a splint for it—and perhaps a small cage, so I can keep it as a pet?" She opened her fingers partway, and both her aunt and father saw the little bird struggling a bit in its apprehension over these new strangers.

"But of course I can make a splint, *mi niña*! I will do it at once." Tomás Vasquez turned to Ferdinand de Lloradier. "I'm in your debt, señor, for having saved my daughter's life! It's true that if she had not stopped to help the swallow, she would not have attracted the falcon and would have brought back the water—but then you see, señor, she is a sweet, very good girl, and she has a tender heart for the suffering of others!"

"If you will allow me, I will bring a pail of water directly. It is the least I can do," the young *caballero* offered. "May I introduce myself—I am Ferdinand de Lloradier, and I came from Taos to live here because I admire the Señores de Escobar and Baines."

"We are honored by your presence and, as I say, in your debt for what you've done for my *hija*. Please, *señor*—" Tomás gestured the *caballero* toward the only chair in the living room. "Be at your ease. I will get the water after I have attended to this little bird. Josefina, if there is some coffee or chocolate, perhaps Señor de Lloradier would enjoy a cup? And with it, one of your tasty spice cakes."

"*Pronto, seguramente, mi hermano*," the gray-haired

woman said, favoring their young guest with a hospitable smile.

Ferdinand was touched by the kindness of these two people, as he saw Miranda's father come to take the injured bird gently from her palm. The old man stroked it, soothing it with gentle words as he carried it back into the bedchamber. A short while later, his sister returned from the kitchen with a cup of hot chocolate and a plate of little spice cakes.

During the older couple's absence, Ferdinand had contemplated Miranda, who, very shyly, though certainly aware of his scrutiny, had averted her face and stood with hands clasped, unable to suppress her blushes. He was enchanted. It seemed to him that, through some incredible miracle, he had come upon the most beautiful girl in all the world, with the kindest of hearts and the sweetest of natures. And in a wash of sentiment and, to be sure, not a little self-pity, he told himself that here was the perfect wife for a man who had given up the slothfulness of selfish life in Taos. Already he knew that he was in love with Miranda Vasquez.

As he sipped his chocolate and partook of one of the cakes, while the aunt urged him to take another, Tomás Vasquez emerged and showed his open hands to all of them: He had fixed an ingenious splint for the broken wing of the swallow, and now it cheeped and cocked its head this way and that as it looked at all of them.

"*Gracias, mi padre*. It is such a lovely little bird, and I will take good care of it. And when its wing is healed and it can fly again, if it wants its freedom, I will not keep it in a cage too long," Miranda promised.

Hearing this, Ferdinand was lost. He gave up his very soul to this beautiful, black-haired girl, gazing at the radiance of her face, the luminous warmth of her dark eyes, the sweet tremor of her full red lips. He closed his eyes and imagined what it would be like to come back to such a young wife at the end of a hard day's hunting or, better still, and certainly more heroic, the defense of the *Hacienda del Halcón* against the most formidable of enemies.

Reluctantly, he rose to take his leave, thanking his host and hostess for their hospitality, for Tomás Vasquez had moved to the door to fetch the pail of water. Ferdinand hesitated a moment before bidding them farewell, and then, unable to hold back any longer his impatient yearning, demanded of the *vaquero*, "Señor Vasquez, I am a lonely man, I have sold my villa and my estate in Taos, and I have come here to lead a purposeful life and to be of service, because I believe that this great Texas must stand against its enemies. I ask you—and do not think me presumptuous—to consider me as a suitor for your daughter's hand."

"Señor de Lloradier! But this is—but we are only humble people, and I myself came from Laredo, and we have been poor—" the *vaquero* began, his eyes wide with astonishment as he glanced at his sister, who put a hand to her mouth and shook her head. Miranda, too, overcome by such an unexpected avowal, turned to stare at the *caballero* and then swiftly turned away, her face scarlet again, her bosom swelling quickly.

"Forgive me—I am too bold, but I am sincere, Señor Vasquez, Señorita Vasquez. You see, in Taos I lived by myself except for my majordomo, Honorio, who no longer is with me. I have no one in the world, and I am not a man to go seeking women who bring rich dowries, or who are high in a society that I consider meaningless. Your daughter has those qualities that I believe the truest and the dearest of women have, and to me it does not matter at all that you are poor, or where you come from. Believe me in this, for I mean it truly with all my heart. I have no right to speak this way, I realize, and I know it is sudden, but . . . you see, I have fallen in love with your daughter. It is an honorable love, I assure you, and with your blessing and permission, I would like to court her and make her my wife."

Never in his life had he spoken so eloquently. There were tears in his eyes, and they were true tears, and the gray-haired woman and the gray-haired man stared at him openmouthed, as if they could not believe what they had heard. Even Miranda, aghast at such a bold declaration, regarded him as if he were an apparition from a spirit world.

"Why, Señor de Lloradier, I do not know what to tell you," Tomás began. "I can say only that we are humble, poor people, and you are a *caballero*. I have already heard from the *capataz* how well you are liked here and respected—surely there must be women of your own class—"

"I am not interested in women of a class, Señor Vasquez," Ferdinand patiently explained. "My parents died when I was in my teens. They loved each other dearly, and what virtue there is in me is what I acquired from them. But in the years after their death, because I was wealthy and because I was in Taos and considered a member of that society, I felt myself becoming useless and without purpose. And if I had not met the señor Carlos de Escobar, I might well have wasted the rest of my life. Now that I am here, I tell you honestly, Señor Vasquez, your daughter means more to me than a thousand shallow, stupid girls who perhaps had the good fortune to be born into families of quality and substance and wealth. I would not give a fig for all of them as against your Miranda—and this is why I ask you, honorably and formally, here and now, to be permitted to pay court to her."

"I cannot deny you that, but I warn you again, señor, that we can offer you nothing—"

"Señor Vasquez," Ferdinand almost fiercely interrupted, "that is not quite so, for your daughter is a treasure in herself. All I ask is the chance to be worthy of her and to be considered as an eligible suitor. If your daughter does not accept me or return my love, I shall gracefully withdraw. But I sincerely hope that, in time, I may have the honor one day of calling you, Señor Vasquez, *mi suegro*." With this, he bowed toward the astounded father and aunt and, going up to Miranda, gently took one of her hands and brought it to his lips and kissed it, saying, "I thank you, Señorita Miranda, for the privilege of meeting your father and your *tía*, and I beg your forgiveness if I have in any way embarrassed you. I wish you only to believe that all I have said in your hearing is from my very heart. I shall await God's will and your approval of me, if it is to be. *Adiós*."

With this, he turned and let himself out of the cottage and went back toward the *hacienda*, trembling in reaction to the impulse that had forced him out of his shell and into expressing what he truly and fully believed was the most honest avowal of his entire life.

Back in the cottage, Miranda's father and aunt, still dazed by the scene they had just witnessed, could not speak for a moment. Finally, Josefina came to her niece's side and, putting an arm around the girl's shoulders, murmured, "If truly he means what he says, *querida*, it would be beyond even our wildest hopes that you should have so fine a husband. But as he says himself, it is important for you to return his love, for I do not believe in marriage without love, no matter what the difference in station. Now let us see if he is sincere."

Miranda suddenly burst into tears and put her arms around her aunt. "You must guide me, *mi tía, mi padre*, for I know nothing of men. But he was so brave to kill the falcon and to think of saving the little bird and then to wish to bring water, which is the work of a *criada*. Oh, Tía Josefina, it is all like a dream, and I do not know if it will ever be more than that—but yes, yes, if I am worthy of him, I would truly wish to love such a man—"

Her aunt and father shook their heads and breathed deeply, as Josefina Vasquez comforted her niece.

Six

Exhilarated as he had been by the day's hunt with John Cooper and Carlos—as well as by its romantic aftermath—Ferdinand de Lloradier had hoped that the morrow would bring a repetition, for the weather continued stimulatingly cool, ideal for riding and hunting. But John Cooper and Raoul Maldones spent most of the morning making a tour of the *Hacienda del Halcón* in the company of Miguel Sandarbal, and not until the following day did John Cooper invite the young *caballero* from Taos to join him and Carlos on a renewal of their earlier hunt. Ferdinand was bursting with enthusiasm as he mounted his horse and drew out the rifle from its saddle sheath to make sure it was primed and loaded. He could hardly wait to divulge the news of his meeting with Miranda Vasquez.

"You recall, Carlos," he exclaimed, as they set out, "you were teasing me the other day about not having a wife. Well, *por todos los santos*, I think I have found a girl who would make me the happiest man in all of this your Texas."

"And who is that, *mi amigo*?" Carlos smilingly looked over his shoulder.

"She is Miranda Vasquez."

"Why, yes, I know her. A beautiful, sweet, gentle girl. And old Vasquez is one of our best *vaqueros*. You show good taste, Ferdinand, and I pray that your suit will be successful," Carlos told him.

"I agree," John Cooper chimed in. "Vasquez and his sister have brought her up to be kind and thoughtful, as they are themselves, and Vasquez is most industrious, never shirking a task that Miguel has set him.''

"The only problem,'' Ferdinand mused, "is that she doesn't think she's good enough for me. That's nonsense, and I've already asked the señor Vasquez to allow me to court her.''

"Good!'' John Cooper said. "I think more of you now for having told me this, Ferdinand.''

"I mean it, John Cooper. I only met her the once, you understand, when I came back from that hunt of ours the other day. She had found a little swallow with a broken wing, and she was so sweet and tender toward it—I lost my heart to her.''

"You are a true romantic!'' John Cooper said with a chuckle. "I wish you joy. If I can help, especially if you need someone to influence the Vasquez father and aunt, I'd stand as your best man.''

"You're most kind, John Cooper! Ah, I feel better already. Today I think I shall kill a brace of wild boar, and perhaps a mountain lion thrown in for good measure!'' the young *caballero* boasted.

"This time,'' John Cooper proposed, "we'll head a little farther east and see what Yankee and his cubs can flush out.''

An hour later, the three riders had gone several miles beyond the place where, two days ago, they had shot the partridges. The weather was not as cool as it had been the previous days, and the air had grown oppressive, suggesting a coming storm. Dark clouds gathered in the sky. Yankee, Maja, and Fuerte loped ahead, Yankee uttering quick little barks as he glanced back, as if urging his cubs to keep up with him.

They neared a stagnant creek to their right, surrounded by a thick growth of mesquite, and beyond was a dense grove of live-oak trees. Yankee's hair suddenly bristled along the back of his neck, and his ears flattened. With a growl, he slunk forward, lowering his muzzle, his yellow eyes intent on something that had seemed to move just within the trees. John Cooper Baines turned back to Ferdinand and Carlos, gesturing in Yankee's direction and signaling that they should ready their rifles.

Suddenly Yankee uttered an angry bark and loped forward, followed by Maja and Fuerte, one on each side of their sire. At the same moment, a huge wild boar charged out of the trees and, with a raging bellow, turned straight for Carlos de Escobar. Startled, Carlos's palomino whinnied shrilly and reared on its hind legs, pawing the air with its front hooves. Maja and Fuerte raced for the wild boar, while Yankee wheeled directly behind it.

The little red eyes of the boar fixed on the uprearing palomino, and the frightened horse, trying to escape, twisted to one side, flinging Carlos from the saddle. The Spaniard uttered an agonized cry, for he had been thrown against a sharp rock, his rifle jarred from his hand.

Controlling his own horse, Ferdinand de Lloradier drew his rifle, brought it to his shoulder, and hastily pulled the trigger. But there was only a flash of powder as the rifle misfired. With an oath, the *caballero* flung his useless weapon to the ground and reached for a pistol at his belt. Maja and Fuerte had closed on the boar and nipped at its sides, as it wheeled to menace each in turn with its razor-sharp tusks. Yankee, fearless, lunged at it and nipped its left haunch, but this only seemed to infuriate the *jabalí* even more, as it turned again and bore down upon Carlos, who lay groaning, unable to move.

John Cooper Baines had "Long Girl" at his shoulder and, squinting along the barrel, pulled the trigger. The raging boar had come within five feet of Carlos when the ball struck it in the left side and reached its heart. The savage animal's momentum carried it forward as, with an agonized bellow, it toppled to one side upon Carlos's chest.

"A miraculous shot, thank the good God for it!" Ferdinand breathed hoarsely as he reached for a kerchief and mopped his sweating forehead. John Cooper had flung himself off his palomino and rushed up to Carlos, and now the *caballero* emulated the tall Texan. From the looks of it, one of the boar's tusks had gashed the Spaniard along the right side of his chest. The two men rolled the dead boar off Carlos's body, and John Cooper tore open his brother-in-law's shirt to peer at the wound. "It's not at all deep, thank the Lord for that," John Cooper exclaimed. "I'll bandage it, and we'll get you back to the *hacienda*."

"My—my arm's broken, I think," Carlos panted. "When I was thrown, I fell on a rock, and I heard the bone crack—damnation, what a thing to have happen after our luck the other day!"

"If only my rifle hadn't misfired," Ferdinand said. "I was sure I had loaded it and primed it carefully—"

"That will happen even with the best of guns," John Cooper put in. "I remember once, when I was aiming at a bear—well, no matter. We've got to make a splint, then get Carlos back to the ranch."

They managed to stanch the flow of blood from the flesh wound dealt by the boar's tusk, and then John Cooper made a splint by breaking off two small oak branches, which he whittled down with his hunting knife. "You'd best hold Carlos by the shoulders, Ferdinand," he said, "while I try to set his arm. He could be crippled if it isn't attended to at once—my father taught me that a long time ago." Then he said to Carlos, "I'm going to have to hurt you, *mi hermano*."

"I'm glad I'm alive, thanks to you. A little pain is nothing." He closed his eyes as Ferdinand, kneeling behind him, gripped his shoulders. "Just do it, and don't tell me when you're going to, John Cooper."

"Of course. You're a brave man, *mi hermano*. But then, I've always known that you were and still are—" As he spoke, John Cooper felt for where the bone was broken and then, suddenly, gripped both hands to Carlos's arm and snapped the bone back. Sweat bursting on his face, Carlos arched his body in agony, and only by grinding his teeth did he suppress the outcry of pain. Swiftly now, John Cooper applied the splint, and Ferdinand, having torn his shirt into strips, used the pieces of cloth to fix it tightly into place.

"The worst is over, *mi hermano*," John Cooper murmured as he fashioned a sling around Carlos's neck. "Now we're going to see how to get you home."

"If you two will help me onto my horse," Carlos said, "I think I can stay straight in the saddle and hold the reins with my good hand. We'll take it slowly. I could use a little tequila or brandy right now, I'll admit."

"You can drink yourself into a stupor, *mi hermano*, once we get you back safely," John Cooper said, chuckling. "Ferdinand, you hold his horse, and I'll give him a little boost."

Suiting action to words, the two men carefully helped Carlos onto his palomino, which by now had quieted. John Cooper patted the animal's neck reassuringly.

"I—I think I can manage now," Carlos said. "My arm throbs as if it were on fire—but I felt it snap back into place. *Gracias, mi hermano, gracias por mi vida.*"

It was midafternoon when they returned to the *Hacienda del Halcón*, and as Ferdinand ran off to fetch Pablo Aguirrez—the resident doctor at the Double H Ranch—John Cooper accompanied Carlos to his bed and made him comfortable. At the Spaniard's insistence, John Cooper promised to immediately send two *vaqueros* to the site of the accident, to bring back the dead *jabalí* so that its meat would not be wasted.

Teresa rushed into the room, greatly upset at the sight of her husband's bandages and his arm in a sling, but as she knelt at the bedside, Carlos assured her that he would be all right.

Dr. Aguirrez arrived a moment later, and after a brief examination, he turned to John Cooper and admiringly declared, "Señor Baines, your quick action and skill served to set the arm into proper place—I myself could not have done better. I will rebandage the chest wound, which does not look bad, then all that is required is sufficient rest and tender care—which I'm certain Señora de Escobar will supply in abundance." The affable black-bearded *médico*, who had left Mexico City two years ago, fleeing the political upheavals, proceeded to clean and dress the tusk wound with great skill, and as John Cooper watched him work, he felt fortunate that he and Miguel had persuaded this man to settle at the Texas ranch and resume his practice.

The very next afternoon, John Cooper went to Don Diego's old study and, seating himself at the *escritoire*, began his regular monthly letter to Fabien Mallard, the ranch's factor in New Orleans. The Texan's mood was troubled, for just a few hours ago he had received news of the skirmish on the Rio Grande between Jim Bowie's Texas Rangers and a Mexican patrol. It was the worst in a long series of such incidents, and John Cooper had a hard time keeping his mind on business matters.

He was rereading the finished letter when there came a knock at the door. He called out "*¡Adelante!*" and the door opened to reveal a smiling Doña Inez, who hurried toward him, holding two letters in her hand.

Rising quickly, he said, "You look as if you've had good news, *mi madre*."

"The very best in the world! And because Dorotéa told me that you were about to send a letter off to New Orleans, I asked the courier not to leave until I give him the letters I am going to write to both the señor McKinnon and my adorable Francesca."

"You've received an answer to your letter to the señor McKinnon, then?"

"Oh, yes!" Dona Inez answered happily. "And a letter from Francesca as well. "Let me read to you Señor McKinnon's letter, dear John Cooper—" When he nodded, she read aloud:

Most respected Doña Inez de Escobar:

When I received your letter, knowing that I was going to have to visit New Orleans on business, I made certain of posting this reply immediately.

I want you to know that I think I owe my life to your daughter Francesca. But at the same time, please be assured that in no way did I encourage her to look upon me romantically. The fact is, two months ago the daughter of the owner of our sugar-cane plantation, Matilda Heskins, did me the honor of accepting my proposal of marriage, and we have set the date for the day before Christmas. I have taken the liberty of writing a letter to your daughter and had my foreman leave it at the convent school she is attending. I did my best to break the news so that she would not be hurt, and to convince her that her feelings for me have touched me very deeply, and that one day she will find a man who will love and honor her as she deserves.

My wife-to-be and I plan to spend our honeymoon in New Orleans, but I should like your advice as to whether you think it wise for us to visit Francesca—we both want to express our very best wishes to her.

I am enclosing a copy of the letter that I wrote to Francesca. If you ever come to New Orleans at a time when I shall be visiting there, or, indeed, if I should ever have occasion to come to Texas, I should be privileged and honored to make your acquaintance. I remain at your service.

Yours sincerely,
Jack McKinnon

"He is a very decent man, Doña Inez," John Cooper declared.

"Yes, yes, I am sure of it. And what he wrote my sweet Francesca was ever so tender. I—I shall keep it to myself, except to say to you that he told her he would always remember that he owed his very life to her, and that he would try to make the most of that life so that she would be proud of him. I think he explained things beautifully, dear John Cooper."

"And how did Francesca take the news?" John Cooper asked.

"Very sensibly. I can tell from her letter that she cried a little, but she understands. I think Francesca is growing up fast, and in a way, perhaps it was good that all this happened."

"That's true, dear Doña Inez. Sometimes we can't always understand why things happen, but there's inevitably a reason. In fact, I think it would be good if Francesca were to meet Señor McKinnon and his wife when they're on their honeymoon."

"I do, too, John Cooper, and I am going to write him to suggest that, as well as send a letter to my darling girl and tell her how proud I am of her, and how proud her dear father in heaven would be, if he could know how she has behaved." Doña Inez took a handkerchief from the pocket of her dress and, turning away, dried her eyes. "I shall write both letters right away, and thus the courier will be able to take them tomorrow with yours, if you have no objection."

"That'll be fine. And now I think you and I should go see Carlos and tell him about this news, for it will make him feel very happy and help get him well again all the sooner."

He offered his arm to Doña Inez, much as he might have done if he had been presented at the court of Spain to a noblewoman. The mature widow made him a curtsy, then kissed him on the cheek and whispered, "God bless you, dear John Cooper! There have been two men in my life who have given me the greatest joy. One of course was Don Diego, and the other is you."

In the dark of night, with a quarter moon casting its sickly glow over the Caribbean sky, the abandoned *Salamander* rolled gently in the placid waters. On its decks were the dead crewmen and officers who had put up so valiant a fight against unequal odds. One man remained alive, the Argentine priest, Angelo Camporata, who for the last several hours had knelt on the deck, clutching his rosary. Now he looked up at the sky, and crossing himself and then touching the silver crucifix of his rosary, he earnestly implored, "*Señor Dios,* You Who sent His only Son, our dear Lord *Jesu Cristo,* to live among us, I pray not for my own safety. I am but a humble servant, and I ask your intervention not for my sake, but for those poor captured American sailors, and for the two young men, Enrique and Benito Duvaldo, that they may survive the wretched slavery that the cruel pirates seek to inflict upon them. O *Dios,* if it be Your divine will, let me be the instrument whereby they gain their freedom; and if my own humble life is to be spared, I swear I shall continue, for the rest of my days, my work in Your name."

He bowed his head and moved the rosary beads as he prayed silently now, and when he glanced around, seeing the lifeless bodies on both sides of him, he could not help weeping softly. Padre Angelo Camporata knew nothing of seamanship, and he suppressed a shudder as the abandoned brig yawed with each new swirl of waves or gust of wind. He could console himself only with the thought that, since the pirates had boarded before their cannons had done much damage to the hull, the ship would probably remain afloat. Where it would go, however, without a helmsman and crew—indeed without a mast or sail remaining intact—was in the hands of Him to whom he prayed.

Padre Camporata had no shrouds, no coffins for the dead, yet it occurred to him that he must give them burial at sea, for seamen expected this, and it was their final right. Summoning all his strength, he rose at last and mournfully began to lift the dead bodies one by one and, praying aloud, drop each over the rail into the dark water below. When this grisly task was done, he wept aloud and again knelt to pray for the souls of these brave, unfortunate men. And then, because he was exhausted, and he had had no water or food since breakfast, he went to the galley and found a pannikin beside a hogshead of water. He drank thirstily, then rummaged through the cupboards until he found a half loaf of stale bread and some strong-smelling cheese. This was his supper, and when he had finished, he thanked God for this sustenance and then went to the captain's cabin, stretched himself out upon the bunk, and, after a last prayer, fell asleep.

He awoke the next morning and promptly went down on his knees to thank God for having spared his life. Then, fortifying himself with more of the bread and cheese, washed down with cold coffee he discovered in a pot beside the galley stove, he went out onto the deck. The sun was bright and the water calm, and Padre Camporata put a hand to the bridge of his nose to shield his eyes from the glaring sun. He squinted toward each side of the horizon, but there was nothing in sight except the clear blue water of the Caribbean. He saw the fin of a shark cut through the surface, then disappear, and he shuddered at the horrid thought that perhaps those valiant crewmen he had been forced to bury might have drawn the attention of these predators of the deep.

He stood on deck throughout the long afternoon, and then, just as the sun began to set, he spied the distant black outline of a ship. With a cry of joy, he looked around him and saw that an American flag still fluttered from one of the masts that the cannonballs of the *Dos Hermanos* had felled upon the deck. He hurriedly untied it and began frantically to wave it.

The ship seemed to come closer, and as he waited, he prayed aloud for this salvation, which might enable him to fulfill his promise to the young Duvaldo brothers. Twilight began to fall, but by now Padre Camporata, to his joy, could make out an American flag, and even see the faces of the seamen at the rail staring across the water toward him. He saw a small dinghy being lowered with two seamen at the oars, and as it approached, tears ran down his cheeks and he clasped his hands, again pledging that what life remained to him would be in the service of the needy and the poor.

Looking about, he saw a rope ladder fixed to the rail of the quarterdeck and, testing it, found it sturdy enough to bear his portly weight. As the dinghy pulled alongside, he let himself down carefully, and one of the seamen reached up to steady him and help him into the rowboat. "May *el Señor Dios* bless you, *mi hijo!*" he exclaimed in his halting English. "I am the only survivor. We were attacked by *piratas*, who killed many of the crew and took the others as *esclavos.*"

"I'll wager it was those damned Obeiras," the seaman who had helped him angrily declared. "Pardon me, Father, but they've been plaguing the coast for some years now, and there's a gallows ready and waiting if anybody ever catches up with them!" He took up his oar and, with his fellow, began to row back to the American ship. "You were lucky they didn't cut your throat, Father."

"Yes, my son. Very lucky."

Fifteen minutes later, on the quarterdeck of the merchantman *Revere* out of Searsport, Maine, the bespectacled, plump priest was explaining what had happened to him to Captain Edmund Marsh. Already the resourceful Yankee shipmaster had sent a skeleton crew aboard the *Salamander* to clear away the wrecked masts and set up a jury rig to sail the crippled brig back to port.

"No doubt about it," the gray-haired captain said to the priest, "those were the Obeira brothers. I hear tell they're sailing out of Florida these days, from somewhere near Pensacola. That's why, the last time we put out from the States, Father, we added six guns, just so we could fight them if they crossed our bow. I'm thinking it would be an act of justice if we could be the ones to sink that accursed ship and send it and its crew to Davy Jones!"

"I am told you are sailing for New Orleans, Captain Marsh."

"That's true, Father, though the poor *Salamander* will make for Mobile, which is closer. In any case, you'll have to go to the authorities in New Orleans and tell them your story about the American crewmen who were seized, as well as those two young fellows from Argentina."

"*Seguramente*, Captain Marsh. But first I shall go to see the bishop of that city—he is my superior, and I must report to him, since I am setting foot upon the *Estados Unidos* for the first time. Until then I do not wish to trouble you, and I require very little for my physical needs—a crust of bread and a cup of water—"

"Nonsense, Father! You'll sit at my table tonight, and we'll give you a fine dinner. And there's a spare cabin aboard, so you shall have a comfortable bunk on which to sleep. You deserve it, after what you've been through."

The *Revere* tied up along the great levee of New Orleans at late afternoon of the second day after it had stopped to rescue Padre Angelo Camporata from the abandoned *Salamander*. After the little priest had thanked Captain Marsh for his kindness, he hurried down the gangplank in search of a calash driver who could take him to the Cathedral of Saint Louis, where the captain had told him he might find the bishop of the diocese. As a final courtesy, the captain had given him a handful of coins to pay for the transportation to the church and for food and lodging for a day or two, until he could make arrangements to continue his journey to Texas.

A gray-haired housekeeper, answering to the priest's knock at the rectory door, took him directly to the study of Bishop Martin Larosse, a tall, gentle man with snowy-white hair. Padre Camporata went down on his knees and bowed his head before his superior, and then began in Spanish, "*Excelencia*, I do not know if you speak Spanish, but I am from Buenos Aires, where I was an ordained priest with my own church and loyal parishioners."

"I am French by birth, my son, but since there are many Spanish in this city, I have learned to speak that language fluently. May I be of some assistance to you?"

"I fervently hope so, *excelencia*. You see, I fled my country for my life, because of the tyrannical government in Buenos Aires, and after my ship was attacked by pirates, I was rescued and brought here to New Orleans. . . ." He went on to explain, with great agitation, how he had been pronounced defrocked, his meeting with the Duvaldo brothers, and what had happened to them and the surviving members of the *Salamander*'s crew. "*Excelencia*, they begged me to intercede for them, to find my way to a señor Baines at the Double H Ranch in Texas, for that man was a friend of their dead father, whom the *porteños* had murdered because he, too, would not bow to their will."

"You are exhausted, my son," the kindly bishop interposed, holding up a slim hand. "Take supper with me, and I shall hear you out at length. I promise I will do what I can to help you. Already what you have said of your experiences tells me that your good deeds have proved your faith and worthiness, and I strongly suspect that you were wrongfully, perhaps illegally, removed from God's holy church."

This surprised Padre Camporata, for he had never thought to question whether the bishop of Buenos Aires did indeed possess the authority to declare him officially defrocked. "I—I cannot express in words what I feel toward Your Excellency," he stammered, "for being so generous to me, an unworthy stranger—"

"Nonsense, my son. What you have told me attests to your faith and devotion. But come now, my housekeeper has already informed me that supper is ready. I have an excellent cook here—one of my sins, alas, is gluttony, and I pray constantly to be forgiven for it. But today I am happy that you will share my repast, for it will perhaps justify my indulgence." He chuckled. "Man is a most rational creature, my son; he invents excuses to justify what he wishes to do in the first place. I do not think that is good theology, mind you, but no matter. Tonight we shall forgo theology and talk only of ways in which I can be of help to you.''

The little priest's eyes again filled with tears. He had not expected so gracious a reception, and now he saw that his prayers, while he had been alone on that wrecked ship, had truly been answered. He vowed, more than ever, that he would work twice as hard for the redemption of all those whom he could help, all who had suffered as he had from oppression and tyranny.

He could not help exclaiming over the kingly banquet— for such it seemed to him—that the bishop's cook had prepared: *pompano en papillote*, a bowl of wonderfully redolent gumbo, sweet yams cooked with butter and herbs, and the tastiest pudding he had ever put a spoon to, as well as a powerfully strong coffee on which Creoles doted in this city by the Gulf.

During the meal, the bishop plied him with questions, asking about the churches in Buenos Aires, the rituals and the services, and Padre Camporata expatiated on his experiences. The elderly housekeeper beamed to see the bishop so delighted with his suppertime guest and, without being asked, brought a decanter of excellent tawny port to conclude the repast.

"Another glass, my son," the bishop smilingly proposed. "It's good for your circulation. And a good night's sleep will give you back the strength that was so sorely taxed by your harrowing experiences. Tomorrow, while you report to the authorities at the Cabildo, which is just next door, I shall summon a young man from my diocese to act as your companion, escort, and interpreter for the time being. Also, out of church funds, since my parishioners have been very lavish and generous, I shall see that you have sufficient money to purchase a horse and supplies to get you to the ranch in Texas."

"I do not know how to repay Your Excellency—"

"Hush, my son! Speak not of payment, for I, too, am but an instrument of a higher power, and I sense what this mission of yours may mean to those wrongfully imprisoned young men. At dawn tomorrow, I will say a mass for your sake, that you may safely and swiftly reach this Señor Baines, who will aid you as I cannot. And now, my son, I will have my housekeeper show you to your room for the night. I shall join you at breakfast tomorrow, and there I will tell you how I plan to reinstate you in Mother Church. I take it that you have no desire to go back to Buenos Aires?''

"I love the country I served so long, Your Excellency, but if I were to return there now, I should cast my life away for no purpose. I alone cannot stand against so many who venerate evil instead of good.''

"Then perhaps I can find a place for you here as a deacon in this, my church, until another post arrives. There are many little parishes in this city, some of them predominantly Spanish, that are in need of loyal priests who will spread His holy word.''

"It would give me a new life, Your Excellency—and I promise that I will try not to be unworthy of your great confidence in me. I still find such kindness hard to believe, my being such a stranger, and this our first meeting.''

"My son"—the white-haired bishop smilingly interrupted as he again held up his hand—"I am sixty-five years of age. I have been a priest since I was nineteen. Do you think that, in all these years, I have not learned to read the hearts and minds of men? In you, Padre Camporata, I see a man of dedication, purpose, and honesty, and one can ask for no more from a priest. Now it is time for you to sleep. Go now with Sister Luisette.''

Seven

The venerable bishop handed Padre Angelo Camporata a little leather pouch with drawstrings. "In this, my son, you will find two hundred dollars in gold, which should surely be ample to provide for the horse and the supplies you will need for your journey to Texas. And this young man"—he turned to a tall, slim, black-haired youth—"is Mathieu Farigo. He is a Cajun, he speaks Spanish, and he knows the terrain of Louisiana as well as that of Texas. When Mathieu was but a child, his parents were stricken by the pestilence of yellow fever, which so often descends upon our city in the summer. One of our nuns discovered him all alone in the little house where his parents lay dead, and he was raised in our orphanage. You will find him trustworthy, strong, and brave, and he will protect you along the journey, as well as lessen its difficulties for you."

"Your Excellency, I shall never be able to thank you enough—" the balding little priest began, but the bishop smiled, shook his head, and lifted his hand in a benediction.

"By the good deeds you will perform in the years to come, you will more than repay me. While you were at the Cabildo this morning, *padre*, I was thinking about the political problems that beset you and drove you into exile. In my study, I did some reading into the church law concerning the defrocking of an ordained priest. Ultimate jurisdiction in such cases resides in Rome, of course, but until such appeals can be made, I have composed a document that will stand you in good stead wherever you may go in this country. You may consider yourself still a priest, and I have appointed you an emissary of goodwill for this diocese from this day forth. I count on you, of course, to write to me and tell me of your progress. That in itself will reward me for the little help I tender you now, my son.''

The *padre*'s face shone with gratitude, and he humbly knelt as the bishop made the sign of the cross over his head and, touching him on the right shoulder and then the left, said, ''May He watch over you on this journey and speed you on your way. In the name of the Father, Son, and Holy Ghost, amen.''

Mathieu Farigo was a soft-spoken young man and, to the *padre*'s surprise, remarkably well versed in theology. Yet he was eminently practical, as he proved at once by going with Padre Camporata to a livery stable and there arguing the purchase price of two sturdy mounts and saddles for the journey, not relenting until the owner agreed to a price that seemed unbelievably low. This done, the Cajun went to a warehouse that specialized in selling food supplies to travelers. There the saddlebags were filled with jerky, flour, coffee, and salt, as well as a sack of oats for the horses and a razor, soap, and hand brush for the priest and his companion.

Mathieu Farigo brought with him his own long rifle, as well as a sharp hunting knife. In the pockets of his jacket he had placed pouches containing gunpowder and ball for the rifle. Seeing this, the priest nervously commented, ''Señor Farigo, is it necessary to carry weapons on this journey?''

''Yes, Father, because one may encounter not only hostile Indians but also outlaws who rob and sometimes kill the innocent traveler. It is well to be armed and wary. But rest assured, Father, I abhor violence, as does any good Christian, and will resort to it only if there is no other choice. And besides, if one wishes to obtain fresh meat during so long a journey, the hunting knife and rifle will help us to supplement what would otherwise be a monotonous diet. And now, if you are ready, we shall begin our journey. We shall follow the river road as far as Baton Rouge, in order to skirt the swampland, and then make our way westward by a trail I know well.''

"I follow you with implicit trust, my son," the priest replied, though he did not fail to make the sign of the cross as they mounted their horses and set off.

The first part of the journey was the easiest, and by nightfall they had covered almost twenty miles. The young Cajun chose a campsite on high ground well away from the river, sheltered by cypress and live-oak trees. After dismounting and helping Padre Camporata to climb down from his horse, Mathieu put a forefinger to his lips and pointed to a jackrabbit in the distant underbrush. Creeping silently toward it, he drew his hunting knife and, suddenly stepping forward, flung it between the tips of his right median and forefingers, felling the rabbit with an unerring throw.

"I'll make a fire, and we'll have rabbit for supper, Father," he called back to the priest.

"I have never seen anyone throw a knife more swiftly, my son. Not even the *gauchos* in my homeland."

"You see, Father," Mathieu smilingly explained as he fell to skinning the rabbit, "I did not live at the orphanage all my life. When I was about twelve, the good sisters found me a place on a little farm not far from New Orleans, where an elderly couple were managing as best they could after their own son had died. I planted yams, beans, and corn, fished and trapped, and did what I could for them. They both died in their sleep some years later, one a few days after the other, and then I went back to the sisters."

"You have led a remarkable life for one so young, my son."

"All in all, it has been a good life, Father, and I am thankful. Now, let us gather some firewood so that we may cook our dinner."

Padre Angelo Camporata soon adapted himself to the physical demands of riding horseback and found the experience exhilarating. The companionship of Mathieu Farigo, who continued to fascinate him with a mixture of worldly and theological knowledge and common sense, more than compensated for any hardships encountered.

On the fourth day, as they were riding past a dense

thicket of flowering shrubs, the priest suddenly uttered a cry of pain, for a bee had stung his right hand. Mathieu halted his horse, dismounted, and helped the priest down from his horse. "The weather is unseasonably warm, Father, and that's why wasps and bees are still dangerous. Attracted by those flowers, I've no doubt. That's a bad sting—I'll see what I can do to help ease your pain."

With the tip of his razor-sharp hunting knife, he deftly and lightly cut out the imbedded stinger, then sucked the wound clean. Next, delving into a side pocket of his jacket, he produced a little flask, opened it, and poured a brownish, syrupy liquid upon the wound. "This is an ointment I made that is good for cuts and stings and the like, Father," he explained. "One of the doctors gave me the recipe when I worked at the sisters' hospital in New Orleans. Now let me bandage your hand, and I promise you that by tomorrow there should be no swelling and certainly no pain."

"Again I marvel at how much you know for one so young, my son," the priest exclaimed. "Surely I am fortunate in having you as my guide and companion. And the more I come to know of you, the more I think that your talents could be of immense use to one of the outlying settlements here. Perhaps it is none of my business, my son, but someone like you would be a great blessing to such people."

"I shall go where my bishop sends me, Father. It is true, I should like to be of greater service than I am in New Orleans, but like you, I am only His humble instrument."

"And you have a rare humility for one so young, as well," the priest declared. By now the Cajun had wrapped a neat bandage and tied it securely. "Already the pain is gone, my son. It is a marvel."

Shortly after noon on the fourteenth day of their journey, the two men rode through the gate of the Double H Ranch. Esteban Morales, the assistant foreman, had been out riding with two other *vaqueros* to round up some runaway steers, and he and his men had just returned as they saw the priest and the young Cajun ride in. He bade the *vaqueros* take his horse to the stable with their own, then hurried forward to greet the newcomers.

"A good day to you, *mi padre,* and you, señor. You are welcome to break your journey and to rest with us, if you are going on. And there is food and drink for you, if you are hungry and thirsty."

"Thank you, my son." The little priest slowly dismounted. "This is my guide, Mathieu Farigo, and my name is Angelo Camporata. I am from Argentina, and I have come to see Señor John Cooper Baines, who I was told owns this *estancia.*"

"That is true, *mi padre.* He is inside now, I believe. I will go to him and tell him that you are here to see him. From Argentina, you say?"

"Yes, my son. Tell him, if you will, that I come on behalf of young Benito and Enrique Duvaldo, who begged me to find him and to tell him what has happened to them."

"At once, *mi padre.*" Esteban beckoned to a nearby *trabajador.* "Juan, kindly take the horses of these two visitors of ours. Excuse me, Father, for not introducing myself. I am Esteban Morales, assistant *capataz* of this ranch. If you and Señor Farigo will follow me, I will take you to John Cooper Baines, *el Halcón.*"

"He is called the Hawk on this ranch?" the young Cajun inquired with curiosity.

"Yes, it is a name his blood brothers, the Jicarilla Apache, gave him because of his courage and his swiftness to avenge a wrong."

They reached the *hacienda,* and Esteban held open the kitchen door for them, saying, "Perhaps, before I fetch the señor Baines, both of you would like some refreshment or some *comida*?"

"No, thank you, my son. My message is urgent, and I made a vow to deliver it as swiftly as I could."

"I respect your purpose, *mi padre.*" Esteban solemnly nodded. He ushered them into a small salon just off the main hall of the *hacienda.* "Wait here a moment, and I'll bring him to you."

John Cooper had been playing with his little son James, to the delight of Dorotéa, who lovingly watched the tall Texan in his buckskin jacket holding the child in his arms.

He emerged from the bedchamber now, saw Esteban

Morales patiently waiting for him, and his eyes widened in question: "*Qué pasa*, Esteban?"

"A priest and a young rider have come to see you, *Halcón*," the assistant *capataz* replied. "The priest says that he has come from Argentina, and that he has an urgent message from the Duvaldo brothers."

"I had thought they would be here by now—this is most important! Thank you for telling me, Esteban. I'll go out to them right now."

A few moments later, John Cooper strode into the room where the two men were waiting and said, "I am told that you wish to see me—I'm John Cooper Baines. *Mi padre*"—he nodded politely to the priest—"Esteban said that you've brought a message from Benito and Enrique Duvaldo."

"I did indeed, my son. This man is Mathieu Farigo, whom the kind bishop of New Orleans sent along with me as a guide. I could never have arrived here in this relatively short time if it had not been for his help. But, yes, it is true, and it is almost a miracle that I am here to tell you what has become of those unfortunate young men."

"Unfortunate? What happened to them? They had written that they planned to come here, after their father's death—"

"Yes, Señor Baines, that is what they said to me. And they were on their way here when a terrible disaster befell them. You see, señor, we were attacked shortly out of Havana by a ship commanded by two brothers named Juan and Manolito Obeira. They killed many of the crew, and the others they took aboard their ship to be sold as slaves in Havana. And that is what they intended to do with those fine young men."

"Sell them as slaves? But they are white!"

"*Es verdad*, Señor Baines—but the *capitán* of our ship, before he was killed, said that the Obeiras were unscrupulous pirates who sold their victims into slavery. They were afraid to harm a priest, however, and so they spared my life, leaving me alone and adrift on the hulk of our ship. No doubt they believed I would die of starvation or thirst; but I prayed, Señor Baines, and the next day a ship appeared and rescued me, then brought me to New Orleans, where I went to see the bishop, who sent the señor Farigo with me to find you."

"Pirates, you say?" John Cooper scowled, rubbed his chin with a hand for a moment, deep in thought, then went on: "*Mi padre*, could you identify those men who captured Benito and Enrique?"

"Yes, my son, I surely could never forget them. They were Spanish renegades, and they base their operations from somewhere near Pensacola, in Florida. At least that was what I was told by the *capitán* of the merchant ship that rescued me. Indeed, the civil authorities in New Orleans, to whom I reported, had also heard the same rumor."

"And they sell their booty and slaves in Havana, no doubt, to stay out of trouble with the government here. Well, Father, I will do whatever is necessary to rescue Benito and Enrique Duvaldo, as soon as we decide the best course of action. But come—you have journeyed a long way, and you and your companion will be our guests at the *hacienda*. I have rooms for you, and tonight you'll have supper with us. Also, you'll be able to meet Señor Maldones, who will be as much interested in your news and shocked by it as I am." He turned to Esteban Morales, who was standing at the threshold. "Esteban, take the padre and Señor Farigo to the guest rooms, and then tell Rosa we will have two very important guests for supper tonight."

"It will be my pleasure, *Halcón*. Come with me, *mi padre*, Señor Farigo," the assistant *capataz* genially urged.

John Cooper Baines stood alone in the salon, a worried look on his face. This peaceful time that had followed Dorotéa's abduction and safe return had been too good to last. Heitor Duvaldo had been Raoul Maldones's best friend, and Raoul was now John Cooper's father-in-law; for this reason alone the tall Texan knew he could not turn his back upon the plight of the young Duvaldos. From what he remembered of Benito and Enrique, when he had met them on his first visit to Argentina, they were fine, strong boys. He hoped they would have the courage and character to withstand their present fate until somehow he could arrange their rescue.

His jaws tightening with resolve, his eyes narrowed and angry, John Cooper Baines went in search of Raoul Maldones to tell him what had happened to his best friend's sons.

*   *   *

At dusk, the *Dos Hermanos* moved slowly past the grim fortress of Morro Castle and entered the Bay of Havana, as one of the crewmen, trained for such duty, took soundings with a weighted line so that the ship could avoid running aground. As soon as they had dropped anchor, some two hundred yards from the main wharf, Juan and Manolito Obeira gave orders to have the captured seamen from the *Salamander* taken out of the hold and loaded into the longboat and rowed ashore, under close guard. The Obeiras themselves chose to go ashore in the dinghy along with their two prized prisoners, Benito and Enrique Duvaldo.

When the Obeira brothers had first come to trade in Havana, they had been clever enough to give sizable bribes to all those in a position to help them, and hence, whenever their ship came into port, the sergeant of the guard at the wharf knew in advance what was expected of him. Now, when the two oared boats from the *Dos Hermanos* neared the shore, the blue-uniformed sergeant saluted the Obeira brothers and smilingly called out, "Was it a successful voyage, señores?"

"Most satisfactory, *mi amigo*," Juan Obeira replied. "Have the goodness to summon a carriage for us, and a wagon big enough to carry a dozen *esclavos* to our warehouse near the slave market, if you please."

"At once, señor."

"This is for your trouble—" Manolito Obeira tossed a gold coin to the sergeant as the dinghy pulled up to the wharf.

Juan stepped ashore and helped his brother out of the boat, then turned to the head oarsman. "After you unload these two prisoners, row back to the ship and bring ashore the rest of the booty. The first mate will show you where it is. Bring everything, don't forget—and be quick about it! We'll be at our warehouse. Remember, the sooner we complete all our business, the more of the evening we'll have to enjoy ourselves!"

The sergeant of the guard wasted little time, and within ten minutes he had already herded the chained prisoners from the longboat into a wagon, then ordered the driver to proceed to the Obeira warehouse.

At the Obeiras' direction, Benito and Enrique Duvaldo were kept apart from the others, and finally loaded into a large, open carriage, with an armed guard sitting behind them. Juan and Manolito took a seat across from the young brothers, and Juan told the driver to take them to their warehouse.

Manolito gave the youths a crooked grin as he appraised them, then turned to his brother. "Juan, *mi hermano,* I think we've a fine prize in these two intelligent *niños.* They have brains, you can tell; they don't fuss the way they did when we first took them. I'm still laughing at what they dared to say when we told them we were bringing them here to sell as slaves—that they were white and citizens of Argentina! But now, you see, they know that a good slave keeps his mouth shut."

Indeed, the two Duvaldo brothers did not deign to reply to this sarcastic comment, but exchanged a meaningful glance. Each of them was hoping that Padre Angelo Camporata in some way would manage to escape the doomed *Salamander* and get to Texas to tell John Cooper Baines what had happened to them. So far, escape had been impossible. Having overheard the comments of the bloodthirsty crew of the *Dos Hermanos* during the journey to Havana, Benito and Enrique were all too well aware they were in the hands of cutthroats who would enjoy having an excuse to mistreat them.

It was dark by the time the carriage reached the warehouse, and Juan Obeira ordered a guard to convey the youths to a separate room and lock them up. Goaded on by the impatient jeers of the swarthy sailor, Benito and Enrique were ushered down a dark corridor, the clanking of their manacles and the difficulty they had in walking reminding them, with every step, of their dismal plight.

Meanwhile, the Obeira brothers walked to the office of the warehouse. On the threshold, a fat, nearly bald man, in a white linen suit and with a thick black mustache whose tips had been stiffly waxed, awaited them, beaming and rubbing his hands.

"*¡Bienvenido, mis amigos!*" he said with a cultured

lisp, waving them to chairs, then seating himself behind a huge mahogany desk. "I trust that our meeting this time will be even more profitable than the last."

"Have no fear of that, Señor Marconado," Juan Obeira said, smirking. "We boarded an American brig on its way to New Orleans and brought back a good dozen seamen to be sold as slaves. But the real prize is two young brothers from Argentina, passengers on the ship. When we saw them, we thought at once of you—didn't we, Manolito?"

"That is the gospel truth, Señor Marconado," his crippled brother agreed with an emphatic nod and a tap of his cane. "We remembered your conversation with us the last time, how you wished to find agreeable young men you could install in your famous Casa de Belleza. Young men of good breeding, I believe you said."

"*Es verdad, mis capitanes,*" the fat man genially agreed. "Many of my customers are rivals of mine in our government, and it is understood that, when men are with beautiful *putas,* they talk loosely. The trouble is, some of these customers prefer to do their loose talking to young men, if you catch my meaning." He shrugged. "In any case, the young man I used to employ as a servant recently met with an unfortunate accident, so I must replace him. These new *esclavos,* if all goes well, will be able to hear treasonable speeches and report to me, which will assuredly strengthen my position with *el gubernador* Santiago de Nuñez." He lowered his voice. "You understand, *mis capitanes,* that in my post as procurator general, I must be most careful in my dealings with you, for if our little arrangement should be bandied about the island, undoubtedly *su excelencia* would seek to remove me from office. And I enjoy this double life, for it gives me wealth and luxury, as well as power. Now, then, besides the *esclavos,* what else have you brought to me?"

"Our men are unloading the cargo from the American brig at this very moment, and it will be brought directly here, Señor Marconado," Juan Obeira unctuously replied.

"You say that you boarded this American ship? I hope you left no witnesses. The young American government, I believe, begins to be in league with the British as regards measures taken to prevent the spread of slavery."

"Have no fear of that, Señor Marconado," Manolito Obeira said, laughing evilly. "We left no one aboard that hulk save for a terrified priest, and he is doomed to die of starvation or thirst."

"We would not bring bad luck upon us by killing a priest, you must understand that, Señor Marconado," Juan explained.

"All the same, you had better hope that he was not rescued by Providence," the fat government official complained irritably, scratching his plump cheek with a well-groomed finger, upon which was a huge emerald ring.

The two Obeira brothers gave each other an uneasy glance, then Manolito spoke up cheerfully: "I tell you, Señor Marconado, the masts of this American ship were shot down by our expert gunners, and the ship will drift where the wind or current takes it. Forget the priest—ah, here is something far more important for our conversation, the cargo we took from the *Salamander*."

The boatswain and the first mate, along with several other crewmen, had driven two wagons in front of the door of the warehouse, and Luis Marconado himself accompanied the Obeiras in his eagerness to see what loot had been taken, so that he might learn his share.

At the orders of the two slavers, the men of the *Dos Hermanos* carried the gold, silver, and jewels into the office, then stacked the sacks of coffee beans, casks of wine, and the other more valuable items of captured cargo to one side of the office for eventual inspection.

"Here is a pair of ruby earrings that the young Argentine passengers had when we searched their belongings," Juan Obeira declared as he opened the velvet case and presented the earrings to the delighted government official.

"Magnificent! Notice the filigree silverwork—whoever made these is a master craftsman! I will give them to my mistress, Rosalie Castillo. She will be beside herself with delight. I'm indebted to you, Señor Juan!"

"It is my pleasure," the younger Obeira brother chuckled. "Manolito, show him the chest of money that we found in the captain's cabin. There are gold and silver coins there, to a large value—we have not bothered to count it all, because we did not wish to touch it until you could see the entire contents. In this way, you know that our partnership with you is an honest one.''

"I've never had any reason to doubt that, *mis amigos.*" Marconado rubbed his hands with glee as he lifted the lid of the chest. Then, giving the Obeiras a quick, steely glance, he suavely added, "Besides, you are both wise enough to know that crossing me would have its disadvantages. The arrangements we have made between us to facilitate your coming and going would, I fear, have to be terminated if you played me false.''

"You shall have a third of the contents, as agreed, since you financed our expedition, Señor Marconado." Manolito gestured toward the chest with his cane. "As for the wine, let that be a present to you.''

"You are most generous. I shall remember this. And the slaves?''

"You will have a third of the proceeds from the sale of the seamen," Manolito said. "But since we experienced a certain risk in boarding that American vessel, we think it only fair, Juan and I, that you give us a decent price for the two young Argentinians. And as you yourself have said, Señor Marconado, they can be of invaluable service to you.''

"Yes, that's only just. I agree. Gentlemen, show me these young men. If they are all that you claim, I shall have my majordomo call for them and take them to the Casa de Belleza. Tonight you will be the guests of honor at my villa. And I have no doubt that there will be a few young *criadas* who will make your evening as pleasant as you have made my day with this gift of the earrings.''

"Thank you for your hospitality, señor." Juan Obeira gave him a mock little bow, though the government official interpreted it, in his vanity, as a mark of tribute to his high rank in the Cuban government.

"And after the sale," Manolito added, "once you have received your share from the slaves, we shall go back to Pensacola.''

*   *   *

It so happened that six braves of the Jicarilla Apache, the tribe with which John Cooper had once lived, were visiting the Double H Ranch, bearing gifts from the tribe's chief. When John Cooper suggested that they join him and Padre Camporata on a little adventure, along with six *vaqueros* from the Double H Ranch, the warriors readily assented, happy to be given an opportunity to prove their mettle to *el Halcón*.

In fact, it was only the second morning after the little priest's arrival when John Cooper Baines and Padre Angelo Camporata prepared, along with the others, to leave for New Orleans, from where they would proceed to Pensacola. Young Mathieu Farigo accompanied them as well, for he would return to his service in the diocese of New Orleans. John Cooper had spent a good part of one day with the Cajun and had verified the priest's high praise of his diversified skills and keen mind. "I'm thinking, Mr. Farigo," the tall Texan told the Cajun, "that you could be invaluable to the settlement on the Brazos as a kind of doctor. The growing community there would be grateful to have someone such as you in their service. You might think about visiting there someday, if your bishop will permit you."

"I have seen what a large community you have here, Mr. Baines, and I admire the spirit of the people of Texas. I am sure the same holds true for the settlement on the Brazos. It would be God's work, indeed, to help them, but of course I am the servant of the bishop. If he should agree, I would welcome the opportunity. Also, I have done some thinking on the subject of increasing my knowledge of medicine, and there is an elderly doctor, one of the parishioners in our diocese, who would be glad to teach me what I need to know to increase my skill, if I am truly to practice medicine."

"Write to me, then, when you've learned whether this will be possible. I like you, and from what Padre Camporata has told me, I think you could contribute much to that settlement."

John Cooper had already taken his leave of Dorotéa and the children, and Raoul Maldones, who, as *capataz*, had reluctantly agreed to stay behind, wished the Texan Godspeed and success with his mission of rescue.

As the fifteen men started along the trail that led to New Orleans, the little priest turned to John Cooper. "Do you know, Señor Baines, I have been thinking about those wicked men who boarded the ship, killing so many innocent people. If indeed they return to their secret base after finishing their business in Havana, how will we find them? And even if we do, they still greatly outnumber our meager forces."

John Cooper continued to look straight ahead. "I have found, *padre*," he began, "that it is easier to hunt a dangerous animal with a few good men, rather than with many. The Obeiras will not be expecting an attack against their secret base of operations, and the Jicarilla Apache are superb trackers, hunters, and warriors, who can move in darkness and in silence. If we can take those pirates by surprise, we can learn exactly what they have done with Benito and Enrique Duvaldo. If, on the other hand, we went directly to Havana, we might be able to get help from the authorities—but we also might spend a great deal of valuable time searching the island in vain. And there is always the chance that the civil authorities might resent our intrusion into their country. I suggest, *padre*, that you leave the worrying to me, and pray that we find the Obeiras in Pensacola, and not out on the high seas on another voyage of piracy and murder."

"If there is justice, Señor Baines," the little priest solemnly answered, "they will be there when we arrive. This I now believe, after the miracle of my own salvation and the good fortune I have had in being sent to you!"

Eight

Luis Marconado had agreed to pay the Obeira brothers the sum of six thousand *pesos* for Benito and Enrique Duvaldo, and although Juan and Manolito suspected that they could have obtained more at a private auction, from other wealthy buyers, they did not haggle over the price. The patronage of the procurator general was indispensable if they wished to continue their lucrative operations in Cuba, so both of them unctuously pointed out to the fat official that it was out of their friendship and admiration for him that they agreed to so paltry a price.

Delighted with his acquisition, as well as with the division of the gold, silver, jewels, and other valuable items of cargo seized from the *Salamander,* Marconado effusively thanked them in return and promised to support them in their future endeavors. The very next day, he and an armed coachman arrived at the warehouse and had the manacles removed from the two Duvaldo brothers, warning them there was no possibility of their escape, and that if either of them tried it, they would both receive a severe flogging.

Benito and Enrique had already decided to wait and see what their new situation would be, so that they could plan the best way to deal with it and, in the meantime, spare themselves additional discomfort and perhaps even harsher treatment. As they were ushered into the waiting carriage, however, their new master wasted no time in again emphasizing that escape from the city would be virtually impossible, since both police and port authorities were in league with him. He very pompously explained his important role in the current Cuban government and reminded them that there was no court of appeals to which they could make any complaint, even over the fact that they happened to be white slaves, and not black.

"I shall take you at once to a beautiful house, *muchachos*," Marconado affably informed them as he leaned back and smiled, contemplating the magnificent scenery of the main street of Havana, with its palm trees and its neatly cobbled pavement, lined by the luxurious tropical shrubbery and gardens of the rich villas along the way. "It is known as the Casa de Belleza, and to this elegant address come the most important people in all Havana. They seek distraction, good wine, good food, and, most of all, the companionship of adorably lovely ladies who are gifted in the arts of love."

The two young men tried to hide their dismay at this revelation, for they had been brought up in a pious, respectable household. They did, however, exchange a woebegone look, and Marconado, noting this, burst into bawdy laughter, mopping his brow with a silk kerchief steeped in French cologne. "But really, you are like little children, *muchachos*! You surely are not going to tell me that in your country of Argentina there are no such establishments where men of affairs and wealth can while away a few hours in the arms of beautiful, enchanting young women! I assure you it goes on throughout the civilized world, and that even the most faithful of *esposos* at times needs the exquisite stimulus of variety in the pleasures of *amour*." Then, frowning, he sternly added, "Understand me, I am not the least concerned with your attitudes or silly notions about my affairs. As slaves, you have only to obey, and your well-being will be assured. Disobedience, sulking, insubordination—these are subject to immediate and severe punishment. A word of warning should suffice, for both of you seem highly intelligent. Now then, listen attentively. If you thought that I meant to employ you to service those who prefer the company of men, be disabused of that notion at once. I admit that I have customers of such predilections, but if you do everything I say, there should be no need for you to be more than, shall we say, friendly. No, *muchachos*, you will be there to bring wine and food to the patrons, to assist as attendants, and to lend a sympathetic ear. Indeed, what I wish most is that you keep your ears open and your mouths shut, and that you listen very carefully to any idle conversation that may pass between the patrons and the girls of my establishment. I owe you no explanations, but I am sympathetic enough to make your lives easier by telling you that, although I have great influence here in Havana as the procurator general, there are those who would try, out of envy and spite, to topple me from my lofty position. Some of these, indeed, may frequent my establishment, and that is why I ask you—no, I order you!—to be attentive at all times, to retain whatever fragments of conversation you believe will be of interest to me, and then, when I summon you to an accounting, to tell me truthfully what you have heard and from whom you have heard it. If you fail me in this, you will be treated worse than the lowliest *puta* in Havana. Do I make myself perfectly clear?''

"*Sí, señor,*" Enrique mumbled.

"You will call me *patrón*—that is the title by which a slave addresses his master! Do not forget it, or I will infer that you are being disrespectful, and then I shall have Teófilo Nogueira, who acts as a guard at my fine establishment, give you a taste of the lash. He is an expert at it, let me assure you. He has practiced with those young señoritas who do not show enthusiasm for their work, or respect for the honorable patrons they have the privilege of servicing. You, I trust, will know better.''

Benito and Enrique nodded, trying to hide the revulsion and anger that surged through them.

Marconado eyed each of them in turn and then chuckled lewdly, hugely pleased with himself. In his waistcoat pocket reposed the little velvet case containing the ruby earrings that had belonged to the mother of his two new slaves. He looked forward to a reunion with his beautiful, passionate mistress and to the gratitude she would show when he affixed these lustrous, dark-red jewels to the lobes of her dainty ears.

The carriage moved down past the central square and thence eastward, until it came to a halt before an iron gate set in a high stone wall. As an armed guard opened the creaking portals, Enrique noticed with dismay the jagged pieces of broken glass set into the top of the wall. The carriage moved through the gate, up a gravel drive bordered by a sumptuous lawn and, beyond, a garden of oleander, honeysuckle, jasmine, and hibiscus. Ahead was a mansion of two stories, with wrought-iron balconies decorating the second floor, and as Enrique peered curiously out the carriage window, he saw a man in a white suit emerge onto one of the balconies, his arm around a slim young brown-haired girl clad only in a silken shift and sandals. He saw the girl sinuously press herself against the man, one of her hands disappearing between their bodies, while the other pressed the back of his neck. He watched them share a long kiss before the voice of Luis Marconado recalled him to reality.

"Well, there is your new home, *muchachos*! It's the Casa de Belleza, the House of Beauty, and it's well named, indeed. You're to be a credit to it and to me, never forget that. Now, you, what's your name—" He jabbed his fat thumb at Enrique.

"Enrique Duvaldo."

The thumb pressed pitilessly against Enrique's neck just below the ear, and the youth uttered a strangled cry of pain. "Did I not tell you to call me *patrón*? And, moreover, each man who enters this house will be called that, and our little friend, Teófilo, will see to it that you do not forget this title of respect. You are, Enrique, *un esclavo,* nothing more. Drum that into your brain, and you will survive without too much difficulty. That goes for you also—Benito, is it not?"

"*Sí, mi patrón,*" the younger brother hastily answered.

This pleased Marconado, and he grinned, revealing tobacco-stained teeth. "You show more wisdom than your older brother. Let him take counsel from you. All right, now, Enrique, open the door for your master. And you will follow me into the house, and there I will introduce you to Señora Consuela Zagora. She runs my establishment, and she, too, has her rules, as you'll soon learn. What are you waiting for, *estúpido*?" Another jab against his ear reminded Enrique of his new duties, and he scrambled out of the carriage to hold the door open for the fat politician, who chuckled with sadistic pleasure at the youth's discomfiture.

"I could not have chosen a better day for your initiation into your new duties, *muchachos*," Marconado commented as he advanced, gesturing for them to precede him. "This is a

Saturday, and that is always our most profitable and busiest time. You'll learn quickly, and if you do not, there are ways of making you respond with the proper alacrity."

With a proprietary air, Luis Marconado put his hand to the brass knocker on the front door of the villa and struck thrice. Almost immediately the door was opened by an opulently contoured woman in her late forties, who still retained vestiges of what must have been an astonishing beauty twenty years earlier. She had black hair, high-set cheekbones, and keenly alert dark-brown eyes. Her mouth was ripely sensual, and she wore a black silk evening gown audaciously cut to the cleft of her well-rounded, closely spaced breasts. Around her full throat was a necklace of pearls, and her earlobes were adorned by costly pearl earrings.

"*Bienvenido*, Luis," she exclaimed in a throaty voice.

"*Gracias*, Señora Zagora." He gave her a brisk little bow. "I have brought you two charming *muchachos*. Have Teófilo garb them properly. They will serve as attendants in place of that other lad, and I wish them to mingle with the *clientes* and make themselves as useful and attentive as possible. They are not, for now, to be involved in any erotic games, however much our more debauched customers would bid for such degenerate sport. If they misbehave, however, or try to escape—" His lips curled into an evil grin.

"I quite understand, Luis."

"I shall not be with you this evening, but as you know, I rely always on your good judgment and on the invaluable aid of Teófilo," the fat *político* drawled. "And now, Señora Zagora, I bid you a successful and profitable night, for I shall be off to my engagement with the Señorita Castillo. I do not wish to be disturbed, but you know where to reach me if anything unusual should occur."

"Of course. I shall handle matters to your satisfaction, as I always try to do, dear Luis." She turned to Benito and Enrique. "Come along with me, *muchachos*!"

As he turned back to his carriage, Luis Marconado called a last warning to the Duvaldo brothers. "Remember now, *muchachos*, do what you're told, and be sure that if you don't, I shall hear of it, and you won't like the consequences!"

When he was gone, Señora Zagora closed and locked the door, then declared, "First, you will have something to eat. Then Teófilo will see that you're bathed and given the attire you will always wear as attendants in the Casa de Belleza. Since you are *esclavos,* and I am not yet sure that you will be docile, you will sleep at night in the cellar, where we have punishment rooms for those who do not obey the rules of this establishment. I am sure that the señor Marconado has warned you about the impossibility of trying to escape. First of all, in the clothing you will be wearing, you would be recognized instantly by the civil guards and the *soldados* if you managed to get as far as the streets. And I do not think you would care for Teófilo's punishment when you are returned here."

"We shall not try to escape, señora," Enrique dully answered, glancing at his brother, who nodded assent.

As she led them through the main salon of the elegant bordello, Benito and Enrique were wide-eyed at the lavishness of the decor. Their feet sank into thick red carpets, and all about them were ottomans, *chaises longues,* and armchairs upholstered with rich damask, velvet, or even satin. There were tapestries on the walls and gilt-framed oil paintings, all depicting erotic mythological scenes, such as Zeus and Europa, Leda and the Swan, Danae and the Shower of Gold.

Suddenly this atmosphere of ornate luxury was hideously dispelled as a hunchback hobbled toward them, with bony chin, long, crooked arms with powerful, thick-knuckled fingers, and little black eyes that gleamed with malevolence.

"Ah, Teófilo, *mi corazón,*" the madam cooed, "you are just in time to take charge of these new *esclavos.* Señor Marconado has just purchased them to replace Pedrillo. See that they are bathed at once and given the customary clothing, and you may as well feed them something first—it will doubtless make them more cooperative. When that's all done, bring them back here, because we shall have many guests this evening, and they will be most useful."

"At once, my dove!" The hunchback briefly scrutinized the two shrinking youths, all the while fondling the handle of a wicked-looking dagger suspended from his waist. He snarled in a cracked, reedy voice, "You'll call me *patrón,* and you'll bow your heads and not look at my face when you speak to me, *comprendéis*?''

"*Sí, patrón,*" Enrique replied.

The hunchback's thin lips twisted in a sardonic smile. "That is a good beginning. Your names, quickly!"

"I—I am Enrique, *patrón,* and this is my brother, Benito," Enrique explained.

"Those names will do as well as any others. Follow me down the stairs. I will feed you first, and then I will have two of the serving women bathe you. You're well made, both of you—"

"A word of caution, Teófilo," the madam interjected as they turned to leave. "They are not to be offered to any of those who have peculiar tastes, you understand."

The hunchback frowned. "A pity, for there is the señor Delregado, who has a positive mania for charming young boys. Oh, well, he's not coming tonight anyway. Now then, you two, follow me!"

The little hunchback was remarkably agile and as swift in movement as a rat as he led them down a hallway, opened a door, and gestured that they were to descend a narrow stairway. The brothers obeyed, though they both felt a shiver of revulsion at the nearness of this deformed, evil little man who would be, they sensed, the temporary arbiter of their destinies.

He descended after them, hurrying them on toward a doorway at the very end of the underground corridor. They passed several heavy barred doors and paused, drawing in their breath, as they came upon an open, cagelike cell about six feet wide, with a hideous sight in its dim interior. Against the far wall, bound spread-eagled by thin cords at wrists and ankles, was a naked young man, his back to them. He was blindfolded and gagged, but from the looks of him, he was long past crying for help. There were ghastly wounds on his shoulders, back, buttocks, and thighs, attesting to the result of a severe flogging.

Directly behind them, Teófilo cackled gleefully, "I'm glad you had this little view, *muchachos*. That is Pedrillo, the young man whose position you are to fill. He had a protector in the city who tired of him and sold him to the

Casa de Belleza. Unfortunately, he tried to steal the clothing of one of our customers, in order to aid his escape. As you see, *muchachos,* I was obliged to discipline him just a bit, and I'm afraid I got carried away. Now he's dead.''

The dwarfish man cackled evilly, and as Enrique and Benito turned in horror to contemplate him, his eyes narrowed, he drew the dagger from his belt, and, pointing it at them, fairly spat out, ''That is merely a warning to you both, for I swear to you, *por los cojones del diablo,* that if you are disobedient in any way to the señora Zagora or to me, or, indeed, to even a *puta* in this elegant *casa,* you will spend some time in this *calabozo.* And since you are not to be offered for the delectation of our wealthy *clientes,* I will not need to be gentle with the whip. A word to the wise is sufficient, *no es verdad?* Now, get along with you!''

On arriving at the end of the corridor, the two brothers glanced nervously at the grotesque hunchback, who hobbled ahead of them to open the door and nod them inside. The room appeared to be a combination kitchen and washroom. Against the left-hand wall was a large, sunken stone tub, with clay ewers of water alongside the edges. Nearby were low benches, stools, and wooden bowls filled with sweet-smelling oils and ointments. On the opposite side of the room were a large brick fireplace, an iron cookstove, and a work table covered with pots and pans. Two fat black women, clad in yellow robes and sandals, were busy basting chickens in a stone oven and stirring a kettle of pleasantly odorous stew.

''Hercula, Lisandra,'' the hunchback announced, ''here are two *muchachos* with empty bellies. Feed them, then bathe them, and dress them in the clothes they'll need to work here. I shall be back to collect them in an hour, mark you well!'' As the two women turned to bow their heads to him, he sarcastically added, ''You're not to trifle with them— it's the master's orders!'' He turned on his heels and then, thinking better of it, whirled around to jeer at the two bewildered young men: ''Tell me this, has either of you taken a woman to bed yet? The truth, *muchachos!*''

''No, *patrón,*'' Enrique stammered, and Benito, scarlet with embarrassment, shook his head.

''Excellent! Then you will be the only virgins in the

Casa de Belleza, which in itself is unique." He cackled hideously. "Remember what you saw in that punishment cage, *muchachos*! Until then, *adiós*!"

With this he hobbled off, and both young men breathed a sigh of relief. The two Negresses, whispering to each other in a dialect that neither Benito nor Enrique could comprehend, gestured that they were to sit down at the table, and when they had done so, promptly served bowls of stew and a loaf of freshly baked bread. The black woman named Lisandra disappeared into a pantry and brought out a carafe of dark red wine, which both Benito and Enrique found to be extremely potent.

After the brothers had eaten—the best meal they had had in many weeks—the black women approached them and, to their huge embarrassment, took them by the elbows and led them toward the sunken bath. Lisandra, giggling hilariously, gestured that they were both to strip naked. When Benito demurred, his older brother whispered, "We have to do what they say. You saw what was done to that poor fellow in the dungeon! Benito, I like this no better than you do, but we must submit."

When both were naked, their hands covering their intimate parts, Lisandra, still giggling, motioned them to step down into the sunken tub, which was about four feet square and three feet deep. It was made of lustrous white marble, and after the two black women had emptied the ewers of water, they refilled them from a hand pump set against the wall. Tirelessly, they brought the ewers to the tub and emptied them, until the water was up to the brothers' knees. Then the black woman called Hercula indicated that they were to seat themselves, and to the utter mortification of both Benito and Enrique, she and Lisandra calmly drew off their robes and, each taking a cake of soap and a brush, joined the young men in the tub and proceeded to scrub them from head to toe. During this operation, both Benito and Enrique closed their eyes, particularly when the Negresses soaped and lightly brushed their private parts, uttering peals of salacious laughter and continuing to make jokes in some incomprehensible dialect, apparently concerning the young men's virility.

This done, the two women rinsed and dried them, then

promptly brought them blouses of red silk and trousers of black, which, with *calzoncillos* of fine white silk, and sandals, constituted their attire.

Only a few minutes later, Teófilo Nogueira appeared to collect his novices, pausing to exchange ribald comments with the two black women in the same dialect, so that once again both Benito and Enrique turned crimson as they guessed what was being said.

"And now, *muchachos*," the hunchback addressed them, "you begin to earn your keep. You will come upstairs to the salon of welcome, and you will stand there and serve wine, rum, little cakes, and the like to the *clientes*. You will be humble, you will obey the orders of the *putas* as you would mine, and you will make yourselves as useful as you can. I shall have my eye on you, and there will be others there who will report to me, when I'm not watching, as to your debut in the Casa de Belleza. For your sakes, *muchachos*, I trust it will be a favorable report. Come now, follow me, and quickly!"

As the evening drew on, Benito and Enrique Duvaldo had little time to bemoan their unhappy destiny, for the bordello was thronged with customers who came first to the large reception salon, where Señora Zagora welcomed them and the brothers were kept busy serving champagne, fine French wines, brandy, and rum. Carrying heavy silver trays, the two young men circulated among the customers, submissively offering the drinks. There was a buzz of conversation, and the youths, who of course spoke Spanish fluently, were easily able to eavesdrop on conversations ranging from the flippant and lascivious to serious speculation on the economic future of Cuba and particularly the pact between Britain and the United States against the slave trade.

At least two dozen men entered the villa between the hours of seven and nine, and after they had had their drinks and the time to put themselves completely at their ease, the astute madam introduced the girls of the establishment in a highly dramatic fashion.

At the end of the salon was an arched doorway hung with red velvet drapes. In front of the drapes was a low stage, perhaps a dozen feet wide by six feet deep. Two *mestizos* sat in the corner, one with a violin and the other with a guitar, playing popular airs and folk tunes of the Caribbean, and as each girl drew aside the drapes and mounted the stage from a tiny stairway, the musicians altered the melody or the rhythm to suggest the origin or the temperament of that particular girl.

Eager to select their partners for the evening, the highly excited throng reacted noisily. Benito and Enrique, their immediate work having ended, were permitted to stand at the back of the salon and observe what took place. For them, it was an incredible revelation.

Señora Zagora numbered some thirty ladies of the evening in her establishment, ranging from a slim fourteen-year-old Caribee Indian of exceptional svelteness, a mocking face, and impertinent manner, to a golden-haired woman in her middle thirties from Marseilles, who, like many of the prostitutes in this elegant house, had sought employment here once her lover had tired of her and abandoned her without means of support.

The Caribee girl, Talame, was chosen by a white-haired, elegantly groomed man in his early sixties, whom Señora Zagora effusively greeted as *"excelencia,"* and who, as Benito and Enrique Duvaldo discovered, occupied a minor post in the office of the treasury. Talame appeared dressed in her native garb, with a heron's plume in her hair and a skirt and jacketlike garment made of thick plantain grass into which garlands of flowers had been woven. The lecherous old official applauded raucously when she had finished her dance, then he scrambled to his feet and, in a thin, piping voice, implored Señora Zagora to accept his bid for Talame's services for the night for the sum of five hundred *pesos*. When the girl, who had sunk to her knees and bowed her head at the conclusion of her dance, glanced up at her madam, the latter nodded with a beaming smile, and Talame scampered down from the platform to hurry to her white-haired suitor and lead him away by the hand to one of the private rooms on the second floor of the villa.

The golden-haired woman from Marseilles, whose provocative costume of a thin black satin peignoir emphasized the voluptuous contours of her ripe figure, attracted no fewer than six of the avid customers, each of whom shouted out his bid to Señora Zagora. The eventual victor, at a bid of six hundred and fifty *pesos,* was a squat man with porcine features, enormous bushy black eyebrows, and a sharply pointed spade beard, whom she addressed as Don Arturo de Magnante and who turned out to be the affluent owner of one of the largest sugarcane plantations in Cuba.

One by one, the girls of the establishment were auctioned off, and the imaginative method of presentation stimulated the bidding. To Benito and Enrique it was a strange new world, and the staggering sums offered for the carnal favors of the women who mounted the stage and danced or took provocative poses led them to conclude that Luis Marconado must surely be enormously rich.

After the bidders had left the central salon with their chosen partners, Teófilo appeared and sarcastically remarked, "Now you see how things go, *muchachos.* But why are you standing here with your mouths open? Ascend the stairs to the second floor and wait in the hallway. The *criadas* who visit the rooms to see if the *clientes* require food or refreshment will come out to tell you what you must bring them. Remember, listen to what conversation you can, and retain anything you think will interest the señor Marconado. First, of course, you will tell it to me, and I will see how quick-witted you are."

It proved to be a tiring evening and night for the two young Argentinians, for it was not until about two in the morning that the amorous customers halted their demands for more rum or champagne or wine, or the maids their urgent whispered commands to bring fresh towels and bed linens to the rooms. Finally, when the house was quiet, the little hunchback beckoned to the brothers and bade them follow him down to the cellar, where he locked them into a tiny, windowless cubicle containing two cots, a chamberpot, and a washbasin, and in which all sound seemed to be sealed off. Exhausted, stricken with anxiety over this incredible and unexpected stoppage of their journey to find John Cooper Baines, they flung themselves down on the cots and promptly fell asleep.

* * *

The next morning, the youths were awakened by Teófilo, who unlocked the door of their cubicle and bade them come to the kitchen for breakfast.

"You will tell me what you heard last night that may be of interest to our *patrón*," he directed.

The two black women who yesterday had fed and bathed Benito and Enrique now served them breakfast, which consisted of hot chocolate, eggs cooked with shallots and herbs, and biscuits with honey. The little hunchback shared this meal, his beady little eyes darting from one boy's face to the other to appraise the veracity of their remarks. Enrique had volunteered that, in one of the guest rooms to which he had been summoned to bring a carafe of red wine, the client, a corpulent, thickly mustachioed man in his late forties who wore a magnificent diamond ring on the third finger of his right hand, had tossed him a silver *peso* as a tip and sarcastically declared, "Keep this for yourself, *muchacho*. Señor Marconado makes enough on our foibles to buy his way past all actions to turn him out of office."

"Ah, well done, *muchacho*," the hunchback complimented him. His lips curled in a vicious sneer. "That was the esteemed Señor José Lartigo. He happens to be an attaché in the office of the minister of the interior, and he is one of the *patrón*'s most outspoken rivals. You have done well for your first night. Keep it up, the both of you, and I may permit you—as a special dispensation, you understand—to enjoy the favors of one of the charming señoritas who dwell with us."

After the hunchback had left them, Enrique turned to his brother and murmured, "We must play along with them, as long as we are captives here, Benito. They may think we are so obedient that they will relax their vigilance. Then we may find some way of escaping. But the best course for now is to do whatever we are told."

"I suppose so," Benito gloomily agreed. "This morning, before you woke, I said prayers for the spirit of our dead father, and I prayed that he would understand why we are in a place like this, instead of helping to avenge his death."

"He knows, assuredly, little brother." Enrique put his arm around Benito's shoulders. "What happened to him, as to the good Padre Camporata, and even ourselves, in a way, was the doing of those *porteños*. One day, for all the evil they have done, they will have to face retribution, and it will be a harsh one in the eyes of heaven, be sure of that, Benito."

Nine

By the end of the first week, Benito and Enrique Duvaldo had successfully passed their onerous probationary period as slaves at the Casa de Belleza, and both Señora Zagora and the little hunchback praised them at the conclusion of their second Saturday in service.

"Word will be sent to the *patrón,* you may be sure of it, *muchachos,*" the madam said, beaming. "Keep this up, and your lives will be pleasant, and there will even be rewards, as I have no doubt Teófilo has already suggested."

Indeed, these were forthcoming on the following Monday, for the little hunchback took Enrique aside and ingratiatingly commented, "Señor Marconado is pleased with you, *muchacho.* He has given permission for you to enjoy one of the señoritas, and it will even be of your own choice. Of course, it must be during the week, when there are not quite so many clients, you understand. As for you, Benito," he said, turning to the younger Duvaldo, "you can wait your turn, since your brother is older. Moreover, as a reward to both of you, you will not be locked into that damp cell each night, but instead enjoy a small room on the second floor of the villa, beginning with tonight. You are wise to have taken my warning to heart, for it would have grieved me to have had to punish such intelligent *muchachos* as you are." This last was said with a mocking smile, as the hunchback fingered the handle of his dagger. Both Benito and Enrique humbly bowed their heads and murmured a phrase of thanks for his kindness.

On the following day, during the time of *siesta,* which

was normally from two to four in the afternoon, Señora Zagora had set Benito to work mopping the colored, ornamental tiles of the patio, while Enrique had been bidden to bring piles of fresh bed linen to the guest rooms on the second floor. In addition to the prostitutes who dwelt in this luxurious villa, there were perhaps a dozen *criadas*, some of them *mestizas*, who made the beds, and who sometimes—for a fee, to be sure—took part in the nocturnal activities, especially when an elderly client's flagging energies needed additional stimulus. As Enrique proceeded down the western hallway of the second floor, a young *criada*, no more than fifteen, stuck her head out of one of the doors and called, *"Venga aquí, pronto!"*

Obediently nodding, Enrique moved toward the room, as the *criada* held the door open for him. There, standing by the little balconied window, clad only in a yellow silk shift and sandals, was an enchantingly slim, brown-haired girl, whom Enrique had observed the previous Saturday evening in the company of a uniformed, bemedaled captain, one of the heads of the civil guard of the city of Havana. A stocky, black-bearded man in his late thirties, the captain, Enrique had observed, was not only dictatorial in manner, but also brutally possessive, judging from the way he had gripped the girl's arm above the elbow and virtually dragged her up the stairway.

As Enrique entered, the girl turned and smiled at him. *"Buenas tardes, muchachito.* They tell me your name is Enrique, *no es verdad?"*

Flushing hotly under her smiling scrutiny, the older Duvaldo brother stammered, *"Sí, gracias, señorita."*

"I am Madalena Cortez. I am told also that you are *un esclavo."* There was a tinge of curiosity in her tone.

"Yes, Señorita Cortez—"

"No, no—Madalena. There is no need to call me señorita. But how is it that you are *un blanco* and yet *un esclavo?"*

"That is—well, to tell you the truth, señorita—I—I mean M-Madalena"—Enrique floundered, as the little *criada* put her hand to her mouth to suppress a titter of amusement at his embarrassment—"my brother and I are from Argentina, and we were on our way to New Orleans when a ship attacked us, and we were brought here and sold as slaves. That is how it is."

"Oh, *pobrecito*!" She approached him and put a hand to his cheek. "It must be difficult to have been a free man, and now be in the hands of that awful little Teófilo. You do not want to make an enemy of him, *muchachito*."

"I have done my best not to, Madalena. Thank you for your kindness to me."

She was perhaps an inch taller than he, slender, yet with high-perched, pear-shaped breasts whose nipples thrust boldly against the thin stuff of her shift. Her sleek waist merged into lithe haunches and firm, lovely long legs. Her exquisitely satiny skin had a faint olive tinge, and her face was a pronounced oval, with a dainty aquiline nose, thin, shapely nostrils, and a small but ripely moist mouth at which Enrique now stared, as if hypnotized by its inviting sweetness.

"That is very wise, Enrique. You cannot be much older than I am, and I am seventeen," she murmured, as she put both hands to his cheeks, her fingertips lightly stroking the outline of his jaw and then his chin.

He was trembling now, bemused by her loveliness and her nearness, and by the spicy scent that emanated from her supple body, for she had bathed only about an hour ago, and the *criada* had massaged and oiled her thoroughly.

"Yes, I—I am seventeen," Enrique confessed.

"That is very nice. I like you very much. You are not like the others. Tell me, Enrique, have you ever had a girl?"

He could only shake his head, the hot color flooding his young face from temples to throat.

"Oh, *qué maravilloso*!" she breathed. Then, turning to the little *criada*, she said softly, "Lumisetta, change the linen quickly, then leave us."

"*Sí*, Señorita Madalena, at once!" This time the *criada* could not suppress a fit of giggling, until Madalena looked sternly at her and hissed, "I have only to mention to the señor Teófilo that you are very impertinent, Lumisetta, and you know what will happen." That immediately silenced the *criada*, who industriously set to work changing the bed linen and then hurried out of the room with a frightened look on her pretty face.

"Now, that is better," Madalena Cortez murmured. "Do you like me, Enrique?"

"*Sí*, v-very much, M-Madalena," he nervously stammered.

"Then why don't you kiss me, *amorcito*?" she whispered, as she wound her supple young arms around his neck.

The blood began to thunder in Enrique's veins, and shuddering, he leaned toward her, their lips fusing. Awkwardly, never having touched a girl in this way before, he put his hands on her sides, just above her hips, and then almost at once withdrew them, as if he had touched a hot stove, fearful of offending her.

Madalena uttered a soft, throaty laugh, pressing herself against the embarrassed youth, her slim fingers stroking the nape of his neck as she insinuated her tongue just between his lips. He uttered a soft moan, feverish with the sensual ardor of her caresses, yet not sure of how to proceed, and, not wanting to dispel this ecstatic moment, he stood there helplessly.

"*Querido, amorcito,* don't be afraid. I want you to love me, *comprendes*?"

Thus encouraged and emboldened, Enrique dared to cup her firm, thrusting breasts with his palms, and at this, Madalena, uttering a faint, happy little sigh, arched eagerly against him, so that their loins pressed together. Wildly aroused, he shuddered, for truly this was the first time he had ever known such intimacy with a girl, and he found himself blushingly embarrassed to realize that she could not help but feel the urgent rigor of his young manhood.

Suddenly, she moved away from him, her eyes sparkling, her lips moist and quivering, as her dark eyes intently studied his flushed face. "It is true, then? You have never had a girl before, never?"

"I swear it, M-Madalena." His voice broke with the emotional strain of his converging physical excitement and embarrassment at his own naïveté.

"But that is wonderful, truly it is! I will tell you something that should make you want me as I want you, *querido*. The very first evening, when I saw you last week, I told myself, 'Madalena, here is a dear, sweet young man who is honorable and who is not at all like those who come to this house—certainly not like *el capitán* Maximiliano Orozco—' " As she spoke this name, her lips compressed in a grimace of revulsion, and then as suddenly she moved closer to him, her hands sliding to his waist. "I want very much to teach you, *querido*. I want to make your first time one you'll never forget, for you will have many women, I know that, because you are kind and good and honest. And when you are very old, *muy viejo*, you will say to yourself that once you met a girl in Havana who taught you how beautiful it is when two people wish to make love with all eagerness and joy. Come, come to the bed, and I will show you, *querido* Enrique!"

She took him by the hand and led him to the low, wide bed, gently pushed him down onto his back, and then went to draw the shutters so that no one might peer in from the balcony. Then, standing proudly, an enchanting smile on her cameolike face, she let the shift crumple to her ankles and was naked. His eyes widened with awe and delight at the sight of her superb young contours, the marvelously uptilting young breasts with their dusky-hued nipple buds, the sleek, shallow niche in the smooth mound of her belly, and the thick, crisp thatch at the juncture of her long, supple thighs. His breath quickened, and he could no longer restrain the manifestation of his virility.

"Lie very still, *querido*," she whispered as she came to him. "I see how much you want me already—how flattering it is to know that it will be with me, this your first time! I am so glad that that awful Señor Teófilo did not yet have you punished, or we could not dare to do this. Besides, I heard Señora Zagora say yesterday that you would be permitted to pick one of the girls here. I hope it would be me that you would have chosen, if she had shown all the girls to you, Enrique."

"Oh, yes—oh, yes, Madalena—you're the loveliest—the sweetest—oh, Madalena, how beautiful you are!"

"That is very sweet. I think already I am more than a little in love with you, and that will make it all the better for us both, you'll see, *querido*." She clambered onto the bed with a miraculous fluidity and suppleness that made him catch his breath at the sheer beauty of her body. Her fingers gently husked him of the silken breeches, and when, in a last manifestation of naïve embarrassment, he tried to hide himself with his hand, she laughed softly, pushed his hand away, and bent her head to apply a kiss on the tip of his rigid member. "But that's not something to be ashamed of—oh, no, quite the contrary, *querido*!" she teasingly scolded. "There is not a man in all the government of Havana, no, nor that detestable *Capitán* Orozco, either, for that matter, who would not give a thousand *pesos*, gold *pesos*, mind you, to have what you have for a girl! I can hardly wait, and I promise I will make you very happy. It will be exactly as if we were *novios*."

She moved upon him, her lips nibbling at his throat, his chest, and finally his mouth, as artfully she positioned herself and let herself sink down. Enrique uttered a strangled cry, his eyes rolling to the whites at the indescribable bliss of their union. And then, very tenderly, murmuring endearments to him, kissing and stroking him, praising him and assuring him that she truly desired and loved him, the lovely young prostitute initiated him as if, just as she had said, they were young sweethearts who had come together for their very first time.

Enrique Duvaldo did not tell his brother how he had been initiated into the mystic pleasures of Venus. To begin with, he respected Madalena and was almost pathetically grateful to her for the compassionate tenderness she had shown him. An older, hardened woman might have mocked his shyness, made a travesty of this, his first act of love. Instead, she had flatteringly wooed him, and he did not doubt the sincerity of her amorous fervor. And, too, instinctively he believed that it was unworthy of a man to gossip to another over this act, which was the most secret, intimate, and thrilling of all his young life.

Moreover, if he had told Benito, it would be a kind of taunt of superiority, because, after all, he was older than his brother, and it would make Benito's ordeal harder to bear. All the same, before he went into the central salon that evening to resume his duties as attendant, Enrique stole out to the garden, picked a bouquet of hibiscus, and brought them to Madalena's room as an impulsive gesture of love.

During the next week, there were several private parties, given by prominent government officials, and Benito and Enrique, though detesting their roles as spies, had much to report each morning to the little hunchback. One of the men, a señor Manuel Bogodas, who held an important post in the colony's treasury, had, in Benito's presence, told his buxom, Junoesque companion of the evening that it would be a good thing if a reform movement swept corruption out of the present government. Darkly, he had hinted that "one of the first to go would undoubtedly be a man who, as almost everyone in Havana knows, has his hands deep in enterprises that should in no way be connected with proper government." Teófilo Nogueira interpreted this as a slur against Luis Marconado and expressed his pleasure over the young Argentinian's alertness and memory. Then, to Enrique's anguished despair, he mockingly added, "Yes, indeed, *muchacho*, I think you've earned a session with one of our delightful señoritas, just as your brother Enrique already has had with Madalena." At this, Benito cast a wondering look at his older brother, who bit his lip, blushed violently, and turned away. "Oh, come now," Teófilo mockingly went on, "I fear I have offended your tender sensibilities, Enrique. But then, how was I to know that you would fall in love with a whore?"

At this vile epithet, it was all Enrique could do to keep from flinging himself on the hunchback and throttling him. Fortunately, he was able to quell that impulse, though he clenched his fists and ground his teeth to keep from blurting out a remark that the hunchback might have used as pretext not only to punish him but also—and this would have been far worse—to inflict a sadistic reprisal upon Enrique's delightful *inamorata*.

Satisfied with the effect of his words, the hunchback tilted back his head and emitted that hideous cackle that passed for laughter. "Ah, Cupid's arrow has struck a vulnerable spot, I see! Forgive me, *muchacho*, if I have destroyed your illusions." Then, his lips tightening into an ugly scowl, making his face still more grotesque, he hissed, "Do not think that simply because you have passed your probation thus far that you have total liberty to behave as you wish. Remember, both of you, you are still *esclavos,* and you will be to the end of your days. Now off with you to your duties!''

As they climbed the stairs to the second floor to begin the distribution of bed linens and towels for the evening ahead, Benito wonderingly whispered, ''Is it true what he said, Enrique? Did you—were you—''

''I didn't want to tell you, because you'd think I was boasting. And then besides, it was wrong of him, despicable of him, to mention it—it was so beautiful, I can't tell you— but you will find out for yourself. It is a wonderful thing, and for a time I forgot that I was here as a slave, in a place where powerful and wealthy men come to treat the poor women as little better than slaves. They, too, Benito, are as chained as we are to this place, and it is worse for them, for if they do not please their clients, they are turned over to Teófilo. Madalena told me he treats them little better than he did that poor young man we saw when we were first brought here.''

''I will never forget that!'' Benito avowed. ''Oh, Enrique, if only—I pray every night that we shall find deliverance from our servitude!'' His voice was strained, betraying his despair and anxiety.

''All we can do is pray, and keep our eyes open for a way to escape that will not fail. Until then, we must go on as we have been, so that we won't be punished. Now, brother, let's do our work.''

On the third Saturday of their confinement in the bordello, the salon was filled with clients, some of them wearing the bright uniforms of the civil guard, or *policía.* There were two lieutenants, one gaunt, graying, and nearly bald, the other a mere stripling of not more than twenty, with effeminate bearing, of whom the malevolent little hunchback whispered to the Duvaldo brothers that his penchant was to have a *puta* dress like a man and seduce him as if he were a woman. There was also the stocky, glowering *capitán,* Maximiliano Orozco, to whom Benito was obliged to serve two large rum punches, which only seemed to make him more out of sorts. He began loudly to demand that the madam display the girls, and as a consequence Señora Zagora rather reluctantly began the evening's parade somewhat earlier than she had planned.

Madalena Cortez was the third girl to appear. She was barefoot, and the madam had garbed her in a tattered peasant's shift, the flimsy garment ripped over one shoulder to expose a breast. In this guise, Madalena danced to the frenetic rhythm of the violin and guitar, the tune resembling that used in the voodoo celebration in honor of Mam'zelle Erzulie, the Haitian goddess of love.

The stocky *capitán* kept time to the music by clapping his hands and shouting obscenities, his face growing more and more florid, until at last he bawled, "I'll take this bitch, and I'll give five hundred silver *pesos* for her services for the night! There will be no other bidders, *comprenden ustedes, señores?"*

The music ended, and the slim young girl stopped dead in her tracks on the stage, casting an imploring look at the beautifully gowned and bejeweled madam. Señora Zagora almost imperceptibly shook her head and made a gesture that indicated Madalena had no choice—nor, indeed, did she, for *Capitán* Orozco was a personal friend of Luis Marconado, and it was most advantageous to have a strong arm of the military on the side of this corrupt government official.

Lurching from his seat, *Capitán* Orozco made his way forward and jumped onto the stage, his eyes glinting with animal lust. Seizing poor Madalena by the back of her neck, he pushed her down the steps toward the arched door and ordered: "To your room and on the bed, slut! And quickly, or you'll suffer for it!"

Enrique, horrified by all this, took a step forward, but Señora Zagora, who knew only too well what had gone on between the two young lovers, shook her head and put her finger to her lips to command the youth's silence. Almost frantic, Enrique watched the brutal officer cuff Madalena across the cheek and then, giving her a prod with his booted foot, angrily order her to hasten up the stairs.

The two of them disappeared, and at the madam's sign, the musicians resumed their playing, this time choosing a popular Creole air that broke the tension. Enrique, still fuming, joined his brother in bringing more trays of drinks around to the guests, and the bidding resumed at a more leisurely and orderly pace.

As the central salon emptied, the little hunchback approached Enrique and hissed, "Tonight, *muchacho*, you've had a little lesson in balancing accounts. You see, you've been a very good boy, and so you were rewarded. But just to show you and Madalena that life in the Casa de Belleza does not go the way slaves pray it will, I had Señora Zagora present your sweetheart like a captured slave destined for the block, just the way *su excelencia* the good *capitán* likes them." As Enrique reddened in anger, the hunchback emitted his horrible cackling laugh. "We are here, *muchacho*," he added, his eyes narrowed and piercing, "to make money for the *patrón*, not to let you fall in love with a stupid little *puta*. Now go about your duties, and beware that you do not end up like Pedrillo!"

Enrique forced himself, with a supreme effort, to refrain from striking out at his evil tormentor, but he could not suppress his anxiety over the knowledge that Madalena was at that very moment in the hands of the cruel Cuban officer. As Teófilo hobbled away, Enrique felt a fierce, unreasoning hate take possession of him, and perhaps for the first time in his young life, he felt the urge to kill, to obliterate that grotesque, mocking face and the devilish mind that fed on others' misery.

Dully, stolidly, he refilled his tray with glasses of various spirits from the bar, and, together with Benito, ascended the stairs to the second floor, where they would wait for the inevitable calls from the *criadas*, who in many instances were closeted with the prostitutes and clients they served.

Enrique had hardly reached the top of the stairway when a young maid opened the door and called impatiently, "*Aquí, aquí, pronto, muchacho!* Bring rum for Señor Iglesias. He is dying of thirst!"

As he crossed the threshold, to see a corpulent bald man reclining on the bed with his head and shoulders propped up by lace-trimmed pillows, while a buxom, seminaked young Portuguese woman playfully tweaked at the thick black hairs on his chest, Enrique heard a scream of intolerable agony from the other end of the corridor. He stopped abruptly and turned his head, only to have the man irritatedly call out, "Idiot, don't you understand an order? Bring me a rum, or I'll have you thrashed by Teófilo!"

There was no choice, and Enrique moved toward the bed, bending to proffer the tray. The fat bald man seized a glass of rum punch and said with a sneer, "Leave another on the night table and then away with you. And take that sullen look off your face, or assuredly I'll see that you're flogged before the night's over!"

"I beg your pardon, señor, I did not mean to offend you," Enrique mumbled as he obeyed.

He had hardly left the room when another scream, even more piercing and agonized, rang out. This time, unnerved, he dropped the tray with a crash, and the maid began to upbraid him in voluble and profane Spanish. Then there was another cry, but this in the voice of a man, hoarse and agonized: "Bitch, you—you've killed me—you—*ahhhh*!"

Doors opened all down the hallway, and the girls and their clients hurried out, alarmed by the sounds that had emerged from the last room. Presently, the door opened, and Madalena, weeping bitterly, stood on the threshold, a bloody knife in her hand. She was naked, and the angry, darkening weals of a riding crop blemished her breasts, belly, and thighs, as well as her back and buttocks.

Pitifully, she turned to them, glanced down at the knife, and then sobbed, "I couldn't help it—he . . . he said he would kill me. He whipped me so hard—I . . . I couldn't help it, I swear by all the saints. I had this knife under my pillow—he's always been cruel to me, this *Capitán* Orozco—I . . . I had to save my life—don't you understand, all of you?"

Drawn by the hubbub, Señora Zagora and the little hunchback hurried up the stairway and confronted the weeping young prostitute. "What's this, Madalena?" the madam angrily demanded.

One of the maids said, "She's killed *Capitán* Orozco, Señora Zagora!"

"Oh, you accursed fool! Now look what you've done! One of the señor Marconado's best friends, useful to all of us in giving us the protection we need for this fine house—oh, I could kill you myself! Teófilo, go send Alonzo to the head of the civil guards to have him arrest this stupid little murderess!''

''Oh, please, Señora Zagora, please understand—I didn't want to hurt him. He whipped me so terribly—he said he was going to kill me. Look at me—you can see what he did with that terrible riding crop of his. I had to protect myself—''

The madam interrupted with a venomous hiss. ''Shut up! I want to hear nothing more from you, you stupid trollop! Luisa, and you, María,'' she ordered two of the *criadas* who had come out into the hallway, ''hold her by the wrists and don't let her go until the *policía* come here to take her to the *calabozo*, where she belongs! Oh, what a scandal for my fine house—what will Señor Marconado think?''

Then, realizing she was still the head of this profitable institution and that it was, after all, the most profitable of all nights for this fleshly commerce, she fawningly held out her arms to the gaping men and the *putas* and, in as syrupy a tone as she could muster, implored them, ''Please, señores, go back to your rooms and try to forget this dreadful scene. I tell you what I shall do, since you have been so shamefully interrupted—your bills for tonight will be cut in half. That should make up to you in some small part for the annoyance you have suffered tonight. Again, my humble apologies, señores.''

Greatly mollified, most of the spectators went back into their rooms with their companions for the night. Only Enrique stood, trembling as with fever. He turned to the madam: ''What—what will they do to her?''

''I'll tell you what they'll do, my fine young lover!'' she hissed angrily. ''They'll put her to the garrote. That's what's done with murderesses, you may take my word for it! And it won't be an easy death for her, either, because she's a lovely bitch—oh, why did she have to disgrace our house on a night like this?''

Half an hour later, summoned by one of the sentries of the establishment, four members of the civil guard entered the house and took Madalena Cortez into custody. The lieutenant in charge of the detail informed Señora Zagora that the prisoner would undoubtedly be brought before a judge on Monday morning for a hearing. He asked the madam to give him what details she could, and wanted to know if there were any witnesses. Unctuously, Señora Zagora declared, "No, *señor teniente*, but all of us here heard the slut's admission that she had taken her knife from under her pillow and stabbed poor *Capitán* Orozco. You understand, of course, that this house is under the protection of Señor Luis Marconado."

"I know that well, señora," the lieutenant replied, inclining his head respectfully. "I shall take your word for it, since you are in charge, and I know you. There's no need to involve your guests and cause undue embarrassment. I thank you for summoning me so promptly, and you may be sure that this misguided señorita will pay the extreme penalty if the judge finds her guilty of murder. I bid you and your guests a most pleasant good night."

As predicted, Madalena Cortez was brought before a judge the following Monday, and although the elderly, bewigged magistrate listened patiently to her frantic pleas that she had killed the officer in self-defense, it was no use. "Madalena Cortez," he intoned, "I find you guilty of murder, the penalty for which is death. I hereby sentence you to die by the garrote at noon on Saturday, December thirty-first, and may *el Señor Dios* have mercy upon your soul!"

One of the *criadas* had gone to the trial and hurried back to report the outcome to the madam and Teófilo. When Enrique heard the news, he was beside himself. He burst into tears and clenched his fists, hoarsely sobbing. "But I saw how he treated her, and she told me once before how cruel he was to her. It's not fair—she only tried to save her life! Anybody would have done the same thing against that monster!"

Benito, nervously glancing around, whispered, "Please, Enrique, there's no help for it. You mustn't do anything rash—you'll only get yourself in trouble, and then perhaps we'll never be able to find Señor Baines."

"Oh, my God, I feel so helpless, so useless—I love her, don't you understand, Benito? And she'll be put to death in the most horrible way. I know what the garrote is, because once our father told me how they sentenced a murderer in Buenos Aires to die that way. God, oh, God, save Madalena, please, I beg of You!''

Ten

Brigadier General Santa Anna excitedly paced back and forth, his brilliant black eyes fixed on a huge map of Mexico and the United States occupying almost an entire wall of his study at the villa of Mango de Clavo. In his right hand he clutched a report from *Coronel* Luis Dominguez, which had just been brought to him by courier. It detailed the colonel's recent engagement against a rebel group who called themselves Texas Rangers, and Santa Anna could hardly restrain his joy at the news that fully half of the enemy had been killed on the field of battle.

His wife had returned to the villa, so Santa Anna had whisked away his beautiful half-breed mistress and, for the past three weeks, had been an exemplary husband, holding banquets in his wife's honor and toasting her to the fawning, bemedaled officers who were his frequent guests. She had not been taken in by this effusive show of connubial admiration, for she knew very well that her husband was a notorious womanizer. However, as long as he did not bring scandal upon their household, thereby jeopardizing his plans to place himself in the palace of Mexico City, she saw no reason for not letting all the world believe that the two of them were inseparable in thought and spirit.

In his study now was a young officer, promoted on the field of honor by Santa Anna himself some six months ago. Ex-*capitán*, now *Comandante* Marco Cienfuegos had ingeniously deployed his men to surprise and surround a village of renegade Yaqui Indians, valiantly killing some seventy of

132

the foe before the last survivors, along with a few of the women and children, broke and ran to safety in the mountains.

The officer had been a guest of the villa all during the week, and Santa Anna, in the presence of other friendly officers, had affixed the insignia of *comandante* to the young man's uniform, saluted him, then hung around his neck a little medallion that bore two words, "Guanjuato" and "Medina," the former referring to a memorable episode in the fight for Mexican independence, the latter to a battle at which Texans had been almost annihilated outside of San Antonio. Indeed, it was at Medina that the young Santa Anna, then a mere subaltern, had conceived his fierce hatred for the *tejanos* that was to preoccupy him for the rest of his life.

"*Comandante* Cienfuegos—" Santa Anna stopped pacing and brandished the report in his hand. "It is fitting that you have been party to this great news. *Coronel* Dominguez, like you, has struck another blow against the enemies of our people—in this case those accursed *americanos* who continue to settle arrogantly upon our great Mexican soil. It is true that the central government foolishly granted them that permission, but long ago they began to abuse it."

"This I know, *mi general*," the round-faced, black-haired major put in. "Unfortunately, others in our government ignore this danger. It takes a farsighted strategist like yourself, *mi general*, to understand that each American settler on the land of Texas represents another enemy against our great country."

"I see I have made no mistake in your promotion, *Comandante* Cienfuegos! Yes, you have a keen perception of the meaning of history. And if I have my way, we shall continue these attacks against the *tejanos* until not a single *gringo* settler remains upon Mexican land. The bungling fools in Mexico City do no more than haggle over and reword the agreement they have made with the Austins, while in the meantime the *tejanos* increase by droves—I do not exaggerate! It is up to men like you and me, Cienfuegos, to take precautions, lest they grow into so menacing an army that we shall have to devote many regiments to win back land that originally belonged to us."

"I could not agree with you more, *mi general*!"

"*¡Bueno!* And now, that is enough serious talk for the moment. Tonight, there will be a ball, and some of the most influential citizens of Veracruz and their families will be in attendance. You shall be the guest of honor, and I am certain we shall find an especially lovely señorita to accompany you in the dance. Now then, let us drink a glass of wine together and make a pact that we shall both stand firmly against these barbarian invaders who would destroy our customs and traditions and flout our laws."

The major, rising to his feet, hastened to pour from a nearby decanter into the general's goblet, then into his own. They clinked them together. "Damnation and extermination to all *tejanos*!" Santa Anna exuberantly declared, and both men drained their glasses.

On this same December day the settlers on the Brazos had called a town meeting, presided over by Simon Brown. These Texans and their families were well aware they had not yet felt the brunt of Santa Anna's vindictive harassment, and like the true pioneers they were, they prepared for the worst.

"Men," Simon Brown began, "you all know how we had to fight off Indian attacks some months back, and how, just a few weeks ago, some of our new Texas Rangers ran into a Mexican patrol and lost more than half their men. It's pretty obvious that our neighbors south of the Rio Grande would like nothing better than for us to give up this settlement and go back where we came from and let them have their so-called Mexican land. Well, as you all know, we came here in good faith after Mr. Austin assured us that he had contracts with the legitimate government in Mexico City, granting us land and a chance to bring up our families and live in peace. We've kept our part of the bargain, but they haven't kept theirs—"

"That's right, sonny!" old Minnie Hornsteder exclaimed from her place on one of the benches drawn up in front of the little platform on which Simon stood. "That miserable specimen of a man who calls himself Santy Anna, he won't rest until he clears us all out of Texas. But I don't think there's one of us here tonight who wouldn't like to stand up to that blowhard and tell him where to get off. We've got to have more men join the Rangers, and we've got to build more stockade walls and have good sentries, 'specially at night, that's my opinion. 'Course I'm only an old woman, and some of you probably think I'm a meddlesome old busybody, but I tell you, folks, if we all stick together and show enough gumption, it'll be till hell freezes over before that miserable critter with all his shiny medals and fancy uniform comes around again and says this is Mexican land, so help me!''

There were cheers and good-natured laughter at Minnie Hornsteder's vehement exhortation, for all of them loved her and knew how she had plunged herself into helping everyone in the settlement after her husband's death.

''As usual,'' Simon went on, ''Mrs. Hornsteder has said what just about all of us feel. I know it's asking a lot of you, especially the men with families, to risk your lives joining up with a group that's pretty young, and not too large, especially after the news we've had of how many Rangers were killed by those Mexican soldiers. But if there are any single men who'd like to keep this foothold we have here in Texas safe against spiteful attacks—for that's what they really are, when you come right down to it—then I urge you to come to me after this meeting and indicate whether you want to sign up and for how long. I know that Jim Bowie will be back here before too much longer, and he'll be very grateful for any recruits.''

When the meeting was over, five men came forward to the platform to tell Simon Brown of their inclination to join Jim Bowie's Rangers. One of them was Thomas Blake, a newcomer to the settlement. He was tall, a little past thirty, with a short black beard and large, widely spaced dark-brown eyes. His features were genial, and already the settlers here liked him, because it was known he had bravely saved the life of another man during an Indian attack, although he never brought the subject up himself.

''Good evening, Mr. Blake.'' Simon warmly shook hands. ''It's downright good of you, new as you are here, to want to take on a risky job like the kind the Rangers are offering.''

''I have no ties, Mr. Brown, and I believe in this

settlement and would like to help defend it. It's sort of paying my dues, if you know what I mean.''

"I do, Mr. Blake, and the sentiment does you credit. Well, I don't have to ask you if you can shoot a rifle, after hearing how you helped Mr. Eberle hold off that Wichita war party before the two of you got here with that nice daughter of his.''

Thomas Blake looked uncomfortable at being thus complimented, and he asked, "When do you figure Mr. Bowie will be back here?''

"I'm pretty sure he'll make it before Christmas. If he doesn't, one of his captains will be along to take volunteers. Don't you worry, you'll get all the action you want.''

"Thanks, Mr. Brown.'' Thomas cordially nodded and walked away. Out of the corner of his vision, he could see the golden-haired, blue-eyed Doris Eberle standing nearby, talking with her father. She caught sight of him and could not help blushing self-consciously.

Thomas hesitated a moment, wanting very much to say good evening to Doris, yet not wanting to disturb her conversation with her father. But when she glanced at him and sent him a quick little smile, he turned toward them and sauntered up in the most casual way, as if this meeting were purely by accident. "Good evening, Mr. Eberle. And to you, Miss Eberle,'' he smilingly offered.

"It's good to see you, Tom,'' Doris's father said, offering his hand. "And for goodness sake, stop calling me Mr. Eberle—the fact is, I'm only maybe about fifteen years older than you, and my hair isn't white—not yet.'' He chuckled heartily. "After all, when two men have crawled on their bellies together and fired rifles at Indians who were after their scalps, there's no need to stand on ceremony and use titles, now is there?''

"Of course, you're right—Roland. And I'd like it fine if you'd call me Tom in exchange. There, now, that weighty problem's settled. Anyway, I just wanted to let you know that I went over to see Mr. Brown about signing up with the Rangers when they next come back to ask for recruits,'' Thomas Blake declared.

"You know, I almost feel like signing up myself," Roland confessed.

"Daddy, don't you dare!" Doris turned to him with a reproachful cry. "You came all this way to find me after I was fool enough to run away, and I'm not going to stand here and let you ride off with those Rangers and maybe get yourself killed like those poor fellows we just heard about."

"That's kind of you to say, honey." Roland put his arm around her shoulders. "I'm glad you still like your pa. I promise you one thing, Doris—I'll never give you cause to want to leave me again, at least until you decide that you've found the right man. Well, now, I'd better get back to my cabin. I'm writing a letter to old Henri Montfournier in St. Louis—you remember, honey, I told you I'd turned over my trading post to him while I was trying to find you. Now that I have, and now that I'm here in Texas and like it fine, I think I'm going to settle down. I could do a lot worse. I'm going to offer old Henri a chance to buy the post, lock, stock, and barrel, and he can take his own sweet time paying me off, so long as he sends me a little money every so often."

"That's wonderful, Daddy!" Doris cried, giving him a hug.

"You'll excuse me, Tom? I think that's even better than Thomas," Roland Eberle said with a smile.

"I like it fine, too. Good night to you, sir."

Roland Eberle chuckled at this mark of respect and trudged off to his cabin. Doris hesitated a moment, twisting her fingers in front of her, her cheeks scarlet with blushes. She knew that she should follow her father, but the presence of Thomas Blake held her like a magnet.

"I don't want to fret you any, Miss Eberle—"

"You can call me Doris—I'd like that," she said faintly, and her blushes deepened at her own audacity.

"I'd like that fine, too, I would. I realize that you really don't know me from Adam, and you probably still don't know the whole story of how I met your father—but that's all history. He saved my life, and I saved his, so we're sort of bound together. I'm real glad it happened that way, because, Doris, you see, well, if it had been otherwise, I wouldn't be here talking to you this evening and telling you that I like you an awful lot. Don't think I'm fresh, and I don't mean any harm—''

"I—I know," she whispered, so faintly that he could scarcely hear.

"But I think you're a fine, beautiful girl, and one day, maybe after we've gotten to know each other better, there's something I'd powerfully like to say to you and to your daddy, too. And now I'll bid you good night and ask your pardon if I said anything that didn't set well with you."

"B-but you didn't at all, Mr. Blake! G-good night!" Flustered more than she cared to admit, Doris gave him a blushing nod, then turned and ran toward her father's cabin.

Three days after John Cooper, Padre Camporata, Mathieu Farigo, and the *vaqueros* and Jicarilla braves had departed on their journey to New Orleans and Pensacola, Carlos de Escobar determined to test his recuperation from his broken arm. Fortunately, the break had been a clean one and easy to set, and although the arm was still weak, he felt hardly a twinge of pain now as he mounted his palomino, his new Belgian rifle in the saddle sheath, and headed toward the eastern boundary of the great ranch. This time of year, he knew, there was plenty of wild game, from deer to boar to jackrabbits, as well as partridges, hawks, and sometimes a bear. Last year, he remembered, John Cooper had even killed a mountain lion, the first seen anywhere near the ranch since the move from Taos.

Carlos set off at a gallop, happy to be out of doors once again. Despite his slight disappointment at not being able to accompany the others to Pensacola, he felt at peace with himself and content with his life. Here, in this community of family and friends, he was free from the stifling class distinctions of moribund old Spain. The children given him by his gentle Apache wife, Weesayo—Diego, Inez, and Dawn—were all growing up fine and strong; and Teresa's child, little Luisa, would celebrate her first birthday next month. Perhaps— but he would not ask too much of the good *Señor Dios*, after all the boons he had been granted already—sweet Teresa would bear him her first son. If it were a boy, he would name him Carlos, after himself. But if it were to be a girl, then for a certainty he would name her after his loving wife.

He rode for about an hour, but there was no game stirring, and when he turned in his saddle to look around him, he was again aware of the immensity of this great territory of Texas. He thought to himself that this land would be as difficult to conquer as to defend; surely, if the Mexicans ever sought to occupy it by dint of arms, they would need many regiments.

Carlos frowned at the thought, then decided to head back to the ranch. It was not really important that he bag any game today; besides, he doubted whether he could aim and fire his rifle accurately with only one good arm. There would be many more days for the hunt, and perhaps he could take Teresa with him. She was a superb horsewoman, and now that he thought of it, they had not ridden out together on a hunt since they had come here to Texas. It was high time they did. For that was how he remembered her best, how he had wooed and won her, first by fencing with her, and then by riding together. His face brightened as he turned the palomino's head back toward the ranch.

Little Inez and Dawn de Escobar had begged Teresa to let them have a picnic with Julia Sandarbal, who was ten now, and Juan, who was five. Bernardo, the teenaged son of Esteban Morales, who had inherited his father's gift for whittling toys out of wood and making dolls out of straw and a bit of cloth, had already begun his work on the Christmas *piñata*, but Inez, now eleven, and Dawn, now eight, had begged and pestered him to make each of them a doll before then, and this he had done. So when Teresa gave Dawn and Inez permission to have a picnic near the Frio River, and Julia and Juan Sandarbal came with them, Bernardo somewhat reluctantly agreed to accompany the four children as escort, carrying a burlap sack into which he had put two straw dolls. The one for Inez represented a pretty girl with yellow hair, the hair being made of reeds from the river; Dawn's doll was that of a small Indian girl with black pebbles for the eyes and tiny little moccasins with beads, which Bernardo himself had sewn in with great care.

As the four children hurried toward a soft, sandy bank on the northern side of the Frio River, Bernardo hung back a bit, although, as the oldest, he took his responsibility as guardian seriously and kept his eyes peeled for any possible danger. Also, at Teresa's insistence, he had brought with him Yankee and the wolf-dog's two offspring, Maja and Fuerte.

At the river, Bernardo presented the dolls to Inez and Dawn and was resoundingly kissed and hugged by both of them, to his furious embarrassment. He made light of his artistry, regretting that he had not had enough materials to make the dolls more lifelike, but the children were enchanted by them. Julia, something of a tomboy and as blond as her beautiful mother Bess, somewhat enviously inquired, "Bernardo, I've heard your father play the flute. I'd like to have a flute, too—maybe you could make me one?"

"Most certainly, Julia. It's very easy. Besides, I've wanted one for myself, so I'll just make two."

"I want one, too," Inez complained, making a long face.

"Very well, then, three," Bernardo affably agreed, only to be confronted by little Dawn, who declared that if her sister had one, there was no reason why she should not have one also. So that made four. Juan, caught up in the spirit of things, insisted that he, too, had every right to a flute. Bernardo sighed and nodded. "There will be five, *mis amigos.*"

This settled, Bernardo, who had also carried the picnic basket, began to distribute the food prepared by Rosa Lorcas. There were slices of ham seasoned with cloves and raisins, several breasts of roasted chicken, freshly baked biscuits with a pot of honey, and cooked sweet yams liberally smeared with butter. There were also apples and slices of melon and a small sack of pecans and walnuts from the trees near the Frio River. And, finally, there was a large leather flask of fresh milk.

The children were so intent on the tastiness of the food and the pleasantness of the sun and the gentle rushing of the water that they did not see a brownish form slink through the underbrush across the shallow river and, flattening itself on its belly, contemplate them with gleaming yellow eyes.

It was an old mountain lion, whose right paw had been infected by a prickly thorn when it had charged a wild deer just across the Rio Grande and, missing its prey, had landed on a cactus. The beast had yowled and tried furiously to nip out the thorn, but to no avail. For a week it had limped, growing ravenously hungry, unable to lope after even the slowest game. It had managed to catch a baby jackrabbit two days ago, but that had only whetted its appetite. Now, its eyes fixed on the group of chatting and laughing children, the smell of their food in its nostrils, the pangs of hunger became unendurable.

Bernardo sat on a boulder and laughed as Maja and Fuerte nudged the children and begged morsels of food, while Yankee, showing more pride and restraint, remained back and only whined occasionally, as if to remind the children not to forget him. Bernardo fed Yankee himself, giving him part of a breast of chicken and half a biscuit, both of which the wolf-dog bolted down with a purring sound of contentment.

Since he was the oldest, Bernardo felt obliged to show some manners, so he let the children have their pick of what was left in the basket before he helped himself again. Besides, he reasoned, after agreeing to make five flutes, and having already made two dolls, he should have a decent share of Rosa Lorcas's tasty *comida*. He reached into the basket and seized a thick slice of ham and another biscuit, divided the biscuit in half with a forefinger, and inserted the ham, doubling it so that it would fit inside neatly. Then he put his lips to it, and the first bite was delicious.

The old, wounded mountain lion saw this and growled softly. Its eyes scanned the shallow ford of the river. Slowly, silently, it edged out of the thicket and, crawling with its head down and its eyes narrowed at the group of children just ahead, cautiously set first one paw and then the other down onto the pebbles. The pressure on its infected paw was agonizing, but in only a few more steps it would be close enough to leap and strike.

Yankee, who had been whining at Bernardo for a piece of the biscuit and the ham, was first to see the terrible predator. The dog uttered a low growl, his ears flattening along his skull, his hair bristling along his neck. Moving quickly, he slunk to the water to confront the approaching mountain lion, and with a bark directed Maja and Fuerte to come to his aid.

The mountain lion saw Yankee and knew that the moment had come if it wished to assuage its hunger. With a ferocious yowl, its tail lashing, it sprang at the wolf-dog, displaying its terrible fangs. Boldly, Yankee met the charge, feinting to one side and nipping the mountain lion above its right shoulder. As the beast whirled and swiped at Yankee with its good left paw, Maja and Fuerte attacked from the other side, nipping at the flank and leg, and the enraged beast snarled and turned to flail at them with the injured paw.

Dawn and Inez had leaped to their feet, uttering shrieks of terror, while Juan began to cry and crawled on all fours away from the scene of the picnic. His sister Julia ran to him, to pick him up and help him escape, while Bernardo looked desperately around for some weapon—but there was none.

Yankee attacked again, springing at the mountain lion's right side, and then, as the beast hissed and swiped in retaliation, darted as nimbly to the left, to close his jaws on the mountain lion's left side. With a screech of pain, the big cat rolled over onto its back, thrashing with its claws, trying to defend itself from all three enemies simultaneously. But Maja and Fuerte at once sprang forward to bite at the exposed belly of the predator, and the cat quickly rolled over again to all fours and lunged at Yankee.

Bernardo, very pale, picked up a large rock and said, "Children, stay together behind me. Come, I will protect you, all of you—come close together, at once!"

Instinctively reacting to the orders of one older than themselves, Inez and Dawn and Julia, who was holding Juan, huddled back within a narrow circle as Bernardo courageously stepped forward, preparing to use the rock as a weapon. He cursed himself for not having thought to bring even so much as a knife. How dearly he wished he had done so now!

*   *   *

Carlos had ridden back through the gate of the Double H Ranch, and some impulse had made him ride beyond the stable, on toward the Frio River. The sun had come out in all its brightness, and the day had turned out to be most beautiful. He reminded himself to tell Teresa that, very shortly, the two of them should go out hunting together, to recall those wonderful days before she had agreed to become his wife, when he had been half in heaven and half in hell, not knowing, for all his fervor and sincerity, whether she would accept him. . . .

In the distance, he perceived the huddled group of children and saw the wolf-dog and the two cubs lunging and springing this way and that against—oh *Dios*, it could not be—yes, a puma!

With a commingled oath and prayer, he drew his rifle out of its saddle sheath, hastily inspected it to make certain it was primed and loaded, then spurred his palomino toward the river.

Now Yankee alone stood against the wounded mountain lion, his cubs, Maja and Fuerte, having suffered claw wounds and withdrawn to guard the children. The wounds were not serious, but enough to dampen temporarily the reckless courage of the cubs. Yankee lunged this way and that, as the mountain lion opened its ferocious jaws and swiped its deadly paws at the wolf-dog. Yankee feinted, then darted to nip again at the cat's left side, but the cagey old mountain lion whirled and, with a savage screech, raked its left paw against the wolf-dog's side, opening a gaping wound.

Yankee uttered a scream of agony but, valiant to the very end, drew back and lunged again at the ferocious animal. By now Carlos had his rifle at his shoulder and, straining to keep the weapon aimed with his one good hand, watched for the instant when Yankee would not be in the way. At last, when he felt he could hold the rifle up no longer, he triggered the shot. His aim was true, and the mountain lion, with a last swipe at the bleeding wolf-dog, uttered a wild yowl, then collapsed in a heap, its tail lashing a last few times.

Disregarding his arm, Carlos virtually jumped from the palomino and rushed to the children, sobbing in his anguish,

"Oh, *Dios*, are any of you hurt? Dawn, Inez, *mis niñas*, are you all right? And you, Julia, and Bernardo—what horror—oh, *Dios*, poor Yankee!"

The wolf-dog, staggering on its paws, turned its head and stared at Carlos, its bright eyes gleaming, its mouth gaping as the life-blood poured from its wound.

Carlos could not restrain his tears as he splashed through the shallow water toward the wolf-dog and held out his hands to it. Yankee barked faintly, then crumpled to his side. With the last bit of strength, the heroic wolf-dog thrust out its tongue to lick Carlos's trembling hand, then was still.

The children were crying now, and even Bernardo wept, as Carlos walked over to Maja and Fuerte to inspect their wounds. But the two cubs, seeing their sire stretched out lifeless on the streambed, uttered mournful yowls and moved past the Spaniard, each to nudge Yankee's lifeless body and to yowl again, as if believing that perhaps they could bring him back to life.

At last they came obediently to Carlos, nuzzling him, but all the same pausing at moments to turn their heads back to the dead wolf-dog.

Carlos sobbed aloud, offering a silent prayer for the sake of noble Yankee, and vowing to give John Cooper's longtime companion the decent burial he deserved.

Eleven

Early Saturday afternoon, on the twenty-second of December, John Cooper Baines and his party reached New Orleans. None of the young Jicarilla braves had seen such a city before, and to them everything was truly worthy of wonder, although they all agreed that they would not want to live in such a dirty and crowded place. John Cooper reminded them that one of their tribesmen, a young man named Lortaldo, did indeed live here, was studying medicine under one of the city's doctors, and so far had got along quite nicely.

That gave the braves pause to think, and from their hushed comments, John Cooper gathered that their estimation of Lortaldo had increased considerably.

As they passed the city's main square, Mathieu Farigo, the tall, black-haired young Cajun who had escorted Padre Camporata to the Double H Ranch, took his leave of the others, and the Texan warmly shook hands with him and reminded him, "Think about what I've said, Mr. Farigo. I'm sure the bishop will see the good of your coming to the Brazos settlement one day, perhaps even to work as a doctor."

John Cooper and his companions rode on to the house of Fabien Mallard, where they were warmly welcomed by the genial factor and his wife, Hortense.

After hearing the Texan explain his mission, including the story of the capture of the young Duvaldo brothers on the high seas, the factor exclaimed, "Even here in New Orleans, we have reason to know the names of Juan and Manolito Obeira, *mon ami*. They are Spanish renegades who should have swung at the end of a rope long ago." He turned to Padre Camporata, addressing him in Spanish. "And you say, *padre*, that you heard they are based in a secret cove near Pensacola?''

''*Sí, Señor Mallard, es verdad*,'' the priest said, eagerly nodding.

The factor frowned and then turned back to John Cooper. ''I know that coastline, for some years ago I myself did a little trade with an honest Spanish merchant in Pensacola. There are many secret inlets and coves where a ship like the *Dos Hermanos* could hide without being detected; no doubt the Obeiras have set up a comfortable little retreat. The swamps alone provide as good a defense as a military fortress. Yours is a difficult mission, indeed.''

''We count on the element of surprise,'' John Cooper retorted. He gestured toward the six young Jicarilla braves. ''These men are magnificent trackers and skilled warriors, and the young *vaqueros* I have brought with me from the ranch are some of the best marksmen we have. My only fear is that in bringing them with me, I've weakened the defenses back home—and I can only pray that, in the meantime, that devil Santa Anna doesn't take it into his head to try another attack against us. So speed is of the utmost importance, both for us and for the Duvaldos.''

''I can help you. I know the captain of a well-armed schooner, who is due to transport some cargo of mine to Santo Domingo. He won't leave until after the new year, and the journey to Pensacola wouldn't take him more than three days. He knows the coastline as well as any American seaman in this port.''

''Sounds like just the man I want, Fabien. Where can I find him?''

''At the Hotel de la Salle, on Esplanade Street. His name is Ross Meyerle, and he's a big red-bearded man, originally from Baltimore. You won't have any trouble dealing with him—he speaks his mind and is one of the most honest captains I know.''

''I certainly couldn't ask for a better recommendation, Fabien. As always, you're a good friend, and a useful one.''

*   *   *

After arranging temporary lodging for the *vaqueros* and the Jicarilla braves in one of Fabien Mallard's warehouses, and leaving them money to buy food and supplies, John Cooper brought Padre Camporata with him to the Hotel de la Salle. The clerk at the desk directed the two men to the restaurant-saloon in a newly built wing of the hotel, and John Cooper, recalling the factor's description of the man he sought, spotted him at once, seated at a table by himself, puffing at a meerschaum pipe, a tankard of rum before him. He looked to be almost as tall as John Cooper, but stockier, with a bristling, thick red beard, bright blue eyes, and a massive forehead.

John Cooper and the little priest made their way toward the captain's table, and John Cooper introduced himself. "Excuse me for interrupting you, Captain Meyerle. My name's John Cooper Baines, and my factor, Fabien Mallard, suggested I meet with you."

The big man scrutinized the two visitors only for a few seconds, then said, "Why, it's a pleasure, then, Mr. Baines, because he's a fine man, and I like doing business with him."

Ross Meyerle extended his hand, and John Cooper shook it, saying, "And this is Padre Camporata from Buenos Aires. If you've a few minutes, Captain, I'd like to tell you a story and enlist your aid—for which, needless to say, you'll be well paid."

"Perhaps Mr. Mallard told you that I'm due to sail to Santo Domingo in two weeks?"

"He did, but what I have in mind will occupy perhaps a week, at most," was John Cooper's reply.

"Then talk away. Let me order you some rum—it's exceptionally good here."

"Thank you, but no." John Cooper turned to the little priest and said in Spanish, "But I'm sure you're hungry, *padre,* and would like something to eat."

"I'd recommend the gumbo, *padre,*" Captain Meyerle interjected, in surprisingly good Spanish. "I always stay at this hotel when I'm in New Orleans—it's not too costly, and they treat me very well. Probably because it's in the American quarter."

Before the *padre* could respond, John Cooper smilingly put in, "You're my guest, Padre Camporata. And here's a waiter—'' He snapped his fingers, and the aproned waiter hurried to the table. "A gumbo for the good *padre* and me, if you please, and some of your prawns—''

"My son, you are much too generous. I am not used to such feasting—'' the little priest began.

"You've had a long, hard journey," John Cooper interposed, "and you've borne yourself like one of us, without complaint. I'm sure you're as hungry as I am, *mi padre*." Then to the waiter he said, "Make that a large plate of prawns, and some biscuits and honey, and your good, strong Creole coffee."

Turning back to the Baltimore captain, John Cooper went on: "Fabien Mallard says you know the Florida coast as well as anyone in these parts."

"I wouldn't make such a claim, Mr. Baines, but I know it very well. What do you have in mind?"

"Just this." Quickly, John Cooper related the story of the capture of the Duvaldo brothers, Padre Camporata's rescue, and the probable return of the pirates to their hideout near Pensacola. When he mentioned the name of the Obeiras, Captain Meyerle took a long swig from his tankard, then set it down with a clatter on the table.

"Those Spanish devils! Oh, yes, I outran their *Dos Hermanos* about three months ago, and I was very lucky. I say 'devils' because they surely must have the devil on their side to have lasted this long—at least three countries would like to swing them from a yardarm, and I myself would be happy to be the first to pull the rope. So you say that they have their headquarters near Pensacola now? If that's true, I have one or two ideas where it might be. I take it you want to engage my ship to bring you there?"

"Exactly. Or land us nearby."

Captain Meyerle frowned. "It will be dangerous. There's a lot of swamp near there—alligators, snakes, and the like. If they're where I really think they are, it won't be easy approaching by land. And they'll have the sea entrances watched, no doubt. You and the good father here certainly aren't thinking of tackling the job by yourselves?"

"Oh, no. I brought along a dozen or so good men, well armed, and we're counting on surprising them, Captain Meyerle," John Cooper declared.

"Well, it could be done, I suppose. All right, then, if you're after them, I'm on your side, for certain."

"When could you board us, Captain?"

"Tomorrow at dawn. The sooner the better, because I want to be at Mr. Mallard's disposal, as you can well understand."

"That's perfect. All we ask is that you land us as close as you can, then wait for us perhaps a day or so. There's no reason you can't be back in time to fulfill your obligation."

"I'm curious to know—what if you do catch up with them?"

"We might be able to make them sail their own ship with us back to Havana. You see, Captain Meyerle, they're the only ones who can tell us where those boys are right now. We can turn them in to the governor of Cuba and get him to issue an order to release Benito and Enrique, and perhaps also the unfortunate American seamen who were captured from the *Salamander*."

"By God, Mr. Baines, I wish I could see you to the end of this adventure of yours!" Captain Meyerle clenched his fist and brought it down on the table, making the tankard jump. "My *Marylander* has a dozen guns—"

"We wouldn't ask that of you, but thanks for your offer. We must do this on our own, Captain. Besides, if you were to take us on to Cuba, you wouldn't be back in time to fulfill your obligation to Mr. Mallard, and I'm not about to interfere with that. Now, as to payment—will five hundred dollars be sufficient?"

"For sailing you to Pensacola and helping you exterminate those Spanish murderers? I'm the one who ought to be paying you—and I've no doubt that England and even Spain itself would award you twice that to bring those murderers to justice." Captain Meyerle stood up and offered his hand. "Come to the levee at the very end of the wharf, and you'll find the *Marylander* ready to sail at dawn tomorrow. Even if it's a Sunday, we're all God-fearing men on that ship, and it's for a cause that I think would make the Lord Jehovah Himself forgive us for sailing on His holy day."

*   *   *

One of the Apaches accompanying John Cooper was Dejari, the same young brave who, several months before, had summoned John Cooper to the side of a dying Jicarilla shaman from whom the Texan had learned of the existence of a second silver mine. When John Cooper had asked Dejari, back at the Double H Ranch, if he and his comrades would help to find the captors of Benito and Enrique Duvaldo, Dejari had replied simply, "You are the blood brother of our *jefe, Halcón*. When I came with the others, he said to me that if you should require any service of us, you had only to speak, and it would be as if he himself had commanded. As for me, I tell you what you wish to do is a good thing, *Halcón*. You would punish evil men who seek to enslave free men. I do not need to remind you of the story of those two mines and how the Spaniards made slaves out of the *indios* many moons ago. The Great Spirit punished them, and I believe that He will aid you in punishing these men equally."

John Cooper and the priest had returned to Fabien Mallard's warehouse and there, sharing the rude quarters for the night with the others, flung themselves down on cots and almost immediately fell asleep. Over the years, the Texan had learned to exist on only a few hours of rest, for his mind worked constantly to anticipate what must be done upon wakening. Thus, well before dawn, he rose refreshed and uttered a low whistle. Dejari at once awoke and sprang to his feet, then wakened his companions. These warriors, like Dejari, were in their twenties, tireless, the best hunters and trackers, the most skillful marksmen with bow and arrow, as with rifle and knife, of the entire stronghold. The priest, wakened by the sounds, blinked his eyes and eased himself from his cot with a groan. "How I might wish the good *Señor Dios* had given my weak body more strength for this endeavor," he murmured as he crossed himself and began to touch the beads of his rosary.

"*Padre*," John Cooper gently answered, "in spirit, you are as strong as any of these striplings. Do not be ashamed of yourself—it was your courage and faith that let you survive the Obeiras. Without you, we might never have known what happened to those boys. As for food, Captain Meyerle will have breakfast aboard the *Marylander* for us."

The *vaqueros* had awakened now and joked among themselves as they dressed. John Cooper was delighted by how well they got along; these were some of the best men on the ranch, and among the first to volunteer when John Cooper, in the presence of Raoul Maldones and Miguel Sandarbal, had summoned all the *vaqueros* and *trabajadores* and explained his mission and the need for six courageous volunteers who might well risk their lives.

Fabien Mallard had arranged the previous night for the horses to be stabled, and now the fourteen men walked down to the great levee and to the end of the wharf where Ross Meyerle's two-masted schooner was preparing to sail with the morning tide.

The red-bearded captain greeted John Cooper as he came up the gangplank. "You're right on time, by the Eternal! Once we get under way, we'll find something for all of you to eat down in the galley. I've had my coffee—that's all I need for now. Also, I've said my prayers. But I'm not of your faith, by the way, Mr. Baines."

"If you say prayers, you pray to the same God I do, Captain Meyerle," John Cooper replied as he moved to let the Indians and the *vaqueros* come aboard.

"Do you know what I've just remembered, Mr. Baines?" The bluff captain chuckled and shook his head. "We'll be making Pensacola around Christmas Day. It's not exactly the way I planned to spend this holiday—you see, I met a gently bred widow of about my own age the other day, and I was hoping, being a bachelor myself, to squire her about during the holidays before I sailed for Mr. Mallard. But perhaps when I come back with the story of your adventure, she may like me even more, who knows?" He turned to cup his hands and call out to the first mate, "All right, then, McGregor! Get the gangway inboard and cast off. Set the main and fore sail and make for the channel."

"Very good, Captain!" The first mate, in turn, nodded to the boatswain, a burly but good-natured Connecticut man, who transmitted the captain's orders. The crew moved swiftly to their stations, releasing the vessel from its moorings and unfurling the sails, and as the wind caught them, the schooner began to move quickly away from the wharf and out toward the middle of the wide Mississippi, heading briskly downriver for the Gulf of Mexico.

Forty-eight hours later, on Christmas morning, the *Marylander* skirted the Gulf Coast east of Mobile Bay. The day was overcast, with a dull, gray sky and sporadic gusts of wind. Captain Ross Meyerle, standing on his quarterdeck, squinted through a telescope at the distant shore.

"We're some twenty miles from Pensacola, Mr. Baines," he told the blond Texan, who had come to join him after a swift breakfast of coffee and biscuits in the galley. "But if my guess is right, I think your quarry will avoid Pensacola Bay itself—too crowded for the comfort of their likes."

"I'm going to rely entirely on your knowledge, Captain Meyerle," John Cooper declared. "If you wanted to have a retreat near here where you could bring your ship and hide it, where would you pick?"

"In the swampland, Mr. Baines, so that you couldn't be approached easily by land. But close enough to Pensacola to buy supplies and carry them in. And it just so happens that we're approaching a place that fits both those requirements— Perdido Bay. I say we sail in and have a look around."

"Is it possible to go by foot?" John Cooper asked.

"Yes," the captain slowly replied, "but it's not the kind of travel I'd personally recommend. It'd be easier to do our scouting from the bay itself. Ashore you've got alligators, poisonous snakes, to say nothing of a few spiders I'd rather not have bite me. There's quagmire, or you could call it quicksand, if you like, that'll suck you down and kill you if you're not careful. There's a trail around the bay that the Seminoles use, I hear, but they grew up in the swamps, and they know all the dangers. Still and all, I'd recommend we try and catch a gander at 'em from out in the bay—I've got my telescope here, and I doubt if they'll be fast enough to catch us, even if they do see us."

"Whatever you say, Captain Meyerle," John Cooper replied, releasing a deep breath. "But let's hope they don't spot us, because I'm still counting on the element of surprise. But the first thing is to find that ship. If it's not in this bay, as you suspect, then they might have taken to sea again, in which case I'll have to think about getting to Havana."

Captain Meyerle scowled. "I certainly wish I could help you there, Mr. Baines, but like I said, I've got customers lined up, and it wouldn't be fair—"

"I'm not asking you to sail me to Cuba," John Cooper smilingly interrupted. "Like *I* said, Captain Meyerle, I plan to persuade the Obeiras to take me there."

The bluff, red-bearded captain stared incredulously at John Cooper, then slapped his thigh and burst into laughter. "By the Eternal, Mr. Baines, I've taken a liking to you, damned if I haven't!" Suddenly he called out a quick string of orders to the boatswain, who swung the schooner's wheel, heading the *Marylander* closer to shore, toward a narrow break in the sandy coastline. "We'll be entering the bay in a few minutes, and then we'll see what's what. I've told my cook to make some plum duff and some cake, and we've a few roast chickens for you and your party, Mr. Baines. It is Christmas, after all. At least you'll have a good meal tucked in your belly if you have to hit those swamps."

"I couldn't have asked for a better man to have brought me here, Captain Meyerle."

"That's kind of you to say, but wait until I find that ship for you before you start complimenting me—"

Padre Camporata emerged on deck, and he greeted the two men, wishing them a happy Christmas. "This is a joyous day," he said, "and I am saddened that we cannot celebrate it properly, in God's holy temple. Nevertheless, I shall not forget to say prayers expressing my thanks, and also asking that we find those two evil men this very day and bring them to justice, whatever hardship I must endure."

"Surely you do not intend to go ashore with the others, Father?" Captain Meyerle asked, a shocked expression on his face. "You can stay on board with my crew—it will be no trouble."

Padre Camporata shook his head. "No, my son, I am needed to identify those evil men, and no one else can do that. Excuse me—" he insisted, as John Cooper sought to add his protesting voice to the captain's. "I am sorry, but on this point I must be adamant; no one but *el Señor Dios* Himself will move me."

The little priest turned his back and moved away. By now, the *vaqueros* and the Jicarilla Apache braves had breakfasted, and they, too, came out on deck. As the *Marylander* entered the bay, they lined the rail on both sides, curious about this part of the young country that, until now, none of them had ever seen. Dejari approached John Cooper and said in a low voice in Spanish, *"Halcón,* one of your men, the *vaquero* Corte, says that he once had a cousin who worked for a year at a trading post near this place. He says the swamps here are full of snakes, and large, swimming lizards that can eat a man—the *caimáns.*"

"Es verdad, Dejari," John Cooper said, nodding. "There will be dangers for all of us, but I will not lead you into them unless it is your will and that of your companions."

"You need not ask that of us, *Halcón.*" Dejari looked hurt, and he seemed to stiffen and draw away a step. "Did I not tell you that our chief, Pastanari, commanded us to be of aid to you in no matter what you undertook, no matter how great the danger? We are with you, *Halcón.*"

"As I am with you, my brother." John Cooper took Dejari by the shoulders and gripped him hard and smiled at the young Jicarilla Apache. "With such courage, with such resolve, we shall do what we have set out to. Forgive me for even questioning your willingness."

"I have already forgotten it." A brief smile flickered on the young brave's face. "I remember once, when I rode to tell you of the dying old shaman, Potiwaba—you did not tell my *jefe* that I lost my horse on the journey because I wished to count coup over a buffalo. You might well have done this, and I should have been sent to live among the squaws and the old women for having failed my mission. I owe you much."

"We shall not talk of debts or owing, Dejari, but of friendship and purpose. Your skill and that of your companions will see us through all dangers, I am confident of it."

All this while, Captain Meyerle had been squinting through his telescope, studying the swampy inlets and coves that made up the shoreline of Perdido Bay. The *Marylander* had sailed perhaps three miles up the bay when he suddenly uttered a hoarse gasp. "By the Eternal, I think I've sighted something! Take the glass, Mr. Baines, and see for yourself. Notice that little cove over there to the right—see how narrow it is at first, then broadens and is lost in all those cypress trees with the Spanish moss dangling from them."

"I see—yes, there's something dark glimmering through the moss and the trees," John Cooper excitedly agreed. "And I think I can see the top of a mast."

"I'll stake my berth as captain of the *Marylander* that that's the *Dos Hermanos,* Mr. Baines!"

"Can we go a little farther and then look back at an angle?" John Cooper proposed. "We will get a better view of the outline of the ship itself, so that Padre Camporata here can identify it."

Captain Meyerle nodded. "I'll have the helmsman hold this course so that we won't appear suspicious, if anyone is watching." He handed the telescope to the little priest, who put it to his eye at once, moving to the rail to get the best possible view of the target, as the *Marylander* moved slowly up the bay. Suddenly he uttered a cry: "Yes, yes, I recognize it from the broad hull, and from the shape of those rails—I shall never forget that—how the seamen came closer to us and then boarded us, and so many brave men died—" He crossed himself and handed the telescope back to the captain, who in turn scrutinized the ship and nodded.

"Yes, no doubt about it, that's the *Dos Hermanos,* Mr. Baines. Well, we've found your quarry for you, and now we'll figure out the best place to put you ashore. It will have to be in the direction we're going, because if we put about here, anyone watching from shore might figure what we have in mind. We can drop you off, then tonight we'll double back on the other side of the bay and wait for you near the ocean entrance."

"I agree with that." John Cooper nodded.

"We'll hold this course for a few miles, so mark in your mind where that cove is. Remember, once it's dark, it's very easy to get lost in those swamps."

"The Apache is trained to see better in the dark than many white men see in broad daylight," John Cooper declared confidently. "But we should be in striking range by dusk."

"Well, then, that's settled, gentlemen. But just to be on the safe side, I'll get the chart from the helmsman and mark it, to show you where we'll rendezvous. Then we'll have our Christmas dinner, and pray for the day's success."

Twelve

After putting ashore John Cooper's party, the *Marylander* continued up the wide bay, waiting for dusk before doubling back along the western shore, out of sight of the cove where the *Dos Hermanos* lay hidden.

Meanwhile, John Cooper, Padre Camporata, the *vaqueros*, and the Jicarilla Apache began their stealthy journey to find the retreat of the Obeira brothers. The *vaqueros* were armed with rifles, braces of pistols, and knives, while the Jicarilla had brought their bows and arrows, which could be just as effective—and deadly silent—in the thickly grown swamp. The braves carried knives as well, while John Cooper himself had brought along his Lancaster rifle, the Spanish dagger he customarily carried in a sheath hung from his neck, and a brace of pistols holstered at his waist. The pockets of his buckskin jacket were stuffed with pouches containing powder and ball for his rifle, for he and all the *vaqueros* had provided themselves with ample ammunition to wage a long siege, if need be, against the pirates.

Only the faint, overcast light of late afternoon penetrated the thick cypress overgrowth as the men moved cautiously forward over the marshy ground. As they proceeded into the swamp, John Cooper took hold of the little priest's arm. "Let me help you, *mi padre*," he said in a low voice. "You're not at all used to a place like this." Then, turning back to the *vaqueros*, he called softly, "Dejari and his friends will go ahead of us, since they're more used to tracking. Follow me and move carefully, and make sure your footing is secure." He chuckled grimly. "I can think of far more entertaining

things to do this Christmas evening, *mi padre*, than to stalk
several miles through swamps like this, even to mete out
justice.''

"What you are doing, my son, will surely earn you
many happier holidays spent with your beloved family, of
that I am certain."

John Cooper became sober at these words, thinking of
his Dorotéa. Before he had left the ranch, he had entrusted
her Christmas present to Carlos, who surely had given it to
her by now. It was a music box that had been inlaid with
mother-of-pearl, and inside, little red garnets spelled out the
words *Te amo, mi Dorotéa*.

In front of John Cooper, Dejari moved in a crouch, his
hunting knife drawn and ready. Once inside the gnarled
clumps of cypress lining the shore, the party found itself in
murky swamps, with six inches of water underfoot. It was not
yet sunset, but they could hear the calls of night birds and the
croaking of giant bullfrogs, and from the far-off distance
came the eerie cry of a loon.

Because he had lived with the Indians for so many years
and knew how to track and to hunt, John Cooper soon
adjusted to the half-light of the swamps. It was like a ghostland,
with stagnant pools of water interspersed with thick bushes,
huge cypress trees with festoons of Spanish moss, and giant
growths of creepers and ivy that in the gloom looked like
deadly serpents.

Behind John Cooper and the priest, one of the *vaqueros*
muttered to another, "*Caramba, mi compañero*, if I did not
know better, I'd be terrified of the *brujas* and *diablos* who
live in this dreadful place!"

"I, too, Sancho," the other *vaquero* grunted as he pushed
away a tangle of creeper vines.

It grew dark quickly as the party continued heading
inland, hoping to intersect the Seminole trail that circled the
bay. To the right, a sudden swarm of fireflies lent a grotesque
glow to the desolate surroundings. Out of the corner of his
eye, John Cooper saw a water moccasin, several yards away,
slither from the base of a cypress tree into one of the stagnant
pools and disappear. Instinctively, his right hand moved to
the Spanish dagger hanging from his neck, and he placed

himself between Padre Camporata and the snake, just in case. "It will be a long march, *mi padre,*" he murmured. "But it's far wiser to go slowly in a strange place than to push ahead too quickly. So far, the footing seems secure."

"When there is danger, my son," the little priest replied, "I think of the great Psalm that says, 'Though I walk through the valley of the shadow of death, I fear no evil, for Thou art with me; Thy rod and Thy staff they comfort me.' From this I never fail to draw courage."

"As do I, *mi padre.* Careful now, there's some brackish water just ahead, and what looks like a log floating at the edge of it."

Hardly had he spoken when the supposed log stirred, and the jaws of a huge alligator gaped open. They were about to close on the bare leg of one of the Jicarillas, just ahead, but John Cooper uttered a cry of warning, drew his hunting knife and, dropping his rifle onto a bush, flung himself forward, lunging with all his strength to send the blade of the knife deep into the eye of the *caimán,* toward the brain. There was a hideous, bellowing roar, as the alligator thrashed about, lashing with its powerful tail, and John Cooper struck again in the same place as, mortally wounded, the hideous beast rolled over in the foot-deep water, exposing its underbelly. Twice more the Texan struck with all his might, and the *caimán* gave a final slash of its huge tail, then drifted off, belly-up, in death.

The little priest, terrified at having witnessed this demonic struggle, was praying under his breath and crossing himself repeatedly. Panting, his buckskins soaked and bloodstained, John Cooper rose to his feet, retrieved his rifle, then turned to the priest. "That was a close one, *mi padre.* These creatures, it seems, have ways of protecting themselves by looking like dead logs. But I view this as a good omen. It tried to take us by surprise, but we had the better of it. Let's hope we're as successful with the Obeira brothers when we reach them."

They started to move forward again, but Bimante, the brave who had been attacked by the *caimán,* turned to the Texan and, in his Jicarilla Apache dialect, thanked John Cooper for what he had done.

John Cooper answered, "I did not think we would run such risks, my brother; if I did, I would not have asked you to come with me."

"I would have come whether you asked or not," the Jicarilla said with finality. "I, like my companions, follow you as if you were our chief."

They resumed their arduous journey, and finally the braves scouting ahead passed back word that they had reached the dry ground of the Seminole trail. Here the party turned south, following the trail back toward the cove where they had seen the *Dos Hermanos*. To their right now was a vast stretch of stagnant water, extending as far as the eye could see in the shadowy gloom. Certainly even the Seminole seldom ventured off the trail here. In this wilderness, time appeared to have stopped at some prehistoric age, and man seemed out of place. No doubt the Obeiras counted on this to shield them from any enemy who might be foolish enough to seek them out in their lair.

The croaking of the bullfrogs increased now, and the men could make out rows of them sitting upon fallen tree trunks and along the banks of the huge expanse of murky water. Here and there, dark, ominous shapes floated, like driftwood, and John Cooper, out of perhaps a boyish impulse, picked up a rock and flung it at one of them. Instantly, the jaws of a *caimán* opened with a bone-chilling hiss, and there was a thrashing of water as the beast disappeared beneath the pitch-black surface.

Three miles to the south, Juan and Manolito Obeira were carousing in celebration of this Christmas night and the rich profits they had gleaned on their last trip to Havana. They had brought back on their ship six comely trollops from Havana, promising to return them after the holidays, when the *Dos Hermanos* would set forth on another piratical expedition, the plunder from which would again be disposed of through Señor Luis Marconado. The Obeiras' first and second mates, the boatswain, and six other veteran crew members had joined them in this revelry. Except for a handful of guards and a skeleton crew aboard the *Dos Hermanos*, the rest of the pirates had been dropped off at Pensacola, from where the Obeiras usually outfitted their ship for an impending voyage.

The Obeiras' hideaway in the swamps was a rambling, bungalowlike affair that had once belonged to a solitary fisherman. The Obeiras had had their ship's carpenter renovate it, adding white columns and a portico, in imitation of the newly fashionable Greek-style mansions of Southern plantations. It was on a rise inland, about a quarter of a mile from the secret cove where their ship lay at anchor. Five sentries were posted in the woods around the house, but in the years since the Obeiras had chosen this desolate part of the Florida coast for their secret base, no one had ever disturbed them. Indeed, aboard the ship itself, the sentries and skeleton crew had drunk themselves into a holiday stupor and lay sprawled on the deck, as the waves lapped gently against the hull and along the shore of the peaceful cove.

Inside the house, Pablo Zaraza, the burly chief gunner of the *Dos Hermanos,* and perhaps the one member of the crew in whom the Obeira brothers had complete confidence, slouched drunkenly on a luxurious brocade-covered ottoman, a prize from a Dutch ship whose masts his cannons had felled a year ago. He was holding a half-empty bottle of rum in his left hand, while his right clumsily fondled the naked bosom of one of the six *putas* who had accompanied the Obeiras on their return from Havana. He lifted the bottle to his lips and took a lengthy swig, then belched and swore. "*Por los cojones del diablo, mis capitanes,* we've had a good year, and here's to a still better one!"

Juan Obeira, himself dandling an attractive young prostitute on his knee, leaned over to reach for a bottle standing on a teakwood taboret and, finding it empty, hurled it with an oath against the fireplace, where it shattered. He grasped the neck of the prostitute on his knee. "Fetch me a fresh bottle, *querida,* and be quick about it!"

"*Seguramente, mi amorcito,*" the girl purred as she slipped off his lap and hurried to the corner of the room, where an array of bottles stood on a broad oval table. There were decanters of Madeira, fine French wines, Spanish sherries and ports, rare old brandies, and other, less refined spirits.

She chose a bottle of rum and hurried back to him. Juan took it by the bottom and, with careless impatience, smashed off the neck against the edge of the taboret, then tilted back his head and poured a copious libation down his throat. "Ah, I've a devilish thirst!"

"You always do, *mi hermano*." Manolito Obeira, on another sofa, uttered a tipsy chuckle. Then he turned to the girl beside him and snarled, "You bitch—be careful! Don't you know that one of my legs is crippled! And you try to sit on it! Do that again and I'll have our bo'sun, Pedro Aguilar, trice you up and teach you manners!"

"Forgive me, *capitán ilustre*," the girl, a slim, tall, *mestiza* of not more than twenty, babbled as she hastily slid off his lap to her feet. "But you're so much a man, *mi capitán*, so perfect in knowing how to please a *mujer*, that I didn't think . . . Say you forgive me!"

Manolito sniggered, savoring this obvious flattery born of the girl's terror, and benevolently he nodded. "Come here, *querida*. I will show you how I forgive you."

Hesitantly, the girl approached, but he made a sudden gesture. "To your knees, because if I am *ilustre*, you don't stand on your feet to address me, *comprendes*?"

When the girl obeyed, her face pale with justifiable apprehension, the crippled slaver reached out and grabbed a handful of her luxuriant hair, which fell nearly to the middle of her back, and twisted it until the traction made tears come to her dark eyes. Then viciously, using the palm of his other hand, he slapped first one cheek and then the other.

"Now maybe you will remember that even I have imperfections, little slut!" he hissed.

His brother, across from him, guffawed with raucous laughter. "That's the way to treat women, *mi hermano*!" He squinted drunkenly around and saw that several of the crewmen whom he and his brother had invited to share their orgiastic celebration were sprawled on the floor in various stages of drunken stupor. The women who had been fondling and caressing them huddled nervously near the oval table, occasionally offering the bottles of spirits, not certain what they should do next.

"Eh, Manolito, you and I and faithful Pablo here, we

seem to be the only ones with energy enough to continue this fiesta of ours,'' Juan joked. ''Pablo, tell those girls to take off all their clothes and do a dance for us. I seem to recall that you play a hornpipe when you're in a good mood— now's the time!''

''*Sí, mi capitán.*'' The Spanish gunner grinned from ear to ear and, fumbling in the pocket of his greasy vest, pulled out a battered hornpipe, put it to his mouth, and began to play a jaunty sailors' jig.

Manolito slid a razor-sharp rapier out of the solid hardwood sheath that served as his walking cane, leveled the long, thin blade at the frightened girls, and hissed, ''You heard my brother! All of you, off with your clothes, and be quick about it! If not, I'll be happy to show you how I can cut them off you without so much as scratching your fine skins!''

With little cries of alarm, the prostitutes hastened to comply, for by now they had experienced the full gamut of the brothers' mercurial whims, which alternated from the merely vulgar to the outright sadistic. Though each of them had been promised a substantial fee for accompanying the Obeiras to the Florida retreat, there was not one of them who by now did not sorely regret her greediness and who considered herself woefully underpaid for what she was enduring.

About a mile and a half from the sprawling house, John Cooper's party had come upon treacherous quagmires. One of the *vaqueros*, Xavier Matzano, had strayed a little off the narrow path all the men were following, when suddenly he uttered a cry as he felt his booted feet sink into the soft, yielding muck. There were sucking sounds as he struggled to free himself, but two of the other *vaqueros* quickly came to his aid, seizing him by the armpits and dragging him out of the bog. ''*Jesu Cristo,*'' he breathed, crossing himself, ''it was as if invisible hands were pulling my legs down, and I did not have the strength to escape them—*gracias, mis compañeros!*''

''*De nada,*'' the vaquero named Sancho gruffly reassured him. ''Never you mind, *amigo*. There'll soon be some serious fighting, and you won't have time to remember this little nastiness.''

"All the same," Xavier said, emptying the muck from his boots, "if I never come here again, it'll be far too soon!"

The party had advanced only another hundred yards when one of the Jicarilla braves leaped to one side as a dark, slithering coil dropped from an overhead branch and fell almost at his feet, then began to unwind. It was a deadly cottonmouth, and the Jicarilla brave, moving as fast as a badger, stamped with a moccasined heel upon the serpent's head, then drew his hunting knife and, squatting down, struck and struck again until the snake was still.

"It won't be long before we come to their place, hombres," John Cooper whispered. "Padre, you've been very courageous, and you've hardly uttered a word all this time. Do you still have some strength left?"

"Yes, my son—but do not worry about me. I trust we have come through the worst of the dangers?"

"Not quite. There'll be sentries ahead of us, and I'm afraid we might have to break one of the Holy Commandments in disposing of them."

"I hope that can be avoided, my son, but I will not shrink from what must be done to stop these evil men. Alas, His will is not always simple to follow, and you must do what you think best." The padre shrugged. "I do not know if that is good theology, but it is what I believe right now, after seeing for myself what you and your men have gone through, Señor Baines."

A few minutes later, Dejari, who had been scouting ahead, came running silently back along the trail.

"I have seen a house, Halcón, and guards. There are at least three of them—one where this path comes into a clearing, a second on top of a small hill in the clearing, and the third beyond him and to our left, near the casa. It is a very large one. You can see lights from it—look there!" He turned to point through the trees and to his left, and John Cooper nodded. Oil lamps could be seen flickering dimly in the distance, like fireflies.

"We shall silence the sentries for you, Halcón," Dejari murmured.

John Cooper nodded. "The *vaqueros* and I will wait until you tell us that all is clear, Dejari. *Vaya con Dios.*"

The brave and two of his companions crouched low and moved forward along the trail. When they were almost out of sight, John Cooper saw them pause behind a thicket, reach back to draw arrows from their buffalo-hide quivers, then fit the arrows to the bowstrings and move forward again.

It was the depth of night, and all was still. Only an occasional night bird and, from the watery swamp whence they had come, the faint croakings of bullfrogs broke the stillness. By now the cool evening air had settled, and a miasmic fog had begun to rise through the bushes and the overhanging garlands of Spanish moss, making the terrain still more terrifying and ghostlike.

John Cooper motioned to the *vaqueros* to remain back with him and the priest. A few minutes later, they heard the twangs of the Jicarilla bowstrings and, beyond, a choking sigh; then a faint gurgling scream that was swiftly silenced.

It was several more minutes until Dejari returned. "We are at the rear of the *casa*, *Halcón*," he whispered.

"Good—we shall join you there. You go first, and send your companions around one side to see if there are other sentries posted at the front. We'll see if we can get in through the back, then signal you when we're ready." John Cooper turned to the *vaqueros*. "At this close range we'll need pistols and knives—we can leave the rifles hidden behind the house. Are all your pistols primed and loaded?"

"*Sí, Halcón—sí, patrón—seguramente, patrón!*" the *vaqueros* chorused in whispers.

They moved cautiously ahead, across the dark clearing and over the rise to the back of the house. There was a narrow door, evidently leading to the kitchen, and John Cooper tried it and grinned. "They didn't bolt it," he whispered. "Gently now, *mis amigos*—put your rifles under that bush, but don't make a sound. Then follow me." He turned to the priest. "There will be danger now, *padre*, if the pirates have guns—I do not want you to be hurt. I think it will be safe if you stay here beside the door and say prayers for us. Here—take my rifle, but be careful, because it's loaded."

"As you wish, my son." The priest permitted himself a

faint smile as he took "Long Girl." "I was only thinking, Señor Baines, that if you bring me before those evil men, they will think that I have come back from the dead."

John Cooper returned the smile. "Wait here now, *padre*, and we'll try to get this over with as quickly as we can."

John Cooper signaled to Dejari at the corner of the house, and then, their pistols cocked and ready, the six *vaqueros* followed the Texan through the back door. The Jicarilla Apache, making short work of silencing the two guards at the front of the house, moved for the front door.

John Cooper led his men through the dark kitchen. Down the hall, from the direction of the main parlor, they could hear the sounds of breaking bottles, oaths, and the cries and squeals of young women as someone played a lively hornpipe.

Abruptly the music stopped and someone growled, "I want another drink. This playing music's thirsty work, *mis capitanes*!"

At that moment John Cooper and the *vaqueros* made their entrance, pushing aside the thick velvet drapes at the other end of the parlor. Almost simultaneously, Dejari and his braves slipped through the front door, arrows notched and their bows held in readiness.

"*¡Diablo!* What are these—alarm!—*capitanes*—" Pablo Zaraza swore thickly and then, flinging aside his hornpipe, reached for the hilt of his cutlass, which lay unsheathed at the end of the ottoman.

Dejari's arrow took him in the throat, and he toppled to the floor, dying in a welter of his own blood.

The naked girls screamed and huddled back against the wall, while the drunken crew members on the floor crawled into the far corner or just lay there. Juan and Manolito Obeira, both openmouthed, stared disbelievingly at the sight of these armed men. John Cooper, a pistol in his right hand, walked across the room and picked up Pablo Zaraza's cutlass.

"Who the devil are you?" Juan Obeira snarled out of bravado. His voice was thick with inebriation, and he swayed on his feet as he tried to stand. The frightened girl he had been fondling slipped away from him and hurried to the far corner of the room, from where she contemplated this incredible sight of armed *vaqueros* and Indian braves led by a tall, blond giant of a man.

"We have some business with you, if you are the Obeira brothers," John Cooper drawled.

"Business? What kind? How did you come into this house without the sentries stopping you?" Juan slurred.

"There are no sentries anymore, señor," John Cooper replied with sarcastic courtesy. "As you can see, there's no sense resisting, and your fellows here seem to have had too much to drink. They'd best sleep it off, I'm thinking, or they may not wake until eternity is over. But as I've said, I have business with the Obeira brothers." He advanced slowly, his pistol leveled at Juan Obeira.

With an oath, Manolito yanked his sword from its walking-stick sheath and limped toward the Texan with surprising agility. "You'll not shoot me down in cold blood," he taunted John Cooper. "If you've guts enough for a fair fight, I challenge you now."

The man was obviously drunk, and John Cooper coolly transferred his own pistol to his left hand and the dead man's cutlass to his right. Manolito lunged clumsily, then uttered an angry, befuddled cry as the Texan's blade struck the thin, sharp sword from his hand, sending it quivering to the floor.

"Now we'll resume our discussion—Señor Obeira, I presume?" John Cooper put the point of his cutlass to Manolito's throat, but the man remained silent. "Very well," John Cooper said. "If you refuse to identify yourself—" He nodded to one of the *vaqueros*, who, without having to be told, ran to the back of the house to fetch Padre Camporata.

"As I was about to say," John Cooper continued, "we are after two young men, Benito and Enrique Duvaldo, whom you took off the brig *Salamander* a month or so ago."

"Can you prove any of this?" Manolito said with a sneer. "All this is fancy talk. We will admit to nothing."

Just then Padre Camporata entered the room, his eyes wide with wonder. "You have done this already? But it is a miracle, indeed—"

"They offered ittle resistance, *padre*," John Cooper said. "Unfortunately, we had to kill one of them—"

Even as the Texan was speaking, however, the Obeira

brothers, both staring at the little priest, simultaneously uttered disbelieving cries, and Juan surreptitiously crossed himself.

"I do not believe it—but I see him, as I did on the deck of the *Salamander*—"

"You fool, you're telling them what they want to know!" Manolito snarled.

"It does not matter what you say, señor," John Cooper again interposed. "The identification of this good priest is enough."

He turned to Padre Camporata, who nodded once and said simply, "Those are the men."

"Thank you, *padre*. Now, señores, since I am told that you are the captains of the *Dos Hermanos*, you are going to take us all to Havana. There we shall visit the governor, and you will inform us and him of the identity and whereabouts of the man who bought the Duvaldo boys from you as slaves."

"You cannot make us sail our own ship back to Havana," Manolito snarled.

"Perhaps I can't," John Cooper agreed. He turned to Padre Camporata. "Padre, I think it is best that you and one of the *vaqueros* escort these women into one of the other rooms, where they can get dressed."

Blushing furiously, the little priest nodded, then instructed the girls to pick up their garments and follow him out of the room.

As soon as they had left, John Cooper continued, "No, señores, perhaps I can't make you sail your ship, but these men whom you see with bows and arrows are Jicarilla Apache. You have probably never been to the Southwest, but if you had been, you would know that they are great warriors, hunters, and trackers. Moreover, they know methods of extracting information from even the most unwilling. I can easily turn you over to them and see what imaginative ways they have of persuading you to loosen your tongues. If I were an Apache, señores, I think I should try tying you to a tree out there in the swamp, capturing some of those water moccasins, and—"

"No, no! You are a fiend from hell! Not the snakes—" Manolito was sweating. Blustering, he added in a syrupy voice, "Come now, *mi amigo*, be sensible—why not let us tell you where the boys are? You have the upper hand of us, and there is no need for us to go with you to Havana.''

"You're forgetting that we need a ship to reach Havana, and yours is the only one at hand," John Cooper reminded them. "But first I wish to hear from your own lips your admission—is it true that you sold those boys in Havana?''

"Yes, yes, have done with this nonsense!" Juan put in.

"And to whom?"

"To the procurator general himself, *su excelencia* Luis Marconado," Juan disgustedly admitted.

"That is helpful and sensible on your part to cooperate like this," John Cooper said. "Still in all, both of you will take us on your ship to Havana."

Juan looked at his brother and shrugged. "After all," he said, "who cares about two young *esclavos*? Why should we risk our lives for their sake?" He turned back to John Cooper and, with a sly smile, wheedlingly asked, "If we agree, señor, and we lead you to them, will you be finished with us?"

"For my part, yes. What the authorities will do to you in Havana, I cannot be certain," was John Cooper's answer.

Juan drew closer to his brother and, in a hoarse whisper, explained, "So it will be an annoyance to take these men to Havana. But we have powerful friends there, don't forget that, Manolito. They won't be able to do a thing to us. And if we have to return Señor Marconado the money he paid us for those boys, we'll get it back from him the next time we've finished a commission for him."

John Cooper gave an order in the Apache tongue, and two braves approached each of the pirates and, after searching them, forced their hands behind their backs, bound their wrists with rawhide thongs, and gagged them.

This done, the Indians went to the unconscious and incapacitated crewmen, rolled them over onto their stomachs, and bound their wrists and ankles as well.

At John Cooper's order, two of the *vaqueros* and Padre Camporata remained at the house, while he and the rest of the party retrieved their rifles and moved toward the cove where the pirates' ship lay at anchor. A long wooden wharf had been built from the shore out into the water, and at its end a longboat was tied.

There was still no moon out, and no guards were in sight, so John Cooper thought it safe to commandeer the longboat. Silently the eleven men rowed out to the ship and clambered aboard the rope accommodation ladder. It was a simple task to round up the drunken sentries and crewmen and bind them before they could recover from their befuddled, drowsy state. After this was done, John Cooper and the six braves went back to the house and ungagged Juan and Manolito Obeira, then marched them down to the ship. Padre Camporata, the two *vaqueros*, and the prostitutes followed.

"How do you expect me to sail to Havana, *gringo*, with not even a full crew, and hardly any provisions aboard?" Juan Obeira grumbled.

"As for the provisions," John Cooper calmly answered, "we'll see what we can round up from your larder. Judging from the food and bottles of liquor I saw when we entered your house, Señor Obeira, I'm sure we can find enough to feed those who will work the ship."

"But it's a good week's sail to Havana, and there certainly won't be enough—" Manolito angrily began, but his brother sent him a warning look, and he lapsed into silence. However, John Cooper had noticed this interplay between the brothers and sarcastically put in, "If you're thinking of setting a false course, señores, forget it. The captain who brought us here taught me enough to steer a course south by southeast, and Cuba would be pretty hard to miss."

Juan cursed under his breath and then sullenly declared, "I'll have you know, *gringo*, that the man who bought those boys you're so anxious to find is none other than the procurator general of Cuba itself, high in favor in the government. He's commissioned us many a time to bring slaves to him— that is no crime. We have done nothing wrong under Cuban law."

"We'll see about that," was John Cooper's resolute answer.

Thirteen

An hour before noon on the day after Christmas, under the watchful eyes of the armed *vaqueros*, the skeleton crew of the *Dos Hermanos* drew up the anchor and unfurled the sails. During the morning, the Jicarilla Apache warriors had ransacked the Obeiras' house and brought back all the food they could find, and John Cooper, searching the ship from bow to stern, had discovered two barrels of flour, some salted pork and beef, and a sack of coffee. "We'll eat on rations, but none of us will starve," he told the *vaqueros* and the Indians.

So that the Obeiras would not instigate trouble with the crew, John Cooper had ordered them locked into a small cell below deck—which, ironically, happened to be the very same cell that not long ago had held the Duvaldo brothers. The Cuban prostitutes had, to their surprised delight, been given the luxurious captain's cabin for their accommodation.

The rendezvous with the *Marylander* went as planned, and John Cooper met with a smiling Captain Meyerle aboard the *Dos Hermanos*, to receive some last-minute tips on navigation and to say good-bye.

By the end of the day, a brisk squall sprang up, and the *Dos Hermanos*, by now out of sight of land, encountered heavy seas. Fortunately, out of fear for their own lives, the pirate crewmen, assisted by the *vaqueros*, frantically worked at the sails and the ropes, and when the squall subsided a few hours after midnight, one of the pirates, a wiry Spaniard, announced that he wished to speak to the *"capitán gringo."*

John Cooper had already flung himself down on the mate's bunk to get a few hours of rest after his first, taxing stint at the wheel, but he forced himself immediately awake when one of the *vaqueros* brought the Spaniard to his cabin door.

John Cooper scanned the frightened face of the crewman, who looked in his early thirties, with a mutilated right ear and a pearl in the lobe of the left. "What do you want of me?" the bearded Texan brusquely demanded.

"Señor," the seaman began, speaking quickly, "my name is Joaquín Sordoña, and if you will spare my life, I will help you sail the *Dos Hermanos* to Havana, I give you my word. The *vaquero* at the helm now, I am sorry, but he does not know what he is doing. He steers the wrong course, and if another squall strikes suddenly, we will be in much danger."

"You know how to handle the wheel, Joaquín?"

"*Sí, sí, señor*," the man eagerly nodded. "*Mis compañeros* say you are taking our *capitanes* back to Havana and will make them give up the slaves they have brought there. I am afraid for myself, because perhaps if all this is found out, they will send me to the garrote. It is not a good way to die, señor." The man crossed himself and shuddered. "I will not betray you; I will keep you on course, and *mis compañeros*, if you will put in a good word for us when you arrive in Havana, they will help you also. We know that you have taken our *capitanes* prisoner, and so our service to them is at an end, *no es verdad?*"

John Cooper nodded. "Very well, Joaquín—it's a deal. But my men will watch you, and if you betray us, I'll throw you overboard with my own hands, I promise you that!"

"Even that, *señor gringo*, would be preferable to the garrote," the seaman hastily avowed. "Say only that you will put in a good word for me and my friends, and I will be your man to Havana. I will swear it on the Holy Book, or by whatever oath you demand of me."

John Cooper nodded to the *vaquero*, and together they accompanied Joaquín Sordoña back on deck, where Padre Camporata, unable to sleep for all the excitement, was standing at the rail, his eyes upturned to the now-starry sky. The seas were calmer, and the moon had come out, seeming brighter than it ever did on land.

John Cooper related the seaman's offer to the priest,

who turned to the wiry Spaniard and, holding out his crucifix, said, "Swear on this, my son, that you will not be guilty of treachery, and we shall believe you."

The seaman leaned forward and kissed the cross, and when he had sworn, John Cooper led him to the helm. A few minutes later, the *Dos Hermanos* was back on course to Cuba.

It was almost dawn on the last day of December, 1827, when the *Dos Hermanos* dropped anchor in the harbor of Havana. The Obeiras' seamen had faithfully kept their part of the bargain and had worked industriously. Now they lowered a dinghy over the side, and with two *vaqueros* at the oars, John Cooper and the priest took seats in the stern. The blond Texan had ordered the rest of his men to keep the Obeira brothers locked in the cell and to stand guard over the crew until he learned from the governor what disposal should be made of them.

A few minutes later, as he and Padre Camporata clambered out of the dinghy and onto the wharf, a uniformed sergeant of the guard halted them. He was not the noncommissioned officer with whom the Obeiras usually dealt, but he knew the ship well. "You come when everyone sleeps," he complained. Then, scowling as he scrutinized John Cooper's blond-bearded, sun-bronzed face, he exclaimed, "I don't recognize you from that ship. Where are the Obeiras?"

"Under lock and key in the hold, *amigo*," John Cooper answered. "With me is Padre Angelo Camporata, who was left aboard the American ship *Salamander*, after the Obeiras had boarded it, killed half the crew, and transported the rest here to slavery. The *padre* was left to die, but as you see, he didn't. We mean to call now on the governor of your island."

"But, señor, that is impossible—do you know what hour of the day it is? His Excellency will be sleeping, and you have no official business with him—"

"We shall wake him, then," John Cooper interrupted. "And if you delay us, I shall tell him that it was you who kept him from learning news about treason and corruption in his own government."

A worried look crossed the sergeant's face. "Now, a moment, *por favor*, señor—there is no need to take that tone with me," he weakly protested. "I merely do my duty. I am a poor man—my name is Paco Algorcada, and as you see, I am only a *sargento* and have no authority—"

"Then perhaps you will win a commission as *teniente* by finding a carriage for Padre Camporata and me and seeing that we reach the governor!" John Cooper swiftly cut in.

For a moment the sergeant hesitated, but the fluent Spanish this stranger spoke, together with his air of authority and the decisiveness of his words, had made an impression that could not be lightly dismissed. To be sure, the sergeant thought, there was the possibility that his superiors would reduce him to the ranks if he failed to help convey an important message to His Excellency Santiago de Nuñez.

Taking a deep breath, the sergeant nodded. "I will find you a carriage, señor. And for you, too, *padre*—" This he said with an unctuous smile, at which the priest made the benevolent gesture of the sign of the cross over the man's forehead, to his grateful *"Gracias, mi padre."*

Some fifteen minutes later, John Cooper Baines and the little priest leaned back in the carriage, and the sleepy driver, scratching his head perplexedly, directed his horse toward the luxurious villa that was the private residence of *el gubernador*.

Once there, John Cooper tossed him a silver coin and ordered him to wait; then he and the priest walked down the inlaid stone pathway, flanked on each side by dazzling flowers, leading to the magnificent house. It was full dawn now, but not a sign of life stirred as John Cooper boldly ascended the low stone steps of the veranda and, putting his hand to the ornamental knocker at the heavy front door, struck three times. When there was no answer, he repeated this, until finally shutters were drawn on the windows of the second floor, and a querulous voice called down, "Are you drunk or mad, señores? His Excellency is asleep. Be off with you, vagabonds, rogues, before I have the *policía* take you to the *calabozo* where you belong!"

John Cooper cupped his hands to his mouth and called back in fluent Spanish, "I am sorry, but we have urgent business with *el gubernador*. I am John Cooper Baines of the

Estados Unidos, and with me is Padre Angelo Camporata. It is of the utmost importance that we see the governor now, so that justice can be done!''

The servant who had opened the shutters now stuck his head out the window, grumbled and shook his fist, then disappeared. A minute later, footsteps could be heard in the hallway, and the door was opened by the same servant. He was still wearing his nightclothes.

''Lower your voices, *por amor de Dios*!'' he gasped, a finger to his lips. ''*El gubernador* is an old man, and his sleep is precious.''

''So is the sleep of two young men captured by pirates and brought here to be sold as slaves,'' was John Cooper's immediate reply.

''All right, all right, in the name of heaven come in, and keep your voices down, I pray you! His Excellency will never forgive me if I waken him for no good reason—'' The servant moved to one side as John Cooper and the priest crossed the threshold.

''I am the valet of His Excellency,'' the elderly man explained as, squinting, he scanned the faces of the two intruders. ''Santa María, you wear the clothes of an *indio,* yet you are *blanco,* and you speak our tongue with ease!''

''My son,'' Padre Camporata interposed, ''we surely did not mean to disturb the well-earned repose of your illustrious governor. But the señor Baines here has just come from Pensacola, Florida, and with his men he captured the infamous Obeira brothers. I myself witnessed these pirates board an American ship outside of Havana and kill many of the crew, and afterward, according to the confession of several crewmen, they brought the survivors and two young men from Argentina here to be sold to the señor Luis Marconado as slaves. Upon my hope of salvation, my son, I tell you that all of this is true. This news must reach the ear of the governor swiftly.''

''The señor Luis Marconado? But that is beyond belief! He is the procurator general of all the island . . . oh, *Dios,* what am I to do? *El gubernador* has not been in the best of health, and I fear that—well, say a prayer that he does not have me flayed alive for wakening him at this unheard-of hour!'' The servant shook his head and mumbled to himself, then ascended the stairs. As an afterthought, he turned and called back, "Wait there, and do not raise your voices again, I implore you!"

He was gone perhaps five minutes, and then out onto the landing came a tall old man with sparse white hair and a little goatee. He was also in nightshirt and slippers, and he scowled down at John Cooper and the priest. "Señores, Rodrigo has told me why you have come to my villa at an hour when all God-fearing citizens should be peacefully sleeping. Am I to believe what he has related to me concerning the señor Luis Marconado?"

"*Excelencia*," the priest spoke up, "it is gospel truth we bring you. I was left on the *Salamander* among the dead members of the crew killed by the bloodthirsty pirates of the *Dos Hermanos*. They believed that I, too, would die, and thus my blood would not be on their hands. But faith and a miracle saved me, and I came to Texas to find the señor Baines, here, and he and his brave, loyal men captured the Obeira brothers in their hideaway in the swamps of Florida. They confessed to everything that your valet has told you. The two young men who entreated me to reach the señor Baines and inform him of their peril are Benito and Enrique Duvaldo. I am told that Señor Luis Marconado purchased them from the Obeiras to serve as *esclavos* in his brothel, which he calls the Casa de Belleza."

"*Mi padre*, I know you would not lie. This is serious business. Rodrigo!"

"*Excelencia?*"

"Since I am up, you may as well bring hot chocolate for my guests and me. Then go back to bed, for you look more in need of sleep than I myself."

"At once, *excelencia*, at once!"

"Señor Baines, Padre Camporata, I will show you into my study. We shall sip hot chocolate, and it will clear my old brain. Then you will tell me your unbelievable story from the beginning, sparing no details. My own procurator general involved with piracy?" The old man shook his head as he slowly descended the stairs, leaning on the beautifully turned and carved balustrade to support himself.

John Cooper moved to one side respectfully, inclining his head, for even in his nightclothes, the governor of Cuba was a man of admirable dignity, and his features were those of an old *hidalgo* who had served his country long and well.

The valet, who had gone to the kitchen to prepare the chocolate himself, reappeared in black trousers and a jacket, such as he would normally wear in service, and hurried into the study with the tray. John Cooper and the priest thanked him, and Santiago de Nuñez smiled at him as he accepted the cup, then gently said, "Now go back to sleep, Rodrigo. I promise I shan't reprimand you for having wakened me from a very sound sleep."

Then he turned back to John Cooper and the priest and, after a sip of his chocolate, said, "Please, refresh my drowsy mind with these amazing facts. The charge you bring against Señor Marconado is a very grave one."

John Cooper deferred to Padre Camporata, and the little priest eagerly expatiated on the pirate attack on the *Salamander* and all his adventures since that time. When he had finished, nearly a half hour later, the old governor shook his head and exhaled a long sigh.

"*Madre de Dios,* it is like a story out of the *Arabian Nights.* It is true that I had heard some disquieting rumors the past few months concerning the divided interests of my procurator general, but no formal charges have ever been made. Since he is a high government official, I cannot summarily punish him until a thorough investigation of this deplorable situation has been made and a trial has been conducted. However, what I shall do at once is to close down the Casa de Belleza—I have been looking for an excuse to do that in any case. I will issue an edict decreeing that this action is being taken pending a formal investigation, to be conducted by my solicitor general."

"I thank Your Excellency," John Cooper replied. "I should be very eager to see young Benito and Enrique as soon as possible."

"Will it satisfy you if I send an official courier and one of my aides to that iniquitous house later this morning? At that time I also will have your prisoners taken into police custody. Until then I shall ask you to be my guests, and we shall all catch up on our sleep for a few hours. The young men will be brought here, I promise you, and I should like to hear from their own lips what they know about this regrettable affair.''

"I can ask for no more than that, Your Excellency, and you have my profound apologies for having awakened you,'' the blond Texan answered.

"There is a room down the hallway for you, Señor Baines, and one for you also, Padre Camporata—please make yourself at home. As for me, if you will excuse me now, I'll go back to my own bed. Rodrigo will waken me at about eight-thirty, at which time I'll dispatch the men to the Casa de Belleza.''

"Thank you again, *excelencia*.'' John Cooper rose to his feet and stretched and yawned, then chuckled. "I'll confess that a few hours of sleep would certainly be welcome after the past weeks—but now that we're here and I've had the privilege of meeting you, Governor Nuñez, I can tell you that I feel it was more than worth the effort.''

"You are much too kind.'' The old man smiled faintly as he rose and walked toward the stairway. "The first door on your right, Señor Baines; and yours is across the hall, *padre*. I will see you both at breakfast. And thank you for bringing this vital matter to my attention.'' He shook his head and, with a rueful expression, went slowly up the stairs.

John Cooper and the priest joined Governor Santiago de Nuñez for breakfast in the ornate dining room of the villa, and even as they ate, a young courier presented himself, and the governor ordered, "García, take this at once to the house of Señor Benitez, my aide.'' The valet had brought him pen and paper, and he now dried the letter by sprinkling sand on it from a little ivory container, blew on it, then folded it and handed it to the courier. "You will accompany him in delivering this to the person in charge of the Casa de Belleza at once. Then you and he will bring back to my residence the persons of Benito and Enrique Duvaldo, who are being held as slaves there. With the utmost haste, García!''

"At your command, *excelencia*." The courier bowed, then hurriedly left the dining room.

A little later, the governor sent another courier to the commandant of police, instructing that the Obeiras and their crew be transferred to a police prison, until their cases could be heard, with account taken for those who had cooperated with John Cooper. The prostitutes, the governor decided, could be freed on their own parole.

It was about ten o'clock in the morning when the courier and the aide, a solemn-faced, brown-bearded man in his early forties, were admitted into the foyer of the villa, with Enrique and Benito Duvaldo between them. The young Duvaldos' faces were crimson with embarrassment, for they were still obliged to wear the colored blouses and trousers that marked their service in the brothel. Padre Camporata, who had been anxiously waiting, sprang to his feet, clasped his hands together, and uttered a joyous cry: "My sons, my sons, your prayers have been answered, thanks to Him Who watches over all of us!"

"Mi padre!" Enrique exclaimed as he hurried forward and knelt at the feet of the priest, bowing his head and clasping his hands in prayer, while Padre Camporata, a beatific look on his plump, bespectacled face, made the sign of the cross over him.

"Please rise, my son. I have brought with me Señor Baines—it was he and his brave men who were responsible for freeing you," the priest told the older youth. Benito, in his turn, had come to kneel and receive the priest's blessing. The brothers both rose now and turned to the buckskin-clad Texan.

"You will never know how grateful we are, Señor Baines!" Enrique exclaimed. Then, turning to the priest, his eyes wide with wonder, he went on. "Benito and I prayed every day when we were in that terrible place, *mi padre*. We could only hope that somehow you would be rescued—"

"As you see, I was, my son," the little priest smilingly interrupted. "It is a long story, and now we all shall have the time to hear each other out—"

"My young señores," the old governor said, as he came forward and extended both arms to the youths, "seeing you now, I cannot comprehend that anyone would dare to sell you here in Havana as *esclavos*."

"But it is true, *excelencia*," Enrique vehemently exclaimed. "It was the señor Luis Marconado who bought us from the Obeira brothers. And he told Benito and me that our duty was to spy on the guests of that infamous place and to report their gossip back to him, through a dreadful little hunchback who was responsible for the death of at least one of the *esclavos* who worked there, and—"

"Comprendo, mi joven." The governor comforted Enrique, who clearly was distraught.

"But Your Excellency," Enrique went on, "now that I'm here, I beg of you, in the name of mercy, to save the life of an innocent girl!" Enrique knelt before the old governor, tears shining in his eyes. "It's Madalena Cortez, *excelencia*. There was a *Capitán* Maximiliano Orozco, a cruel man who beat her, and one night I heard her scream and beg for mercy, and then she came out of her room with a knife and wept that she had to kill him to save her own life. And she has been sentenced to die by the garrote, *excelencia*, at noon of this very day! I have not been able to sleep since then, thinking of this dreadful death to which this innocent young girl has been condemned!"

"It's true, *excelencia*," Benito hurriedly broke in. "She's only seventeen, *excelencia*, a sweet and gentle girl, and she was kind to my brother. And *Capitán* Orozco, on that night, I remember, was already drunk and abused her before he took her to her room. Please don't let her die, *excelencia*!"

"You plead most eloquently. I must, of course, examine the facts in the case, but I will do this much at once—I will send my courier, García, to the place of execution. You say it is for this noon?" the governor asked.

"Yes, *excelencia*, yes, and there is not much time!" Enrique groaned.

"García will reach the plaza well before then, have no fear. I shall write an order at once, halting the execution until I personally have had an opportunity to investigate the case. You have my word on this. García!"

"Excelencia." The courier stiffened to attention.

"I will have Rodrigo bring pen and paper again, and I

shall write an order staying this execution. You will ride at once to the residence of the minister of justice, who always presides at such punishments. With speed, you should reach him before he leaves for the plaza.''

"As you so order, it shall be done, *excelencia*." The courier respectfully inclined his head.

The old governor turned and clapped his hands. "Pen and paper quickly, Rodrigo! Bring them to me in the study. And you, García, follow me. Directly after I have written it, you will prepare to leave!''

When the governor had gone, John Cooper turned to the young Duvaldo brothers. "Everything will be all right now, Benito, Enrique. When this is all over, I plan to take you back to my ranch in Texas, just as your father hoped. I remember him well, and how kind and gracious he was to me when I first visited Argentina. And you will be reunited with Raoul Maldones, too, and see Dorotéa, my beloved wife.''

"Señor Baines," Enrique declared, "we, too, remember you well from your visit to our house. It was because of the respect our father had for you that he told us on his deathbed to come to you. In the meantime, the *gauchos* and our own faithful majordomo are defending our land and home, and we hope that one day soon the rule of the *porteños* will be overthrown, and we may return there.''

"I pray for your sakes that it will happen, Enrique.'' John Cooper warmly shook hands with the youth. "But until then you will find life at the Double H Ranch far from dull. You can hunt and ride, and you'll make many friends among the people who live with us. For just like your *gauchos,* our *trabajadores* and *vaqueros* have that rare gift of loyalty, which makes them part of the family, and not simply workers bound to an estate.''

"And the other daughters of the señor Maldones, are they at your ranch, too, Señor Baines?'' young Benito questioningly put in.

"They are going to school in New Orleans, Benito,'' John Cooper said with a chuckle. "María, Paquita, and Adriana. But have no fear—you will soon see them again. Now, have you boys eaten this morning?''

"Just some bread and coffee—it was enough,'' Enrique

said. "Señor Baines, I am sorry, but my mind was on nothing but Madalena Cortez—I pray that courier will reach the plaza in time to save her—"

John Cooper put his hand on the boy's shoulder. "You have heard the governor, Enrique, and he is a man of his word, I am sure of that. You will see your Madalena again." A smile transformed the tall Texan's expression. "I have a feeling that you have more than an ordinary interest in her, Enrique."

"Yes—I love her, it's true. She was so tender, so kind and sweet, and when I think of how that cruel man beat her, I wanted to kill him myself—" Catching sight of the little priest, who had overheard these last words, so violently uttered, Enrique sheepishly hung his head. "No, I know it's wrong to kill. But all the same, I couldn't bear to have her treated like that—"

"Perhaps we can arrange to take her back with us, then," John Cooper said. "But there's no sense worrying— that courier will arrive in time, Enrique. Sit down and rest and think of the new life that awaits you, and of the friends you will make. And," the blond Texan added, "it will be an even better life, if your sweet Madalena accompanies you."

Fourteen

A huge crowd had gathered in the plaza of the city to witness the spectacle of two public executions by the garrote. The balmy weather had attracted many, and there were vendors selling cooked shrimp, pieces of melon, salted fish, spice cakes, and mugs of the potent *taffia,* the native rum distilled from the sugarcane. Others sold printed sheets detailing the crimes of the two unfortunates who were to die, and quoting last statements from them.

A large wooden platform had been erected the night before, and in its center was fixed a heavy chair with a high back. Its legs had been bolted to the platform so that the struggles of the victim would not dislodge it. In the middle of the chair's back, at about neck height, were drilled two holes, about five inches apart. Behind the chair, his arms folded, stood the public executioner, a brawny man with a black hood over his face, with slits for the eyes, nose, and mouth. He wore a black *camisa* and matching breeches, and heavy-heeled black boots. The short sleeves of his shirt bared thickly muscled wrists and forearms. At each side of him stood an assistant, wearing the same garb, but unmasked. They adopted his pose of laconic patience, their arms folded, faces cold and impassive.

Beside the chair, on the floor of the platform, were small coils of thick whipcord, to be used to bind the victims' wrists and ankles to this grim *silla de muerte*. In the breeches pocket of one of the assistants was a velvet-lined case, a fitting setting for a costly necklace—yet this necklace was a deadly one, for with it the public executioner plied his terrible trade,

183

for which he received a munificent fee from the office of the public prosecutor. As the three men on the platform waited, the crowd grew more boisterous by the minute, eager for their morning's entertainment to begin.

The governor's young courier had ridden to the house of the minister of justice, Don Felipe de Tolado, hoping that the venerable minister had not yet left to preside at the execution. Dismounting and hurrying to the door of the mansion, the courier knocked loudly, and an old majordomo appeared, obviously distressed.

"I have come from *el gubernador, viejo*," the courier said, panting. "I have a reprieve for one of the condemned today; I must see His Excellency!"

"What a dreadful day! My master has been stricken with a fainting spell, and the *médico* is with him now."

"Then the execution cannot take place, if he is not there." The courier uttered a sigh of relief.

But the old majordomo shook his head. "Alas, when I brought him his breakfast this morning, Don Felipe was already feeling indisposed. He ordered me to fetch one of the servants and bade him ride to the house of Señor Baptista Paralto, the assistant minister, who was to proceed with the carrying out of the supreme penalty for those two unfortunates."

"Oh, *gran Dios*!" the courier groaned in his frustration. "And you think Señor Paralto will have gone directly to the plaza?"

"I am certain of it. I am sorry I can give you no better news. And now, forgive me—I must go back to my master. I pray he will not be taken from us, he is such a good, kind man!" With this, the majordomo crossed himself and closed the door in the courier's face.

The *calabozo* was just off the east side of the plaza, and now the buzz of conversation rose as four uniformed guards, armed with muskets, escorted the two prisoners out of the jail. It was already a quarter past eleven, and the crowd had begun to express its impatience, since the news had been that the first criminal was to be put to death beginning at eleven o'clock.

The first prisoner walked ahead of the nearly fainting Madalena Cortez, who, barefoot and clad in only her shift, with her hands tied behind her back, stumbled trying to keep up with the two guards prodding her onward. Her face was swollen with tears, and a priest moved beside her, mumbling his prayers, urging her to confess her sins, to make peace with her Maker, and to die in the hope of eternal forgiveness. Yet agonized by the thought of the merciless death that awaited her, Madalena could hardly respond, and her shoulders shook with sobs as she moved closer to the platform.

The prisoner ahead of her was a burly man, a black slave from a sugarcane plantation who had strangled to death his white overseer because, it was rumored, the latter had gone to the slave's hut and ravaged his woman. The slave was as powerfully built as the executioner, and his face was defiant. He looked straight forward and did not heed the priest who walked beside him, urging him to seek repentance and remission of his dreadful sin.

"There they come now!" a gray-haired woman gleefully cried, turning to the stout, nearly bald man beside her. "I hope they save that *puta* for last! You can be sure of one thing, Antonio—the executioner will take his time with her. She's a pretty one! I'll wager you some *rico* has already bribed him to stretch it out as long as he can, so that her struggles can be seen. Now, don't feel sorry for her, you old fool—she deserves to die. Didn't she murder an important officer? What I'd really like to see is to have them whip her first before they throttle her, the murderous little bitch!"

"Now, now, María, why should you hate her? She's one of the poor, like us," the man, her husband, timidly protested.

The gray-haired woman turned on him and shook her forefinger in his face. "I know what you're thinking! If you had a few extra *pesos*, you'd enjoy paying a visit to that *casa de putas* where she used to work, I know you would! I tell you, she's earned the garrote! Ah, just as I thought, she's behind that *negro*, the one who killed the *capataz*. They'll make her watch, to see what will happen to her next. That's good, that is!"

The stout man uttered a faint sigh and rolled his gaze heavenward, but diplomatically said no more, as his wife, her eyes glittering with cruel anticipation, followed the slow procession of the four armed guards, the two condemned, and the priests beside them. There were seven wooden steps leading to the platform, and now, adjusting his wig and black robe, Señor Baptista Paralto, the assistant minister of justice, ascended and faced the crowd. Unfolding a heavy piece of paper, he sonorously read the official order of execution passed upon Simón Ibarra, *esclavo negro*.

Baptista Paralto was a little man, with a long, sharp nose and the austere look of a pious zealot. Earlier this morning, when he had heard the news that his superior had taken ill, he had secretly hoped that the illness would be fatal, for his burning ambition all these years had been to ascend to the post of minister of justice. As he continued reading the lengthy order, the crowd burst into catcalls and demands that the executions begin. Already they had gorged themselves on what the vendors had to sell them, and now they hungered for the sight of slow, expertly prolonged death.

Wishing to make friends with the populace, Baptista Paralto hurriedly finished reading, then pronounced, in as loud a voice as he could muster, "Let the first execution proceed by the law of our government. Executioner, do your duty!"

This was greeted with cheers, and the little man smirked and nodded benevolently at what he believed to be popular gratitude directed at him. Perhaps, he thought, as he descended from the platform, if Don Felipe truly was mortally ill, it would do no harm to pay a New Year's call upon His Excellency, *el gubernador,* to remind him—oh, very humbly, to be sure—of his own qualifications for the vacated post. Indeed, he was already composing his little speech, which would be full of flowery praise for his late predecessor.

The first two guards seized the black man by the shoulders and forced him up the steps of the platform. At the top, the two assistants at once grabbed hold of him, for now the prisoner was their rightful charge. Knowing his powerful strength, they took the precaution of not untying his wrists until they had first forced him down into the chair, while one of them swiftly knelt and looped the coil of whipcord round and round first the right ankle and chair leg, and then the left, until it was certain that the victim could not break free.

Then, cautiously, the other assistant approached from the side of the chair, drew out a short knife, and swiftly cut the bonds of the black man's wrists, only to seize one of these and grasp it firmly, while the other assistant took charge of the other arm. In a few moments, the slave's wrists were bound securely to the arms of the chair.

The priest who had accompanied him now ascended the platform and urged, "My son, it is not too late to seek forgiveness—"

The black man spat at him, then tilted back his head and laughed. "It was no sin—that dog got what he deserved! Let him fry in hell, where he belongs! Go away from me, priest. I can die without you!"

Madalena Cortez, as if hypnotized, raised her head, and her tear-swollen eyes fixed on the platform. The executioner was ready. He made a curt nod to the assistant who held the velvet case, and the latter handed it to him. The hooded man opened it and took out a small coil of whipcord and a cylindrical metal object the length of a pistol barrel. He made another sign, and one of the assistants plunged his hand into the thick black hair of the slave and forced his head back against the narrow vertical upright. Quickly the executioner thrust the two ends of the whipcord through the holes pierced in the chair back, wound them around the victim's neck, then drew the ends back out the holes, where he knotted them solidly. All was in readiness.

The black stared out at the throng of faces before him, a sneer on his lips. Behind him, the hooded executioner threaded the metal cylinder between the chair back and the connected whipcord, then turned it very slowly to one side.

The black's eyes bulged, his nostrils flared, and his fingers clenched savagely against the arms of the chair. The executioner paused, looking out over the spectators, who were now hushed in morbid expectation. Had they lived in another era, long centuries past, they might well have been those who watched the Christian martyrs die under the claws and jaws of the lions in the Colosseum of Imperial Rome.

The executioner turned the metal piece back, easing the

strangling bite of the whipcord. The black slave groaned, his body stricken by a violent shudder. It was well known that friends or relatives of a condemned criminal could at times bribe the executioner to bring a swift, merciful death; but in most cases the hooded man reserved the right to apply death as he chose, and the defiant attitude of this black slave had angered him. His left hand held the metal piece steady, and now he extended his right and twisted the little bar. Once again the whipcord bit into the flesh of the thick neck of the slave, and again his eyes bulged, and a hollow groan was wrested from him. His body tried to arch in the chair, as he strove to lean backward to ease the hideous constriction of the whipcord. There were murmurs among the spectators, savoring the skill of the executioner. Then, once again, the bar returned to the middle of the neckboard, easing the cord's cruel impress.

Yet it was not the prolongation of the black's death that some in the crowd wished to see, but rather that of the beautiful young prostitute, who had now sunk down on her knees and burst into heartrending sobs. "Oh, *Dios*, have mercy on me, I don't want to die," she cried. "Oh, *Dios*, please help me!"

Pitiless, many called out jeering insults at her, while others cried out taunts of the torment she would endure, and said they hoped that the executioner would prolong the spectacle of her death as long as he possibly could.

One of the spectators even cried toward the assistant minister, "End it with this one—give us the *puta*!" Others took up the chant.

At first, conscious of his importance, the bewigged and berobed little man shook his head and held up his hand, as if to imply that justice must not be rushed. But as the angry cries grew, he finally acceded to the will of the mob, thinking also that this would aid his own cause in replacing the ailing Don Felipe de Tolado. He turned to the platform and gave a peremptory sign. The executioner nodded, inclining his head.

Using both hands now, he turned the bar with slow, inexorable force.

There was a gurgling, choking cry, instantly cut off. The black slave's eyes bulged, and blood appeared at the tops of the whites, then from his nostrils. His mouth gaped as he fought for air that could not come into his windpipe. At last his eyes glazed, and he stopped struggling. His head fell limply to one side. Yet even in death, his fingers still savagely clutched the arms of the chair.

The executioner stepped back and nodded. A tall, gaunt man, the prison doctor, ascended the platform, bent his head to the slave's chest, and listened. Then he straightened, took out a small mirror from his coat pocket, and held it to the gaping mouth. After a moment, he turned to the assistant minister and solemnly announced, "This man is dead."

The executioner's helpers busied themselves undoing the whipcords that had bound the black's wrists and ankles, lifted his sagging body in their arms, and bore it down the steps of the platform, where two of the soldiers took it from them and strode away toward the *calabozo*.

As if relieved from the tension of this hideous spectacle, the crowd seemed to exhale a chorused sigh. But, almost instantly, the cries arose again.

"Now it's her turn!"

"Death to that filthy *puta*!"

"*Verdugo*, take longer with this one—we'll pay you well!"

"Yes, let it be a whole hour, if you've the skill, *verdugo*!"

The two soldiers flanking Madalena Cortez stooped now, their hands gripping her slim waist, and lifted her to her feet.

"Oh, no—*por piedad*, no, please, I had to kill him, don't you understand? He beat me so—please, it was to save my life! Have mercy! Is there no one here who will listen to me? Oh, *gran Dios*, save me!" she cried hysterically as the soldiers forced her toward the grisly platform where death awaited her.

The priest continued to exhort her to contrition, to confess the sin of murder and ask for divine forgiveness. But Madalena could see only that hideous chair and the three men who stared at her, and, most fearful of those three, the man in the black hood, whose eyes seemed those of a demon from hell.

Once again it was time for the assistant minister to

exercise his office. Ascending the platform, he unfolded another paper and read aloud—more quickly this time—the sentence of death passed upon Madalena Cortez for the murder of *Capitán* Maximiliano Orozco. The order specified that the prisoner was to be executed at noon—still twenty minutes away—but the little minister skipped that part, not wanting to provoke the crowd's wrath. Pompously refolding the paper, reveling in each moment of this brief public show of supreme power, he announced, "Let the sentence of our honorable court be carried out! Executioner, do your duty!"

Cheers again greeted his announcement, and he hastily descended, wise enough to understand that, henceforth, the unfortunate young girl would monopolize the attention of the mob.

The two soldiers forced her up the steps, and the assistants seized her. She uttered a pitiful scream as they forced her into the chair, but offered no resistance as they bound her bare ankles to the chair legs, then cut the bonds of her wrists, only to replace these with the whipcord fetters that would lash her slim wrists to the chair arms. Then the second assistant, at the executioner's nod, handed him the cord and metal bar.

Madalena closed her eyes, and her lips moved in prayer. Yet just as the executioner was preparing to pass the two ends of the whipcord through the pierced holes of the neckboard and wind them around her slim young throat, there was a cry from the crowd.

"I bring a reprieve from *el gubernador* himself! The execution is not to proceed! Where is the señor Paralto? I have the decree signed in the governor's own hand! Take me to him!"

The executioner halted, glancing at his two assistants, who shook their heads.

Baptista Paralto frowned and, cupping his hands, called out, "I am here—bring me this decree of yours! If this is a joke, señor, I have the power to imprison you, and you have not at all helped this poor girl meet her fate bravely!"

The young courier pushed his way through the crowd until he came face to face with the bewigged minister, then thrust Governor Santiago de Nuñez's decree into the man's outstretched hand.

"See for yourself. I trust you recognize the signature of *el gubernador*?" he said, panting. "I thank God I came in time—it is twenty minutes before the official sentence was to have been carried out. This is your doing, Señor Paralto, and I shall tell the governor about it, have no fear!"

"Gently, gently, señor," Paralto stammered, looking nervously about him.

"You will see also," the intrepid young courier added, "that the decree states that she is to accompany me back to his house, for he wishes to question her himself."

"I was only doing my duty," the little man defended. "You must understand, the people demanded the death of this assassin—yes, I see, I recognize the signature of *el gubernador*. Very well." Looking extremely agitated, he ascended the steps and announced to the crowd: "His Excellency, our beloved *gubernador*, has, in his mercy and wisdom, spared the life of Madalena Cortez—"

This immediately provoked an angry outburst, and the minister waved his arms for quiet.

"Good people of Havana," he implored, "there is no more here for you to see. I bid you go back to your homes and reflect on the justice of our government . . . a justice that, as you can see and hear for yourselves, has been tempered with mercy."

But no one was listening to the bewigged little man, and it took several policemen and soldiers to restrain them from climbing the platform, as Baptisto Paralto took refuge behind the hulking executioner.

Meanwhile, the assistants had freed Madalena Cortez, and the courier himself hurried up the steps of the platform to sustain her, for she was very nearly fainting.

"Courage, *pobrecita*," he sympathetically murmured. "The governor's aide has just arrived with a carriage, and we will take you to meet His Excellency. And there will be a happy surprise for you, señorita. It was the brave young man Enrique Duvaldo who interceded for you with *el gubernador*, and that is why you have been granted your life."

*   *   *

The governor's aide and the young courier rode with Madalena Cortez back to the governor's mansion, but thoughtfully, the aide first had the driver stop at his own house, where he borrowed one of his young wife's dressing robes so that the reprieved Madalena might be more modestly covered when she was presented to the governor.

Enrique Duvaldo had been staring out the window in the salon where he and his brother Benito, John Cooper, Padre Camporata, and Governor Santiago de Nuñez were waiting. When he saw the carriage draw up in front of the mansion, he uttered a joyous cry and bolted out the front door and ran toward the street.

The old governor chuckled. "How wonderful it is to be young and to care so deeply for someone!"

"He's in love with her, *excelencia*," John Cooper averred. "You've reprieved her—but will she go to prison for what she's done?"

"I have the power to pardon a criminal, Señor Baines," the governor solemnly responded. "If the matter concerned only this poor girl, I should most likely order a new trial and take the evidence of the young man who seems to be her friend. However, Señor Baines, in view of the many irregularities of this entire affair, I shall interview her myself and then determine whether, indeed, she was driven to this violent act in order to protect her own life. If that is the case, I have, as I said, the immediate power to pardon her."

"I could ask for nothing better than that, and neither could Enrique," John Cooper responded.

The aide and the courier had helped Madalena step down from the carriage, and for a moment she stared disbelievingly at the luxurious mansion. But Enrique, with another joyous cry, hurried up to her and seized her hands and brought them to his lips.

"Madalena, Madalena, I've prayed so hard that you'd live—*querida, mi querida,* I love you so, I thank *el Señor Dios* for saving you!"

"Enrique, *corazón*," Madalena sobbed as she flung her arms around his neck and clung to him, her body convulsively shaking in the aftermath of her horrifying ordeal.

"It will be all right. The governor is a kind man—I'm

sure he'll pardon you. Madalena, the señor Baines has come to save us all—and the priest, I told you about him, how those pirates left him to die on the ship. A miracle happened, and he was taken to New Orleans by another ship, then brought back Señor Baines and his men to capture those pirates who boarded our ship and made Benito and me *esclavos* at the Casa de Belleza! And now, *querida*, Benito and I will go back to Texas with him, and I—I want you to come with me. I love you, and I want to marry you, Madalena."

"Enrique—my sweetheart—I can't believe . . . This is like a dream—a dream after such a horrible nightmare! Oh, yes, yes, I'm yours—you've saved my life! I belong to you, Enrique, but . . . you don't want to marry a *p-puta*—" she tearfully faltered.

"Not another word! To me, you're the sweetest, loveliest girl in all the world, and no one else shall ever have you. You'll be my wife, Madalena. We'll live on the señor Baines's ranch in Texas, and we'll have a family—"

Now she was laughing and crying, and blushing, too, as she clung to him. The young courier and the aide exchanged smiling glances, and finally the courier gently proposed, "We mustn't keep His Excellency waiting, you know. Come along—you'll have plenty of time to yourselves later on, after he's spoken with the señorita."

They entered the house, Enrique's arm protectively around Madalena's shoulders. When she saw the tall, white-haired governor standing solemnly in the center of the room, she disengaged herself, ran toward him, and fell on her knees. Seizing his hand, she brought it to her lips and sobbingly thanked him for having spared her life.

"You mustn't kneel to me, my child," he gently admonished. "Now then, Padre Camporata, Señor Baines, if you will excuse us for a few moments, I wish to question the señorita and this young man, who, from what you have told me, heard and saw a little of this tragic act for which she was condemned. Come with me, both of you."

Half an hour later, the governor emerged from a study just off the salon, followed by a radiant Madalena and Enrique, who again had his arm around her shoulders and was unabashedly kissing her cheek and whispering impassioned pledges of his profound love.

"I am convinced that both these young people are telling the truth," the governor announced. "I find that Señorita Cortez merely defended herself against the depraved cruelties of *Capitán* Orozco. There are some who, out of prejudice, might condemn this poor girl because she was obliged to earn her livelihood in a disreputable house; I, on the contrary, believe that *because* of that very situation, she was coerced into enduring the cruelties of this high-ranking officer. And when her very life was endangered, she tried to save herself—I find no fault with that. I therefore shall issue a decree formally pardoning her."

"You are a humane and just man, *excelencia*," John Cooper said, respectfully inclining his head.

Enrique turned to the blond Texan. "Señor Baines, would it be all right if Madalena comes with us back to Texas? I mean to marry her, if she'll have me."

"If His Excellency has no objection." John Cooper eyed the governor.

"I think that would be a very happy solution to a tragic set of circumstances, Señor Baines. By all means." The governor permitted himself a warm, compassionate smile. "Particularly if she goes in the custody of this staunch young defender. And, if he marries her, she can begin a felicitous new life—and with my blessing."

Enrique strode toward John Cooper, grasped his hands, and energetically shook them, his face aglow with happiness. "My father told me what a great man you were, Señor Baines—I know it for myself now, and Benito and I will work hard on your ranch, you'll see!"

"Your father's friend Raoul Maldones will find a useful occupation for you, never you fear," John Cooper replied.

"Señor Baines," the governor now put in, "I shall ask you to remain for a few days in Havana—you and Padre Camporata, as well as these two young gentlemen from Argentina—to be on hand for court proceedings against the Obeiras and Luis Marconado, which I shall ask the public prosecutor to begin immediately. I shall send my courier to his house this very evening with instructions on the charges and the defendants.''

"As you wish, *excelencia*," John Cooper said.

"Meanwhile," Santiago de Nuñez chuckled as he turned to look at the enraptured girl who clung to Enrique, "I suggest that Señorita Cortez be taken in charge by my major-domo, who will see that my *criadas* bathe her and give her suitable attire and then conduct her to a comfortable room, where she may have what I believe to be a much-needed *siesta*." He smiled encouragingly at Madalena, who had turned to stare at him as if he were a saint come down from heaven. "If you are hungry, my child, you have only to ask the majordomo, and he will see that you are provided with whatever you desire."

"Señor gubernador," Madalena joyously sobbed, "I shall pray for you and thank *el Señor Dios* for you all the days of my life, and I swear to you, I swear it by all the saints, *excelencia*, that I'll make Enrique the best wife that ever was, and I'll be worthy of your pardon!"

Fifteen

The courthouse was crowded as Don Florian de Vargas, the tall, solemn-faced, black-bearded public prosecutor, addressed the presiding judge—the very same judge who had sentenced Madalena Cortez to the garrote: "Most honorable *Juez* Cardoso, the case now before you has three defendants— Juan and Manolito Obeira, who are accused of piracy, contravention of the slavery laws, bribery of high-placed colonial officials and officers of the city of Havana, ruthless murder of the seamen on ships they attacked—specifically, the American brig *Salamander*—and a host of other infractions, too numerous to list here. The other defendant, the señor Luis Marconado, procurator general of Havana, this government accuses of being in conspiratorial league with the Obeiras."

"This is stated in the document signed by *el gubernador*, Don Florian," the elderly, stern-faced judge nodded. "Proceed with your exposition of the evidence pertaining to these accusations."

Near the rear of the courtroom, John Cooper Baines turned to the little priest beside him and whispered, "You see no jury here, *mi padre*, nor are the Obeiras represented by a lawyer. In the *Estados Unidos*, a jury of a man's peers decides whether he is innocent or guilty, and he has the protection of the law until that time. Indeed, that is one major issue over which we differ with our Mexican neighbors, and that's one of the reasons they'd like to drive us off the land on which they allowed us to settle."

The priest whispered back, "So it was in my country of Argentina, Señor Baines. If the judge is against your beliefs,

196

he has the power to find you guilty—just as I was condemned by the *porteños*. I think I should like to see this jury system of yours adopted in Argentina, and here, too—yet these wicked men whom you captured cannot escape the judgment of *el Señor Dios*, even if such a system existed here and their peers were to find them innocent."

"True enough. In my heart, *mi paare*, I cannot feel sorry for them. Yet even if there were a jury, your testimony alone would be enough to convince them that the Obeiras are pirates and murderers," John Cooper bluntly whispered back.

To the left of the judge's bench was a large prisoners' box, in which Juan and Manolito Obeira and Luis Marconado sat. The first two were manacled, while the arrogant *político*, nattily dressed, his pudgy fingers decorated with jeweled rings, had drawn his chair a distance apart, as if to suggest that he did not wish to be contaminated by the Obeiras' nearness. From time to time, as he listened to the public prosecutor, he put a perfumed silk kerchief to his nostrils, and whenever he glanced at the two brothers, his fleshy mouth curled in a grimace of contempt.

The public prosecutor dealt first with the Obeiras and called upon Benito and Enrique Duvaldo, as well as Padre Angelo Camporata, to testify to what they had witnessed aboard the *Salamander*. In addition, since Governor Santiago de Nuñez had ordered the captured American seamen, whom the Obeiras had delivered to the auction mart for sale as slaves, to be freed and brought to the court, these men also testified as to how the bloodthirsty pirates had boarded the American ship, killed nearly half of those aboard, and chained and sold the rest, save for the priest.

After all these witnesses had made their statements, the judge ordered Juan and Manolito Obeira to rise, then solemnly declared, "I have heard the evidence and weighed it carefully, and it is my judgment that the public prosecutor has proved his case against you. Do you have anything to say before sentence is passed?"

The two brothers remained silent, and the judge hastened on. "Then I sentence you both to death by the garrote, the execution to take place tomorrow at noon. May God have mercy upon your souls—more mercy than you showed your innocent victims.''

Juan and Manolito turned to each other, ashen-pale, and began to whisper as they resumed their seats. The judge turned to the prosecutor. ''We will now take up the case of Señor Luis Marconado. You may proceed, prosecutor.''

As the latter prepared to speak, Luis Marconado called out, ''Does anyone think that I would participate in piracy? I, the procurator general of Cuba? I have had no hand in these murders, and there is no proof that I did, or even that I have been involved in this illegal slave trade. Yes, I will willingly admit that I purchased those two *muchachos,* but I was told in good faith that they were already slaves. I admit also that I am the owner of the Casa de Belleza. But since when has this been a crime, to furnish entertainment to appreciative patrons who represent the best of society in this colony?''

At this, Juan and Manolito Obeira turned to glare at the fat official, and Juan muttered, ''You lying dog, you're in this as deeply as we are, even if you never boarded a ship and cut down a man with a cutlass, or shot him with a *pistola!*'' And then, incensed, he sprang up, his manacles clanking, and cried out to the judge, ''*Excelencia,* the señor Marconado is a liar! Manolito and I accuse him of having backed our ventures many a time and split the profits with us!''

The judge banged his gavel angrily. ''Silence!'' he shouted. ''You are out of order!''

''Excellency,'' the public prosecutor now put in, ''the statements we have just heard from the condemned are, in my opinion, simply attempts to have someone else share his fate, or perhaps a futile endeavor to induce Your Honor to mitigate the sentence.''

''This I will not do,'' the judge declared. ''They have been proved guilty of their murderous deeds upon the high seas. I am satisfied with the incontrovertible evidence provided against them by those who saw their men board the American ship. But I must call your attention, Mr. Public Prosecutor, to the fact that you have not yet presented your case against the señor Luis Marconado, and it is a serious charge, the more so because he stands so high in our government.''

At this, Marconado sat back with a satisfied sneer, as he eyed the Obeira brothers, and once again put the scented kerchief to his nostrils, confident that he would get off scot-free.

At that moment, young Benito Duvaldo, out of curiosity, turned his head to look around at the spectators seated on the benches behind him. He saw a young woman sitting a few rows back, and was about to turn away when some impulse made him take a longer look. Then he put his hand over his mouth to stifle a startled gasp, for affixed to the dainty earlobes of the attractive young woman were his mother's priceless ruby earrings.

Enrique, not understanding the reason for his brother's gawking, nudged him with his elbow and muttered, "Behave yourself, *mi hermano*."

"But, Enrique," Benito whispered back, "look there—at that young woman in the white dress. Look at her earrings. Those are the ones our father gave us, which belonged to our dead mother. I know they're the same ones—look for yourself, Enrique!"

Enrique turned to look, and he, in his turn, could not suppress a gasp of surprise. "But you're right, Benito!"

"Please, señores, señoras," the judge irritatedly called, "let there be silence in this court while the public prosecutor continues his case!"

But Benito had sprung to his feet and, pointing to the young woman with his right forefinger, exclaimed, "*Excelencia*, the woman in the white dress—she's wearing the earrings that belonged to my mother, and which Juan and Manolito Obeira stole from us when they captured the *Salamander*!"

A loud murmur of surprise spread through the courtroom, and Luis Marconado compressed his lips and looked daggers at the younger Duvaldo.

"Come forward, young man," the nearsighted judge beckoned. "Ah, of course, I recognize you—you and your brother gave valuable testimony, which led to the sentence I have just passed on those two murderous pirates."

"Yes, and we're telling the truth now, *excelencia*," Enrique chimed in as he, too, approached the judge's bench.

"Before our father died on his *estancia* in Argentina, he had given us a pair of ruby earrings that belonged to our dead mother, as a remembrance. And just as my brother has said, when those two men"—he pointed to the Obeiras seated in the prisoners' box—"captured the *Salamander* and butchered those who resisted, they took the earrings from us and said that we were slaves."

"Bailiff, you will bring forward the woman in the white dress, the one these young gentlemen have just identified," the judge ordered.

Rosalie Castillo half rose, as if wanting to flee, but the bailiff was already striding toward her with an air of great importance and severity. "You'd best come with me, señorita," he muttered. "There are *soldados* outside this courtroom, and they would only bring you back, and it would be embarrassing. That's a good girl!"

Luis Marconado frowned as his gaze followed the approach of his young mistress toward the judge's bench. He glared at her, his look eloquently telling her to reveal nothing, if she valued her well-being.

"Now, then, señorita, your name?" the judge demanded.

"Rosalie Castillo, *excelencia*."

"Señorita Castillo, how did you come by these earrings? The truth, señorita!"

The young woman turned a frightened glance over her shoulder at her lover, then regarded the judge and tremblingly faltered, "They—they were given to me."

"Yes, that I can understand. But by whom, Señorita Castillo?" the elderly judge pursued.

"By—by my *patrón*, the señor Luis Marconado," she confessed in a low, shaking voice. Again there rose a loud murmuring from the startled spectators.

The judge rapped his gavel. "Most interesting. Thank you for telling me the truth, Señorita Castillo. Now, then, Juan and Manolito Obeira, you have heard the charges made by these young gentlemen, Benito and Enrique Duvaldo, to the effect that you stole the earrings from them aboard the *Salamander*. What do you have to say to this?"

Juan bit his lips, leaned over toward his older brother,

and whispered, "Maybe if we tell the truth, they'll send us to prison instead of the garrote."

"Yes, yes, tell him, Juan, tell him everything!" Manolito panted, unconsciously putting his hand to his throat, as if already he felt the bite of the terrible whipcord.

"Well, *excelencia*"—Juan slowly rose to his feet— "the fact is that what those *muchachos* say—well, it's true. You see, *excelencia*, we gave those earrings to the señor Marconado, and he told us that he would give them as a gift to his mistress."

"And why would you give the procurator general a gift, especially one of such value?" the judge sternly questioned.

Juan looked down at his seated older brother, who feverishly nodded. "Because, *excelencia*, the señor Marconado backed us on our voyages, with the agreement that he would receive a share of whatever cargos we took from the ships we captured. As well, of course, as a share of the profits made from the sale of the slaves we brought to Havana."

"You lying dog, it's not true!" Marconado rose to his feet and, brandishing his fist in the air, glared at the Obeiras, his face livid with fury. "*Excelencia*, do not take the word of these condemned pirates against that of the procurator general of Cuba!"

"Silence!" the judge commanded. "I alone will weigh the relative merits of the testimony given in this court. And indeed, señor, it is my inescapable conclusion that you were in league with these wretches, and thus in a sense—truly in a moral one, if not by the letter of the law—you have been as responsible for the deaths of innocent victims as have they and their men. As such, and as a demonstrated purveyor of stolen goods, as well as an abuser of your high office, you deserve the same fate. Therefore, in the presence of the public prosecutor, and with the authorization of His Excellency, *Gubernador* Santiago de Nuñez, I sentence you, Luis Marconado, to the garrote. I further decree that you will be the last on the execution platform, for this will give you more time to pray and to reflect on your complicity with these murderous scoundrels. I leave it for the sages and philosophers to consider how, in so short a space of time, one of our most respected citizens and government officials should have fallen to such depths of degradation! Bailiff, you will call the guards and remove the condemned. The priest will attend them before they are brought out tomorrow. I am certain they will have further confessions to make before they die!''

Manolito Obeira had sprung from his seat and, despite his clanking manacles, had seized Luis Marconado by the throat with his wiry fingers. It took two soldiers to break that hold, which nearly accomplished what the executioner would do on the morrow. During this hubbub, Juan Obeira, craven now at the thought of the hideous death he was to suffer, cried out piteously to the judge, "*Excelencia, excelencia, piedad, por amor de Jesu Cristo,* we told you the truth! We convicted this thief who sent us out upon the seas to plunder others! Surely you will grant us mercy because of this?''

As the soldiers bundled all three men away, the judge rose from his bench and scathingly called after Juan Obeira, "I can give you no mercy; only *el Señor Dios* Himself can see fit to pardon you for all that you and your brother and your accomplice have done.''

As John Cooper Baines rose from his seat in the back of the courtroom, the governor's young courier approached from behind and respectfully touched his elbow. "Señor Baines, *el gubernador* asks that you, the *padre,* and the *hermanos* Duvaldo return with me to his residence. There are matters still to be decided, and he has promised to aid you in your return to the *Estados Unidos,* for he is grateful for the service you have rendered the loyal citizens of Havana.''

Santiago de Nuñez gave a formal dinner in the mansion's huge refectory, ordinarily used only for occasions of state, and Padre Camporata, the Duvaldo brothers, Madalena Cortez, and John Cooper were the honored guests. The governor's cook had prepared a veritable feast, which featured the tastiest viands, fruits, vegetables, wines, and cordials of the island. A servant poured out a rare old French brandy for the governor, John Cooper, and the young Duvaldos, and even Padre Camporata decided to accept a small libation to toast the miraculous good fortune that his prayers had brought to these worthy people.

As they took coffee and one of the servants passed around bowls of nuts, raisins, little candies, and other tidbits, Santiago de Nuñez leaned back in his huge hand-carved chair and, after a few puffs on one of the slender cigars of which he was especially fond, genially declared, "My young friends, Benito and Enrique, I shall make restitution to you in gold from our island's treasury equivalent to the *dinero* that was taken from you. And here—" He beckoned to the major-domo, who, smilingly nodding, hurried up with a little velvet case and, again at the governor's gesture, moved to the places where Benito and Enrique sat. "Here are the earrings that are rightfully yours—a priceless heirloom, indeed. I hope that this action will make you think more kindly of us and help you forget that you were brought here and forced to toil in that infamous *casa de putas* as *esclavos*."

"Your Excellency has been wonderful to us," Enrique enthusiastically declared. "We shall certainly have the happiest memories of Havana." He turned to look lovingly at Madalena, who blushed and lowered her eyes.

The governor chuckled, took a sip of his brandy and then a puff at his cigar. "A happy ending, señores, señorita— and I am very grateful that I was able to bring it about. But now, Señor Baines, this concerns you. I shall have our *soldados* search the residence and warehouses of Señor Luis Marconado for any booty that is hidden there, and it will become, under law, the property of the treasury of Cuba. However, I shall sign a decree awarding you the *Dos Hermanos* out of thanks for your role in putting a stop to the unlicensed slave trade and bringing to justice these three villainous rogues. And with this goes my personal heartfelt thanks for having opened my eyes to the misconduct of my subordinates. I am old and perhaps do not have many more years in office, but I shall always pride myself on knowing that I had a small part in putting down corruption in the highest places. Oh, yes, there is one more thing—those men of the *Salamander* who were seized and brought here as slaves have, of course, been given full liberty. They have said they would like a berth on an American ship. I am setting aside an amount of gold to compensate them, also, for the distress caused by the Obeira brothers and the señor Marconado. It may be, Señor Baines, that now you are the legal master of the *Dos Hermanos*, you may wish to engage them as members of your crew."

"Your Excellency is far more generous than I could ever have asked—but would you not prefer to keep the ship and let it be sold and the proceeds returned to your own treasury?" the blond Texan countered.

The governor smiled and shook his head. "Not at all, Señor Baines. You have earned a reward, and since I would not insult you with gold, perhaps you will accept, with all my gratitude and that of the people of Havana, the ownership of this ship. I know that you will use it in honorable ventures, which may help cleanse the stain of piracy and murder from its sails and decks. As I've no doubt, you will wish to change the name."

"*Gracias, excelencia.*" John Cooper inclined his head. "Then I shall find a captain who will take us back to the United States. You see, *excelencia*, all of us here who have enjoyed your hospitality and kindness plan to go to my *estancia* in Texas." He turned to Padre Camporata. "I have thought of how you could be of great service to people who would need you, *mi padre*. You were exiled because you showed compassion for the needy and the oppressed. Our *estancia* is a community of many loyal *trabajadores* and *vaqueros* and their families, and they are devout parishioners in whose service I am certain you will feel joyous and fulfilled. Our community grows constantly; perhaps it can be a beloved sanctuary for you."

"You—you are most kind to offer this, Señor Baines," the little priest replied, clearly touched by the offer. "I told you that the bishop of New Orleans was good enough to take me into his diocese; I should, of course, write to him to obtain his permission—"

"Of course—and I hope that he'll grant it. I admire your courage and tenacity, *padre*. A man who could follow us through the Florida swamps without complaint is a man the people of the Double H Ranch would admire, respect, and love." And then, with a twinkle in his eyes, John Cooper raised his voice so that Enrique and Madalena could hear him as he said to the priest, "And perhaps, who knows, once you have the bishop's permission, your first official act as a priest on our *estancia* might be to marry these two lovebirds you see before you, Enrique Duvaldo and Madalena Cortez!''

John Cooper did not witness the spectacle the next noon in the plaza, but the governor's aide was present and reported that Luis Marconado had died badly, fighting the guards who had to drag him up the platform to the chair, and then weeping and screaming for mercy, even before the whipcord was put around his neck. By contrast, the Obeiras had died with resigned courage. Since the Casa de Belleza had been officially closed, the governor had ordered his aide to do what he could toward relocating the young women who had been prostitutes there into more honorable employment. Some of them were given posts as seamstresses, others as *criadas*, while a few, the younger ones with more stamina, found employment in the refining mills of the island's sugarcane plantations. The hunchback, Teófilo, when he learned that he was to face prosecution for the torture and murder of one of the *esclavos*, committed suicide with a small dagger, before anyone could stop him. Madam Zagora, Enrique discovered, had taken a position as ''governess'' for a wealthy *hacendado*.

John Cooper spent this third day of January visiting *cantinas* and *posadas* near the waterfront, in search of a suitable captain to sail the *Dos Hermanos* back to the United States. It was in an out-of-the-way *taberna*, however, that the bartender directed him to a morose-looking man in his late forties, with gray sideburns and a short beard, who sat at a table in the back, nursing a mug of *taffia*. ''Señor, he is *americano*,'' the bartender whispered, ''and he has been here nearly a month. His ship was taken by pirates, like those accursed Obeira brothers who died today, as you may know, señor. They set him adrift in a small boat. By great good fortune, he was rescued by a Spanish ship. He has no money, but he has found a kind widow who lets him stay at her little house and feeds him in return for the work he does in repairs and errands.''

''*Gracias, amigo*,'' John Cooper thanked the genial Cuban. ''He may be just the man I'm looking for. Give me two mugs of your best *taffia*, please.'' He threw down a silver *peso*, and the bartender was about to give him change, but John Cooper waved it off and strode with the two mugs toward the table where the gloomy man sat, staring into space.

"Good evening, friend," John Cooper said lightly. The gray-bearded man looked up, startled, his blue eyes narrowing with suspicion, then, scanning John Cooper's buckskin costume, he said under his breath, as if to himself, "I haven't drunk all that much—the saints preserve us, it's a blond Indian—"

"Not quite, but I'm an American, like you—so the owner of this pleasant little *taberna* tells me. My name is John Cooper Baines, from Texas. I've brought over another mug for you, and I'd like to talk with you for a bit, if you've nothing better to do."

"Nothing better—" The bearded man checked himself and uttered a hollow little laugh. "No, Mr. Baines, I've certainly nothing better to do. I've been cooling my heels here for a month, wondering how the devil I'm to get back to Charleston. I had my own ship, you know, but that was before I was boarded by pirates on my last voyage here, my men cut down or made to walk the plank, and I myself put into a dinghy without food or drink."

"You've had a hard time, indeed. But I don't know your name."

"Sorry—this is the first time I've had a chance to speak English in weeks. I forgot my manners. I'm Amos Blanton, and by all means sit down, sir, because I'm hungry for good talk and, better still, news from the States."

"Well, I'll admit that, since my home's in Texas, I don't get much wind of what's going on along the eastern or southern coasts. I did, however, have occasion just recently to come through New Orleans, on my way to smoke out the Obeiras—the late Obeiras, I should say."

"Aye, those murdering devils—though they weren't the ones who took my ship," Amos Blanton gloomily volunteered. Then he started with surprise and leaned forward across the table. "Do you mean to say, Mr. Baines, that you were the one who captured those pirates? I heard as it was an American, but I didn't figure—"

"I can't take credit for it singlehandedly, Mr. Blanton. I brought with me six *vaqueros* and six Jicarilla Apache braves—I'm a friend to the chief of that tribe, for at one time I lived in Taos. But the Obeiras' ship, the *Dos Hermanos*, has just been awarded to me by the governor, and the reason I'm here now is that I'm in search of a man to sail it home for me."

Blanton's eyes brightened. "Do you mean that?"

"I have a habit of meaning what I say, Mr. Blanton— *Captain* Blanton, if you'll take the post. The ship is mine now, legally, but I've not much experience sailing, except for one trick at the wheel, which I'd rather not repeat. I've been thinking, now that I have this ship—if a good man like you could be persuaded to run it for me, my factor in New Orleans could dispose of whatever cargo you thought best. Both of us could turn a neat profit."

"Aye, that we could, for certain. But where am I to get a crew?"

"When the Obeiras captured the *Salamander*, they took aboard a good dozen American seamen, together with two young brothers from Argentina whom I personally knew—it was, indeed, to rescue those boys that led me here," John Cooper explained. "The governor has since freed the seamen, and I'm sure they'd like to get back to the States, as you would. You could do worse than enlist them. From what Benito and Enrique Duvaldo told me, they were good men."

"I can't believe all that you're telling me, Mr. Baines. After a month in this dreary hellhole, living off a kind widow's charity—well, it's like a promise of heaven after what I've been through," Amos Blanton confided.

"I wouldn't call it heaven, exactly," John Cooper said with a chuckle, "but I promise you there'll be no more hell. I'll take a chance on you, Captain, if you'll do the same with me."

"It's a deal, Mr. Baines. And I promise that you won't be disappointed with your choice. I've spent some twenty years at sea, starting as a cabin boy, then second mate, then first, and for the last seven years I had my own ship."

"Sounds just like the man I want. And you've no ties here? What about that widow?"

Blanton looked down into his nearly empty mug and frowned. "I'm fond of her, and that's a fact—I won't lie to you, Mr. Baines." He lifted the mug to his lips, took the last swig, and set it down. "We've been good for each other, I guess. She was grieving for her late husband, and I for my ship. She speaks no English, but I think she's sweet on a fellow who works in a sugar mill. She took me in out of Christian kindness, and I'll say prayers for her in every port I'm sent to, until I draw my last breath, Mr. Baines. But— well, if you do engage me, would I be greedy if I asked for a mite in advance? You see, Mr. Baines, I'd like to give her a few *pesos,* because there were times when, not having any money on me, as you could expect, and she not much more, she still fed me and gave me a roof over my head."

"Of course, I'll give you an advance. I'll tell you what, Captain Blanton. Here's a hundred *pesos.* Pay your debt to her, and get yourself a good meal—for all she's cooked for you, I think you could stand a little more flesh on your bones. Then get yourself some fresh clothing, and perhaps tomorrow afternoon you can come down to the wharf and see the ship the governor gave me. I'll welcome your ideas on rechristening her—I don't want to sail under a name that's associated with pirates and murderers. I'd like a good American name— but we'll think about it tomorrow, after you've seen her, Captain Blanton."

The gray-bearded sea captain lifted the fresh mug John Cooper had brought to the table and clinked it against the Texan's. "I'm grateful to you, Mr. Baines. But my way of showing gratitude is good hard work. I'll satisfy you on that score, you've got my word on it."

"Good. Suppose we say four o'clock tomorrow afternoon at the wharf. Meanwhile I'll round up the people who came here with me, my *vaqueros* and Indians, the boys, and also a priest."

"That'll be good luck. He can bless our first voyage together, Mr. Baines."

"That's exactly what I was thinking," John Cooper

laughed as he drank from his mug and looked across the table at the gray-bearded man, whose face, for the first time, showed eagerness and animation.

It was on Monday, January 7 of this new year, that John Cooper, Benito and Enrique Duvaldo, Madalena Cortez, Padre Angelo Camporata, and the *vaqueros* and Jicarilla Apache braves boarded the *Dos Hermanos*. The surviving sailors from the *Salamander* had, to a man, eagerly volunteered for service with Captain Amos Blanton. From the very first, Blanton demonstrated his expertise both in managing a crew and in assembling and loading a cargo, in this case mostly finished Spanish goods and produce transshipped from Cadiz.

Before leaving, John Cooper paid a call on the old governor to thank him for all his kindness, and Santiago de Nuñez shook his hand and said, "If your destiny should bring you here again, Señor Baines, I hope that it will be on this same ship that is now your property, and which I trust you are going to use in trading ventures that will be touched with profit and honor, not disgrace and the shedding of blood."

"Perhaps I might return someday—I don't know, *excelencia*. But if I do, you may be certain I'll come back here and shake hands with you again. God bless you, and please accept the thanks of all of us."

The American seamen weighed anchor before twilight to catch the outgoing tide from Havana harbor, and the ship, its sails filled by an offshore wind, moved past Morro Castle and out into the Gulf of Mexico toward home—a word John Cooper now thought of with the utmost longing, for he greatly missed Dorotéa and the children.

That first evening, in the captain's cabin, John Cooper and Amos Blanton conferred over the selection of a fitting name for the ship, and it was Blanton who suggested "New Venture."

"A perfect name!" John Cooper exclaimed. "It holds true for both of us, now that we're partners in this new venture. First thing tomorrow we'll have one of the men paint out the old name and substitute what you and I have chosen tonight. Yes, Captain Blanton, I think it's a good name."

"And an appropriate one, Mr. Baines, as you said."

Sixteen

Apart from a brief squall as the *New Venture* neared the Mississippi delta, the journey to New Orleans was uneventful and took only a little over one week. For Enrique and Madalena, there was no thought of time, as they stood at the rail in the evening, watching the moon, embracing, and whispering plans for their future together.

The ship docked at New Orleans in the early afternoon, and John Cooper lost no time in paying a call on Fabien Mallard to inform him of this unexpected new enterprise and request that he handle the cargo Amos Blanton had assembled. The genial factor shook his head in disbelief at John Cooper's story.

"I swear, John Cooper, you could fall into a bottomless pit and come up with gold in your pockets! I will have no trouble selling your cargo, and I assure you I can put this captain and this ship of yours to good use. By the time you get back to your ranch, I'll have the *New Venture* at sea again, loaded with goods from my own warehouses. I'll have to take a look for myself, of course, but from what you tell me, she sounds like a sturdy ship, and we could use her on the growing coastal trade between here and the East, or even westward to Corpus Christi—yes, John Cooper, no one could ever accuse you of not diversifying your occupation! Oh, by the way, Hortense asked me to give you a little gift for Dorotéa." Fabien rummaged in a drawer, then handed John Cooper a tiny, daintily wrapped jewel case. "Hortense found this cameo brooch in a quaint little shop off Chartres Street last week and told me that it was perfect for Dorotéa. The outline of the face has an uncanny resemblance to your sweet wife."

"How kind of you, Fabien! You thank Hortense for me. I wish one day the pressure of affairs would ease enough to allow you both to come and visit us at the Double H Ranch."

"I might just take you up on that someday, John Cooper. Hortense has been after me to take a vacation! Well, it's getting late, and we'd better get down to the levee if you want that ship of yours unloaded before dark. And Hortense would never forgive me if I didn't have you home in time for dinner!"

John Cooper was in a hurry to start back to Texas, so the very next morning, after arranging with Fabien Mallard to outfit the others for the coming journey and to have a pair of packhorses loaded with supplies needed at the Double H Ranch, he hired a calash and had the driver take him and Padre Camporata to the residence of the bishop of New Orleans. There the little priest, after relating his incredible adventures in Florida and Cuba, asked if the bishop would not grant him permission to go to Texas, where his services as a priest would be supported by the growing community at the Double H Ranch. John Cooper added his persuasive pleas to the little priest's, and the bishop, shaking his head and smiling, gently interrupted.

"There is a saying, my son," he addressed John Cooper, "that God works in mysterious ways His wonders to perform. From what you have told me, I have seen these signs, and yes, Padre Camporata has my permission. My son—" He turned to the priest. "All I ask is that you send back frequent reports of the work you do with this good man for the people who live with him."

The *padre* knelt and kissed the bishop's ring, tears in his eyes, but the graying man bade him rise. "I also ask you both one other thing—that you join me for breakfast, for which my cook has prepared something special." And although John Cooper was impatient to be on his way, he, as well as the little priest, accepted the invitation with gratitude.

*   *   *

It was not until noon that John Cooper, Padre Camporata, and the others, with the two loaded packhorses, assembled at the stables where they had left their mounts several weeks ago. Amos Blanton was there, too, to bid his benefactor farewell. He had spent the evening as a guest of Fabien Mallard and had already struck up a friendship with the personable factor.

"You'll find that M'sieu Mallard is a shrewd business-man, as well as a gentleman, Captain Blanton," John Cooper explained. "I'm sure you and he together will come up with some excellent ideas on how to use this ship to advantage. He knows markets, tariffs, and plain old horse-trading better than anyone I've ever met, and best of all, he's a loyal and honest friend."

"Then it'll be a pleasure to do business with him, as it is with you, Mr. Baines. And by the way, my crew wants to thank you, too—it seems every one of them is happy on the *New Venture*. I never thought I'd live to see the day again when I could say that about a ship after I lost mine, Mr. Baines."

John Cooper shook the captain's hand. "Fabien Mallard will keep me informed about your future voyages, sir, and we can keep in touch through him. I wish you all the best."

The gray-bearded captain gripped John Cooper's hand with both of his and stared gratefully into the Texan's eyes. Then, smiling, John Cooper mounted up and gave the signal to the others, and they set off toward the levee road, on the first leg of the long journey back to Texas.

It was nearly five hundred miles to the Double H Ranch on the Frio River, but John Cooper counted on reaching his Dorotéa by early February. He had, after all, an escort of twelve armed men—his six trustworthy *vaqueros*, and the six Jicarilla Apache braves led by Dejari. The latter group would have a far longer ride home, but they would enjoy his hospitality at the ranch and rest for a day or two before resuming their journey to the stronghold.

It was a morning on the second week of their journey when John Cooper cantered his horse up to Dejari's and leaned forward to engage the young brave in conversation. "I should be most grateful, *mi hermano,* now that we are in Texas, if you and your companions would begin to watch for signs of Mexican *soldados.* My fear is that we shall see more and more of them in areas that until now they have not visited. They seem intent on harassing the *gringo* settlers whom their own government has given permission to come here."

"Pastanari has mentioned this at the council fires, *Halcón,*" Dejari answered. "He thinks that one day there must be war between the Mexicans and the *gringos.*"

"If that were to come—and I pray it will not—would he be on the side of the *gringos?*" John Cooper added, before Dejari could answer, "I should not blame him if he sided with the Mexicans, for many of the white-eyes have lied to, betrayed, and killed the *indios* of the plains."

"It is true that not all white-eyes are like you, *Halcón,* but still, I do not think Pastanari would side with the *mejicanos.* My people have not forgotten, in days long past, how the *conquistadores* treated all *indios* like slaves. Surely you do not forget the mines of silver, and the bones you saw there of the *indios* who were forced to their labor by the *soldados* and the *padres,* and whose souls were smothered so that they could not reach the Great Spirit when death ended their miseries? Surely if the *gringos* are vanquished, and there is no one to stop the *mejicanos,* it would be the story of the *conquistadores* all over again."

"Particularly if a man like Santa Anna commands them," John Cooper soberly added. "Yes, he is today's Cortez, and when he takes full power in Mexico City, as I fear he will before too many years have passed, then all of us must be on guard."

But no Mexican patrols, nor hostile Indians, were encountered all the way to San Antonio, where John Cooper halted his escort of *vaqueros* and Indians long enough to reprovision. For Dejari, he bought one of Jim Bowie's special knives, which had already earned a legendary reputation from Natchez south to the Gulf, and, so that he should not slight Dejari's *jefe,* Pastanari, he purchased one for him as well. Dejari was ecstatic over the knife, a magnificently forged, razor-sharp weapon that could be used for cutting, slashing, thrusting, or even throwing, since it was superbly balanced to the hand. To the five other braves, John Cooper gave presents of sharp new hunting knives, and for their squaws he bought several bolts of bright calico, together with needles, threads, and scissors. This surprised Madalena Cortez, until John Cooper informed her that the Jicarilla Apache women were as competent with needle and thread as any frontier housewife.

These gifts cemented the ties between the Hawk and the people whom he rightly called his blood brothers. Even so, to these braves, who knew John Cooper well, a simple handshake, or the Apache gesture of friendship—placing one's hands upon the other's shoulders—meant far more than any gift could have.

As they continued on from San Antonio, heading northwestward now, the uninhabited stretches of barren land grew longer. Here Mexican patrols rarely ventured, for there were too few settlers to make it worth the cost and time of an armed troop.

Early on the second evening out of San Antonio, the little caravan stopped and made camp by an almost-dry streambed. The *vaqueros* soon had supper cooking, which consisted of two rabbits and a prairie chicken that one of the Jicarilla braves had brought down earlier with his bow. To this was added coffee, *frijoles*, and, as a contribution from young Madalena Cortez, delicious pan biscuits, smeared with wild honey one of the Indians had removed from the stump of a rotted tree after smoking out the angry bees.

Padre Angelo Camporata sat beside John Cooper in front of the cooking fire, a look of content on his plump face. He had attacked his food with gusto, and now he embarrassedly admitted to his friend, "Do you know, back in Argentina, I never considered gluttony to be one of my weaknesses, but now I am not so certain of that. Perhaps all this walking and riding has lost me some of my excessive flesh and therefore stimulated my appetite. You may smile at this excuse—it is a poor one, I know—but then man is an animal who constantly invents reasons to prove why he should do what he really wants to do in the first place."

John Cooper laughed heartily, for he liked and admired

this priest, perhaps most of all because the little man had never once uttered a complaint, even in the dark and dank thickness of the Florida swamp. "I must agree with you, *padre*," he chuckled as he helped himself to more coffee and, though the priest attempted to lift a hand over his mug, refilled his cup too. "Our appetites can be our downfall—but then I don't think *el Señor Dios* begrudges us a decent meal now and then, especially if we are not lazy and do His good work."

"It is true, my son, that sloth and gluttony often walk hand in hand, but the fact is I now look forward to the challenge of serving your community, almost as if I were a young man again. It was good that we stopped off to visit the bishop in New Orleans and receive his dispensation in this matter. But now, since you have chosen my course for me, my son, you must also see to it that I do not neglect this charge and become fat and lazy, despite all I say!"

"I'll make it a point to remind you from time to time, *mi padre*," John Cooper chuckled.

Enrique Duvaldo also welcomed the camping outdoors, particularly at night, for then he could steal away a few moments with his beloved young Madalena. Yet he had been the most circumspect of suitors since their departure from Havana, and although he longed for her, he had contented himself with a few kisses and tender caresses.

This evening, she had baked two of the biscuits, larger than the others, especially for him and smeared them liberally with the tasty honey. When he had turned to thank her, she had sent him such a piquantly engaging look that he felt his heart melting with longing and joy at the knowledge of her affection for him. And, since Benito had become engrossed with two of the *vaqueros* in a discussion of the flora and fauna in this part of Texas, and Padre Camporata and John Cooper Baines were also deep in conversation, Enrique decided that no one would miss him if he took a little walk under the moon and stars with his lovely Madalena.

They slipped away and walked hand in hand, and for long minutes there was silence between them. Yet it was more eloquent than any words, and from time to time Enrique shivered with longing, as Madalena's slim fingers gave tender little squeezes against his palm. Finally, when he had judged himself to be a sufficient distance from the campfire so that the two of them could not be seen, he halted and turned to her, took her into his arms, and kissed her lingeringly on the mouth. "Oh, Madalena, *querida, corazón*," he said, "do you know what I wished this evening when you gave me those biscuits?"

"No, *amorcito*, what did you wish?"

"That I could ask Padre Camporata to marry us right now, so that we could be husband and wife, and so that, from this moment forth, you would be mine to cherish and to protect for all the days of my life. *Es verdad*, Madalena, that is truly what I wished and what I have prayed for ever since we met—" He blushed, now remembering the circumstances under which he had made the acquaintance of this enchanting girl.

She, too, blushed, but taking comfort in Enrique's sincerity and obvious respect for her, she tactfully steered the conversation to another course. "You read what is in my heart as well, my dearest Enrique. But we must be very good, and as soon as we reach the *estancia* of the señor Baines, the *padre* will marry us. They are both good and honest men, Enrique, and we must try to make them proud of us."

"Yes, and if there were more men like them, Madalena, the Argentina of my murdered father would be free now, and the merciless, greedy *porteños* would be dealt with in the same manner as the *patrón* for whom we were both slaves, Luis Marconado."

She shivered and put a hand over her eyes, as she whispered, "Do not remind me of him, because all I can think of is—" Her voice broke, and she could not finish the sentence.

To his horror, Enrique realized that he had unwittingly stumbled onto a still more agonizing topic, for of course it would have reminded his sweetheart of the horrid death to which she had very nearly been subjected. He hastened to make amends by blurting out, "And yet, now that I think of it, my darling, if Argentina had been free, I'd never have come here, and so I'd never have met you—so I'm very happy that I came to Havana, even as I did, Madalena."

"And I, too, am happy, very much so, *querido*, my husband-to-be!" she tenderly breathed, and once again they were locked in each other's arms in a long, fervent kiss.

"I love you so, *mi* Enrique!" Madalena sighed as they finally released each other, and to Enrique it seemed that never before had his name been pronounced so beautifully, with such tenderness. She took hold of his arm and hugged it more tightly to her as they prepared to continue their stroll.

Suddenly there was an ominous rattling sound, then a hiss, and Enrique, instantly alert, was petrified to see, only five feet from Madalena, a rattlesnake coiled on a low, flat rock.

"*Querida*," he whispered, "do not move. Do not even breathe and, *por amor de Dios*, don't turn your head. I will take care of it—let go of my arm, now, slowly. Make no sudden movement. Pretend to look ahead, and please, *please*, as you love me, do not turn your head at all!"

"*S-s-st—*" she stammered in her terror, her fingers releasing his arm. As she did so, he silently and carefully drew the pistol from his belt and cocked it, then, grasping her right wrist with his left hand, suddenly jerked her backward and out of range of the rattlesnake's fangs.

With a cry of alarm, she stumbled and fell onto her back in the soft grass, as Enrique whirled to face the dangerous serpent and, just as it drew back its head to strike, triggered the pistol. The explosion shattered the desert silence, and the rattler's head was torn away by the ball. As Enrique watched in horror, the body writhed, quivering in convulsive waves, the hideous rattles sounding even in the death throes.

Madalena, her dark eyes wide with stupefaction, stared at the dying snake and then, scrambling to her feet, flung herself sobbing into Enrique's arms as he stuck the pistol back in his belt.

"*Mi corazón*," she cried, "that's twice you've saved my life. Surely I'm meant to be yours—the good *Señor Dios* Himself has sent this as a sign that we are truly to be one! *Querido, querido*, how brave you were—you are truly *un hombre macho*!"

As she clung to him, her eyes wet with tears, John Cooper and Padre Camporata, drawn by the sound of the pistol, came hurrying up. When John Cooper saw the lifeless body of the rattlesnake, he declared, "I think I've warned you both not to stray too far from our campsite; now you know why. But, Enrique, that must have been a good shot. Your father would have been very proud of you."

"I—I couldn't let it bite her—" Enrique faltered.

"Of course you couldn't. All the same, don't try to slip off again the next time we camp out at night, especially in land you know nothing about. There are other dangers besides the *culebra*, such as the *jabalí*, yes, and the puma, and sometimes even the wolf."

"I—I ask your pardon. I didn't think—" Enrique hung his head, while Madalena still clung to him fiercely, and even glared at John Cooper for daring to censure her adored young lover.

"I think, *mi padre*"—John Cooper's face relaxed into a whimsical smile—"that we had best get ready for a wedding as soon as we reach the Double H Ranch."

"Oh, *gracias,* Señor Baines," Enrique happily exclaimed, and Madalena beamed radiantly as she added her own sincere thanks for the Texan's decision.

It was late afternoon on the first Monday in February when Enrique Duvaldo and Madalena Cortez, riding side by side, and followed closely by Padre Camporata and John Cooper Baines, passed through the gate of the Double H Ranch. The six *vaqueros* spurred their horses and whooped and hollered until Esteban Morales, the assistant *capataz* of the ranch, spied the little caravan and, waving his *sombrero* and hallooing in return, roused the other *vaqueros* and old Miguel Sandarbal, as well as Carlos de Escobar, who was in the stables. Carlos, seeing the familiar buckskin-clad figure of his brother-in-law, ran to the *hacienda* to carry the news to Doña Inez, Dorotéa, and his beloved Teresa, and they followed him out into the courtyard to welcome back the blond Texan.

Waving his hat, too, John Cooper dismounted, hurried toward Dorotéa, and embraced her. "Forgive me, forgive

me, my sweet wife, for being away so long!'' he said, his
voice husky with emotion.

"You were with me in spirit, *mi corazón*,'' she murmured between kisses. ''And Carlos gave me your present on
Christmas Day, so that I could feel your nearness and your
love for me.''

"Where is Raoul Maldones, our *capataz*?'' John Cooper
demanded, as at last he released his beautiful young wife and
turned to the assembled *vaqueros* and *trabajadores* who
had come to welcome him home.

"Here I am, John Cooper!'' Raoul edged his way through
the throng and emotionally embraced the tall Texan. Then he
saw Enrique Duvaldo leap from his mount and hurry to help
down a young woman, whose arm he linked with his as he
led her toward his late father's dearest friend. "*Por todos los
santos*, you've done it, John Cooper!'' Raoul joyously exclaimed. ''Benito, Enrique—and what's this I see? A beautiful señorita—''

"She is to be my wife, Señor Maldones,'' Enrique
proudly said, as he led the blushing Madalena forward. "*Mi
corazón*, this is Raoul Maldones, whom my father loved as if
he were his own brother. This, Señor Maldones, is Madalena
Cortez. Padre Camporata here is to marry us. I hope it can be
arranged soon—perhaps tomorrow?''

This ingenuous remark drew a burst of good-natured
laughter from its hearers, but Enrique did not seem in the
least daunted as he unabashedly put his arm around Madalena's
waist, put his other hand to her cheek, and kissed her ardently
on the mouth.

"Now, there's a true man of the *pampas*, who makes
up his mind and, once having made it up, will tolerate
nothing less,'' Raoul pronounced. ''And what could be more
fitting than to have the good Padre Camporata, an Argentinian as well, marry the two of you?''

Carlos came forward to shake his brother-in-law's hand,
but there was a sad look on his face. ''I wish I didn't have to
tell you this, *amigo*,'' he hesitantly began, ''but we've lost
Yankee.''

"Yankee dead?'' John Cooper said. ''But how did it
happen?''

"He and his cubs helped save the children from an old puma that had crossed the river and come in search of food. I shot the beast, but not until its claws had mortally wounded Yankee—he licked my hand as he died. We've buried him, and there's a marker, *amigo*."

"Like Lije, like Lobo, he was of a breed with great heart and courage," John Cooper sorrowfully mused. "I hope Maja and Fuerte will carry on that legacy and help defend us in the days ahead."

Not wanting to spoil the others' pleasure at this happy reunion, however, John Cooper turned to Dorotéa and declared, "Sweetheart, you and I are going to the kitchen now and bribe Rosa Lorcas to let us have a great feast tomorrow. I've missed Christmas and New Year's, but we'll have a holiday celebration all the same. And we'll have the wedding of Enrique and Madalena tomorrow, as a prelude to the great feast!"

There were cheers at this announcement, and John Cooper smiled, but now he had eyes only for the dark-haired young wife who, her love written in her own eyes, took him by the hand and led him away toward the house.

Seventeen

The very next day, Enrique Duvaldo and his adored Madalena were married in the chapel at the Double H Ranch by the bespectacled little priest, Padre Angelo Camporata. The *hacienda*'s other priest, the young Jorge Pastronaz, presided as assistant. Perhaps a generation apart in age, the two priests had met and talked the day before and found much in common. The younger man admired the Argentinian's courage and defiance of the oppressive *porteños* back in Buenos Aires.

"Padre Camporata," he had said, "each of us is united in the fight against evil, no matter where it is found. You have known more of it than I, and I still have much to learn about my priesthood; and already there are more parishioners here than I am able to minister to with proper attention. I am sure we can work together in harmony for the good of this community."

"I agree, but you must not flatter me so, Padre Pastronaz," the older man smilingly reproved. "You have the God-given gifts of youth and enthusiasm, and what you may not have experienced, I sense that you already feel in your heart. No, we shall not be rivals, but rather spiritual brothers linked by our love for and belief in Him Who made us all."

A dozen men, supervised by Miguel Sandarbal, were already at work constructing a small house for the newlyweds. It was of the strongest timbers, and situated near a little spring that would provide fresh water for cooking and drinking.

When Enrique and his young bride emerged from the chapel, the assembled *vaqueros* and *trabajadores* waved their *sombreros* and cheered lustily. Enrique, lifting his hand to acknowledge this tribute, turned to Madalena, took her in his arms, and tenderly kissed her, which drew another round of loud cheers.

The weather was unseasonably mild, and Rosa Lorcas, aided by half a dozen wives of the community, prepared the wedding supper—a great outdoor barbecue—while music and dancing began in the *hacienda*'s courtyard. Enrique and Madalena, as custom dictated, were first to begin the dance. The Argentinian youth stared longingly into his bride's dark eyes, and her face was radiant with love and happiness as they moved, first to the measures of a stately saraband, and then, to show their youth and eagerness, into a vivid bolero, which drew a rousing "*¡Olé!*" from the delighted spectators.

Soon the other couples joined in, leaving the children and the older folk watching enviously. John Cooper's four oldest children—Andrew, Charles, Ruth, and Carmen—who were seated at the large head table with Doña Inez, proudly watched their father and their lovely stepmother, Dorotéa. Andrew's gaze strayed from time to time toward young Madalena and Enrique, and he observed how the two of them were starry-eyed with love on this day of their wedding. To his growing torment, he was reminded of Adriana Maldones, who was still in New Orleans at the convent school, and to whom he had pledged his heart. He had fervently wished she would come home for the Christmas holidays, but Doña Inez had sent letters to Francesca and to Carlos's son Diego, telling them of John Cooper's absence. And a few days after Diego and Francesca had received those letters, Francesca and the three Maldones girls, along with several others within the close confines of the convent school, had been afflicted with bad colds, which necessitated their taking to their beds. The mother superior, though she knew how much it would grieve them, had suggested they give up the thought of so long a journey to the Double H Ranch until they were completely recovered. As for young Diego de Escobar, beginning his apprenticeship to a renowned New Orleans lawyer, he had written of how he had met a girl and—as though by way of compensation for not having come home for Christmas—had become thoroughly smitten with her. In short, none of the ranch's young people in New Orleans had come home for the holidays, and they might not be home for some time to come. But to Andrew Baines, it was Adriana's presence that was missed most of all.

The dancing ended, and Enrique returned his bride to the head table, accepting, as he went, congratulations from the other dancers. John Cooper stood with his arm around Dorotéa's waist, watching the young couple, then escorted his wife back to their seats across from Enrique and Madalena.

The Texan's face was relaxed and his eyes warm and contemplative, for the obvious happiness of the two seated opposite him recalled to him the unforgettable days of his first youthful courtship; and although he was more a man of action than of spiritual reflection, there nonetheless rose in him a grateful prayer of thanks that, after the loss of Catarina, his journeyings had taken him to Argentina to find the beautiful, courageous young woman who sat beside him and who had given him another fine son. With such inspiration as he now had with this family, he did not fear the future, not even the darkening shadow that Santa Anna cast upon this Texas land from his brooding retreat at Mango de Clavo.

After the company had eaten, John Cooper rose to his feet and, in a loud voice, declared, "As host, it's my great pleasure to welcome as one of us Enrique Duvaldo and his lovely young wife, Madalena. And as a mark of our welcome, and our pleasure in his marriage, I hereby bestow upon Enrique—and I shall write out a deed of grant that will bear out my intention—ten acres of the land of this ranch, to be located at the meeting of the northern and western boundaries. If he wishes to raise horses or cattle, or even to become a farmer, these acres will be his to work as he chooses. May his yield be great and profitable, and may his union with this sweet girl he has brought with him from Havana be just as fruitful."

This drew laughter and applause, and both Enrique and Madalena blushed at the Texan's allusion to the offspring destined them. Around the table, their companions toasted them with wine or rum and again wished them every happiness.

John Cooper could see that the long day and the excitement had made these two young people almost pathetically

eager for their longed-for time of privacy, which, as husband
and wife, was rightfully theirs. He looked at them, his smile
nostalgic, for he well remembered his own honeymoon with
Catarina and how the wondrous magic of first love transformed the most mundane setting into a magical world into
which no one else could intrude.

That was why he now leaned forward to Enrique and
murmured, "Come with me, and I'll have Doña Inez bring
Madalena. Since your house won't be ready for some time,
I'm going to give you the largest guest room of the *hacienda*, and I promise you that no one will disturb you or
waken you tomorrow. And until your house is ready, both of
you will be honored guests here, and we will respect your
privacy."

Enrique flashed him a look of the most ecstatic gratitude
as, in his turn, he bent to Madalena and whispered into her
ear, then rose from the table and followed John Cooper into
the *hacienda*. The Texan had stopped to whisper something
to Doña Inez, who laughed gaily, nodded, and looked tenderly across the table at Madalena.

The music was resumed, along with the dancing, but
shortly afterward Doña Inez came to Madalena to escort her
to her bridal chamber and her waiting, ardent young husband.

Later, in the hallway, John Cooper and Doña Inez looked
at each other, and it was she who most fittingly described this
memorable night. "A time like this, John Cooper, takes us
back to when we were young and hopeful and believed
ourselves to be immortal. What a blessed gift these two
young people have before them! I only pray that they may
enjoy such happiness to the end of their days!"

Since the town meeting held at the settlement on the
Brazos in December, Thomas Blake had fallen deeply in love
with Doris Eberle.

Just a few days afterward, in fact, Blake had bathed and
shaved, dressed in his Sunday best, and called at Roland
Eberle's house. Doris had been in the kitchen preparing
supper, and Thomas Blake had taken advantage of her absence to declare his intentions to her father.

"Mr. Eberle," he had nervously begun, "I want to level with you, sir. I thank God our differences have been resolved, and I want you to know that I don't hold the slightest grudge against you."

Roland looked slightly mystified. "Why, that's the way I want it, Tom, but—"

"Good. Because, you see, Mr. Eberle—and I'm not calling you Roland on purpose, sir, because I want to do things formal and proper-like—well, the long and the short of it is, I'm in love with your daughter Doris, and I want to marry her, if you've no objection."

Roland's face lighted. "I haven't the least, Tom. You're a good man, brave, trustworthy, and reliable. You're not like that cowardly, fast-talking Roy Fenwick who very nearly ruined her life. I think you could make Doris happy. Of course, you understand, she's the one who'll have to say yes, not I—but you'll certainly have my blessing. Nothing would make me happier than to see her with the right man, starting her life all over again, as if she'd never met that scoundrel!"

They had shaken hands, and then Doris had come out of the kitchen, flushed and lovely from her chores over the stove, and, seeing them both smiling, had demanded, "What are the two of you plotting behind my back?"

Thomas had come to her and taken both her hands in his and said, "I've just asked your father for permission to marry you, Doris, if you'll have me. I know it's awfully soon, but I don't see much point in waiting to do everything I want to do to make you happy."

She had turned scarlet and then, seeing her father smiling gently at her, exclaimed, "Daddy, I'll bet you just want to get rid of me!"

"Now, that's a wicked thing to say, honey," he had chuckled. "No, I don't want to get rid of you—but I do want to be sure this time that you've found a good, honest man I'll be proud to call son-in-law. And in my book, you couldn't do better than Thomas Blake. But don't think I'm trying to influence you, honey. If you don't love him, just say so!"

Doris's blushes deepened, and she turned to one side and, in a very faint voice, murmured, "But I do love him— the only thing is, Daddy, we really haven't had any time for sparking together. And a girl likes to be made to feel a fellow really wants her.''

"Honey," Thomas eagerly exclaimed, "if it's sparking you want, you won't have to ask twice. And we can do that after we're hitched just as good as any time!''

"Well, I never!" She stamped her foot and tried to look angry but, seeing them both grinning, broke down even this token show of primness. "All right, then, you both seem to have it planned in advance—but it just so happens, Thomas, that I like you a whole lot, and I'd be proud and happy to be your wife.'' Then, turning to her father, she had heatedly declared, "But you're going to have to give a girl a chance to romance her fellow a little, Daddy. I promise I'll marry him by Valentine's Day, if that's all right with you.''

The three of them dissolved into laughter, and Doris hugged and kissed Thomas Blake, while Roland Eberle beamed with paternal satisfaction.

Despite Doris Eberle's wishes, however, she was not to enjoy a leisurely courtship, for a few days later, Thomas Blake, along with Moses Wilson and several of the other Texas Rangers at the settlement, was summoned away by Andy Worringer, the lanky ex-farmer Jim Bowie had appointed captain of the Rangers at the Eugene Fair settlement. The tall, blond-haired Worringer, not quite thirty, was of an invariably cheerful disposition, but his good humor masked a deep-rooted sorrow, which, indeed, had made him volunteer for this service. A year ago, a Mexican patrol had visited a little village south of San Antonio, where Andy had maintained a small farm, and when the already drunken sergeant in charge of the platoon had demanded tequila from Andy's wife, who had been home alone with their infant son, she had refused. Enraged, the sergeant had drawn his pistol and callously shot her dead, in sight of the other settlers. The baby, dropping from her arms, had begun to scream, and the corporal of the platoon had put a ball through the baby's head. Then, as contrition suddenly struck them, the two soldiers had mounted their horses and ridden off with the rest of the platoon.

Andy had not discovered what had happened until he had come back for his noonday meal. After burying his wife and child, he had turned over the farm to his hired man and immediately ridden off to find Jim Bowie and join the Texas Rangers.

Before leaving, Thomas Blake told Doris that he did not know how long he would be gone. He warned her that his status as a Texas Ranger might well expose him to danger, and that, in fairness, she should think of this and perhaps reconsider her acceptance of his hasty proposal. Doris, however, would hear none of it, and, indeed, promised to marry him in February, courtship notwithstanding.

As it turned out, the Rangers, having patrolled as far south as the Rio Grande, returned three weeks later, so the couple had only a few days to enjoy before they were married.

It was on an overcast Tuesday evening, within a few days of Enrique and Madalena's wedding, when Thomas Blake and Doris Eberle stood before a minister in the settlement's little church and were married.

Roland Eberle stood behind his daughter, and as the minister pronounced the words that made the couple man and wife, he watched Doris turn toward her husband, her face radiant with happiness. Roland felt a warm glow of love for his daughter, and despite his own joy, he could hardly hold back a tear when it came his turn to kiss the bride.

Meanwhile, outside the church, Simon Brown, Minnie Hornsteder, and a dozen settlers' wives had already begun the preparations for the wedding feast. Slaughtered pigs and carcasses of beef were turning on the spits, and long wooden tables were crowded with plates heaped with biscuits, roasted sweet yams, ears of winter corn, stuffed squash, okra, and an assortment of freshly baked cakes, as well as pumpkin, rhubarb, and wild raspberry pies. The settlers stood by, eager to begin the bounteous repast, and the pleasantly cool night air increased their appetites.

They fell to it as soon as the couple emerged from the church to a rousing cheer. The atmosphere of celebration and companionability was infectious, and Simon turned to old Minnie Hornsteder and remarked, "Sights like this, Minnie, make me proud to be a Texan."

"You and me both, sonny," Minnie declared, pausing for a moment from her labors of turning a slowly roasting spitted pig, which she smacked now and then with a wooden spoon so that the cracklings and juice would drip off and the flesh of the animal would be thoroughly cooked.

"How old Henry would have loved these doin's, bless his ornery old soul! I'm sure he's up in heaven looking down and wishing he could grab hisself a plate and pile it high!"

The young scout gave her a knowing look and put his hand on her shoulder and murmured, "I'll tell you one thing, Minnie—he's in heaven, for sure, and he's mighty proud of you right now."

"Simon," she testily retorted, giving the turning pig an extra-hard whack with the spoon, "you just hush your big mouth and leave me at the cookin'. Can't you see folks is hungry as all git-out?"

Simon shook his head and gave Minnie an admiring glance, which she did not fail to notice, although she pretended to bristle and waved her wooden spoon at him until he burst into hopeless laughter.

"Land sakes, Simon Brown," she said with a chuckle when he had at last recovered, "you're sure a cure for the blues and the sulks, you are, teasin' a poor ole widder the way you do. Why, if I didn't know you wuz so stuck on your sweet wife, I'd tell all the single gals here to be on their lookout when you come stalkin', and that's no lie!"

His face sobered. "Now, that would be a real fib, Minnie, and you know it."

"I reckon so," Minnie sighed. "Well, I think this meat's just about ready to be cut up and served—and I got first dibs on it, sonny, 'count of all the work I done preparin' it—" She stopped turning the spit. "Hey, they're startin' the music! That's nice. Music while you eat, and then later to dance by. Simon Brown, d'ya think your sweet wife would mind if you danced just one little jig with poor old Minnie Hornsteder?"

"She'd chew me out if I didn't, Minnie. And even if she didn't, I'd ask for the very first dance with you, and you know it," Simon teased.

There was a suspicious moisture in the widow's eyes— which she attributed to the smoke of the cooking fire—but the warm look she gave the young scout spoke volumes for her gratitude at his trying to cheer her up and make her forget the dark memories that still sometimes troubled her.

Now the music of fiddles and fife rose in merry country tunes, some from the Ohio Valley, others from the Appalachian foothills, still others from back on the East Coast— "Yankee Doodle" was, by all odds, the favorite of these patriotic frontier folk. But there were also songs from the Cajun region of Louisiana and, perhaps most appropriate to the wedding ceremony being celebrated tonight, Spanish love serenades that had been sung in the Southwest for well over a hundred years. When the first jig began, Simon Brown, true to his word, squired Minnie Hornsteder out into the cleared-away space beyond the tables and benches and joined her in the lively reel. There was applause from the onlookers as the widow showed that she had lost little of her spryness and stamina.

After the dance, he led her back to their table and brought her a plate piled high with roast beef and suckling pig, sweet yams, corn, and biscuits. Then he served his wife, Naomi, who squeezed his elbow and whispered to him, "You're such a good, sweet man, Simon—no wonder Minnie likes you so much."

"Now, you hush up talk like that, sweetheart," he whispered, reddening visibly. "It's just when I think of what happened to her poor husband—" He nodded at his rifle, which was leaning against the bench, mostly concealed by the table. "We'll never be caught defenseless like that again, so help me God!"

He glanced around the table and saw, to his approval, that Moses Wilson, too, had taken the precaution of keeping a weapon at the ready, even on such a day of celebration. Minnie Hornsteder and Simon himself had invited the freed black man to join them at their table, a hospitable gesture for which the young Wilson had obviously been grateful. Simon hoped it would help make up in part for the many slurring insults some of the slave-holding settlers and their families had cast at the black man ever since he had arrived at the settlement after having saved Emma Sturtevant and her slave woman from the Kiowa Apache.

Emma herself had pointedly moved to another table and turned her face away, ordering her slave Bessie to bring her a plate of food. The white widow sat alone, for recently she had exchanged hot words with her cousin and her cousin's husband, and no longer feeling welcome in their home, she had moved to rented lodgings. Now, quickly finishing her food, she rose to return to her cabin, and Bessie dutifully followed, taking her little son and daughter with her, though from their expressions it was clear they wanted to stay and enjoy the celebration.

Moses Wilson, hurt by the fact that Bessie had avoided even looking at him, abandoned his plate and rushed after the slave woman, catching up with her at the edge of the crowd.

"I don't want to cause you no trouble, Miss Bessie," he said as he walked beside her. "I can understand why you don't want to have any truck with me, 'specially since that Mrs. Sturtevant won't free you. Only you know, Miss Bessie, it's not right to have slaves in this settlement, because that was part of the agreement Mr. Austin made with the Mexican government."

Bessie stopped in her tracks. "Go on home, children," she said, shooing them onward, then turned to face Moses Wilson. "Miz Sturtevant's affairs don't happen to be none of your business, Mr. Wilson," she said sharply, turning to go. Then, seeing the hurt look on his face, she seemed to think better of it. "I—I'm sorry, truly I am. I don't know why I should speak so sharp to you. You saved my life—I won't ever forget that. Only, it's—well, Miz Sturtevant don't favor colored folks none. She'll never free me, if you want to know the truth, so it's no use you payin' any attention to me."

She began to walk away again, but Moses stayed at her side. "I just don't want you to be angry with me, Bessie. I know that you don't have a husband, and—and I was just thinking—"

The widow's eyes widened, and she cut him off abruptly. "You'd best save your sweet talk for someone who kin marry you, Moses Wilson. Sure as you're born, I cain't, not so long as Miz Sturtevant owns me."

"Maybe that will change." They were nearing Emma Sturtevant's cabin, and Moses let her go on alone, deciding he had better not cause any trouble for her. "Good night, Bessie," he called to her. "Anyway, I'm glad you're not angry with me."

"No. Good night to you, too, Moses," she murmured back, then disappeared into the cabin.

He walked slowly back to the gathering, thinking forlornly that here, in this frontier settlement, with the chance for a new life, there shouldn't be such a thing as slavery. No matter how he looked at it, it made no sense to him. Even with slaves to help, folks here had to work hard; they had to build their own homes, lay in their own crops, bring up their own children. And because they had to deal with hostile Indians as well as with Mexican soldiers, they had no choice but to be strong and work together. Yet slavery divided the people, and not only black from white. It just didn't make sense.

Yet Moses remained in a hopeful mood, for he was an optimist at heart, and certainly Bessie's attitude toward him this evening had been the most cordial since their first meeting, when he had driven off the Kiowa Apache. Perhaps he could even earn enough money to buy Bessie's freedom. After all, Mrs. Sturtevant, for little more than room and board, could easily hire a servant to take over Bessie's duties.

The prospect so filled his mind with new hopes and longings—for until now he had never really thought of marrying and settling down—that he went back to the table and finished his meal with a hearty appetite, all the while watching the happy new bride and groom with envy.

Eighteen

Before Eugene Fair and Stephen Austin had founded this flourishing settlement on the Brazos, the fertile valley here had been the hunting grounds of the spirited and periodically dangerous Tawakoni Indians. Like the Tonkawa, who ranged more toward the interior, they coveted horses. Yet after the coming of the whites, the larger herds of wild horses had moved off toward the north and west, and the Tawakoni had begun to cast covetous eyes on the sturdy and, better yet, already trained mounts that the whites had brought with them from their homes to the east.

On this February evening, a band of twenty-five Tawakoni braves, led by their war lieutenant, Pitanse, had come to the Brazos Valley from their nomadic camp some thirty miles away, in search of horses and whatever else they could find. They had made a grudging truce with the Waco—another tribe who frequently harassed the settlers in this area—and now, since the Waco themselves were on the warpath against a renegade tribe of Tonkawa far to the west, Pitanse had urged his braves to consider a surprise night attack against the settlement. In the afternoon, one of his scouts had climbed a tree on a hill not far from the whites' stockade and had observed the preparations for the wedding of Thomas Blake and Doris Eberle. He had reported back to Pitanse, who had grunted with approval and declared, "The white-eyes will not expect us. They will be drunk and will roll on the ground from all the *wasichu tiswin* they will have swallowed today, and we shall open their corral, drive out their horses, plunder their supplies, and perhaps take white-eyes women to be the squaws of those of you who count the most coup!"

The name of Pitanse meant, roughly translated into English, "His Head Is Hot," and it well suited the young, tall, sullen-featured Tawakoni, because he was forever daring to override the decisions of his elders at the council. Indeed, because of this, he had broken away from the main body of the tribe. Others, even younger than Pitanse but as feverishly eager to prove themselves brave warriors, especially against the hated white-eyes, had joined him and elected him their leader. He had already led them on two successful raids in the past four months, which had won for them over thirty horses, four captive Mexican women and one white girl—all of whom had been made squaws of the victorious band—several old rifles and muskets with ammunition, and a few precious sacks of grain and sides of salt-cured meat.

When he announced his decision to his men, they unhesitatingly approved, for he had already proved his valor and wisdom as a leader. On the wooden shaft of his lance were six notches, representing his personal victories over four whites and two Mexicans. And since he was as expert with the knife as with the lance, and an excellent marksman as well, and had emerged from these campaigns without so much as a scratch, his men regarded him as invincible. One of them now admiringly said, "After tonight, we shall know you not by the name of Pitanse, but rather that of *Egraldo*, 'He Whom All Fear,' " and Pitanse had chuckled and patted the brave's shoulder, hugely pleased with this flattery.

"Do not forget," he cautioned his men, "that the white-eyes here outnumber us as the swallows outnumber the eagle. We must surprise them and flee quickly, so my plan is this: First our fleetest men will climb the stockade and open the corral to drive out the horses. The rest of us shall follow and strike from the other end of the settlement. You, Morgardo, and you, Distande—to you I bestow the honor of striking the first blow against these wicked *tejanos* who drive us from our hunting grounds and our camps!"

The two warriors exchanged a glance of joyous pride to be thus honored; each was armed with an old musket, a hunting knife at his belt, a bow strung over his shoulder, and a quiver of arrows ready at his back. Now, as Pitanse nodded and raised his hand, the half-naked Tawakoni braves, their chests and faces painted red, yellow, and black to symbolize their war against the *gringos*, moved out silently toward the stockade, splitting up in two bands at their leader's signal.

By now it was nearly midnight. And it was true, as Pitanse had predicted, that many of the settlers had eaten and drunk well to celebrate the wedding, and some, indeed, had already slid off the benches and onto the ground and begun to snore in a drunken stupor. But the musicians, though weary, still played on, for there were a few diehards yet eager to dance and forget their troubles. Consequently, no one heard when one of the guards on the stockade was felled by an arrow to the throat, or noticed anything amiss when Morgardo and Distande were boosted up the posts of the stockade wall and, holding themselves near the top, cautiously peered over. The large common ground where the wedding feast had taken place was now almost empty, save for a fiddler, a few dancing couples, half a dozen supine revelers who had drunk more than was good for them, and a handful of settlers seated at the tables, reminiscing about the olden days.

Morgardo, a squat, haughty-faced brave of twenty summers, nodded to his older companion, who was wiry and nearly as tall as Pitanse. Morgardo gestured toward the gate of the corral, where there were at least fifty horses. Not far from the corral was a large stable, where even more horses were quartered.

Morgardo deftly swung over the top of the stockade onto the firing platform, then quickly lowered himself to the ground, dropping the last few feet. He regained his balance like a cat and, crouching as he ran, made a beeline for the corral gate.

Distande watched him, and as Morgardo drew out the round wooden centerpiece that held both sections of the swinging gate together, the older brave turned, cupped one hand to his mouth, and emitted a hoot-owl screech, the signal to Pitanse and his men to be ready to attack.

Simon Brown heard the call. Without a second thought, he put down the pipe he had been smoking and retrieved his rifle from its place on the bench. Swiftly examining it to make certain it was primed and loaded, he moved toward the sound of the owl.

At the same moment Morgardo swung the corral gates

wide and, with another, louder, hoot to startle the horses, ran swiftly toward the young scout, who had his back to the Tawakoni brave. As Morgardo drew his knife and lifted it into the air, ready to strike, Simon whirled around and, holding his rifle at hip level, pulled the trigger. The ball buried itself in the brave's belly an inch above the navel, and Morgardo dropped his knife, staring stupidly down at the bloody hole in his paint-bedaubed body. Then he fell like a rag doll, almost at Simon's feet.

"Injuns! Sound the alarm!" Simon shouted, but already Pitanse and the rest of his men had begun climbing over the stockade walls and dropping to the ground.

Minnie Hornsteder, in her nightgown and with her husband's old rifle in her hand, hurried out of her cabin, just in time to see one of the braves prepare to leap down from the firing platform. She swung the rifle to her shoulder, squinted along the barrel, and pulled the trigger. There was an inhuman screech of agony, and the brave fell heavily to the ground, his shoulder smashed by the rifle ball.

The horses had begun to circle the corral, and now, frightened by the war whoops and the sounds of rifle fire, they burst out of the gate and galloped into the clearing, some of them knocking over the wooden benches and tables in their terrified flight.

Moses Wilson had retired to his cabin a little while before the attack, but he had not been asleep, and when he heard the gunshots and the neighing of the stampeding horses, he hurriedly buckled on his holstered pistols, seized his hunting knife and thrust it through his belt, and hurried out toward the corral.

Six of Pitanse's braves who had cleared the stockade now began to fall on the defenseless drunken men lying near the benches. Two of them had already been stabbed to death before Simon Brown, who had quickly reloaded his rifle, shot the nearest brave, twenty yards away, and then, pulling out a pistol, winged his companion, who had been in the act of drawing back an arrow aimed at him.

A twelve-year-old indentured servant girl, who had heard the war whoops and the shooting and had opened the door of her cabin to see what was happening, was seized from behind by one of the braves. Grabbing her by her long taffy-colored hair, he bent her head back, preparing to stab her in the heart before beginning the grisly task of scalping her.

Moses came around the corner of the cabin just in time. Shouting to distract the warrior momentarily, he aimed and fired his pistol, instantly killing the man. Then he pushed the frightened girl back into the cabin and yelled at her to bolt the door.

By now a few of the settlers in nearby cabins had awakened and emerged into the open with weapons, and one of them, Pedro Pondilla, dropped his rifle and staggered back, staring down at an arrow buried in his chest. His eyes glazed, and he collapsed to the ground. One of his neighbors saw what had happened, and with a furious oath leveled his pistol and killed the Tawakoni bowman who had slain his friend.

Meanwhile, the brave named Distande, who had been following the stampeding horses, leaped astride a black yearling and, clutching its mane, rode toward the main gate. An old, white-haired settler who had come out to see what all the noise was about noticed the brave riding down upon him and tried frantically to go back into his cabin, but was too late. Distande fired a pistol, and the old man pitched forward on his porch and lay still, a bullet through his skull.

Pitanse himself, leading the last eight of his braves who had scaled the stockade wall, headed for the settlement's storeroom. Along the way he split his men up, sending four to help out at the gate and two more toward the stables, instructing them to release as many horses as they could and stampede them out of the stockade.

Moses Wilson and Simon Brown had spotted the two Tawakoni sneaking toward the stables, however, and simultaneously raising their pistols, they fired and dropped both warriors as they were about to pull open the door.

"Some of those Injuns went toward the storeroom, Mr. Brown," Moses panted as he reloaded his pistol. "I'm gonna scout back there and see if I can be of any help. How many of 'em do you reckon there are?"

"I can't tell in all this darkness and confusion, Moses. But it's the horses they went for first, so they'll try to get them out the gate. I'll head there and rally some of the fellows along the way. Good luck!''

Moses hurried off, crouching like an Indian, his hands gripping his pistol butts. He moved in the shadows, following the direction Pitanse and his two remaining companions had taken.

Emma Sturtevant, who had been wakened by the firing and the screams of the wounded and dying, called to her slave in a frightened voice, "What's going on, Bessie? Go out and see!''

"Yassum," the slave woman timidly responded, obviously reluctant to do her mistress's bidding. Drawing on a tattered old robe, she gingerly opened the door and peered out. Pitanse, just then passing by, spied her and, with a triumphant grin, seized her by the wrist and dragged her out the door, then shoved her against the wall and put the point of his knife to her throat.

"No talk, no make sound, or I kill, savvy?" he muttered in his guttural pidgin. Bessie's eyes widened, fixed with horror on his savage, painted face. He called out something in a language she could not understand, and the two other braves entered the cabin, a moment later emerging with a screaming Emma Sturtevant. One of the braves struck her backhanded on the mouth to silence her, then threw her to the ground. With mocking jibes, he and his companion tore her nightshift from her, leaving her naked. Pitanse, who was still holding Bessie, ordered in the Tawakoni tongue, "The white will be my squaw! Bind her quickly! You two shall have this other one as a reward.''

Emma started to scream again, but one of her captors clapped his palm over her mouth, and the other touched her naked left breast with the tip of his hunting knife.

It was at this moment that Moses Wilson appeared. Seeing Bessie pinned with her back to the cabin wall, he raised both his pistols and fired the right-hand one point-blank at the Tawakoni leader. Pitanse's knife pricked Bessie's throat and drew blood as it jerked in his faltering hand, then he crumpled to the ground, dead from a ball in the brain.

Only an instant after triggering the first shot, Moses fired the other pistol, killing one of the two men holding

Emma Sturtevant. The other brave, whose back had been turned, rose with a bloodstained knife in his hand. Moses, drawing his own knife, put himself between the burly warrior and Bessie.

With an animal growl, the brave rushed straight at him, slashing diagonally with his knife, but Moses ducked at the last second and, bracing himself against the charge, drove his own knife up into the brave's belly. The Tawakoni's slash had gashed Moses high on the arm, but now the brave rolled over and over, moaning and clutching at his belly in a slow and agonizing death.

Bessie's two children appeared at the open cabin door. "You'll be all right now, honey," Moses said, taking her by the elbow. "Go back inside with the children, and I'll carry Mrs. Sturtevant in—" He had to grip the half-fainting slave woman by the elbows and hold her up. "Look at me, Bessie, honey . . . that's better. Now, you go back in like a good gal, and it'll be over soon. Just bolt the door and don't let anybody in until you hear me tell you it's all right, understand?"

"Yes—yes—oh, thank you, oh, my God, Moses, you saved my life again! I thought I was dead—his knife—" She put her hand to her throat and drew away her bloodstained fingers.

"Just a nick, sweetie. You go wash it with some good cold water, and you stay put, and that's an order!"

"I—I'll do whatever you tell me," Bessie quavered as she stumbled back into the house, collecting the children as she went.

Moses quickly turned to pick up Mrs. Sturtevant, who he had assumed had fainted, but as he bent down, he saw otherwise.

"Oh, my Lord!" he whispered, then remembered the Tawakoni's bloody knife. The man had driven his blade into Emma Sturtevant's heart.

Half an hour later, the people of the settlement assembled on the common, to count their losses and bind their wounds. The Tawakoni had been driven off, only six or seven of the original band having escaped with their lives, but they had taken with them one of the prize horses in the corral, and the younger men of the settlement would spend some wearying hours before dawn rounding up the other horses that had been stampeded out the gate. And the settlers had lost four of their own men, and one woman. But it could have been much worse, as Simon Brown said.

"I just want to tell you folks one thing," he said, his anger for once showing. "And I want you to remember it. You all know me pretty well by now, and you know I'm not a preaching sort of man. But you're going to hear this, whether you like it or not. I heard some nasty things from a lot of you—and I won't mention any names—when Moses Wilson came here to our settlement. You didn't like him because his skin was black, and you couldn't accept the fact that he was just as free and deserving of respect as you or me. You had to go ahead and make life hard for him, even after he became a Texas Ranger, offering his life to protect you and me."

There was silence, and several of the men and women lowered their heads.

"I saw some of what he did tonight to save all your hides, and if he was a soldier, he'd get a medal for it, no matter if he was black or red or white. I'm telling you now that Moses Wilson has earned his place here. He's a good, decent man, and I trust him with my own life. I don't ever want to hear any more talk against him, because as long as you've elected me the head of this community, I'm going to have a say-so about things like this."

There were murmurs of assent, and Jeremiah Whelks, one of the men who had most reviled Moses Wilson, shame-facedly stepped forward and said, "I know who you're talkin' about, Mr. Brown. I'm here to make amends, if I can. I once said I'd be damned if I'd let a nigger handle my weapons. Well, from what I've just found out, he's a better man than I am. Fact is, I was so scared I didn't even come out of my cabin and lift a gun to help." He turned toward the black man. "Moses Wilson, I ask your pardon for saying what I did. You won't ever hear it again from me, or from any other member of my family. Nosiree, you won't!"

Nineteen

The young Jicarilla brave Lortaldo had been assiduously pursuing his medical studies with Dr. André Malmorain of New Orleans. Although Lortaldo greatly missed his beautiful young Pueblo wife, Epanone—especially since he had received a letter from her saying that she was expecting the birth of their first child—he had, for the time being, no way of getting back to the Double H Ranch to be reunited with her.

He had written her a tender, consoling letter in which he enclosed a little silver bracelet with an amethyst set in the central link—a gift he had purchased out of the generous wages Dr. Malmorain paid him. In the letter, he explained that perhaps it was not so bad that he could not rejoin her for the holidays, because Dr. Malmorain had been showing him the secret of the ingredients that New Orleans apothecaries used to compound remedies for various illnesses. Also, he told her, during the recent yellow-fever epidemic, he had helped Dr. Malmorain at the city's hospitals, which had been filled to capacity. His experience there had made it obvious to him that even the most knowledgeable doctors had not the slightest idea as to the causes of the fever, for surely if they did, they would have been able to prevent its spread. He had said as much to Dr. Malmorain, who, Lortaldo recalled, had simply smiled, shaken his head, and said, "You have hit upon a flaw that none of us in this profession would like to admit, Lortaldo—and there are doctors far more skilled than I who have no better answer than simply to try all the measures we know to alleviate the effects of the fever before its very temperature kills the patient. There are times when I have thought that these remedies are worse than the disease itself; but perhaps you, Lortaldo, young and dedicated as you are to the noblest ideals of medicine, perhaps you will be the one who one day learns what causes this abominable pestilence.''

Now, in the first weeks of February, another dreaded disease had struck New Orleans—diphtheria. So far only a few, seemingly isolated, cases had been reported, but on the sixth day of the month, three cases were reported at the Ursuline Convent School. Summoned to the hospital by his colleagues, Dr. Malmorain examined the patients—two young students and a middle-aged *dueña* called Señora Josefa—and agreed to the diagnosis of diphtheria. Señora Josefa, whose case was more advanced than the others, died a day later, but the two girls lingered for a week, until at last Dr. Malmorain, seeing the congestion of the windpipe, daringly decided to perform a tracheotomy as the only hope of saving their lives. The older doctors objected, but they could offer no other alternative, so Dr. Malmorain went ahead with the operations, Lortaldo closely assisting him. To everyone's great relief, both operations were successful.

The mother superior of the convent had gone to the hospital the day after this double operation, and Dr. Malmorain had told her, ''Mother Cécile, I do not wish to cause you alarm, but in view of these three cases, my suggestion is that you close your school temporarily. From what I believe, it is a highly contagious malady, and I can only pray that others among your people have not been affected.''

''I shall take your advice, Dr. Malmorain,'' the kindly nun replied. ''You may recall that, during the Christmas holidays, quite a few of our girls were afflicted with the ague and were deprived of the pleasure of going home. Well, m'sieu, they can take this opportunity to do so. Do you think a month will be sufficient time?''

''That would be a good start. I would also suggest that you have the sisters burn the bedding used by the three infected patients, and, indeed, it would not be a bad idea to replace all the bedding of all your pupils. We do this with yellow fever, and to my view, diphtheria is quite as serious, particularly if it is allowed to spread.''

Later that evening, in the assembly hall of the school building, Mother Cécile addressed her pupils, informing them of her decision to close down the school for at least a month. "I shall send dispatches to your parents, *mes filles,* as soon as it is safe to return." Then, with a faint little smile, she added, "To be sure, when you return, there will be work to be made up, but most of you have shown such excellence in your studies that there should be no real problems. And now our sisters will aid you in preparing your plans for the journeys homeward. We shall pray for you all and hope to see you back perhaps sometime in March." With this, she made the sign of the cross and left the hall.

When Adriana Maldones and her sisters, Paquita and María, heard the news from the mother superior, Adriana informed the young girls, "Now that we no longer have dear Señora Josefa to counsel us, we must make our own decisions— but I am sure she would have told us to go to the Double H Ranch and see our *padre,* to tell him of all that has happened."

"But how shall we get there?" Paquita wailed. "Surely the sisters will not take us!"

"I will speak to Francesca," Adriana said, with a sudden air of authority. "She will probably be seeing Señor Mallard, who is the factor for Señor Baines. He will arrange a way for all of us to get to the *hacienda.*"

And so, that evening, with the mother superior's permission, Adriana Maldones and Francesca de Escobar engaged a calash to take them to the home of Fabien and Hortense Mallard, where Francesca related what had happened at the school, including the sad death of Señora Josefa, and asked if it were possible for an escort to be arranged for them and the other two girls to the Double H Ranch.

"It would be my great pleasure, Mam'selle Francesca," Fabien replied, his mature wife nodding in confirmation. "As it happens, I was about to send a letter to M'sieu Baines, informing him that M'sieu Blanton, the captain of this ship of his, the *New Venture,* has drummed up an order for two hundred head of beef cattle. M'sieu Baines can drive them to Corpus Christi, where the *New Venture* will board them in the hold and transport them back here to New Orleans. I can have the courier accompany you, along with a few other trustworthy men, and I'll lend you my carriage, so that you will not have to ride horses. But if I may be so bold to ask, would you not wish to take young Diego de Escobar with you?''

"Oh, my, of course!" Francesca gasped. "What a dunce I am to have forgotten! It's just that I have heard so little of him since he became an apprentice to that lawyer—Señor Allary, I believe his name is.''

"Correct. Well, then,'' Fabien declared, ''we'll see if M'sieu Allary can spare Diego's services for a time. Even if there's not room in the carriage for him, I'm sure he would be eager to ride horseback and help out with the escort. I'll go and speak to him first thing tomorrow morning and arrange for the rest of the escort.''

That same evening, while Francesca and Adriana were visiting Fabien Mallard, Dr. Malmorain conferred in his office with Lortaldo.

"The convent school is to be closed down for the time being, Lortaldo, because I am worried about the spread of the diphtheria. I am sure that the Maldones and de Escobar girls will go to Texas for a visit, and the thought occurs to me that you should accompany them, if that can be arranged. You've been working very hard the last few months, and it's high time you took a vacation. Besides,'' he smiled, ''you told me that Epanone is going to have a child. I'm sure you'd like to see him—or her, as the case may be.''

Thus Lortaldo, who took Dr. Malmorain's advice and visited the office of Fabien Mallard the next morning, learned of the proposed trip and eagerly accepted the factor's invitation to join the escort. In fact, M'sieu Mallard said he had just returned from a visit to Diego de Escobar, who would also be going.

Their departure was planned for the very next afternoon, and by twelve o'clock most of the party had assembled in front of Fabien's warehouse. Francesca stood anxiously by her luggage, and when her cousin Diego appeared on horseback, she hardly recognized him.

"My, how grown-up you look, Diego!" she exclaimed. "How distinguished! I could already mistake you for a lawyer—except for the rifle, of course!"

"Fabien gave it to me this morning," he said. "And my employer presented me with this hat," he added, straightening his new silk top hat, which was just like the ones most lawyers wore. "Yes, Francesca, I mean to be a good lawyer, and Señor Allary is a wonderful teacher. But it's so pleasant to see you—and you've changed too. You're a very beautiful young woman now!"

Diego could say this lightly, without any pangs of regret, for although formerly he had had eyes only for Francesca, he had since been captivated by the pretty little seamstress Marie Duval.

"Why, thank you, Diego!" Francesca couldn't keep from giggling. "Gracious me, when I think how it was when we were on the ranch, and how you used to tease me! I thought you were a terrible boy! But now I'm glad you're coming with us. Did Señor Allary give you any trouble getting time off?"

"Oh, not at all. The lenten recess is coming up soon, so the courts will be closed, of course," he said knowledgeably. "Where are the Maldones girls? Fabien told me they're coming, too, and I've never met them."

"They're already sitting in the carriage," Francesca said. "They are in mourning for poor Señora Josefa, their *dueña*, who, as you probably heard, died of the diphtheria."

Diego glanced at Fabien Mallard's sturdy black carriage but could not see into the window openings from where he sat on his horse. There were gunnysacks of provisions tied atop the roof, and still more in a compartment behind the rear axle. Two personable-looking Creole men stood beside their horses, with rifles thrust into their saddle sheaths, and each wore a belt with a holstered pistol as well. Fabien was nearby talking to Lortaldo, who was holding a horse by the halter.

After exchanging a few more words with Diego—mostly about the Maldones girls—Francesca entered the carriage, and as the last bags were loaded by the Creole escorts, Hortense Mallard arrived to bid everyone a safe and speedy journey. Fabien called to Diego: "How would you like to drive the carriage, young man? Lortaldo's never handled a team before.''

"That would be fun!" Diego enthusiastically agreed and, attaching his horse's rein to the back of the carriage, nimbly clambered up to the driver's seat. As he did, he glanced into the carriage and caught sight of the brown-haired, lovely young Adriana Maldones, and his eyes widened with surprise. Francesca had told him how these three girls had come from Argentina at great risk to their lives, but she had said nothing of how remarkably beautiful Adriana was. She had mentioned, however, Diego now recalled with disappointment, that Adriana and Andrew Baines were as good as pledged to each other.

Diego had not completely forgotten the winsome Marie Duval, but all the same, Adriana's vivid beauty made an instant impression upon him, for he was now entering that period of adolescence when he was more than usually susceptible to the charms of the opposite sex. As he settled in the driver's seat, Diego thought of what Francesca had said about Adriana and Andrew, then reminded himself that it would be at least a two-week journey to the ranch, and much could happen in that time. Certainly he would have many opportunities to talk to Señorita Adriana before they arrived, and if she liked him, it might not be too difficult to oust Andrew from the preferred place in her affections. After all, he reasoned, if the three girls had been in the convent school all this time since they had come from Argentina, there had been no chance for Adriana to renew her friendship with John Cooper's oldest son.

Diego straightened his new hat again and, seeing that all was in readiness, called his last good-byes, then picked up the reins and shook them, directing the horses forward at a brisk trot. He was smiling to himself. This belated holiday might turn out to be even better than Christmas! And since Fabien Mallard had presented him this morning with a new Belgian rifle, as well as a pistol and holster to wear so that he might defend the lovely occupants of the carriage, he almost wished that someone would attack them so that he could prove himself a hero. That, certainly, would impress the enchanting, dark-eyed Argentine girl. He whispered to himself: *"Adriana."* Even to say the name was music, and as Diego rode along, feeling quite important, he leaned over the side of the seat and glanced down at the door, secretly hoping that those two dark eyes would peek up at him, as if in answer to his fervent whisper.

"¡Amigo!" someone next to him shouted. Diego sat up quickly as one of the Creole escorts rode alongside. "I thought perhaps you had fainted," the man said, "but I see that you are all right."

Diego blushed slightly and returned his attention to the road. The Creole, he knew, was named Maurice Colbert. Fabien Mallard had described him to perfection: a dashing young man of twenty-five, with a little waxed mustache and trim Vandyke beard. With his plumed cap, he almost looked like a fop, but Diego knew this man had already won a reputation as a duelist who had nerves of steel. Just last month he had killed two notorious blackguards, one after the other, in a duel under the famous Three Sisters oak trees.

"Amigo," the Creole now repeated, "I see that you are a skilled driver. With luck, and no disturbances along the way, I believe we can reach our destination by Mardi Gras. Tonight we shall make camp where our route leaves the river road, if it pleases you. There's a place I know, well away from the swampland, that will be comfortable for the charming *señoritas.*"

He said all this in such pure Castilian as to make Diego blink with surprise, and, indeed, the Creole had addressed him with deference, as if he, Diego, were the leader of the expedition.

"Señor Colbert," Diego replied with a tone of self-importance, "you have but to lead the way, and I will have the horses follow as speedily as I can make them."

"But not too speedily," the Creole advised, "or they will quickly tire. *¡Su servidor!*" The handsome Creole doffed his plumed hat, then spurred his horse forward to join his companion and Lortaldo.

They reached the proposed campsite just after sundown, and once Diego had watered and fed the carriage horses, he made himself useful by helping the two Creoles to prepare the evening meal. He had assisted Adriana out of the carriage, but she had avoided talking to him, and now observing that she was conversing animatedly with Francesca, he volunteered to bring them their plates of food.

Maurice Colbert, observing this, murmured to his companion, the jovial, stocky Philippe Morléac, "The young señor de Escobar has already become a cavalier. Handsome as he is, and, as I've heard, the heir of a great *hidalgo* of Spain, he will leave many a broken heart behind."

"Like you yourself, Maurice," Morléac twitted him. "Except that you are not the heir of an *hidalgo*, and not quite so handsome."

"Have a care now, *mon ami*"—Colbert pretended high dudgeon as he put his hand to the knife at his belt—"or you will have me to deal with under the Three Sisters one fine dawn!" Then, he and his friend burst into laughter at the little jest.

For her part, Adriana Maldones found Diego's attentions highly flattering, yet they only served to remind her that she was coming closer and closer to her beloved Andrew, who had risked his life to join his father, the señor Baines, on the expedition that had saved her father and brought them all to this wonderful new country. To be sure, Diego was handsome enough, his manners could not be faulted, and he certainly knew how to handle horses—but it was Andrew she truly loved. No other young man, save John Cooper's son, could have had the courage to disobey his father's orders in order to come along on so perilous a venture—why, they might all have been put before a *porteño* firing squad! Adriana shivered at the thought and crossed herself.

After supper, Maurice Colbert extinguished the cooking fire, then himself took the first guard duty. Since they were on high ground, and the moon was bright in the sky, one sentry could circle the camp and see a good distance in all directions.

For safety's sake, however—and since the carriage was roomy enough—all four girls reclined on the comfortable padded seats and were soon fast asleep. Lortaldo, taking an evening stroll around the campsite, noticed a small, silver-barked tree and, believing it to be the same kind from which his people stripped a medicinal bark, took out his knife and carefully cut away pieces of the bark, which he put into a leather pouch he carried. He looked at the moon and smiled gently, thinking of Epanone. How loyal and sweet she had been all this while, waiting faithfully for him at the Texas ranch, until he could finish his studies and rejoin her. And now she was carrying his child. Lortaldo gazed for a long time at the starry sky, feeling truly blessed by the Great Spirit to have found her as his squaw.

When they rose to resume their journey early the next morning, they were greeted by overcast skies and a fine spray of rain. The wind blew strongly from the southeast, and Maurice Colbert frowned and said to Diego as he rode up beside the carriage, "The weather is from the Gulf, and there may be much rain accompanying our journey, if this continues. It will slow us, but there's no help for it. Keep your horses on as solid ground as you can, m'sieu."

The rain subsided somewhat when they stopped for a brief lunch, but it persisted as a drizzle almost until twilight, when it stopped abruptly. Diego had handled the horses extremely well, and the dashing leader of the escort complimented him as they made camp and prepared the evening meal. "*Mes félicitations,* M'sieu de Escobar. You have made the charming *demoiselles* quite comfortable the way you have driven the carriage today."

"But of course!" Diego roguishly replied, glancing over to where Adriana stood talking with Francesca. "It would not be gallant to discommode such lovely young ladies."

"*Tiens,* you have a little Gallic blood in your veins, I perceive, m'sieu," Colbert chuckled. "No doubt you will break the ladies' hearts before you are too much older—though I fear you will find more of them back in New Orleans than between here and Texas."

Diego smiled in assent but did not pursue this topic. As long as Adriana was nearby, he was not greatly concerned with the relative sparsity of attractive females at the Double H Ranch. It did not even occur to him that he had already nearly forgotten the charming little seamstress Marie Duval.

Since they had lost some daylight because of the overcast skies, Colbert was of the opinion that they should start out earlier the next morning, providing that the rain had stopped. "That way we can be out of the swampland as soon as possible; after that the ground is a bit higher," he pointed out to Lortaldo and young Diego.

The next morning, although the skies were still cloudy, there was no hint of rain, and the escort moved more swiftly. They were able to cover nearly sixteen miles before stopping for lunch, and then, since the weather continued pleasant and there was even a hint of the sun, Colbert determined that they push on until they could no longer see the road ahead of them. "We'll gain a little of the time we lost yesterday," he explained.

The rain and overcast, however, returned for most of the first week of the journey to the Double H Ranch. The wind was steadily from the southeast, indicating that a prolonged storm was brewing in the Gulf. Colbert and Morléac had brought tarpaulins with them, stored in the rear compartment of the carriage, but even when these were erected as crude tents, and used to cover the windows of the carriage, they could not entirely keep out the dampness. It was hard to find dry wood for the cooking fires, and in consequence the meals were cold and skimpy. But for Francesca and Adriana, as well as the younger girls, the journey was an exciting adventure, and even the discomforts seemed to enhance it.

Adriana and Francesca had already become friends at the convent school, and now they grew even closer. One evening, Francesca confided how at first she had thought young Diego de Escobar to be a brash know-it-all who went out of his way to make himself objectionable and to prove his masculinity. But after getting to know him better, she confessed, she had developed something of an infatuation for him. Yet in almost the same breath, and with a wise little nod—as if to indicate she was quite mature enough by now to perceive her own earlier follies—she casually added, "Of course, even if I'd fallen desperately in love with him, it would never have been correct. We're cousins, you see. And besides, well, there was an older man—would you believe, a man nearly thirty—who I think was really head over heels in love with me. Of course he was a good, fine, and honorable man, and because he was promised to someone else, even though it had to break his heart to give me up, he did so for her sake." She did not add that she had recently met Señor McKinnon's lovely bride, when the couple had visited her in the hospital during the Christmas holiday.

"How romantic!" Adriana clasped her hands and sighed. She, however, was thinking of Andrew Baines, and she could almost, by closing her eyes, summon his image before her, even hear the impassioned words he had poured out to her the last time they had parted. He had written faithfully, and even though the nuns regularly read all the girls' correspondence, the meaning of his letters had been clear enough to her. Yes, they were promised—as good as betrothed, as far as she was concerned—and she could hardly wait to see how much older Andrew must look by now. Surely he would make a fine man, and she would have no one else as her *esposo*, when the time came. True, it would be with her father's permission, for a well-bred Argentine girl did not marry without parental approval.

All the same, she thought as she continued to listen to Francesca's confidences (which, to be sure, were not strictly governed by the truth, at least as far as Jack McKinnon was concerned) that it was flattering to see Diego de Escobar so interested in her.

Even as the two girls were whispering about him, Diego had absented himself for a few moments from the cooking fire and moved off toward a clump of bushes. When he returned, it was with a bouquet of wild flowers, and affecting the most nonchalant air, he strolled up to where the three Maldones girls and Francesca were sitting awaiting their supper. Stooping down, he handed the bouquet to Adriana with the offhand remark "I thought perhaps you might enjoy these flowers, Señorita Adriana. I just happened to see them, and after the long, dreary days we've had on our journey, I thought they should be yours, for your loveliness has brightened each of these days—at least for me."

As Adriana blushed and accepted the flowers, Francesca regarded Diego almost openmouthed and was hard put not to let a giggle slip out; she clapped her hand over her lips and looked away, lest she spoil his gallant approach. She was surprised that she did not feel at all jealous, and thinking about this, she understood that at last the two of them had been totally released from the infatuation they had once shared back on the ranch. She also thought that she was very lucky to have a mother like Doña Inez, whose tactful letter had undeniably helped her over a most trying period in her life. Indeed, as Adriana reluctantly thanked Diego—Paquita and María giggling all the while—Francesca told herself that she was truly grateful that the trials of her own last two years were now behind her.

The rain continued off and on through the second week of their journey. Diego de Escobar had to exert great care in keeping the carriage wheels from becoming mired in the soggy, rutted road, but once the party had left the swampland of Louisiana behind, they made much better time.

On their fifth day into Texas, the sky finally cleared, treating them to a magnificent sunset. Philippe Morléac had shot a deer, and that evening they all had venison for supper, a great treat for the Maldones girls, who had never tasted deer meat, and for Francesca as well, who fondly remembered the times when John Cooper and Diego's father, Carlos, would go hunting and return with a fine buck.

The girls were on their way back to the carriage to retire for the evening, as Lortaldo, Diego, and the two Creole escorts enjoyed a second cup of coffee, when suddenly Adriana uttered a piercing cry. From out of the darkness, an arrow grazed her right arm, just as she was about to open the carriage door. Almost simultaneously, Philippe Morléac swore aloud, his eyes wide with agonized surprise, as he looked down and saw the shaft of an arrow embedded in the fleshy part of his left thigh. Without a second thought, he pulled the arrow out and reached for his rifle nearby.

"Les peaux rouges, mes amis, gardez-vous!" Maurice Colbert shouted as he drew his pistol and fired at something moving in a dark thicket to his right. There was a hoarse grunt of pain and the sound of a body falling, and then

another volley of arrows, as Morléac, Colbert, Diego, and Lortaldo grabbed their weapons and hurriedly spread out in a semicircle around the carriage, under which the girls had taken refuge.

Diego saw an Indian break out of the darkness and run straight at him, his head bald save for a topknot, a lance drawn back in his hand. Flinging himself to the ground, Diego rolled over twice and, cocking his rifle as he stopped, fired upward. The ball took the warrior in the chest, and he toppled forward, dead.

Meanwhile, Lortaldo aimed his pistol as another brave rushed in from the opposite side. Holding his fire until the tomahawk-wielding Indian was almost upon him, he brought his attacker down at the last second with a shot to the heart.

Morléac and Colbert were firing their rifles and pistols into the shadowy thickets now, but both must have seen their targets, for the shrieks of the wounded attested to the accuracy of their marksmanship.

Colbert moved swiftly toward the carriage, reloading as he did. He called to his companions: "Try to find cover. I don't know how many there are, but it seems they do not have firearms."

"They're Kiowa," Morléac said, just as another brave came running at him from behind, crouching low as he did, his tomahawk descending toward the Creole's skull.

"Prends garde!" Maurice shouted to his friend. He had not finished reloading, but oblivious of his own safety, he leaped at the Indian and grabbed the tomahawk with both hands, just in time to deflect the blow. The two men wrestled briefly on the ground, then the Kiowa broke loose and, unarmed now, scrambled away to safety.

Lortaldo and Diego had placed themselves behind the carriage wheels to protect the girls, who huddled behind them. Little María and Paquita screamed with fear each time an arrow shot from the dark bushes beyond thudded against the side of the carriage or skidded past them on the ground, but Francesca and Adriana kept up the younger girls' courage by hugging them and assuring them that the men would protect them.

There was a lull in the fighting, during which time the

men reloaded and Colbert whispered that the Kiowa were probably preparing their last, all-out assault.

Sure enough, without even a war whoop to signal their sudden onrush, three paint-bedaubed Kiowa burst from the bushes and came straight at the carriage, while two more braves, crouching in the shadows beyond, released arrows. One of the shafts ricocheted off the wheel behind which Diego was crouching, and the young man coolly aimed his rifle and fired at the nearest attacker, who grunted, clutched at his shoulder, and stumbled to the ground, then got up and lurched away. The second brave was also winged, apparently by Lortaldo, and the third attacker saw this and seemed to lose courage. Colbert and Morléac held their fire, waiting for a sure shot, but the Kiowa attackers had apparently had enough, for they all melted back into the night, dragging their dead and wounded behind them.

Colbert got to his feet and, his rifle at the ready, moved to the edge of the camp to make sure the attackers had indeed fled. He returned a few moments later, brushing the dirt from his clothes and complimenting his three companions on their heroic stand. "We must see to your wound, Philippe. I hope you'll be able to ride with that leg of yours."

Lortaldo, who had already checked Adriana's arm and quickly bandaged it after assuring himself the wound was only superficial, now helped Philippe Morléac to a place by the fire, where the young Jicarilla cut away a piece of the Creole's blood-soaked trouser-leg and inspected the wound.

"I think you are fortunate," he said, after skillfully probing the flesh around the wound and eliciting only grunts from his stoical patient. "Many times the arrowhead remains embedded in the flesh." Searching the ground near where Morléac had been sitting when they were first attacked, Lortaldo picked up the discarded arrow and satisfied himself that the head was still attached. Then, after washing the wound with brandy supplied by Maurice Colbert, he took from his leather pouch some tree moss and a square of cinchona bark, applied them to the wound, then bandaged it with a strip torn from a blanket.

As he was doing this, Adriana approached Diego and said, "How brave you were!"

"Oh, it was nothing." Diego tried to be modest, but all the same he could not suppress a smug grin of satisfaction and pride at his accomplishments.

Francesca eyed him wonderingly. She had sensed the note of triumph in his response, yet she knew that Adriana's feelings for Andrew Baines would not change because of this incident. So, to deflate Diego somewhat and put things back into proper perspective, she archly commented, "Oh, it was nothing? And by that I suppose you mean Señorita Adriana's life is worth nothing? For a boy who is studying to be a lawyer, Diego, I should think you would be more careful in your choice of words."

Diego turned as red as a turkey cock's wattles and mumbled something, then strode off, furious with Francesca.

"You really were too hard on him," Adriana meekly protested. "He did save my life."

"Just don't tell *him* that," Francesca replied, "or he'll be impossible at the ranch. Don't you know, dear Adriana, that boys should never be allowed to be too boastful? They easily become swellheaded."

Satisfied that she had put Diego in his place, Francesca, in a more mollifying tone, added, "But it's true—he really was very brave. And, you know, he saved my life too."

Twenty

The intermittent rain had mired the carriage road leading to San Antonio and the Double H Ranch, and Philippe Morléac, because his leg wound did not permit him to ride, had taken over the driving duties. He was not as experienced in handling a team as was Diego, and hence it was a few days later than expected when the little party finally made its way under the broad wooden archway that bore the insignia of the Hawk.

The alert old Miguel Sandarbal had already informed the others of the approach of the riders and carriage, and John Cooper and Dorotéa, Carlos and Teresa, and Doña Inez hurried out to see who the unexpected arrivals were. John Cooper was first to recognize Fabien Mallard's carriage, but they all were surprised when, instead of the factor and his wife, they saw Diego and Lortaldo and, when the carriage pulled to a halt, the three Maldones sisters and Francesca. A shouting Benito and Enrique Duvaldo and Raoul Maldones rode up, eager to join the happy reunion, and Andrew Baines and his younger brother, Charles, ran from the stables to greet the occupants of the carriage.

When the initial confusion had died down, Maurice Colbert introduced himself to John Cooper, explaining the troubles they had encountered with the roads and the Indians.

John Cooper frowned at this news. "The Kiowa are being driven from their southern hunting grounds by the Mexican patrols, it looks like. The particular group that attacked you must have broken away from the main stronghold in search of food and horses. You're lucky to have escaped as you did.''

"I know, M'sieu Baines." Colbert's handsome face shadowed. ''We were surprised, and I blame myself for having chosen the campsite.''

John Cooper shook his head. "If the Kiowa wanted to ambush you, Mr. Colbert," he said, "you could have had a half-dozen sentries on guard all night, and they'd still have been waiting for you. It speaks well of your ability to have driven them off with no losses on your side. But it's also fortunate it wasn't a larger band. When you return, Mr. Colbert, I want you to take another route—and it'll be with an extra sum of money for the fine work you've done.''

"That's very generous of you, M'sieu Baines; Philippe and I are deeply honored. But we shall not impose upon your hospitality too long. We need only perhaps a night's sleep, fresh horses, and provisions—''

"Nonsense," John Cooper broke in. "There's no reason to rush back tomorrow. I'd like you and your companion to be our guests for a few days, if only to rest and be at your ease and see what a friendly community we have here.''

"You are most convincing, m'sieu—and I am sure Philippe could use the extra rest—although the young Indian doctor who accompanied us has taken good care of him. Oh, I very nearly forgot!'' Colbert clapped his hand to his forehead. "There were two other little commissions my employer bade me execute. One I have in my saddlebag, M'sieu Baines— presents for you and your wife, with the best regards of Captain Amos Blanton.''

"Why, that's most thoughtful of him!" John Cooper exclaimed.

"The other," Maurice Colbert continued, "is right here." He pulled a folded letter from his pocket and handed it to John Cooper. "I do not think it is presumptuous of me to tell you, m'sieu, that M'sieu Blanton is responsible for this as well.''

John Cooper broke out in a smile as he read the letter, in which Fabien Mallard gave details of the order for two hundred head of cattle that John Cooper was to deliver to the coast, where they would be loaded on the *New Venture* and shipped to New Orleans.

"M'sieu Mallard," Colbert continued, "is quite pleased with *M'sieu le Capitaine* Blanton, and thinks the two of you have found an excellent ally who will make much money. But I forget the gift . . ." He went to his horse and opened the saddlebag, from which he extracted two elegantly wrapped little parcels.

"How lovely it is, dear John Cooper!" Dorotéa rapturously exclaimed when she opened her gift—a beautifully carved and embellished tortoise-shell comb.

"Yes, but I'm just wondering," the tall Texan said with a chuckle, as he inspected his gift—a velvet case containing a hand-tooled French straight razor. "Perhaps Captain Blanton is trying to send me a little hint that I should trim my beard more frequently."

"It would do you no harm and would surely make you look younger, *mi corazón*," Dorotéa teased him, and all the listeners joined in the good-natured laughter that this remark provoked.

Maurice Colbert now turned as Carlos de Escobar introduced himself.

"I must commend you on the valor of your son, M'sieu de Escobar." The Creole gestured toward Diego, who pretended to look away and not to be listening to this extremely flattering conversation. "When we were attacked by *les sauvages rouges*, he personally dispatched three or four of them, and showed great gallantry in defending the charming *demoiselles*."

"Diego, come here, *mi hijo*," Carlos raised his voice, and Diego sheepishly approached his father. "I've just been told what you did. You are *muy hombre, muy hombre,* and I'm proud of you. I'm also happy to see that the good training you've had riding and hunting here on the ranch hasn't been forgotten."

"I couldn't let *los indios* hurt the *muchachas, mi padre*," Diego ingenuously explained, but his eyes were now on Adriana, who, to his great chagrin, was talking with Andrew Baines.

Francesca and Doña Inez had already gone inside, and

Paquita and María seemed to have completely forgotten the others, for they were reunited now with their father and with their older sister, Dorotéa. John Cooper chuckled as he saw the three sisters, joined now by Adriana, lead their father off, Paquita taking one of his hands and Adriana the other, while Dorotéa held out her hand to little María, who kept insisting, "*Pronto, pronto,* Dorotéa, Papa is going too fast. We must catch up with him!"

John Cooper took the opportunity to speak to Miguel. "It appears there's still bad weather blowing in from the Gulf, judging from what that fellow Colbert had to say."

"Yes, and it's got me worried," Miguel complained. He nodded toward the Frio River. "I tell you, *mi compañero,* I don't like the looks of that river. It's still rising, and if there is any more rain, it could overflow its banks. This fine, soft ground would be turned into mud and muck, and we'd have the devil's own time working the cattle or the horses."

"Well, Miguel, maybe we'll be lucky and the storm will turn back to sea." Just as he finished the sentence, there was an ominous rumble of thunder, then another, even closer. Suddenly it began to pour, and John Cooper looked at Miguel, and both men burst out laughing. But it was only for a brief moment, because each was thinking of the dangers to the ranch, if this downpour were to continue for any prolonged time.

"We'd best get the *trabajadores* to build some dikes around the *hacienda,*" John Cooper suggested.

"I was just going to say so myself, *Halcón,*" Miguel vigorously nodded in agreement.

In the excitement of welcoming Diego, Francesca, and the Maldones girls, Lortaldo had been almost forgotten. As he was leading his horse to the stables, he was joined by one of the *vaqueros,* who insisted on taking care of the mount for him.

"Thank you, señor," Lortaldo said. "I have been away for many months. Can you tell me where I can find my wife, Epanone?"

"But of a certainty, *amigo,*" the *vaquero* pleasantly

rejoined. "The *patrón* had some of the men build a little cabin, not far from the house of the señor Santoriaga. I will take you there, if you like. *Dios*, this rain! We have had more than we need already—" A sudden bolt of lightning seared the dreary sky, and the *vaquero* hastily crossed himself. "Begging Your pardon, *por piedad, Señor Dios*!"

After they had left the horse with a stable boy, the *vaquero* pointed to an adobe cottage just beyond Ramón Santoriaga's house. "There you are, Señor Lortaldo. Your wife does very well, and Señora Toldavia has been staying with her since she had the child—"

"The child?" Lortaldo's face joyously brightened, and leaving the *vaquero* behind him in the rain, he hurried to the door and knocked. The plump, genial Señora Toldavia opened the door and exclaimed in surprise as Lortaldo hurriedly greeted her and stepped inside, throwing off his traveling coat.

"Epanone—I am here!" he called out.

There was a happy cry from the bedroom beyond, and Lortaldo swept past the curtained doorway to see Epanone sitting up with a little baby wrapped in swaddling clothes. His wife's eyes were beaming with love.

"My darling Epanone—I had hoped that I could come here before our child was born. Forgive me that I could not—" he began.

"But there's nothing to forgive, *mi esposo*. Here is our little son. I have thought of a name for him, if you do not think I am too bold in selecting it," she timidly replied.

"Oh, no—it is your right! What would you call him, my sweet one?"

"I had thought that Wekantisay would suit him best—in the Pueblo tongue, as in yours, my beloved husband, it means 'The Child Who Is Loved.' "

"That is truly the most beautiful name I have ever heard, Epanone—next to your own." He knelt beside the bed, took one of her hands and brought it to his lips, and then, very gently and carefully, took the baby from her and peered down at it. "Truly he is a child of our love and our new life together. Just as you are learning to read and write in the white-eyes language, Epanone, I am learning much of white man's medicines and the ways they have of treating the sick, to which I have added my own people's knowledge of herbs and poultices. Both of us will teach what we know to our child, so that he shall advance beyond us, I can foresee it."

He kissed her gently as he gave the baby back to her, and then he turned to the amiable wife of the *vaquero* and thanked her in fluent Spanish for her kindness to his wife and child.

Maurice Colbert and Philippe Morléac did not start back, even three days later, to New Orleans, for the weather had remained unfit for traveling ever since the afternoon of their arrival. The thunder that John Cooper and Miguel had heard had signaled the onset of a violent storm, which lasted almost until dawn. And all through the next day, a light rain fell, almost without interruption. At sunset it ceased, but resumed with another storm shortly after dawn, even more violent than the first.

Miguel Sandarbal and a dozen *trabajadores* had worked steadily to build dikes around the *hacienda* and were concentrating mainly now on reinforcing the southern side, which faced the still-rising Frio River. Alongside the *trabajadores*, John Cooper, Raoul Maldones, Carlos de Escobar, and even Maurice Colbert labored as if they were the lowliest and newest of the workers who had come to the *Hacienda del Halcón* to earn their daily bread—indeed, it almost seemed as if they were trying to outdo each other as to who could work the longest and hardest. John Cooper had to urge Miguel to go home for supper and rest, and finally took him firmly by the elbow and, with a very straight face and not a word, led him back to his cottage. There Bess forced him to remove his wet clothes and climb into bed, whereupon she brought him a bowl of nourishing broth with boiled vegetables and chunks of meat. Even then he continued to protest, until Bess broke down and brought him a flask of good Mexican red wine to go with the broth, and some freshly baked bread slathered with honey.

John Cooper, who gratefully accepted a bowl of the tasty

broth, shared the meal with his old *compañero* and, when he had finished, declared, "This is exactly where you are going to stay for the rest of the night, Miguel. *Hombre*, at your age you're not immortal, so let's not hear any more of your fussing, is that understood?"

Miguel uttered a great sigh and rolled his eyes, as if to say, "Look at how I am put upon in my declining years," but Bess soothed him at once by bringing out a bowl of *flan* sprinkled with cinnamon, one of Miguel's great favorites. John Cooper reluctantly declined the serving of this rich dessert and said to Bess, "If he dares come out again tonight, I'll send him home in disgrace, with two of the youngest *trabajadores* to guide his footsteps—you have my word on it." And then, to Miguel, he added, "I mean what I say, *mi compañero*. You get your rest."

He went back to the others, nervously glancing up at the sky, which was ominously dark. A distant flash of lightning illuminated the scurrying clouds, and then the rain seemed to fall even more heavily than before.

John Cooper went back into the *hacienda* to change his clothes, for he was soaked to the skin, and the wind had turned cooler than usual. Andrew intercepted him in the hallway and insisted on helping with the dikes, as did Charles, both boys protesting that their other chores had all been completed. John Cooper hesitated, for although he could use Andrew's help, Charles was too young and might get in the way, and he didn't want to hurt the younger boy's feelings. "All right—you can both help, and I'm grateful for the offer, boys," he told them. "Charles, you go see Señor Maldones, and tell him I said to put you to work on one of the dikes away from the river. And you do exactly what he tells you to, just as if I were giving the orders. Go on, now.

"You, Andy, come with me," he said as Charles obediently ran off. "I want to get up a good strong dike between the river and the barn. Floods terrify horses almost as much as fire does, and I don't want to have to deal with a barnful of panicked horses."

Andrew looked suddenly concerned. "Pa—Ma's out in the barn. She wanted to make sure her mare wasn't frightened, and to check on the new colt—you know, the one with the white star on its forehead that was born just when all this rain began.''

John Cooper had a vague sense of foreboding as the two of them made their way toward the barn adjoining the old stables. The river could jump its banks any time now, and— A sudden gust of wind nearly knocked them off their feet in the slippery mud.

"Look, Andy!" John Cooper called over the wind. "The door's blown open!" A swirling gust of rain almost blinded them both as they stared at the barn, about a hundred fifty yards away. There was a forked flash of lightning, and by the unearthly glare they saw Dorotéa, booted and in her riding clothes, hurrying out of the stable with a small lasso in her hand.

"Dorotéa! Dorotéa, I'll help you—what is it?" John Cooper stopped and, cupping his hands to his mouth, shouted out as loudly as he could.

But Dorotéa did not hear him and kept running toward the river. Another, even more violent flash of lightning scissored the angry sky, and by its momentary illumination they could see a little black colt loping about ten yards ahead of Dorotéa.

"See if you can shut and bar the door so it won't blow open again, Andy. I'll go after your mother!" John Cooper shouted, and Andrew nodded and began to run toward the large, flapping door.

The horse stalls all had gates, which the men had been trained to latch closed on every occasion, but John Cooper guessed that the colt must have bolted when Dorotéa opened its stall. Negrito, it had been named, the Texan remembered, even as he watched the frightened animal gallop awkwardly toward the swollen river, whose current already lapped over the banks on either side.

John Cooper found that because of the unsure footing, running after his wife was difficult, and he called out again, "Dorotéa, be careful! Don't go near the river!"

But it was too late. The colt, ears flattened, uttered a frightened whinny at still another clap of thunder and, approaching too close to the slippery riverbank, slid into the rushing torrent, which swept it quickly away. Dorotéa, trying to stop herself in time, deliberately dropped to the ground, letting go of her lasso in order to get a handhold on the soggy turf. But she had been running too fast, and her momentum carried her, too, into the river. At the last second she reached for a clump of bulrushes and managed to grasp hold, but the savage current drew her under and she was forced to let go.

With a cry of horror, John Cooper forced himself through the wind, which was increasing in violence and drowning out his futile cries. Dorotéa's lasso was still on shore, and he headed for it, careful so as not to slip and fall into the river. He picked up the coiled rope, and coming as close to the riverbank as he could, he saw Dorotéa flailing in the current, which was carrying her downstream. "Don't fight it—go with it, *corazón!*" he yelled with all his might. "Watch for my lasso! Try to grab hold of it!"

He trotted down the bank, trying not to lose his footing while twirling the lasso in the air. He saw her head emerge from the foaming water, then flung the loop out and, to his immense relief, caught her around the shoulders. One of her hands came up and seized the rope, securing it under her arms.

"I'm going to pull you in now, *querida!*" he cried, and dug in his heels, then began to back up, both his hands wound around his end of the rope.

Slowly, Dorotéa was brought closer to the bank, until finally she was drawn over the edge and onto the muddy ground. Panting and gasping, spluttering from the water she had swallowed, she finally regained her footing and stumbled toward him.

He put his arms around her and helped her walk until they were a safe distance from the river. After waving to Andrew, to assure the boy that everything was all right, he said to his wife, "You gave me a terrible fright—I was really scared! Don't ever take chances like that again, *mi corazón!* We can always have more colts, but there'll never be another Dorotéa."

She began to weep as what had happened finally sank in, and disengaging the lasso from herself, she flung her arms around him and hugged him desperately.

"Forgive me, but it was such a darling little colt—poor

little *Negrito*! I tried so hard to save him—it was that awful wind that blew the door open, and—"

"It doesn't matter now, *querida*. The important thing is that you're safe. Come on, let's go back to the house. You can get some good strong coffee and soup from Rosa, and you're not going to do anything else the rest of the evening—that's an order, *querida*!"

Her face was muddy and wet, but she gave him such an exasperated look in reply to this lecture that he burst out laughing and kissed her long and hard. "I didn't really mean to sound quite so harsh, honey," he confessed with a boyish grin.

"Never you mind, John Cooper," she murmured. "I rather like your being so concerned about me. And your orders I will always obey—you need never doubt that, heart of my heart, *vida de mi vida*."

Twenty-one

During the next few days, the *vaqueros* and *trabajadores* of the Double H Ranch labored from sunrise to late at night, building dikes, reinforcing the foundations of some of the outbuildings threatened by the overflowing river, and keeping the livestock safe on higher ground. The women and children pitched in as well, helping in whatever way they could, and even old Tía Margarita insisted on coming out of retirement to help the overworked Rosa Lorcas in the kitchen.

On Friday, the seventh of March, the rain at last began to abate to a drizzle, and now the *vaqueros* had to turn their full attention to the cattle, rounding up the strays, getting the herds to ground where there was ample graze, and taking care of any distressed animals.

Shortly after lunch, John Cooper kissed Dorotéa and told her he was going out to the western range with a dozen *vaqueros* to round up some of the prime heads, including a prize bull that had been missing for two days. The bull was a dark gray Brahma, which Fabien Mallard had purchased and sent on to the ranch about six months ago. It had already been mated with ten prime young heifers, and John Cooper looked forward to quality breed calves from the issue. Carlos had named the bull Priam, after the legendary king of Troy, because of its habit of prancing and snorting and calling attention to itself whenever it neared cows and heifers. John Cooper had found the name amusing, but at the moment he was hardly laughing at the task confronting him. The bull had scampered off and had last been seen headed toward the muddiest part of the range.

Carlos, when he learned that the bull he had named was the one now causing the greatest concern, decided to join John Cooper on the roundup. As the two men rode along ahead of the *vaqueros*, Carlos turned to his companion. "What a contrast between last March and this, *amigo*! This year, everything is muck and mire, while last year the weather was glorious. Don't you remember how the peach trees made a cloud of pink against the blue sky, and the plum trees were a rich purple?"

"Only too well, and the memory doesn't cheer me," John Cooper glumly remarked as he peered through the misty atmosphere for some sight of the runaway bull.

"There were bluebonnets everywhere," Carlos reminisced, "and Indian paintbrush, and the wild verbena. And there was just enough rain to make all those things grow to their most beautiful."

John Cooper shot him a look that was at first curious and then sympathetically understanding. It had been just such a March, two years ago, when Carlos had achieved his heart's desire in obtaining the hand of Teresa de Rogado in marriage; no wonder he could remember every last detail of the beauty of the landscape, which had mirrored with his own blissful mood.

"I understand you, *mi hermano*," John Cooper chuckled. "But if I'm not mistaken, I think I see your Priam—over there, between the two heifers. They're all stuck in the mire, it seems, and—he's spotted us, and he's trying to make a run for us, the stupid animal! Trying to run in muck like this is asking for a broken leg, or maybe worse."

"But of course—that's because he's Priam, and like his mythological namesake, he thinks he's monarch of all he surveys," was Carlos's teasing answer. Leaning forward, he patted the neck of his horse, spoke soothingly to it, and deftly turned the reins this way and that to urge the animal to take secure footing in tracking down the prize bull.

John Cooper beckoned to the nearest *vaquero* and said, "Vittorio, follow me. If we can lure him over to that clump of pecan trees and corner him, maybe Carlos can get a lasso on him."

"*Sí, patrón.*" The *vaquero*, a genial, stocky Mexican in

his early thirties, one of the newcomers to the Double H Ranch, enthusiastically spurred his horse on.

John Cooper paused long enough to call back to Carlos: "Get your lasso ready. I'm going to dismount and try to draw Priam closer to those trees, where it's a bit drier. I'll try to get him by the horns, and you get ready to lasso him—and don't miss!"

"That's dangerous sport, *amigo*," Carlos responded with a frown, knowing only too well the risk involved. Although virtually tame, the bull was spirited, and in a moment of panic—particularly if a two-legged animal were to seize its horns and try to impede its progress—it might turn mean.

The other *vaqueros* who had accompanied Carlos and John Cooper moved off toward a group of heifers that had become mired down and which were beginning to bawl as lustily as young calves, believing themselves certain to be swallowed up by the thick, oozing mud. Each of the *vaqueros* lassoed one of the heifers and, alternating brisk commands with soothing reassurances, managed to drag the animals onto safer ground.

The big gray bull paused in its struggle now, uncertain of which way to go, lashing its tail, lowering its horns, and uttering an impatient bellow. Its breath was visible in the chilly drizzle.

"There is a *toro* who seeks a *matador*," Carlos whimsically called to his brother-in-law. "But from what I've heard of your experience in the señor Duvaldo's private arena, and how you saved his *matador*, I think you could take on a whole arena of brave bulls, if you had a mind to!"

"This isn't the time for joshing, Carlos. Just get that lasso of yours ready," John Cooper irritatedly called back as he dismounted and circled slowly toward the bull, placing himself between it and the clump of trees. Vittorio also dismounted; his horse, like John Cooper's, showed its superb training and stayed where it was, awaiting its rider's next command. Vittorio approached the bull from John Cooper's right, so that the three men now formed a triangle around the mired animal.

Carlos remained astride his horse, wanting to get a better angle for the cast of his lasso. He urged his mount forward into the mud as he anxiously watched the bull manage a few awkward steps toward John Cooper. Only the mud prevented it from charging.

Exactly as it might do in the arena, the bull lowered its head, lifted one hoof from the sticky muck, and snorted angrily.

"Now, Priam, you know me, *amigo*—no tricks, now!" John Cooper spoke as if to a wayward child. "We're going to do you a service and get you back to all those heifers you've had your eye on. . . ."

Priam recognized the voice and lifted his head warily, not quite certain of what was intended. John Cooper came closer still, and once again Priam lowered his horns—but this time John Cooper lunged forward and seized them with both hands. "Now, Carlos!" he cried, as the bull bellowed and lurched, trying to break free. At the same time, John Cooper ducked down, so that the bull's head was actually above his own, and Carlos's lasso expertly flew out and circled Priam's neck. John Cooper let go and jumped back, as the handsome Spaniard jerked the lasso tight.

"Good work! Now hold on, Carlos, until we can give you a hand and pull this fellow out of the mud," John Cooper ordered.

Circling the struggling animal, he joined Vittorio, who had already grabbed hold of the taut line between Carlos and the bull. Carlos looped the rope around his saddle horn and ordered his horse to move backward, and the constricting pressure of the lasso around Priam's neck, together with the exertions of the two men pulling on it, forced the animal, for the sake of its own comfort, to take hesitant but definite steps toward one side until at last it stumbled out onto a solid patch of ground.

"We'll take him right back to the pen and see he doesn't get out again," John Cooper firmly declared as he remounted. "Good work, Vittorio! And thanks, *mi hermano*. That's as good a lasso throw as I've seen anyone make on the ranch."

"I hope so," Carlos blithely rejoined. "I have to be good, or else run the danger of being laughed at by the *vaqueros*. I even confess to practicing every now and again."

"I'm glad to hear that," John Cooper said, "because if

you'd missed, we'd soon enough find out that Priam was just a little heavier and a mite stronger than I am.''

Now that the danger was over, Priam docilely trotted along behind the three riders. And, as if it were a happy omen, the drizzle suddenly ended, and the skies began to clear.

At dawn the next day, the sun cast its vigorous rays on the Double H Ranch, as if to announce its return after the long weeks of gloom, and by noon the sky was blue and serene, with drifting cumulus clouds, like small flocks of sheep, placidly tracing their course. The Frio River began to ebb away from the tops of the banks it had overflown, and the weary *trabajadores* took their time as they began dismantling the dikes around the *hacienda* and outbuildings. Everywhere there was the chirping of birds, rejoicing in the bright new day and the advent of the invariably warm Texas spring, which promised flourishing growth for crops, cattle, and sheep alike.

Late in March, a letter arrived from the mother superior of the Ursuline Convent School in New Orleans, declaring that the epidemic of diphtheria was ended, and that school would be resumed by the second week in April. And to make up for the lost school days, the term would be extended to the very end of June, by which time, in any case, life in the city became almost unbearable because of the heat and humidity.

Young Andrew Baines had secretly hoped he could somehow gather the courage to declare to his father, to Raoul Maldones, and to Adriana herself that he wished to marry her before she returned to New Orleans. What concerned him most was the way Diego de Escobar took every possible opportunity to ingratiate himself with the vivacious Argentine beauty. Diego had even gone so far as to send a letter back to New Orleans—delivered by Maurice Colbert and Philippe Morléac, who had left the day after the rain stopped—informing his employer that he, Diego, would have to delay his return so as to serve as an escort for the girls. True enough, Andrew had been able to take Adriana out alone on horseback rides, during which time he had spoken ardently of his love for her and had hinted strongly of his hope they would soon be married. And her response to these overtures had convinced him he was still first in her heart.

As for Adriana, what she had felt a month ago still held true: Although Diego had saved her life when the Kiowa raiding party had attacked the carriage, she would never forget all Andrew had done to help save her father from a *porteño* firing squad. In the past weeks, she had had plenty of opportunity to compare the personalities of both her young suitors. Andrew was straightforward, exactly like his father, whereas Diego was more glib and self-assertive, already adopting the manner of a cavalier who seemed more intent on courting for the technique and the sheer challenge of it than for the actual enjoyment of his heart's desire.

For his part, Diego was still smitten with Adriana, and, indeed, he now admired not only her physical beauty but also her ability to handle horses. In addition he had discovered, somewhat to his dismay, that she was as adept as he with a lasso, and almost as good a shot with a rifle.

She had been given occasion to demonstrate this latter skill one day when John Cooper suggested that the young people have target practice. For the first rounds, Adriana held her own quite commendably, even outshooting Charles and the well-practiced Francesca. As could be expected, however, Andrew Baines won top honors among the young people, surpassing even Diego, who was crestfallen when John Cooper and Carlos, acting as judges, examined the final targets and pronounced Andrew the winner for having come an average of an inch and a half closer to the bull's-eye than had Diego.

Adriana could not help but notice that Diego had a habit of sulking when he was bested by anyone. He gladly accepted praise from the others over his own marksmanship, but when it was announced that Andrew was the winner, Diego had scowled and walked away, turning his back on everyone.

By now preparations were being made for the young people to return to New Orleans, this time with an escort of four armed *vaqueros*, augmented by Diego, who, as before, would drive Fabien Mallard's carriage. Unexpectedly, Lortaldo announced that he would not be returning as yet, since he had decided, at his wife's urging, to take her to visit her village near Taos. He would send a letter back with the others to Dr. Malmorain, who, in any case, had told Lortaldo to take as much time off as he needed.

As it turned out, Lortaldo's decision not to leave with the others came as a godsend to the Double H Ranch, for the very morning after the party had departed, Esteban Morales, while making an inspection of the western range and the new watchhouse, happened upon something that gave everyone on the ranch cause for alarm.

Hurrying back to the *hacienda*, he went at once in search of John Cooper, whom he found near the stables, inspecting a newborn colt. *"Patrón,"* Esteban hurriedly began, "I came upon a dead heifer while I was out riding on the western range. I found a tick in its swollen neck—and I have seen this kind of tick before. It is very bad for cattle, *Halcón*, very bad. And when I was riding back, I kept my eyes open and spotted three more dead animals. One was a calf, one was a steer, and there was a yearling too."

John Cooper frowned. "This is very bad, indeed—and right after all that rain! But we've never had such trouble before, Esteban. Are you sure it was the ticks that killed all four animals?"

"I am afraid so. On each carcass I found at least one blood-sucking tick—and as I said, I have seen this before, *Halcón*, where I worked many years ago. An entire herd was wiped out in a matter of weeks."

Esteban looked very agitated, and John Cooper did not doubt his word. "Then these ticks must have some kind of fever that kills the cattle, for surely the bites alone would not be fatal. I know that animals are bothered by blackflies and lice and ticks, but I hadn't realized that they could kill such large animals. I'm going to ask Lortaldo to take a look, and if you'll be good enough, Esteban, to show us the four dead animals, perhaps he can learn something by examining them."

"An excellent idea, *Halcón*! He knows of many Indian herbs and potions that perhaps could kill these accursed little pests!"

"Let's hope so," John Cooper declared. "I'll fetch Lortaldo, and you go find Raoul Maldones," he directed the foreman. "Together we'll see what we can do."

Less than half an hour later, the four men were mounted up and began to retrace the route Esteban Morales had taken earlier in the day. The young Jicarilla inspected all the corpses, taking a good deal of time, and gouging out two more of the ticks with his own knife. When he had finished, he declared, "My people have for long years used a mixture, a kind of potion, if you wish to call it that, to drive away blackflies and lice. They use sage and garlic and also wormwood. And I have heard also that stinging nettles can be used. My thought is that all four of these ingredients can be put together and reduced in water, to make a strong solution that can be applied to all the cattle. I am certain it will be powerful enough to drive away, if not to kill, these blood-sucking parasites. I agree, also, *Halcón,* that they spread the fatal disease that killed your cattle."

"Can you find enough of those plants around here, Lortaldo?" John Cooper anxiously demanded.

"Oh, yes. I myself have seen sage and wild garlic abundantly, along the banks of the Frio River. And wormwood as well. The stinging nettles may be more difficult to find, but I am sure that some of your *vaqueros* have encountered them. If they have, they will remember where, for to brush against one of the leaves is very painful. We shall ask them."

"Good idea. I will have the *vaqueros* hunt for these four things, Lortaldo. But I do not wish to delay your and Epanone's journey to Taos—"

"Epanone will not object; and certainly Dr. Malmorain would approve of my trying to help you, and gaining some practical knowledge at the same time. He is a kind, good man, and I am eager to learn all I can to justify the faith he has in me."

A few hours later, the dozen *vaqueros* whom Raoul Maldones had sent out to gather the plants Lortaldo had mentioned returned with several sackfuls, including two stuffed full of stinging nettles.

"Now, if Rosa Lorcas can lend me the largest iron kettle you have," Lortaldo said, "and your *vaqueros* can fill it with water and build a fire under it, I shall empty these sacks into it, and we will let it boil down for several hours. The resultant potion, after it cools, can be rubbed onto the cattle." Lortaldo permitted himself a wry smile. "Of course it will not smell good, and with some of those steers with the huge horns, this may be somewhat dangerous."

"Our *vaqueros* know how to work cattle," John Cooper chuckled, "and they will avoid injury. Besides, it's better to put the cattle—and the *vaqueros*—through a little inconvenience than to lose the entire herd."

Then he turned to Miguel, realizing that whenever the old *capataz* was joined by Raoul Maldones, the former was bound to feel a certain regret at not being the one to give the orders. "Miguel, my good friend, would you assign this task, which you have heard Lortaldo explain, to some of your best *trabajadores*? Let us make as much of this potion as we can, and perhaps we should send the *vaqueros* out for more of these plants so that we will have enough for all the cattle."

"Gladly, *Halcón*! I will give orders right away." Miguel hurried off toward the bunkhouse, his face aglow with pleasure. John Cooper murmured to Raoul: "I think, *mi suegro*, that Miguel is much happier when he is made to feel useful."

"I quite agree. At times, it embarrasses me, my dear John Cooper, to think that he feels I am his superior. He has had far more experience on this *estancia* than I, and after all, what I did in Argentina does not necessarily apply to what is needed here."

"But you have already contributed many valuable ideas from your experience there, *mi suegro*. All the same, I owe Miguel a great deal, and I should not wish ever to hurt him."

"Nor I, John Cooper. Ah, he is coming out of the bunkhouse with four men, and they follow him with respect and attention—that is very good."

"Given Miguel's disposition, indeed it is!" John Cooper

chuckled, as the two men exchanged a knowing, sympathetic look.

Within the hour, a huge kettle had been hung from the sturdiest of the cooking spits, and a fire had been built under it. Lortaldo, who had put on a pair of coarse woolen gloves he had borrowed from one of the *criadas*, began to cut up the sage, garlic, wormwood, and nettles, dropping them into the steaming water. Miguel, Raoul, and John Cooper watched intently, all three of them making faces at the pungent odor. "It smells strong enough to drive away much more than ticks," Miguel sourly commented.

"So long as it does that, we shall all be grateful," was John Cooper's answer.

By sunset, the kettle had cooled enough for the *vaqueros* to fill old waterskins with the vile-smelling compound, and several of them rode off at once toward the western boundary to apply this to as many cattle as they could before it grew too dark to continue work. In the morning, the *vaqueros* would gather still more of the plants, and more kettles would be used to make the potion Lortaldo had concocted.

"Are you sure you don't mind staying a day or two longer, to see how effective this is?" John Cooper anxiously asked the Jicarilla brave.

"Not at all, Señor Baines." He grinned almost boyishly. "Besides, it will give me more time to spend here with my friends and my beloved Epanone, and to enjoy Rosa Lorcas's cooking." Then, his face grave again, he added, "I have prayed to the Great Spirit to let my humble wisdom be of service to you and to cure your cattle. Then I shall feel that I have in some way repaid you for all the kindness you have granted to Epanone and me and our child."

"I shall be in greater debt to you by far, if your medicine accomplishes its purpose," was John Cooper's earnest reply.

When the *vaqueros* returned that night from the western range, all of them reported that it was indeed difficult to get the cattle to remain tranquil while the evil-smelling potion was rubbed onto them. Nevertheless, they had been able to apply the potion to some fifty head of prime cattle, which was an excellent beginning.

The next morning, Andrew Baines volunteered to help the *vaqueros* in their labors, but all the while he had a gloomy look on his face. He had decided to throw himself into his work, so as to help him forget that his beloved Adriana would be in the same city as Diego, while he was left behind at the ranch. True, he had managed a few moments in private with her yesterday, before she had entered the carriage, and she had told him she would write often, and, more important, that Diego would not replace him in her heart. These were reassuring words to hear, yet Andrew—far less sophisticated in his feelings than the fickle Diego de Escobar—was nonetheless rueful over the prospect of giving free rein to his competitor. He could only hope that by July, when the Maldones girls would return, he would be able to resume his interrupted courtship and perhaps at last induce his father and Raoul Maldones to grant permission for their marriage. . . .

By that evening, thanks to the unrelenting efforts of the *vaqueros*—and Andrew Baines—nearly all the cattle had received an application of the potion from neck to flanks, and two days later, Raoul Maldones reported that the men had told him they had found only two more dead animals, these near the southeastern boundary and isolated from the others.

"We shall make extra stocks of this compound, then," John Cooper declared. "It is well to have it always on hand, if any new attacks should break out. But it appears, Lortaldo, that your skill has been our salvation."

"I am glad to have been of some help to you, *Halcón*." Lortaldo shook hands with the tall Texan. "Tomorrow, if all remains well, Epanone and I will depart for Taos, so that she may visit her people. Then I will bring her and the child back here, for this is her home now, *Halcón*. I will see you again at that time, but until then, I will pray for the Great Spirit to watch over you and yours."

"Thank you, Lortaldo. And we shall pray for your family, so that you will return safely to us. *Vaya con Dios, mi hermano!*"

Twenty-two

By the second week of April, Lortaldo and Epanone, with their infant child, were well on the way to Taos, where Epanone's people lived. As Lortaldo had said in his letter to Dr. Malmorain explaining his continued absence, the young apprentice physician would be able, in the pueblo, to observe at first hand the effects of proper medical training upon a large and virtually isolated community. The Indians of Taos had only their old, superstitious shaman to perform rituals of incantation and to concoct nauseous potions when illness stalked the village, as it often did. Despite the stipend John Cooper Baines sent each year to Padre Salvador Madura of Taos to be expended on food, blankets, and clothing for the needy, there were still many who were bitterly impoverished and who had no way to appeal for help, save through the compassionate priest.

In fact, just before Lortaldo and Epanone had left, John Cooper had decided to send two *vaqueros* with them, partly as an escort—albeit the route the party would take was fairly safe—but also to carry to Padre Madura a gift for the poor of the village. This "gift," Lortaldo discovered, was one of the silver ingots John Cooper had found in the second mine; it was camouflaged and carefully wrapped, and placed in one of the *vaqueros*' saddlebags with urgent instruction that it be given to no one save Padre Madura himself.

On a sunny Thursday afternoon, the two *vaqueros*, Lortaldo, and Epanone—with the child strapped to her chest— rode up the winding road to the Jicarilla stronghold, knowing that already the signals of the sentries had told Pastanari and the kindly shaman, Marsimaya, of their approach.

That evening there was a great feast to honor this brave who had gone to New Orleans to study the white-eyes' medicine, and who, not long ago, had been wed here, according to Apache custom. After the feast, Marsimaya and Pastanari talked with Lortaldo at great length over what the young brave had learned in the hospital under Dr. André Malmorain.

"This is all new and strange to me, Lortaldo," Marsimaya declared, "but I see in it much that might be good for our people."

"That is why I willingly went to learn all that the white-eyes could teach me, Marsimaya," Lortaldo responded. "In return, remembering the use of herbs and plants that you taught me when I was a boy, I could repay the blood brother of our tribe, the great *Halcón*." He went on to tell Pastanari and Marsimaya of the ticks that had plagued John Cooper's cattle, and how the potion boiled from the plants had been applied to the cattle and prevented the spread of the deadly fever. "I was glad to be able to pay a small part of the debt I owe *el Halcón*," Lortaldo told them. "But I have yet much to learn, and after I have taken Epanone to Taos to see her people, I shall go back to the *wasichu* medicine man and learn all that he can teach me. It is my wish, *mi jefe*—with your permission, O mighty shaman—to serve my people here once I have acquired the white-eyes' skill."

"This is a good thing," the shaman said with a warm smile. "Yes, I believe there is much we can learn from your *wasichu médico*. But now I shall cast the bones before you, Lortaldo, and welcome you back among us in the old way," the shaman said.

He went back to his wickiup and returned with a pouch that contained the sacred bones, and after a suitable period of chanting, he cast them upon the ground, as the firelight leaped and danced, throwing off weird shadows. He studied the bones a long moment in silence, and then he said: "The signs are good; and yet there is some evil, as there is in all of our endeavors, Lortaldo. You will succeed in becoming a mighty shaman—yes, far mightier than I, because of all your knowledge and your good heart. But I see also that there are enemies who will seek to discredit you, and you will find them even among the people of that village from which Epanone comes."

"I do not fear enemies, Marsimaya. I fear only ignorance and stupidity, for those are the true evils," was Lortaldo's solemn answer.

"We have made the *vaqueros* of our blood brother comfortable for the night," Pastanari told the young Jicarilla, "and tomorrow we shall send several of our own warriors to go with you to Taos." He put out his hand to Lortaldo. "You have come back a leader of our people, and you will do much good for us. Your name will be sung with honor around our campfires, and I believe that what you will achieve will be far more important than what a *jefe* like myself can do. I need not tell you, Lortaldo, that we of the Jicarilla no longer seek the warpath, except to defend ourselves when enemies wish to destroy us. I hope only to be remembered as a *jefe* who brought his people peace rather than as a man who counted many great coups in battle. You, Lortaldo, have found the new way, and I, as chief of the Jicarilla Apache, praise and honor you for this."

Three days later, the *vaqueros*, four escorting Jicarilla Apache braves, Lortaldo, and Epanone rode into Taos and headed for the pueblo village to the east of the central square. Porfirio Ercola, the *vaquero* entrusted with the bar of pure silver, tethered his horse to a post and, removing the wrapped bundle from his saddlebag, entered the church, crossing himself and bending a knee in reverence before the altar. Padre Salvador Madura, standing alone before the altar, his hands clasped in prayer, at last turned and saw the sturdy *vaquero*.

"Good day, my son. Have you come to confessional?"

"Alas no, *padre*." Again the *vaquero* crossed himself— although it was difficult to hold the heavy ingot in one hand. "I have come from the *Hacienda del Halcón* with a gift for your poor from *el señor* Baines, who is known to you as *el Halcón*."

The *padre*'s face became suddenly radiant. "You are most welcome, my son! He has never forgotten us, just as *el*

Señor Dios will never forget him." The priest hurried forward to take the carefully wrapped ingot from the hands of the *vaquero*. "Do you have news of *el Halcón*, my son?"

"He is well, and he asks you to pray for his *esposa*, the señora Dorotéa, and their new little son, James." He went on to relate how John Cooper had recently journeyed to Florida and the island of Cuba to save the two young sons of the late friend of his father-in-law, the señor Maldones. "With the help of *el Señor Dios, padre*," Porfirio concluded, "*el Halcón* and his men brought these *hermanos* back to the *estancia*, and one of them was wed to a young girl who had been rescued from a life of shame."

"Wherever he goes, *el Halcón* casts his shadow always for good," Padre Madura smilingly mused. "Say to him that I shall pray for him and his family, and thank him also for this new and generous gift. Did you come all this long way, my son, to bring this to me?"

"The fact is, *mi padre*," the *vaquero* awkwardly avowed, "*mi compañero* and I were ordered to escort the *indio*, Lortaldo, and his *esposa*, Epanone, first to the stronghold and then on to Taos, for Epanone wishes to visit the people of her village."

"Yes, yes, how well I remember that sweet girl! I was so pleased to hear that she had married and made a good life for herself away from the poverty here. You bring me heartwarming news, my son. For you, too, and your companion, I shall pray. Tell the señor Baines that all goes well here in Taos. We keep the faith, and the *alcalde mayor* is fearful of the wrath of Him Who punishes the unrepentant sinner."

"I shall tell *el Halcón* all that you have said to me, *padre*. Perhaps—no, you are busy, and it is not right for me to confess—"

"One should always confess one's sins, my son, for one never knows when one may be taken in the act of committing them, without the opportunity to renounce evil and so save one's immortal soul. Come." He gave the *vaquero* a gentle smile as he urged him toward one of the confessional booths. "It will not take long, for I do not think your sins are many, my son."

*   *   *

Palvarde, spokesman of the Pueblo Indians, welcomed Epanone and Lortaldo into his *jacal*. "My daughter," he said to her, "it is good to see you again and to know that you have not forgotten the place of your birth and your people. And you, Lortaldo," he said, extending his hand to the sturdy young Jicarilla, "I bid you welcome, and I thank you for this mark of respect that you show in returning to us." His eyes strayed to the child Epanone was holding, a smile transforming his serious features.

"Palvarde, I am grateful for your welcome and the kindness you show my wife," Lortaldo replied, as they all sat cross-legged around the fire. "It was her desire to visit here, with the child, and until now I have been in New Orleans for many moons, learning from a white-eyes *médico* the ways in which the *wasichu* heal their sick."

"That is a fine thing, Lortaldo. Here, abandoned in our village and despised by the *alcalde*—who, fortunately for us, and thanks to the vigilance of the blessed Padre Madura, has refrained from more outrages against our people—we depend on the wisdom of our old shaman, Pogramondi. He, as did his father before him, serves as the *médico* of our village."

"I do not scorn the old ways, Palvarde, understand me," Lortaldo earnestly replied. "But under the fine *wasichu médico* with whom I have studied, I have learned much that can be helpful in the treatment of the sick. He has taught me that it is not necessarily the will of the gods that weakens a strong man with an illness that otherwise seems to have no reason or purpose. I speak with no intent to blaspheme the all-knowing Great Spirit, but you see, Palvarde, this *wasichu*, Dr. Malmorain, has shown me that illness can come from poor food or unclean living quarters, or again, the bite of insects. In New Orleans, there is a hospital where fevers are treated, and the lives of many who are taken ill by the fever are saved through the methods the white-eyes use."

"My mind is not closed to what we can learn from the *wasichu*," Palvarde solemnly admitted. "Yet there are many who would resist new ways, for you know well that we are a people to whom customs and traditions are sacred; and there are also those among us, Lortaldo, who will say that the white-eyes cannot know the beliefs of the *indios* who were here long before them and who have survived through all the oppressions the *wasichu* have forced upon them.''

''But does not the Great Spirit tell us that understanding and tolerance will erase fear and hatred, and that it is meant for all of us to be brothers?'' Lortaldo countered.

Palvarde put his hand on Lortaldo's shoulder and nodded. ''I believe this because I am not yet so old that my mind has become closed to the hope that one day the *indio* and the *wasichu* may come together in understanding. But I warn you, not many among us have this view. I fear you may see this when you talk with Pogramondi, but . . .'' He shrugged his shoulders. ''Perhaps he will listen to what you have learned about healing the sick.'' His face was momentarily shadowed, and he shook his head with a doleful sigh. ''In the past few moons, several of the old squaws and the old men have taken to their beds, sung their death songs, and gone to their ancestors in the sky. Pogramondi did all he could to halt their departure, but he said that it was the will of the Great Spirit that their souls be taken into the sky and that even his skill could not change that which was decreed. But there have also been young children who took sick without apparent reason and who died a few days later, and so I myself cannot tell you why this is, or if it is decreed. Come now, we shall eat—then you can share your ideas with Pogramondi, and perhaps our village will benefit from the meeting of the two of you.''

After they had shared a humble meal, Palvarde led Lortaldo toward the *jacal* of the old shaman, and hearing the call of the village spokesman, Pogramondi emerged. He was white-haired, his shoulders stooped, his face painted black and ocher. He wore a necklace made from the bones of antelope, rabbit, and squirrel, and from the center of which hung the skull of a rattlesnake. In his right hand he held a crooked staff, the twisted branch of a mesquite bush, painted with cryptic symbols.

''I come at your call, Palvarde,'' he said in a reedy

voice, his eyes turning to contemplate Lortaldo. "What do you seek of me?"

"You will remember Lortaldo, who wed Epanone here in this village. They have returned to us because it was her wish to visit her people and to have you, our shaman, meet with this Jicarilla who has gone to New Orleans to learn the lore of the *wasichu médico* in the treatment of the sick," Palvarde responded.

"What can the *wasichu* teach us of such matters?" Pogramondi scornfully answered. His bony face was set in a contemptuous sneer. "No *indio* who is true to his people and their teachings would let himself be guided by the *wasichu,* who have, since they set foot upon this land, brought nothing but treachery and poverty to us—and not only to those of our village, Palvarde!"

"I would not presume to rebuke you, Pogramondi," Palvarde evenly responded, "but I would remind you that you forget the good *wasichu* friend of our village, the señor John Cooper Baines, who, as a friend of Padre Madura, has sent many gifts of food and clothing to our people. Surely you must remember that we are far better off now than before that man, blood brother to the Jicarilla of whose tribe Lortaldo is, saw our wretchedness and resolved to help us."

"I have not forgotten that, Palvarde," the shaman grumbled, "but I say that no *wasichu* helps the *indios* without a reason. We do not yet know what price this Señor Baines of yours will demand for his acts of kindness toward us."

"That is unworthy!" Lortaldo vehemently burst out, but Palvarde shook his head and motioned for the young brave to be silent. In turn, he said to the shaman, "We do not come together this day to talk of gifts or prices, Pogramondi. I would ask only that you listen to Lortaldo as he tells what ways he has learned for helping the sick to cast off their malady."

"Ha! I have no need to hear from his lips, or yours either, Palvarde, what a *wasichu* may have taught him. Look you, Jicarilla," he turned and, in a contemptuous tone, addressed Lortaldo. "There is an old woman who is about to join her ancestors, and she lies in her bed wasted with fever. Come with me, and I will show you how I can cure her with my magic powers, which are greater than any *wasichu* can evoke against the evil spirits that struck her down!"

Humbly, Lortaldo replied, "I would eagerly watch you demonstrate your skill, O Pogramondi."

"I rejoice that a stripling still knows how to show respect for his elders," the shaman stiffly rejoined and, with great dignity, walked toward one of the shabbiest little huts at the southeastern edge of the village.

Lortaldo and Palvarde waited outside while the shaman entered the hut and stooped over the straw pallet on which an old, emaciated woman lay, breathing heavily. Beside her, her face streaked with tears, stood her granddaughter, a girl of about fifteen. The shaman gestured that she was to leave the *jacal*, and she stepped outside and stood near the embers of the cooking fire, across from where Lortaldo and Palvarde were waiting.

After a moment, Pogramondi emerged from the *jacal* and haughtily proclaimed, "We must prepare smoke to drive out the evil spirits." He turned to the granddaughter. "Girl, bring wood and build up the fire swiftly, if you wish her to draw breath when the sun next rises into the heavens."

When this was done, Pogramondi squatted, murmuring incantations while taking from his belt a pouch containing a grayish powder. This he liberally sprinkled upon the fire, and billowing, acrid smoke rose at once, its tendrils edging into the opening of the *jacal*, soon filling it with the dense fumes. They could hear the old woman coughing and gasping a few unintelligible words, and Pogramondi triumphantly turned to Lortaldo and declared, "The soul within her fights the evil spirits, and only the Giver of Breath knows whether she has strength enough to withstand them, for they are very powerful."

"More so than your magic, O shaman?" Lortaldo innocently asked with an ingenuous look.

The old shaman glared at him and then, turning his back on Lortaldo, resumed his incantations. A few moments later, he began to do a curious hopping dance, taking his necklace in both hands and rattling the bones, as his lips moved in the mystic prayers of the ritual.

Inside the hut, the old woman's coughing continued, until it seemed that she was greatly weakened. Lortaldo groaned and looked in appeal to Palvarde, who rolled his eyes expressively and shrugged, indicating that he could not interfere with the shaman. Finally, when the dancing and chanting ended, Lortaldo asked, "May I be permitted to see this woman, Palvarde? And you, Pogramondi, have I your permission?"

"Do as you wish," the shaman scornfully answered. "But I warn you, if you bring death upon her, it will be of your doing, not of mine."

Lortaldo inclined his head, saying simply, "I will examine her now, since you have given permission."

He entered the hut and squatted down before the old woman, after first having vigorously waved his arms to dispel the acrid smoke. The old woman feebly tried to lift her head, her eyes seeking his young, earnest face, and she tried to speak.

"No, Grandmother, rest. I wish to look at you and to see what causes you such pain. I will be gentle with you, do not fear."

She watched him, fearful and yet hopeful, as he took her pulse, then touched her forehead and cheeks and throat with his strong but gentle fingers. He observed that she moved her left arm, but that her right seemed motionless. He took hold of the right wrist and slightly lifted it. At once, a feeble little cry escaped her, and her body shuddered.

"Do you not hear?" Pogramondi angrily demanded of Palvarde outside the hut. "He already causes her pain, and yet he can do nothing to remedy it. I should not have given him permission!"

"But if your powers are greater, Pogramondi," Palvarde slyly argued, "what he does will have no effect upon her. And you have granted him permission, remember."

"Very well," the shaman grudgingly assented. "But I call you to witness that, if she is summoned to her ancestors, it was not of my doing."

"This is understood, O Pogramondi," Palvarde said with a nod.

Very carefully, Lortaldo began to touch the old woman's right arm with the median and forefingers of both hands to determine where it pained her most. As he reached the upper arm, she winced and groaned, and tried to struggle. "Gently, Grandmother, I think I know what pains you. It is under the arm, is it not?"

She feebly nodded, her eyes rolling eloquently, and her face expressed both pain and fear.

Carefully, he opened her buckskin jacket and bared the arm. At once, his eyes fell upon a purplish swelling in her armpit, a round protuberance that he knew to be a boil. It had become infected, and this was what had brought about her fever. Back in New Orleans, Dr. Malmorain had showed him a case of gangrene and how a leg had had to be amputated to save the patient's life. Lortaldo feared that the poison of this infection, as well, might have spread too far, yet there was still one remedy that might work.

He smiled at her reassuringly and said in his most soothing tone, "Grandmother, I have found the evil spirit that is hurting you. For me to vanquish it, there will be momentary pain—but I promise that you will feel stronger once it is done. If it is not done, you will surely go to your ancestors. And your granddaughter will be lost without you. Give me permission to cause you this little pain, that I may try to save your life for her."

She searched his face with rheumy eyes and then feebly nodded.

He rose quickly and went out of the *jacal*. "She has a boil, and I must lance it," he explained. "Palvarde, I need a sharp knife, and it must be held in the fire so that the tip is seared. It will be cleansed thus, and when I touch the flesh, there will be no sickness from it."

"What nonsense is this?" Pogramondi grumbled. "Do you, the spokesman of our tribe, allow this upstart to send this woman's spirit into the skies before it is yet time as willed by the Giver of Breath?"

"Once again, O shaman," Palvarde placatingly replied, "it is known that your powers are great. Why, then, should you fear what this Jicarilla does? He is a kind, gentle man, and I am sure that he will not harm her."

"You speak as the elder of the village, and I must listen. But my heart is not in this, let it be known." The shaman turned his back, folded his arms, and closed his eyes, indicating that he had washed his hands of the affair.

While Lortaldo sent the old woman's granddaughter to fetch Epanone, Palvarde went to a nearby hut where a young brave and his squaw were eating their noonday meal. He asked the brave for the use of his knife, which was known to be the sharpest in the village, then took it back to the old lady's hut, where he held the blade in the flames for a moment. Handing the knife to Lortaldo, he said, "My prayers are with you, my son. It would not be well if what you are about to do hastens her end," he added in a voice too low for the indignant shaman to hear.

"It will not endanger her life, Palvarde. Epanone—" he said as his wife appeared, "come help me. I must lance a boil on the old woman who lives in this hut, but first I need you to wash the infected area, which is under her right arm. Did you bring my pouch of cinchona bark and the other herbs that are used for poultices?"

"Yes, I have them here," Epanone replied.

At Lortaldo's direction, the granddaughter fetched an iron pot filled with water and heated it over the fire. This done, Epanone took a strip of clean cloth and, dipping it into the water, went into the *jacal* to cleanse the area around the boil.

"Now," Lortaldo said, joining his wife, "hold her firmly, and assure her the pain will be only for a moment, and that she will be better."

Epanone obediently grasped the woman at the collar-bone, soothingly telling her that her discomfort would ease, once the first sharp pain had come. Even as she spoke, Lortaldo swiftly lanced the boil. There was a spurt of yellowish and purplish matter, and the old woman uttered a scream, at which Pogramondi, outside, turned and hissed, "Do you not hear that, Palvarde? The evil spirits are rejoicing that this *wasichu* is allowed to meddle!"

"Now the infected matter is out, and we shall cleanse the wound again and apply a poultice," Lortaldo told his wife. The old woman lay back, her eyes closed, while fitful tremors assailed her frail body. As Epanone wiped the wound clean, Lortaldo took herbs from his leather pouch and wrapped them in another strip of cloth, then pressed this poultice against the cleansed and open wound. The swelling had gone down, and the flesh around the edges was freed of the suppurated matter.

Next he took a longer strip of cloth and wound it around the old woman's upper torso, to hold the poultice in place. "Grandmother, for a time you must keep this bandage from moving, so that the herbs will send their medicine into the wound. It will not be long, and Epanone will make you tea with the cinchona bark, which will take down your fever. The worst of it is over now, trust me."

"Yes, my son—already I feel better. May the Great Spirit bless you for easing my pain," the old woman faintly gasped.

Soon Epanone had brewed tea from a large piece of the cinchona bark, and she held a cup of it to the old woman's lips and bade her drink as much as she could. "Now you must sleep, Grandmother," Lortaldo told her. "And when you waken, you will be refreshed."

Lortaldo and Epanone emerged from the *jacal* to find only Palvarde and the granddaughter waiting for them. "The shaman has gone back to his *tipi*," Palvarde said with a rueful smile. "He does not wish to speak to you again. And he said that if the old woman dies, you should nevermore be allowed to set foot in our village."

"If she does, Palvarde, I will accept that judgment. But I do not think she will die. We shall wait and see," was Lortaldo's calm answer.

During the next three days, Epanone nursed the old woman, feeding her nourishing broth, putting on fresh poultices, and giving her more tea from the cinchona bark. And by the evening of the third day, the granddaughter ran out of the *jacal,* her eyes shining as she cried out, "*Mi abuela* is well again! She sits up and she asks for food!"

The villagers who heard her outcry murmured among themselves, and Pogramondi, who had come out of his tipi for a moment, turned and went back, his face black as a raincloud.

That evening, at a feast, Palvarde said to Lortaldo, "You have proved that what you learned from the *wasichu* can be of great help to our people. I ask you to stay here and serve us as *médico*. You have respect for the old ways as does Pogramondi, but you have something new, and you have your youth and skill."

"Thank you, Palvarde, but I am Jicarilla, and when I have finished my studies in New Orleans, it will be to the stronghold of my people that I shall return as *médico*. But as elder of this village, it is for you to find someone who understands that incantations and dancing alone cannot prolong life."

"I have already learned this lesson. Perhaps Padre Madura will find us a *médico*, then. And you, Epanone, you will return with your man?"

"Yes, Palvarde. We shall leave tomorrow, I to go back to the *estancia* of Señor Baines, and Lortaldo to New Orleans to resume his studies. But perhaps—" She broke off, her eyes shyly downcast.

"What she wants to say," Lortaldo added with a smile, "is that the Jicarilla stronghold is not far from here, and that when we go to live there, she will persuade me to visit Taos very often, or else she will suffer from the dreaded disease called homesickness."

Epanone blushed so deeply at these words that Palvarde could not help but smile, knowing that Lortaldo had spoken the truth.

Twenty-three

The sun was blazingly hot on this May midafternoon. Miguel Sandarbal and Raoul Maldones were standing near the arched gateway to the *Hacienda del Halcón*, discussing the excellent weather for crops and graze, and remarking on the health of the herd since Lortaldo's successful halting of the spread of cattle ticks. Soon the first drive of the year would begin, and although it would be relatively small—two hundred head to be delivered to the coast for loading on the *New Venture*—more orders for later in the year had come in from Fabien Mallard, and business had never looked better.

Both Miguel and Raoul looked up as they heard the sound of a horse's hooves coming at a trot down the road leading to the great gate. They stared in bewilderment, for astride a spirited sorrel mare was a stocky, black-bearded man in his middle thirties, wearing the garish uniform and insignia of a colonel in the Mexican army.

"*¡Qué diablo!*" Miguel muttered to John Cooper's Argentine father-in-law. "What's a *coronel* of Mexican troops doing here, riding up alone as if he were paying a social call?"

"We can find out by asking, Miguel," Raoul offered, then, in fluent Spanish, hailed the visitor as the man reined his mount to a halt. "*Bienvenido, mi coronel.*"

"*Gracias, amigo,*" the stranger replied. "Permit me to introduce myself. I am *Coronel* Luis Dominguez, attached to His Excellency, General Santa Anna. I have come here with a letter from *el general* for the señor John Cooper

Baines. May I be permitted to present it to him personally, since these are the instructions of my superior officer?''

"What devilment is this?'' Miguel muttered under his breath to Raoul. "A letter from Santa Anna, no less! I wonder what this misbegotten son of an ape has up his sleeve.'' Aloud, he said as he doffed his *sombrero* and made an ironic little inclination of his head, "I will inform the *hacienda* of your arrival, *mi coronel*. If you will be good enough to ride straight ahead to the courtyard, a *trabajador* will take your horse.''

"I thank you for your courtesy, señor. I have come a long distance—all the way from Veracruz. The señor Baines is here, I take it?''

"He is,'' Miguel tersely responded.

Colonel Dominguez controlled his prancing mare with a savage tug on the reins; then, digging his heels into its belly, he urged it at a gallop toward the courtyard. Miguel stared after the officer, then shook his head. "I'm as curious as an old woman to know what's in that letter, Raoul.''

"As am I, Miguel. Let's walk back to the *hacienda*. It will do no harm to let this officer cool his heels until we can tell Señor Baines of his arrival.''

The two men covered the short distance to the *hacienda* while the brilliantly uniformed officer halted his mare in the courtyard and dismounted, looking arrogantly about for a *trabajador* to take the reins and quarter the mare. Catching sight of three *vaqueros* near the corral, Miguel put two fingers to his lips and emitted a shrill whistle to catch their attention, then gestured with his thumb toward the officer. One of the *vaqueros* hastened up to the colonel and, doffing his *sombrero*, took the reins.

"It is a fine mare—be careful with her, *hombre*,'' the bearded, stocky officer growled.

From his saddlebags he now removed a leather case, holding it in both hands as if it were a sacred relic, while Miguel and Raoul took their time catching up with him.

"You do not seem to understand, señores,'' the officer said with a frown as they approached, "that I am the emissary of His Excellency Brigadier General Antonio López de

Santa Anna. The news I bring is of great importance not only to the señor Baines but also to all *tejanos*."

"I am surprised, *mi coronel*"—Miguel could not hold back a sarcastic gibe—"that, being Mexican, you are not familiar with the national proverb, which suggests that *mañana* is as good a time as any. The señor Baines will not run away, I assure you."

"How dare you speak to me like that!" Colonel Dominguez's face hardened, and he haughtily drew himself up. Then, remembering his mission, he shrugged and said blandly, "Forgive me. It is only that I have been on horseback for long weeks to reach here, and I am not the most patient man in the world."

"We shall notify him of your presence," Raoul offered.

John Cooper had spent most of the morning hunting with Maja and Fuerte, wishing to train them to replace their dead sire, Yankee, whose loss he still deeply mourned. Then, after the *comida*, he had ridden out to the western boundary to make a personal inspection of the herds there, after which he had returned to the *hacienda* for a siesta, which Dorotéa had shared with him.

He was just emerging from his bedchamber when he encountered Miguel and Raoul in the hallway.

"John Cooper, you may think you are still asleep and dreaming, when I tell you what has just happened," his father-in-law declared.

"I guess I could stand a surprise, Raoul—what is the news?"

"Well, *mi hijo*," Raoul began, "Miguel and I were out by the main gate, and—"

Unable to contain himself any longer, Miguel blurted out, "It's a Mexican officer, *Halcón*! A *coronel*, no less, who says he has a letter to you from Santa Anna!"

For a moment, John Cooper stared at both men in incredulous surprise. "A letter from Santa Anna himself?"

Both men nodded.

"And no other soldiers accompanied this officer?" he asked.

Raoul shook his head. "He was alone and insisted he see you at once. He said he has come all the way from

Veracruz, and that his mission is of great importance. Indeed, he said it was not only of importance to you, but to all Texans.''

"Where Santa Anna is concerned, I'm sure it concerns all Texans. Very well. Let me throw some cold water on my face, while you take him to the study beside the chapel. Give him some wine and some of Rosa's cakes and make him comfortable. I'll be there quickly," John Cooper directed.

As John Cooper, clad in his usual buckskins, entered the study, Colonel Luis Dominguez rose from his chair and stood stiffly at attention. Miguel Sandarbal and Raoul Maldones, at their ease on a sofa, exchanged an amused look.

"You are Señor John Cooper Baines?"

"That's right. Sit down, please, Colonel," John Cooper affably responded.

"Gracias." The officer resumed his seat. "I have been instructed by my superior, His Excellency Brigadier General Antonio López de Santa Anna, to bring you this letter, which he himself has written in his own hand.''

"I'm greatly honored. And why would General Santa Anna single me out for so much attention?" John Cooper smilingly asked.

The bearded, stocky officer's face tightened with displeasure as he replied, with a note of irritation in his voice, "Señor Baines, I ask you to respect His Excellency, as he respects you. But you will see for yourself, once you read the letter.''

"Very well, then, I'll read it."

The officer opened the leather case and drew out three vellum sheets, the last of which displayed Santa Anna's own wax seal, complete with military insignia and crest. He got up and handed the sheets to John Cooper, then sat back down.

"Gracias. You have no objection if I read it aloud to these two gentlemen, *coronel*?" John Cooper asked. "Allow me to introduce them to you—both act as *capataz* here, the one closer to you being Miguel Sandarbal, and the other my esteemed *suegro*, Raoul Maldones."

"Señores." Colonel Dominguez gave each man a curt nod and remained in his chair.

John Cooper leaned against the desk and considered the three closely written sheets. "Now, then, let's see what's on Santa Anna's mind." The tall Texan eyed the first sheet, cleared his throat, and read aloud:

By my hand, at the villa of Mango de Clavo, this 20th day of April, 1828.
To Señor John Cooper Baines:

This letter will introduce to you my personal emissary, *Coronel* Luis Dominguez. I have chosen him to act as my courier because of the importance of the occasion, and you will understand the reason for his presence, rather than that of an ordinary courier, after you have read the proposal I now set before you.

Señor Baines, it has always been true in history that men of extraordinary ability and talents have been chosen by destiny to act as leaders, and it is given to these leaders to decide the future of their people. Consider the case of Napoleon Bonaparte, the obscure Corsican corporal who became emperor of the French and whose military exploits, though still fresh in our minds, have already assured him immortality. It is such men who decide the destinies of their people, whether it be war and glory, or peace and honor.

Humbly, I submit to you that I myself—as a man who rose from fledgling cadet to brigadier general through personal valor and, more importantly, dedication to the people of Mexico—I am one of those leaders chosen by history.

Here John Cooper paused and glanced at Raoul and Miguel, both of whom were trying their best not to look amused. The Texan cleared his throat again and continued:

"And you, Señor Baines, are known to me as a leader of the *americanos*, more specifically of the *tejanos* who have come to settle in the province of Coahuila, of which the so-called Texas Territory is a part. Thus, we are rivals, and you assuredly speak for your people as I for mine. And this is why I appeal to you.

Together, we can do much good for our peoples. It is true that I had indirectly set myself up against you in my dedicated attempt to recover for my country that treasure of silver which destiny chose you to discover, but which, I submit to you in all fairness and candor, was discovered upon Mexican territory. Thus, we have had our differences, but my letter to you seeks amicably to put an end to all such enmity. This, then, is the heart of my proposal:

I propose that you and I meet to discuss a way to end our dispute over the silver, and to make a pact in which I shall formally agree to cease all harassment of American settlers for all time to come, in exchange for a stipulated portion of this silver. I am apprised by the most learned *abogados* of our country that Mexico has first claim to this silver, since you found the forgotten ingots in caves of mountains located in *Nuevo Méjico*. I hasten to assure you, however, Señor Baines, that the purpose of this meeting is not to argue over legal technicalities. You and I, as men of honor, can strike to the heart of the problem and agree upon a solution felicitous to all concerned.

By the time this letter reaches you, I shall be on my way to the meeting place I propose for our conclave, in the town of Piedras Negras. As a guarantee of my good faith—and, if you are willing to extend to him your hospitality—I propose that Colonel Luis Dominguez remain at your *estancia* as a hostage. Furthermore, you may bring with you whomever you wish and as many escorts as you wish to ensure your own safety, if you should have the least doubt as to the honesty of my intentions.

And finally, Señor Baines, I have already sent

word to high-ranking officials of the government in Mexico City that I have invited you to meet with me at Piedras Negras. You will see from this that there can be no possible trickery, since the government has been officially notified of our proposed conference.

It is my prayer for the good of both our nations that you will accept my proposal. If you decline it and return the person of my emissary, I must warn you, in all candor, that the Mexican government will take it as a sign that you endorse the behavior of many rebellious *americanos* in the settlements; I shall then have no power to control what steps the government may wish to take against them or you. That is why I urge you, in the name of humanity, to meet with me at Piedras Negras.

Rest assured of my esteem and admiration for you, both as a man and as a leader. I herewith sign my hand and seal,

General Antonio López de Santa Anna.''

Miguel Sandarbal uttered a low whistle of amazement and eyed Raoul Maldones. The latter spoke up: "Will you go to this meeting, *mi yerno*?"

John Cooper rose from the desk, his forehead furrowed in thought. *Coronel* Luis Dominguez, his own face impassive, watched the Texan closely.

"It's true I've had my differences with Santa Anna, and just as true that—as he now admits—he was behind the attempts to grab the silver—"

"I protest, Señor Baines!" the officer indignantly interrupted. "You imply that His Excellency is a thief. As the letter said, the silver you found in those mines was situated in Mexican territory. When our republic declared its independence from Spain, we formally assumed all rights of our predecessors, and although it is true that the silver was mined by the Spaniards and the *indios*, the fact remains that in no way could the treasure belong to the *americanos*. No,

Señor Baines, you must not impute to His Excellency such a crime. On the contrary—''

Colonel Dominguez was red-faced with anger, and finally John Cooper cut him off. ''I'll not argue with you, *mi coronel*. My feeling is that people can juggle words as they please to shift their meaning. All right, then—I won't say that Santa Anna tried to steal the silver, if that's what you think I mean.'' He paused a moment, then addressed Miguel and Raoul. ''What happened in the past, like Cortizo's kidnapping of Dorotéa, and Colonel López's murder of my wife Catarina, cannot be forgotten. But just as Santa Anna says here, there is a chance that the two of us can come to some understanding that will help the settlers. That's important—maybe more important than thinking about what's already happened. Besides, Colonel Dominguez stays here as a hostage, and I can take armed *vaqueros* with me to this meeting. And for what it's worth, Santa Anna says he's letting the people in Mexico City know about the meeting. I've got to weigh what's more important in the long run for all of us. That's why I'm rather inclined to accept Santa Anna's proposal.''

''I think, Señor Baines,'' Colonel Dominguez quickly spoke up, ''you will find you have made a very wise decision.''

''I haven't agreed to anything yet,'' John Cooper replied. ''And if I were you, I wouldn't be in such a hurry to make myself a hostage. If you tried to escape from the Double H Ranch, I think Raoul and Miguel here might interpret it as a sign that what your master says in this letter isn't to be believed. And my *vaqueros* are experts at rounding up strays, *coronel*.''

Once again, the stocky, bearded officer stiffened and bristled with indignation. ''Take care, Señor Baines—again you cast slurs upon me and upon His Excellency! He has taken me into his confidence, and I assure you that everything he promises in this letter is exactly as set forth, so there would be no reason for me to try to escape. His Excellency has absolutely no desire to shed the blood of the innocent.''

There was a long silence, and finally John Cooper said, ''Neither do I, *coronel*. And that's exactly why I'm going to take him up on his offer and go to Piedras Negras.''

At these words, Colonel Dominguez rose to his feet, an ingratiating smile transforming his bearded face. "I congratulate you, Señor Baines. You have made a sensible decision. Between men of honor, much can be achieved without recourse to military action. And now, since you have accepted the offer of *el generalísimo*, there remains the formality of my surrendering to you, so that I may remain your hostage until your return from Piedras Negras. However, as you can see, I have not worn a sword, so—"

"That doesn't matter," John Cooper interrupted, amused by this flowery little speech. "If you will give me your word of honor as an officer not to try to escape or attempt any hostile act against any person on this *estancia*, I'll have you put up comfortably, and you'll be well fed, for we've one of the finest *cocineras* in this part of the country."

"You are most gracious, Señor Baines. But then, both *el libertador* and myself had expected nothing less."

"I'm not so sure about that," John Cooper said, then quickly added, before Dominguez could object, "How far would you say Piedras Negras is from this *estancia, coronel*?"

"Not more than eighty miles, Señor Baines—a leisurely three-day journey, at most. By that time, *el general* Santa Anna will be there to greet you."

"Good—then I'll make plans to leave tomorrow. And now, Miguel, Raoul—perhaps we should see about quarters for Colonel Dominguez. I have someone in mind whose company the colonel might find very edifying."

Twenty-four

As it turned out, the person whom John Cooper had in mind to watch over Colonel Luis Dominguez was none other than Ramón Santoriaga, himself a former aide to Santa Anna and now the man in charge of the defense of the Double H Ranch.

"He is a Mexican?" Dominguez said with a disbelieving tone when John Cooper told him of his decision. "And he became a *gringo*? I find that strange. But I am now your hostage, and I shall adhere to whatever terms you set for my sojourn here."

"Fine. Come along, then, and I'll introduce you to Ramón Santoriaga. The two of you are of equal rank, for he was a colonel under Santa Anna too," John Cooper nonchalantly remarked.

A flush of anger darkened Dominguez's bearded face as he followed the tall Texan, Miguel Sandarbal, and Raoul Maldones toward the house where Ramón lived with his family.

Ramón, having already heard of the arrival of the strange courier, and half expecting a visit from John Cooper, saw the four men approaching and came out to meet them. His eyes widened with surprise, however, to see a colonel in full military dress, and he looked wonderingly at John Cooper for an explanation.

"Ramón, this is Colonel Luis Dominguez, who has been sent here by General Santa Anna with a letter asking me to parley with him at Piedras Negras," John Cooper explained. "And since Santa Anna has offered the colonel here as a hostage, I've agreed to the meeting. I thought that there might be an extra room in your house where he could stay, and I don't know of a better and more vigilant guard."

The Mexican officer gave Ramón a look of thinly veiled contempt as he bowed stiffly and said, "I am *a sus órdenes,* Colonel Santoriaga. I am told that you once held my very own rank under *el libertador.*"

"That's true, *coronel,*" Ramón replied. "But I yielded to the stronger appeal of living peacefully with my family and friends here on this ranch. I am now at the service of these good people, in the event they should be attacked by *los indios* or *soldados.*"

"I cannot speak for *los indios,* Señor Santoriaga" —Dominguez sarcastically emphasized the civilian title—"but I do not believe that soldiers would seek to attack this *estancia* without reason. If, of course, revolt against my country's government was being fomented, then naturally the army would be sent in to suppress it. But if there is no revolt here, then you surely have nothing to fear."

"A most logical-sounding statement, *coronel,*" Ramón responded with the utmost seriousness. "Yet in Mexico, what the government wants and what the army does are often two different things, and it is here that your logic falls apart."

"I will not discuss politics or military issues with you, Señor Santoriaga!" the officer bristled. "If you will kindly take me to my room, I shall give you as little trouble as possible!"

"*A sus órdenes, coronel.*" Ramón Santoriaga bowed with impeccable politeness and, winking slyly at John Cooper, led the fuming officer into the house and to a room at the back.

Miguel Sandarbal clapped his thigh and burst into laughter. "I could hardly keep a straight face—what a conceited coxcomb that man is! And did you hear, *mis compañeros,* how our good friend Ramón put him in his place? There's no love lost between those two, I can tell you."

John Cooper nodded and put his arms around both Miguel and Raoul's shoulders. "Now I must ask you both to help me choose the best marksmen and horsemen among our *vaqueros.* I'll ride with twenty-five."

"Your son Andrew will sulk if he isn't allowed to go along," old Miguel declared.

"And Enrique and Benito Duvaldo have been getting restless, I've noticed," Raoul put in.

John Cooper shook his head. "Andrew can sulk to his heart's content, but he's not going, and neither are the Duvaldo brothers. They've been through hardship enough, and you're forgetting, Raoul, that Enrique was just married a short time ago. No, twenty-five good men riding with me will be all I'll need."

"I don't trust that *coronel*," Miguel grumbled.

"He's only one man, and Ramón will watch over him— well, like a hawk, to coin a phrase." John Cooper gave a boyish grin. "To tell you the truth, I don't trust Santa Anna all the way, either, but I'll be armed, and so will my men, and we'll be ready for any tricks. And remember, the silver he wants is safely tucked away in a New Orleans bank vault. I'd have to send a letter to my factor or Eugene Beaubien, president of the bank, to authorize release of any of it. If Santa Anna were to kill me, he'd never get a cent. No, I think I'll take my chances. It's worth the gamble, if only to get him to agree to stop bothering the settlements. I've told you I had a hunch war was coming, but maybe if Santa Anna and I can come to terms, we can postpone that date by a few years. By then Texas will have more settlers and more men to fight, if they have to."

Raoul Maldones reflectively nodded. "When you speak like that, *mi yerno*, I almost wish you had been born on the *pampas* and been a leader against the *porteños*. If there had been men like you, John Cooper, I would not today be in exile, and my dear friend Heitor Duvaldo would not be dead. Allow me to go with you, at least."

"No, Raoul." John Cooper emphatically shook his head. "Only I shall go, so that no member of my family or anyone else essential to the well-being of this ranch will be involved with Santa Anna. It's enough risk that I have to endanger twenty-five *vaqueros*—though I don't doubt there will be enough volunteers. But let's go to the bunkhouse and find out."

As soon as John Cooper had told the assembled *vaqueros* of his plan to ride to Piedras Negras the next day, and his reason for accepting Santa Anna's offer for this meeting, the bunkhouse resounded with clamorous cries, each man insisting that he accompany *el Halcón*.

John Cooper held up both hands for silence. "*Gracias, hombres.* I shall take just twenty-five, and Miguel here, who has known you longer than Raoul, will help select the volunteers. I hope there will be no danger, but just in case, every man who rides with me should be a good shot with a rifle. For the same reason, I would prefer men who have no families, so that if anything should happen, God forbid, we won't be leaving widows and orphans behind us."

Esteban Morales, the assistant *capataz*, who had been talking to the *vaqueros* when John Cooper and Raoul had entered, now exclaimed, "*Halcón,* you saved the life of my son Bernardo once; I owe you this debt, and I am not afraid to go with you."

"No, Esteban, but I'm grateful for the offer. Concepción and your children need you, and so does the Double H Ranch. As I say, I don't want men with families, and for more reasons than I've already mentioned. If it comes to a showdown, men with women and children might be more cautious than they should be. Now, Miguel, you know these men well, and I'll leave it to you to choose the twenty-five who'll ride with me tomorrow morning to Piedras Negras."

At supper that evening, Carlos de Escobar lifted his glass of wine and toasted *el Halcón*. "I wish I were going with you, *mi compadre,* but you know how little Santa Anna thinks of me ever since I left his service. And then besides, I have to be best man for Ferdinand de Lloradier. You know, two days from now he's going to marry that sweet Miranda. He's finally been able to convince her that just because she's the daughter of a *vaquero,* she shouldn't think herself unworthy of him."

"I'm happy to hear that, Carlos," John Cooper said. "I'm sorry I can't be here for the wedding, but you can convey my warmest wishes to the bride and groom. And, as a token of my pleasure over their marriage, tell Ferdinand that, as a wedding present, I'm giving him two dozen head of our best cattle. Whatever profits will accrue from these—and Raoul Maldones will keep a record of it—will be his. You might call it a dowry for Miranda, if you like."

"That is indeed generous, *mi hermano*," Carlos smilingly replied, and Teresa, sitting beside him, added, "You never fail to think of others, John Cooper. But this time, because all of us love you so, look out for yourself and come back to us safely. I'll pray for that."

"Thank you, dear Teresa. You know, now that I've had a chance to think about it, I rather look forward to meeting with Santa Anna. All this time he's remained behind the scenes, hatching conspiracies because he's greedy for that silver. Now it will be out in the open, and I'll be able to see exactly what's on his mind. And he'll know mine, for a change. It should be a most interesting meeting."

That night, in their bedchamber, Dorotéa said her own farewell to her blond husband. "Of course, I worry about you, *mi corazón*. But I know deep in my heart that you'll return unharmed. If you could survive the dangers of getting my father out of prison and escaping from Buenos Aires, you'll come back to me again."

"I plan to, my darling." He held her close and, refraining from giving voice to his own anxieties, kissed her tenderly.

"Dear John Cooper, I'll pray for you every moment you're gone until you come back here to me. Every day I love you more, *mi querido*." She in turn clasped him passionately, and her lips met his in a fervent communion.

The next morning, John Cooper rode ahead of the twenty-five *vaqueros,* two of whom drove a supply wagon at the rear. Watching them go, Miguel Sandarbal stood with his arm around his golden-haired Bess and said with a sigh, "What I wouldn't give to go with *el Halcón* and see this man who calls himself *el libertador*!"

"I'm sure you'd like that, *mi esposo*," Bess wryly replied, "because it would give you an excuse to shirk your duties to me and the children."

"What a dreadful thing to say to me! Have I not been a good *esposo*? How can you think so ill of me? You know how much I love you—"

She burst out laughing softly. "What a sweet, dear fool

you are, *querido*! I was only teasing. You're the most wonderful husband any wife could have."

"Woman of mine, the luckiest day of my life—after the one where Don Diego took me into his service—was when I first saw you," Miguel gallantly exclaimed as he put his hands on Bess's shoulders and kissed her exuberantly on the mouth.

On May 21, at eleven o'clock, the little chapel at the Double H Ranch was crowded with *vaqueros* and *trabajadores* to attend the wedding of Miranda Vasquez and Ferdinand de Lloradier. The Argentine priest, Padre Angelo Camporata, presided, with the young Padre Pastronaz assisting as deacon. Carlos de Escobar served as best man, and his wife, Teresa, was matron of honor.

Young Miranda was radiant in her white *mantilla* and matching silk dress, and Doña Inez had given her a bouquet of yellow roses to carry to the altar. The night before, Miranda had had a last misgiving, confiding to her aunt that she still felt herself far beneath this handsome *caballero,* and that she was afraid she might not make him a good wife. "Tía," she had anxiously declared, "perhaps one day he will be ashamed of me and wish he had married a fine lady with a dowry and a family of much importance."

"You are a silly goose, Miranda," her aunt had chided. "If you were not too old for it, I should turn you over my knee and belabor your backside until reason entered your head! And I warn that if you persist in these kinds of thoughts once you are married to that fine young man, he will assuredly feel the same way as I do." And then, as Miranda's face clouded with the threat of tears, her aunt gently embraced her and murmured, "Have courage, my dear. I am proud of you. You are a good girl, and you have given great joy to your family. And this man is not like the *caballeros* who prance around the señoritas and try to show off how *macho* they are. He respects and truly loves you, of this your father and I are certain. Go to him joyously and resolve to be the best wife you can. You will enchant him, I promise you."

And now, on this morning, there was no doubt in Miranda's mind as she turned to look at her handsome husband-to-be and saw the light of adoration in his eyes and heard him repeat the vows after the priest, with a sincerity and fervor that made tears come to her eyes. They were tears of joy, however, and heartfelt delight in her resolve never to give him doubt that he had taken unto himself a wife who would cherish and adore him.

After the wedding, a low mass was held so that the parishioners could combine their prayers for the long and happy life of the newly married couple with their fervent entreaties that John Cooper's meeting with General Santa Anna would guarantee lasting peace to all *tejanos*.

Colonel Luis Dominguez had attended the wedding with Ramón and Mercedes Santoriaga, but he took little joy in the proceedings. Though himself *católico*, he had little patience with otherworldly rituals, since his own philosophy was that of a man of forthright action, as learned on the battlefield.

Immediately after the mass, he rose to leave the chapel with Ramón and his wife, but as he was crossing the threshold, he encountered a tall nun in the black garb of the Dominican order, who was staring intently at him. He inclined his head respectfully, and then, as her stare persisted, courteously spoke. "Sister, do you know me?"

"No, yet I recognize your uniform, *señor coronel*," the woman replied.

"Yes, I am a *coronel* indeed, attached to *su excelencia, el generalísimo* Santa Anna," the officer responded.

"It was another colonel, in the town of Benicia, I recall now—it was he whom I met. His uniform was the same, and for a moment I thought you were he," was the nun's answer.

"I have never been in Benicia, though I know of the town. Why do you remember this man, Sister?"

Sister Eufemia straightened, made the sign of the cross, and answered in a voice tinged with bitterness, "May *el Señor Dios* forgive my un-Christian thoughts—they are not directed at you, *coronel*. You see, my sisters and I came from the town of Parras, some five hundred miles from this, our sanctuary. And when we came to Benicia, this officer, Colonel Esteban Moravada, arrested two *tejanos* because they had weapons—which they used for hunting—and had them shot. Then he ordered that the town be sacked, and there were innocent women who were brutalized by the *soldados*. This is why I cannot forget the uniform you wear, *señor coronel*. May *el Señor Dios* forgive me for my impious thoughts.''

"Perhaps it will ease your mind, Sister," Colonel Dominguez blandly countered, "if I tell you that I know Colonel Esteban Moravada to be dead. He was once an aide to my illustrious general, as I now have the honor and privilege to be.''

"Then I shall pray for both of you, *señor coronel*, that there may be no more such barbarisms committed in the name of patriotism,'' Sister Eufemia said with intrepid courage, then went on her way.

The stocky, bearded officer turned back to Ramón and Mercedes Santoriaga, a scowl on his face. ''A pleasant welcome, indeed, Señor Santoriaga!'' he declared in a huff, then started back to his quarters at a brisk walk, Ramón hurrying to keep up. ''Did you hear her? She as much as implied that because I wear the uniform of my rank, I am of the type who would burn and sack a village! If such a thing was done, there must have been a reason. From what I know of Colonel Moravada, he was an excellent officer. And officers—myself included—merely follow orders; we do not question them.''

"There you have, in a nutshell, the reason I could no longer remain on the staff of *el libertador*,'' Ramón replied. ''For I believe that even the most disciplined of officers must question the wisdom of an order given to him, if it means that, in carrying it out, he sacrifices his honor—yes, and his very soul.''

"Bah! Living with these *gringos* has addled your mind, Señor Santoriaga! I, for one, shall be happy to go back across the Rio Grande when Señor Baines returns here. But I will tell you this—I have already observed that your *vaqueros* carry modern weapons, and that this *hacienda* is guarded day and night like a fortress. This is not the behavior of settlers who expect to be considered peace-loving citizens of the state of Coahuila! And now, señor, I would like to return to my room and be alone!'' With this, he let himself into Ramón's house, leaving his escort standing outside, waiting for his wife to catch up. When she did, Ramón eyed her and shook his head.

"A most difficult man, *mi corazón*,'' he said. ''I shall be very happy when my role as a jailer is over, and John Cooper comes back safely.''

Twenty-five

As if to make up for the weeks of dreary overcast and drenching rain, the skies were fleeced with slowly moving clouds, whose whiteness intensified the pure, clear blue that spread to the horizon in every direction. The weather was hot, but not oppressively so. And the rain, followed by the nurturing warmth of the sun, had brought about a glorious display of foliage and flowers, so that wherever the eye rested, there was beauty.

John Cooper and his twenty-five men and the wagon moved steadily toward the Rio Grande, and there were no signs now of human habitation for miles in either direction. Here was the vast, magnificent Southwest, virtually unchanged from when the first Indians had come upon the land, many centuries ago. No sight was more beautiful to John Cooper, and nowhere—not in the mountains or in the forests—did he feel more alive or in his element. Even the saguaro, the giant cactus, was now in blossom, and John Cooper remembered what he had learned from the Indians, that a traveler without water in the desert need not die of thirst if he came upon this plant, for its pulp gave off precious moisture for the parched throat and lips, new strength for the weary miles ahead.

Yet all this land, which every *gringo* called Texas, was part of Coahuila Province, and thus, by law, under Mexican rule. If John Cooper had persuaded his late father-in-law, Don Diego de Escobar, to leave Taos to escape the oppressive regime of old Spain, he now had to admit that life under Mexican rule—and that meant the Mexican army—was beginning to look just as bad. He had not reckoned with the human greed and lust for power that seemed to characterize men and nations once they achieved independence from tyranny. The Mexicans had suffered under Spanish rule, but now, in their turn, they were making others suffer—and those others happened to include many Americans. And here was the great danger, that this unwise policy would bring about a clash of two peoples and two nations, the one young and ambitious from its very birth, the other young by rebirth after centuries of peonage under the Spanish yoke.

As he rode, leisurely conversing with the *vaqueros*, John Cooper was more than ever convinced of the importance of this rendezvous, despite all his doubts and misgivings. If he could reach some agreement with Santa Anna to keep this country free of harassing Mexican patrols and render it safe for American settlers wishing to raise families in peace, it might clear the way for future amity between these two nations. Perhaps one day legislators of the American Congress and of the Mexican Republic would sit down together at the same table and forge a pact of mutual friendship and cooperation. It was as if John Cooper could see a generation into the future and clearly envision the benefits his children could derive from this first meeting between him and the man who called himself *el libertador*.

By the end of the first day they had covered nearly thirty miles, or about a third of the way to Piedras Negras, John Cooper estimated. He and the *vaqueros* made camp, and the youngest of them, Fernando Beltorres, volunteered to prepare supper for the entire company. He was a tall stripling of twenty-two, and many of his *compañeros* mercilessly ragged him about being still a boy, since he had neither beard nor mustache. John Cooper had observed how skillfully this "boy" had ridden during the first day of the journey and how ably he had borne himself, fending off with good humor the gibes of the other *vaqueros*. And if there had ever been any doubts over his marksmanship, he had quickly dispelled these when, just before they had made camp, he had pulled his rifle out of its saddle sheath and quickly triggered a shot that had brought down a small antelope in full flight. John Cooper had watched as the *vaquero*, swiftly dismounting and tethering his horse

to a manzanita bush, had hurried forward and expertly skinned
the animal, then cut the most edible portions away.

Now, as he watched the young *vaquero* prepare a
cooking fire and season the meat of the antelope, the tall
Texan looked around at the other *vaqueros* and declared, "I
have never heard that the presence of a beard helps a man
shoot better. It's true, I wear one myself, but I shot just as
well when I was a boy and had no more hair on my chin than
our *compañero* here. And I say to you now, *mis amigos,* that
even I could not have made a better shot with 'Long Girl'
than he did in killing that antelope. So instead of making him
feel unworthy because he does not have the luxurious beard
that you, Darbona, or you, Rogales, can boast of, let us
esteem him highly."

Fernando Beltorres could not hold back a blush as he
continued to busy himself with the supper; all the same, he
shot a grateful look at John Cooper, whom he secretly admired almost to the point of idolatry. And he knew that from
now on, since he stood so high in John Cooper's esteem, the
other *vaqueros* would be bound to show him more respect,
even if they did continue their genial bantering.

Fernando recalled how, like all the others, he had volunteered for this mission. At the time, old Miguel had eyed him
suspiciously and growled, "Not so fast, Beltorres! Haven't I
seen you playing the gallant to Conchita Segura? You know
the rules—*el Halcón* will take no one who is in the way of
getting himself a family or who has one already." To this,
Fernando had blusteringly responded, "*Mi capataz,* surely
you're not so old that you cannot recognize a flirtation when
you see it. Why, I've just been amusing myself a little with
Conchita, and she with me. The fact is, I could disappear
from the face of the earth tomorrow and she wouldn't notice
the difference."

To be sure, this had been pure fabrication on the young
vaquero's part, but he had wanted to go with *el Halcón* so
badly that he had denied his real love for Conchita Segura in
order to accompany the Texan on this vital mission. Afterward he had gone to the chapel to beg forgiveness for his lie
and to swear by all that was holy that, when he returned, he
would more than make it up to her.

Five men stood guard duty during the peaceful night, and early the next morning, after a hearty breakfast on the rest of the antelope meat and the remains of a batch of biscuits Rosa Lorcas had baked prior to their departure, the *vaqueros* and John Cooper continued their journey. They saw in the distance what appeared to be a hunting party of Comanche, but there were only a dozen or so braves, and these veered off to the northeast after a few minutes of scrutinizing the *vaqueros* and the supply wagon.

The little caravan made good time this second day and camped at night in the shade of a large clump of scrub oak. Two of the *vaqueros* clambered atop a little rise to serve as lookouts, and they reported that there was nothing in sight.

This time, John Cooper had used "Long Girl" to contribute to the evening meal, garnering two jackrabbits, shot within half an hour of each other, and a plump quail. He welcomed the camaraderie of the outdoors among the *vaqueros*, where he was accepted as one of them and where there was no need for deception. He thought to himself how much easier life would be if only more people—Santa Anna, for one—could have the good temper of, say, a man like Felipe Rogales, a stout *vaquero* of twenty-eight with an enormous mustache and a roguish sense of humor that sometimes surpassed the bounds of propriety. And John Cooper also relished the adventure and sheer good fun of a journey, the simple but tasty food, the smell of outdoor cooking, and, not least of all, the freedom from napkins and cutlery and chinaware and all the complicated appurtenances of civilized life.

When he had first married Catarina, John Cooper had been restless, reacting badly to domestic ties and preferring to spend endless days riding and hunting in the open. However, as he had grown older, he had mellowed considerably. With Dorotéa, he did not seem to have the same impatience. A journey such as the one he was now taking seemed merely a pleasant change, rather than a painful reminder of the freedom he had lost.

Around the campfire, the younger men pressed him for anecdotes about his life with the Indians, and it pleased him to relate some of the more colorful experiences; most of all, however, he liked to tell of the adventure when he and Lije had raced away from the Sioux village in the dead of winter, at the very time when the great earthquake in New Madrid, Missouri, had turned the course of the Mississippi to flow backward for three days and nights. The *vaqueros* listened breathlessly, and some of them surreptitiously wiped away a tear when he told of how Lije, with an arrow in his side from a Sioux's bow, had leaped to the rock where the brave stood and killed him before he himself died.

That brought on talk from the *vaqueros* of the dogs they had owned in their boyhood, and how one had been smarter or more courageous than another; and in turn they remembered how valiantly Yankee, who had had Lije's blood in him, had given up his life to save the children at the Double H Ranch.

As John Cooper lay down on his blanket and prepared to sleep, he thought to himself that tonight had been a most auspicious omen. This closeness to the *vaqueros*, which made them seem a part of his own family, was warm and good, and it was one of the blessings of the freedom that Americans had brought to this young country. Tomorrow he would arrive at Piedras Negras, and perhaps, when they were face to face, he and Santa Anna could find it easier to establish the ties and loyalties that men of goodwill could develop simply through living together. Yes, it almost seemed possible that he and Santa Anna could come to reasonable terms, and John Cooper slept dreamlessly in that hope.

On the afternoon of the third day, John Cooper and his men crossed the Rio Grande and approached the dusty little town of Piedras Negras. Except in size, it did not differ much from Taos, with its narrow streets and the central square dominated by the church. Beyond the outskirts, not far to the southwest, could be seen the erratically shaped hills surmounted by giant black boulders from which the town derived its name.

As he halted his horse just outside of town, John Cooper turned to Fernando Beltorres. "Well, *amigo*, I don't see any sign so far of the man we've come all this way to meet. At least there aren't any *soldados* in the streets—just *peones* and old women, as far as I can see."

"Perhaps we've come too early, *patrón*," the young *vaquero* respectfully suggested.

"No—wait, there's an officer riding up!" John Cooper declared. As he spoke, a young lieutenant, in full-dress regalia, neared in a cloud of dust. The man raised his hand in salute as he galloped closer, finally reining in the spirited mount ten yards in front of John Cooper. "Are you Señor Baines, the *tejano*?" he eagerly demanded.

"Yes, I am John Cooper Baines."

"I am delegated by His Excellency, General Santa Anna, to conduct you and your men to your guest quarters. If you will follow me—I am *Teniente* Ricardo Manteca—I will lead you to a house that is owned by *el libertador* and which is large enough to receive all of your party most comfortably."

"*Gracias, teniente.*"

"*De nada.* This way, if you please, señor!" The young lieutenant wheeled his horse and trotted off, and John Cooper made a sign for the *vaqueros* to follow him.

Across the central plaza, opposite the old adobe church, stood a large two-story house. It belonged to the elderly *alcalde* who presided over Piedras Negras, but at Santa Anna's order, the man and his family had vacated it and gone to live in a humble *jacal* on the outskirts of town. He had been compensated by the "gift" of five hundred *pesos* and had been urged not to show himself in public during this important meeting, and most emphatically not to contest Santa Anna's claim of owning the most luxurious house in this little village. Similarly, the *alcalde*'s servants had been sharply warned not to let the true ownership of the house be known to the blond Texan, whom they had been ordered to treat with the utmost courtesy.

Dismounting, the lieutenant imperiously clapped his hands, and two *trabajadores* hurried out to welcome the *gringo*. "You will take the horses of these men and quarter them in the stable," the *teniente* brusquely directed. "Tell the *cocinera* to prepare supper immediately for the honored guest of *el generalísimo* Santa Anna, *comprendéis*?"

Then, turning to John Cooper, the officer averred with a smile, "General Santa Anna wishes you and your *compañeros* to rest tonight. He bids me tell you that tomorrow you and he will meet, where he is camped near the black rocks. I shall escort you, when the time comes. Until then, you have only to command these servants, and they will gratify your every wish. *Adiós,* then, until tomorrow, Señor Baines!''

After posting four of the *vaqueros* as guards, John Cooper led the others into the house. As he entered the vestibule and saw the elegant furnishings, he whistled with surprise. Jokingly he turned to Felipe Rogales and said, ''Felipe, you'd best advise your *compañeros* to take off their dusty boots. These are fine rugs, and I haven't seen fancy furniture like this outside of New Orleans. Let us at least be gracious guests and not destructive ones during our stay here.''

They moved into the huge salon, and the *vaqueros,* their *sombreros* doffed, looked wonderingly around. There were tapestries on the walls and stuffed couches and ottomans, for the *alcalde* of Piedras Negras was rich—not from his office, which paid a pittance, but from his ownership of a huge silver mine near Sonora. As it chanced, he was a partisan of Santa Anna, and thus had deemed it an honor to move into a *jacal* while the *gringo* and his men occupied this lavish dwelling.

''Perhaps I may be of assistance, señores.'' The melodious, cultured voice of a servant interrupted the silent awe of the *vaqueros,* and they turned as one man to regard the newcomer. He was the majordomo of the house, a man who appeared to be in his early forties, clad in elegant livery and with a gold chain about his neck to which was affixed the key to the wine cellar, for the *alcalde* prided himself on his collection of fine wines from France, the Canaries, and Spain, as well as some magnificent old brandies, cognacs, and port.

''I am at your command, señores. I am called Baltasar. *El generalísimo* has bidden me to see to your comforts during your stay here, and to try to answer any questions you may have.''

''It is most gracious of the general,'' John Cooper replied in fluent Spanish. ''I am John Cooper Baines, and I thank you on behalf of my men and myself. Perhaps, Baltasar, you can tell me exactly when it is I shall have the privilege of meeting *el libertador*?''

John Cooper had tried to put no sarcasm into his pronun-

ciation of that lofty title, and the majordomo smiled genially
and inclined his head. "You will receive a visit from a
special aide of His Excellency after the evening meal, señor.
As you have probably been told, the general and his staff are
camped beyond the town; I am certain that the aide will
acquaint you with the conditions of your meeting. How many
men do you have here in all, señor?"

"I have twenty-five *vaqueros* with me. Seeing the
elegance of this house, I have already warned them to remove
their boots and to disturb as little as possible the beauty of the
furnishings."

"That is thoughtful, Señor Baines. I shall tell the cook,
then, to prepare supper for twenty-six. Oh, yes—one thing
more. His Excellency bids me ask whether you and your men
would enjoy companions for the night. There are *criadas*,
and young women as well who would be—"

"No, *gracias*, we do not come here for the pleasures
of the flesh, Baltasar," John Cooper wryly interrupted. "And
be sure to tell the cook that my *vaqueros*, like me, are
simple men, who require no fancy preparations or extraordinary dishes."

The majordomo again permitted himself a smile. "I
shall tell the *cocinera*, Señor Baines. May I say, on behalf
of my master, that you show the most gracious disposition;
your thoughtfulness in not wishing to make demands will be
reported to my master."

"Thank you again, Baltasar."

"The supper will be served in the large dining room,
señor, and I shall come to tell you when it is ready." The
majordomo bowed himself out.

"By all the saints!" the *vaquero* Manuel Darbona
muttered under his breath. "This is even fancier than the
house I once was in in San Luis Potosí, where you paid
twenty *pesos* for the tenderness of an esteemed *mujer* to help
you forget your troubles. All the same, I shouldn't have
minded a woman tonight, after the long journey we've had."

Felipe Rogales tapped him on the shoulder. "*Mi compañero*, did you not hear what the *patrón* said? We did not
travel here for such pleasures, remember that well. Are we
to show ourselves creatures of luxury like this illustrious

general we come to meet? We are better men than he by far, and don't forget it, *amigo!*''

The cook employed by the *alcalde* of Piedras Negras had taken to heart Baltasar's communications of John Cooper's wishes. She prepared a simple beef stew in a cauldron, with bits of tripe for additional flavor, and added seasonal vegetables to make it more nourishing. With this, since the weather was intensely warm, she served pitchers of *sangría*, a hearty, chilled red wine to which fruit was added. She offered a delicious *flan* for dessert, served with a black coffee even stronger than that made in New Orleans.

Seated at the long table that the *alcalde* used for formal dinner parties, the *vaqueros* ate and drank with gusto, exchanging anecdotes among themselves, to which John Cooper occasionally contributed. The atmosphere of companionship, on the eve of so crucial a rendezvous, seemed more precious than ever, and John Cooper drank it in, laughing at some joke one of the *vaqueros* had just told, adding a quip to top it, and then, when pressed, again describing one of his own exploits during the years he had spent with various Indian tribes before arriving at Taos.

What he savored most, however, was the feeling of brotherhood and equality between him and these men, all of whom were honest, brave, and willing to risk their lives for one another and for their freedom. Such a feeling strengthened his resolve to meet this arrogant *libertador* and, through his own wits and resourcefulness, arrive at terms that would preserve that precious freedom for all the settlers in the Texas Territory.

Yes, he would go into the meeting with his eyes open, and he had the *vaqueros* to thank for this, too, because here were men who spoke their mind without the sophistry or deviousness that he was certain he would encounter on the morrow.

After the good food and companionship, John Cooper felt drowsy, but the temptation to sleep had to be put off; Baltasar had told him to expect the visit of Santa Anna's personal aide, and for this he had to be alert. Fortunately, the majordomo now appeared, setting a teakwood box of Havana cigars upon the long table and bidding the men help themselves. The tobacco was rich and strong, and this and another cup of coffee helped drive away John Cooper's somnolence.

It was not until a full hour later that Baltasar again reappeared. Inclining his head toward John Cooper, the majordomo deferentially announced, "The general's aide has arrived, señor, and asks to meet with you."

"I will see him at once. Perhaps a private room might be best," John Cooper decided.

"Of course, Señor Baines. I will take you to the study now, and then I will bring Don Pablo to you."

John Cooper followed Baltasar down the beautifully carpeted hallway to a room at the rear of the first floor; then the majordomo hurried off to bring Santa Anna's aide to the blond Texan. A few moments later, a tall, stately white-haired man appeared, dressed in the black velvet costume of an *hidalgo* of old Spain, with a silver chain around his neck bearing the Order of Saint James of Compostela. John Cooper at once recognized this medallion as the very same that had been presented to the late Don Diego de Escobar, the father of the Texan's first wife.

"I have the honor to present to you, Señor Baines, Don Pablo de Vasconcellos," Baltasar formally announced, then discreetly withdrew, closing the door behind him.

"I bid you welcome to Piedras Negras in the name of His Excellency, General Santa Anna," the old *hidalgo* said in a solemn voice. "I am to tell you that he awaits this meeting with impatience, for he has long wished to meet you face to face."

"You may tell His Excellency that the feeling is mutual, Don Pablo," was John Cooper's polite answer. And then, having noted the pure Castilian fluency of the old man, he hazarded, "I should guess you to have come from Madrid, Don Pablo."

"And you would be right. That was the city of my nativity, Señor Baines. Wishing to serve the court, I came to settle in Veracruz with my young wife, María, who died together with our little son during childbirth."

"Forgive me if I bring you pain in reviving such a

memory, Don Pablo." John Cooper used the formal language of diplomacy, matching the aide's Castilian with his own fluent Spanish.

"That was many years ago, Señor Baines, but I thank you for your compassion. I might ask you how you could guess that I had come from Madrid—"

"For one thing, because you wear the Order of Saint James about your neck, Don Pablo. My own late father-in-law, Don Diego de Escobar, was awarded that same honor before he died, when a representative of the Spanish *junta* came to our ranch in Texas to notify him that he had been wrongfully banished and to compensate him for his estates, which had been seized by the crown."

"Don Diego de Escobar . . . but of course, that name is not at all unfamiliar to me! He and his father served loyally at the court in Madrid. It was a court beset by disillusion and family hatreds, and lorded over by Manuel de Godoy, whom my people called the Prince of Peace, without realizing he sold Spain out to Bonaparte and began the dreadful Peninsular Wars thereby," the old *hidalgo* mused aloud.

"It was through that very same man, Don Pablo, that Don Diego was banished and given the forgotten post of *intendente* of Taos, which is where I met him and his daughter and son when I came from Illinois."

"Your reputation is great in Mexico, Señor Baines. You are credited with almost supernatural powers, if you wish to know the truth." The old *hidalgo* smiled disarmingly. "It is said you have fought with a wolf at your side."

"Not quite a wolf, but the offspring of a timber wolf and an Irish wolfhound, Don Pablo," John Cooper smilingly corrected.

"If you wonder why I represent His Excellency, Señor Baines," the old man continued, "it is because he wishes to show the people of Mexico that he has not turned his back on the traditional royalty and nobility of what was once New Spain, before my native land and his were rent asunder by Mexican independence."

"I understand that. I might wonder why you never thought of going back to Madrid, Don Pablo."

The white-haired *hidalgo* shrugged. "After the death

of my wife and little son, I thought of it, indeed. But by then I asked myself if it was not far healthier to plunge into the service of this struggling new republic, so that it would not be crushed under the heel of a Spain that had become corrupted and depraved. I stayed because I believed that Mexico as a republic might surpass the golden era of Spanish achievement in the world. Now, of course, I see that I was far too optimistic. But at my age, Señor Baines, one adjusts to circumstances. I am as loyal a subject of Mexico as ever I was of Spain, be assured of it."

"I have only to hear and see you, Don Pablo, to know that" was John Cooper's sincere answer.

The white-haired aide sighed heavily and then said, with a touch of nostalgia to his voice, "Six years ago, I had the opportunity to visit another struggling young republic, that of Argentina. They, too, alas, are beset with problems."

"And I, Don Pablo, went to Buenos Aires two years ago, after the death of my first wife. I sold some of my cattle and horses to a *hacendado* on the *pampas*, a Señor Raoul Maldones, whose oldest daughter, Dorotéa, I brought back as my wife."

"But this is an incredible coincidence, Señor Baines!" The old man's dignified face was fairly transformed with joy. "I, too, know the señor Raoul Maldones. In fact, I stayed at the villa of his good friend, Heitor Duvaldo."

"It is indeed a striking coincidence. But perhaps you do not know that Heitor Duvaldo is dead, Don Pablo?" John Cooper remarked.

"But no, I did not know that! What dreadful news you bring me—"

"I am truly sorry, señor. Doubtless you were aware of the *porteño* government's enmity to the *hacendados* of the countryside; from all I can determine, Heitor Duvaldo was murdered by the decree of those *porteños*." Briefly, John Cooper described how the younger Duvaldos had been driven to emigrate from Argentina, only to be kidnapped on the high seas. "Fortunately, I was able to rescue them, and they, along with Raoul Maldones, now live on my ranch. The older brother, Enrique, was but recently married to a sweet young Cuban girl whom he met during his imprisonment there."

"How many memories you bring back to me, Señor Baines!" Don Pablo de Vasconcellos sighed again and cleared his throat. Then, in a more forceful tone, he resumed, "But my purpose in coming here tonight is to acquaint you with the personality and temperament of *su excelencia*."

"Can you tell me what Santa Anna really intends when we have our parley?" John Cooper pressed.

"The *generalísimo* loves his country, as I do, and wishes for peace—not only within *Méjico*, but between *Méjico* and *los Estados Unidos*. All I can tell you is that he is strong-willed and intends to carry out his plans. My advice to you is to show yourself to be equally strong-minded, for only then will he respect you."

"You said earlier that I was known by reputation in Mexico. Well, most of what I know of Santa Anna is by reputation—namely, that he is ambitious and determined to take total power in Mexico."

"I cannot affirm or deny such rumors, Señor Baines. It is true that His Excellency wants nothing better than to serve the people of *Méjico*, and that if he were called to the presidency, he would eagerly accept it as his destiny."

"He has offered me safe conduct, as you doubtless know, and sent Colonel Luis Dominguez to my ranch to serve as hostage while I am here in Piedras Negras," John Cooper stated.

"Yes, for he wishes this meeting between the two of you to be on neutral ground, so to speak, so there can be no threat of deception or trickery."

"I hope that to be the case, Don Pablo. Nevertheless, I have come here with twenty-five good men, not one of whom has a family to leave behind, if by some misfortune we should be forced to defend ourselves."

"His Excellency has assured me that you need have no fears as to your safety, Señor Baines. I urge you to trust him, and to weigh your words carefully and listen to his."

"I am grateful to you for your advice, Don Pablo."

The old *hidalgo* rose from his chair. "Then all is settled, señor. Tomorrow morning, I will take you to his camp myself."

"Good—I shall be at your disposal." John Cooper also

rose from his chair. "Thank you for coming, Don Pablo, and when you return to Santa Anna, please convey my gratitude to him for the hospitality he has arranged for my men and me. If all goes as well tomorrow as it has today, I am sure our talks will soon bear fruit."

Twenty-six

Even while John Cooper Baines was meeting with Don Pablo de Vasconcellos, Colonel Luis Dominguez was the supper guest of Ramón and Mercedes Santoriaga, as he had been each evening since his arrival at the Double H Ranch.

For the stocky, bearded Mexican officer, these three days as a hostage had been boring in the extreme. To begin with, he had no love for the *gringos,* and it irked him that he could do absolutely nothing to swing the balance scales in favor of his general. Alone, without troops to command—although he could perceive certain weaknesses in the defenses of the Double H Ranch that a regiment might readily exploit—he found himself in the intolerable position of having to do nothing until John Cooper returned from the meeting at Piedras Negras.

By now, assuredly, the blond *gringo* and his *vaqueros* had reached the rendezvous and were probably at this very moment being instructed as to protocol for the next day, when the thrice-accursed *yanqui* would come face to face with *el libertador.*

Dominguez so far had kept up his part of the bargain, behaving as one must who for all intents and purposes was a prisoner. At least Santoriaga had not placed him under lock and key—though at times Dominguez almost wished it so, for the constant proximity of the man who had once been of his own rank and attached to Santa Anna's regiment grew ever more exasperating. Every time the soft-spoken former officer ventured an opinion—even on so trivial a subject as the weather—it seemed that he purposely went out of his way to antagonize Dominguez. For example, all during the first course he had been praising the fertility of this soil—as if it were not Mexican to begin with!—boasting of the bounteous crops of fruits and vegetables, the healthy, flourishing herds of cattle and sheep, and the abundant supply of pure drinking water.

It was almost too much to take. During dessert, in fact, Dominguez had purposely tried to pick a quarrel with his host. They had been discussing the policies of the Mexican government, and Dominguez had asserted that the real trouble was the lack of a strong leader in Mexico City, clearly implying that, once Santa Anna answered the growing popular call, Mexico would shake off its inertia and go forward as a mighty nation.

But Mercedes's genial husband had refused to be drawn into the trap, saying only, "In *los Estados Unidos, coronel,* the 'popular call' is not so abstract. Every man, whether rich or poor, has the opportunity to vote. This winter, they shall elect a new *presidente,* and it will be done not by military coups or by force of arms, but rather by the will of a united people. How each man votes depends solely on his conscience, his own appraisal of the qualities of the candidates. This is how a true republic functions, *coronel,* and you yourself know that, in Mexico, the humble *peón* has not yet been granted this right. I wonder when the day will come that he will be allowed to participate with the same freedom even the lowliest worker in the United States enjoys."

"Bah, you speak like an idealist, Santoriaga," Dominguez replied, making a point of using his host's surname, which in itself was a veiled insult.

Ramón, however, pretended not to notice this breach of politeness. "Yes, it is true," he blandly responded. "But I've always felt that even a military man must live by ideals—although, of course, these must be reconciled with his obligation to follow the orders of his superiors."

"Ah, I have you now, Santoriaga!" Dominguez triumphantly burst out. "Tell me—just how can you reconcile this matter of ideals with orders given on the battlefield? Let us say that you find a superior's order objectionable because of your own moral scruples. Would you obey it?"

"If on moral and ethical grounds I found it impossible to

obey, I should resign from the service therewith, even if it meant a court-martial" was Ramón's calm reply.

Dominguez's lips curled in a sneer. "Then you would be shot, and your idealism would be for nothing, and your family name would be disgraced. No, *gracias,* the matter of ideals and conscience is out of place in the character of a dedicated officer."

"Let us say," Ramón countered, "that you were ordered by a general to butcher innocent men, women, and children of a town that had held out against your troops. Would you carry out such an order? Would it not sicken you to massacre those civilians who in no way had offered resistance or formed any military danger to the campaign?"

"If I were ordered to kill enemies of my country, I should not hesitate," was Colonel Dominguez's blunt answer.

"There, you see, *coronel,* you and I differ. I think perhaps that is why I decided to come north and follow the ways of these people you call *gringos.* Our Spanish tongue, *coronel,* is most eloquent, and it contains many hidden meanings and nuances. '*Gringo*' can refer to someone who speaks English rather than Spanish, but it also can simply mean 'foreigner.' Yet in *los Estados Unidos,* such a word may be seen as a badge of honor, for it is a nation of all faiths and persuasions, whose people came from many different lands seeking freedom from tyranny. They won that freedom in what is called the War of Independence, and they are bound together by their Constitution, which prevents any one man, even *el presidente,* from becoming a dictator."

"I am not interested in a philosophical or political discussion of the *gringos,* I thank you," Colonel Dominguez stiffly answered, glaring at his host. "And in all this discussion, you forget the main issue: It is simply that, where you now are is not at all *los Estados Unidos,* but part of the Province of Coahuila, and thus Mexican soil. It amuses me to hear you consider yourself virtually an American, as undoubtedly you do. Surely all the views you have expressed to me since I came here bear this out, although you are still, by law, a Mexican citizen."

Again, Ramón refused to be baited. "You are quite correct, *mi coronel.* But may I call your attention to your reason for being here. It is to act as hostage while the señor Baines meets with your general for the purpose of negotiating a working peace between your government and the settlers in Texas. Surely this would not be necessary if the *tejanos* were treated justly in the first place, as free Mexican citizens. As it is, I can only hope our people are guaranteed the freedom from harassment that many of them enjoyed as *americanos*. But I have never been an advocate of war, and still less of needless bloodshed, whether to satisfy the pride of generals *or* governments."

"Then we shall always be at odds, Santoriaga. I have no other hope or ambition except to reach as high a rank as I can, to be looked upon by the government, as by my superiors, as an able, obedient officer who knows how to lead men to victory. And now, by your leave, I shall take a stroll around this *estancia*. The weather has been extremely hot, and I have longed to remove my uniform tunic, except that it is not proper, under the circumstances."

"I would certainly not notify your superiors as to such an omission during your stay with us, *coronel*," Ramón smilingly replied.

But this harmless little jest seemed to add fuel to the already well-kindled fire of Colonel Dominguez's temper. He sprang up from his chair at the table with an angry glare—which did not soften even when he saw the gentle, concerned face of Mercedes plead with him—and without a further word, he stalked out of the house.

"He is a restless, unhappy man, *mi corazón*," Mercedes said to her husband. "And it is obvious he hates you and everything you stand for."

"I am afraid you are right, *querida*. But in all good conscience, I do not hold it against him. He is entitled to his views, as I am to mine. You know, my darling one, why I left the service after my dealings with that man who wishes to rule all Mexico. A few of my friends had a name for him which we dared not utter: *el buitre*."

Mercedes shuddered. "The vulture—the bird that lives upon death," she murmured, as to herself.

"*Sí, mi amor.*" Her husband gravely nodded. "And if he ever has his way and 'liberates' all of Mexico as he

proposes, those evil scavengers will perch on the trees throughout all Mexico, and their prey will be not only the *soldados,*
but innocent men and women as well, and yes, even their
children. A man like Santa Anna, my dear Mercedes, does
not count the number of lives cast away to achieve an end; he
counts only the victory and the glory that come from it. Ah,
no, Mercedes, I have prayed every morning and evening that
John Cooper will somehow be able to convince that cunning,
boastful man that there is more glory to be achieved through
peace than through warfare."

"Amen to that, *mi corazón.*" She rose. "I'll do the
dishes and put the children to bed."

"Yes, my sweetheart. As for me, I'd best go follow our
hostage. He is my responsibility, and if anything should
happen to him before John Cooper's return, it might place us
all in a very difficult position. Heaven knows I try not to pick
a quarrel with him, but he seems bent on making himself
angry."

"I know, *mi corazón.*" She came to him at the table,
put her arms around his shoulders, and kissed him. "I am
blessed in such an *esposo, mi* Ramón."

He turned his face to kiss her on the lips and held her
close for a moment, then rose and said, "A walk before
bedtime will be good for me, also. Don't wait up for me, my
darling. I shall see our guest gets back to his room."

He kissed her again, then abruptly turned and went out
into the night.

He took no weapon with him, knowing that Colonel
Dominguez was himself unarmed. All the same, a twinge of
concern over having neglected this precaution troubled him as
he set out to follow Santa Anna's officer. Just then, the full
moon came out from behind a cloud and illumined the stable
off to his left, and he saw Colonel Dominguez moving stealth-
ily toward the door.

Quickening his footsteps, Ramón called out, "*Mi coronel,*
I'd best accompany you, if you wish to go horseback riding at
this hour!"

The bearded Mexican officer whirled, his face twisted
with anger. "I am quite capable of riding alone, Santoriaga,"
he answered in a tone of savage resentment. "Surely you

can't believe I'm riding off to lead troops against your admirably fortified *estancia*! *Hombre*, have I not given my word to remain here until your precious Señor Baines is safely back?''

''That you have, *mi coronel*.'' Ramón warily approached the Mexican officer. ''But I am personally responsible for your safety. If you come to any harm while you are a guest at the *Hacienda del Halcón*, your commanding officer may take it into his head to seek some sort of reprisal. Come now, be candid with me—if you wish to go for a ride in the moonlight, at least allow me to go with you.''

Colonel Dominguez turned to face his genial host and guardian. ''Since this seems to be a time for honesty, Santoriaga,'' he said in a contemptuous tone, ''let us be quite frank with each other. I despise you as a traitor, and your very presence is odious to me. I wish, at least for a short time, to be removed from you, since all that you stand for offends me as a loyal Mexican.''

''I sincerely regret our personal differences, *coronel*,'' Ramón placatingly answered. ''Nevertheless, in view of my responsibility here, I must insist that I accompany you.''

By now, he stood facing the stocky, bearded officer at a distance of only a few feet. Dominguez had his left hand on the wooden bar of the stable door, and his dark, malevolently narrowed eyes fixed on Ramón's face as if intent on memorizing every feature. Then, with a vile oath, he plunged his right hand inside his tunic, drew out a sharp kitchen knife, and lunged at Santa Anna's former aide-de-camp.

Ramón had just enough time to twist himself to one side and thrust out his right hand to ward off the knife as it descended. Its cutting edge gashed his palm, and with a stifled cry of pain he grasped the colonel's wrist with his left hand and tried to force the knife away.

''Traitor! Lapdog of the *gringos*! I'll ride away from here, once I kill you!'' Dominguez hissed as he tried to jab with the bloodied knife.

Ramón flung himself forward, pinning Dominguez to the stable door, both hands now grasping the Mexican officer's right wrist, trying to twist it to free the knife. With another savage oath, Dominguez thrust up his right knee into his opponent's crotch, and with a dull groan of agony, Ramón stumbled back, releasing his grip on the colonel's wrist.

"Now, you filthy traitor, I'll cut your tripes out!" Dominguez snarled as he lunged again with the kitchen knife.

Dazed by the searing agony in his vitals, Ramón nonetheless found strength enough to dodge to one side as, sinking down on his knees, he wound his arms around Dominguez's legs and twisted him to the ground. Then he flung himself across the Mexican officer's chest, both hands pinning the man's right wrist and again seeking to loosen the grip on the knife.

With an almost insane frenzy, Dominguez clenched his left fist and repeatedly smashed it against Ramón's face, all the while trying to get to his feet and uttering the most blasphemous oaths. Despite the savage pummeling, which bloodied his mouth and blackened his right eye, Ramón held on to the colonel's wrist, doggedly twisting and digging with his wiry fingers, until at last Dominguez uttered a shrill cry of agony, the fingers of his right hand relaxing and the knife falling away.

Again Dominguez smashed his fist against his adversary's face, and Ramón, gasping with pain, twisted to the right, momentarily releasing the officer's pinioned wrist as he lunged for the knife, intending to fling it far beyond them both. But Colonel Dominguez took advantage of this maneuver by seizing Ramón's neck with both hands and, thrusting his thumbs against his opponent's windpipe, trying to throttle him.

Choking and gasping for breath, Ramón dug his own fingers into the Mexican officer's wrists in a frenzied effort to break the stranglehold. Then, with all his strength, he rolled over, and at the same time thrust his own right knee into the officer's groin.

"¡Aiiii!" Colonel Dominguez screamed as his fingers released their hold, and Ramón stumbled to his feet, moving groggily toward the discarded knife.

In his murderous desperation, however, Dominguez tripped Ramón by seizing his ankles and jerking at them. Then the Mexican slowly and painfully got up, breathing hoarsely, and launched a vicious kick with his booted foot against Ramón, who was crawling toward the knife.

The toe of the boot dug savagely into Ramón's hip, and he rolled in pain onto his stomach—but his scrabbling fingers had grasped the knife. Now Dominguez leaped onto Ramón's back and again fixed his strong, thick fingers around his foe's neck.

Ramón tried to twist away, but in vain; he felt Dominguez's fingers constrict his windpipe, and his senses began to fail. He could scarcely see now, but with his last failing strength, he clutched the handle of the sharp knife and thrust backward over his right shoulder, even as waves of blackness threatened to engulf him.

Crouched over his opponent as he was, Colonel Dominguez had not expected this final, frantic attempt at salvation. The knife buried itself halfway in his left chest, and he uttered a shriek of unspeakable agony and incredulity. Then his fingers eased their murderous hold, as he seemed to lean back, his eyes staring, unseeing, at the moon-illumined sky, before he suddenly stiffened and collapsed over his intended victim.

Ramón lay gasping for breath, pinned down by the weight of the Mexican officer's inert body. At last, as full consciousness was restored to him, he managed to roll the gruesome burden to one side and get to all fours, groaning and panting as he drew in great gulps of the warm night air.

After what must have been a full minute, Ramón got to his feet, his face bloodied and bruised, the purplish marks left by Colonel Dominguez's fingers blotching his throat. He stumbled toward the stable door, turned, and put his back to it, then stood leaning there, closing his eyes as the shuddering reaction to his near-death swept over him. Long minutes later, slowly, with painful effort, he forced himself to kneel down and roll Dominguez's body over onto its back.

"*Madre de Dios,* I've killed him! May all the saints aid us now! If Santa Anna finds this out, it will go very badly with John Cooper. If only I'd disarmed him, or called for the *vaqueros* to take him prisoner and lock him up . . ."

He clasped his hands and looked up to the starry sky. "Merciful *Señor Dios,*" he prayed, "do not let what I have done harm John Cooper, or any of the others on this *estancia!*"

Twenty-seven

The skies were overcast on this Friday morning of May 23, the fateful day of John Cooper's meeting with General Santa Anna. The Texan had awakened at dawn, after a dreamless sleep, and was at once alert and eager for what was to follow. He saw to it that the guards outside were relieved, as they had been twice during the night, and the *criadas* entered at about eight, to ask if they might serve breakfast. John Cooper genially told them to bring the meal as quickly as possible.

After they had left, he assembled his men and declared, "Don Pablo de Vasconcellos will come and fetch me to meet *el libertador*. I think four of you should still stay on guard here and keep your eyes open for any movement of soldiers. It's always wise to take precautions. The rest of you will accompany me."

"Are we to take our weapons, *patrón*?" Manuel Darbona anxiously asked.

"I'll know more after I've seen Don Pablo, *mi amigo*. Meanwhile, let us enjoy the hospitality of the illustrious general. Judging from last night's meal, I'd say it beats dried jerky, and maybe even the antelope Fernando killed for us. We may as well enjoy it while we can, *mis compañeros*."

Half an hour later, the *vaqueros* and John Cooper went into the dining room, where the *criadas* served them melon, fried eggs, tortillas, pork cutlets, and strong coffee. It was a hearty meal, and the men ate ravenously, exclaiming over the excellence of the food.

At about ten-thirty, Baltasar reappeared to inform John

Cooper that Don Pablo awaited his pleasure, and the tall Texan bade the majordomo usher in the old *hidalgo*. Don Pablo, dressed as before in black velvet and with the royal Spanish order about his neck, smiled as to an old friend as John Cooper came forward to meet him.

"*Buenos días,* Don Pablo. I trust you've come to take me to His Excellency."

"That is true. And please remember what I told you last night about His Excellency. You are, by nature, Señor Baines, a forthright, honest man. I may say, and not without some cynicism, that this is a rarity in Mexico, particularly with those in government. But I believe that the *generalísimo* will sense your candor at once, and it is my hope that it will lead him to deal as frankly with you as possible."

"You're a most perceptive man, Don Pablo. But let me ask you, before we go—may I take my *vaqueros* with me, and is it permissible to have them carry their weapons? This, you understand, is only for our protection; but I do not wish to offend Santa Anna, if you think he would take it thus."

"No, I think not; he is, after all, a practical man. I hasten to assure you, however, that there will be no treachery. Frankly, he is most curious and eager to meet with you."

"As I with him, Don Pablo." John Cooper turned back to where the *vaqueros* stood waiting for their orders. "*Mis compañeros,* come with me, and bring your weapons. The sentries are to remain behind."

"Then we shall proceed to the stables, Señor Baines," Don Pablo said, following John Cooper out the door. "It would not do to walk. The *generalísimo* enjoys a colorful show, and your entrance on horseback will be more to his liking."

There were manservants already posted at the stable, and at Don Pablo's gesture, they brought out the horses.

The old *hidalgo* mounted with surprising nimbleness, and had begun to ride down the street to lead John Cooper to the place of rendezvous, when suddenly a young lieutenant—not the one they had met yesterday—galloped up to meet them. John Cooper held his hand up to halt the *vaqueros*

behind him as he waited to learn what message this courier
was bringing.

The officer was in his twenties, beardless, with a pleasant, frank face, and he approached John Cooper, reining in
his black gelding as he demanded, "You are the señor Baines?"

"That is my name, *teniente*."

"I come from the *generalísimo*, who asks that you bring
only five men to the meeting by the black rocks. He bids me
tell you that he will have an equal number, but that they will
not be armed. I ask you, therefore, Señor Baines, to tell your
men to leave their weapons behind them."

Don Pablo looked at John Cooper and shrugged, as if to
admit he knew nothing of this change in plans.

"Very well—if that's what the general wants." John
Cooper turned in his saddle. "You, Darbona, Rogales,
Beltorres, Mancrugo, and you, Martínez. Turn your weapons
over to your *compañeros*. The rest of you stay back with the
others and await my further orders. Juan—" He handed his
own rifle and pistols to the nearest *vaquero*.

"It will be done as the *patrón* wishes," the *vaquero*
said, then rejoined his companions.

"I will escort you to meet His Excellency," the lieutenant proffered. He turned to glance at the old *hidalgo*, then
added, "You are to come as well, Don Pablo."

"Forgive me, Señor Baines," Don Pablo murmured,
having moved his horse up abreast of John Cooper's. "I do
not know what this change of plans means, but since he and
his men, like you and yours, will not be armed, I think this is
an honest way of beginning."

"I can't gainsay that, Don Pablo. If you're wrong, we'll
just be buzzard meat."

"You mustn't say such a thing!" the *hidalgo* whispered. "Don't you see how the lieutenant is peering at you,
trying to hear every word you utter?"

John Cooper shrugged. "I'm grateful to you for all your
help, Don Pablo. But perhaps I'd better not display this
dagger around my neck—" Even as he spoke, and while the
lieutenant wheeled his horse so that his back was to John
Cooper, the blond Texan quickly slipped the sheathed dagger
into his open collar, so that it hung inside his shirt. He

remembered how he had come by that knife, during the first dreadful winter following the murder of his parents by the renegade Shawnees. He had been holed up with Lije across the Ohio River and had wakened to find two murderous-looking ruffians staring down at him. One of those men had worn this dagger, and John Cooper, in a fight for his life, had been able, thanks to Lije's help, to kill them both. He had kept the knife and its sheath as a lucky talisman, and perhaps, this morning, he might need all the luck it could bring him.

He glanced back at the five *vaqueros* he had chosen as his escort, and then at the old *hidalgo,* who gave him a comforting nod. Don Pablo's presence somehow reassured John Cooper, yet it could not quite dispel his uneasiness at the sudden interposition of the young lieutenant. It meant that Santa Anna would have to be taken entirely on his word; if there were treachery, John Cooper and his five *vaqueros* would be totally vulnerable. The fact that Colonel Luis Dominguez remained a hostage at the Double H Ranch suddenly seemed of little comfort.

The lieutenant trotted ahead of them toward the southwest, leaving the small town behind and entering a desolate area of irregular ravines and dry gulches, marked by patches of cactus, chaparral, and manzanita. To the east was the river, and rolling hills beyond. Straight ahead, John Cooper saw the giant black boulders that gave the area its name, and after another ten minutes' ride, they came at last into sight of the camp. There were three tents, the smaller, central one about a dozen yards in front of the others. From its tentpole hung the Mexican flag, and near the peak, over the door flap, were sewn the gold stars of a brigadier general, Santa Anna's rank.

The other two tents were huge, beautifully decorated with flags, pennons, and banners signifying military victories, including that of the Battle of Medina. Before each of these two tents a sergeant stood stiffly at attention. John Cooper noted they were wearing the tall shakos with chin straps that indicated they belonged to a cavalry troop of cuirassiers. Flanking the opening to the center tent were two captains, in parade uniforms, one with the shako of cavalry, the other with the headgear of an infantry officer.

The young lieutenant wheeled his horse back to join John Cooper. "Señor Baines," he said, "you and your men may now dismount. The *sargentos* will tether your horses to that clump of trees." John Cooper nodded to his men, and all dismounted, including the old *hidalgo*. At the lieutenant's imperious gesture, the two sergeants left the tents and hurried forward to take the reins of the horses.

John Cooper waited while this was being done, and at last the lieutenant came to him and declared, "I shall introduce you now to the *generalísimo*."

With this, he stepped forward to the entrance of the central tent, parted the flaps, and entered. A moment later, he emerged and held the flaps open, beckoning to John Cooper. As the tall Texan approached, the young officer murmured, "Your *vaqueros* will not take part in this meeting, Señor Baines. They may seat themselves where they wish, as long as they remain in view of our guards." Then he said to the *hidalgo,* "Don Pablo, it is Santa Anna's wish that, at the beginning of this discussion, you not be present. But out of regard for your age, he urges you to take your ease in one of the other tents, where refreshments await. I shall lead you there myself."

Finally the moment had come. John Cooper stepped forward, parted the flap to the tent, ducked his head and entered. He found himself standing before a black-haired, sallow-complected man in the bemedaled uniform of a brigadier general. John Cooper took in the high, sloping forehead, glittering black eyes, and almost femininely sensual mouth.

"At last we meet, Señor Baines." Santa Anna rose from his chair and extended his hand across the table.

John Cooper shook it, and Santa Anna maintained the grasp while he stared boldly into John Cooper's eyes before at last releasing his grip. "Be at your ease, Señor Baines. As you see, I have kept my promise. We meet honorably to discuss our differences, and we are alone. What is said here is for our ears only, so that each of us may state his mind openly and clearly. Do you not agree that this is the best way to begin our conference?"

"Indeed, I do, *excelencia*." John Cooper took a seat in the offered camp chair. Though he maintained a casual air, he was keenly alert, and he studied Santa Anna's expressive face and, even more, the ostentatious uniform with its medals and ribbons that gave eloquent testimony to the pride and ambition of this man who styled himself *el libertador*.

"I believe that we are almost of the same age, Señor Baines. This interests me, for I hold a man must be judged not only by his reputation but also by his years of experience. Indeed, I have heard much of you these last years, for you have become almost a legend in the Southwest."

"Thank you for your flattery, *excelencia*, but I really can claim no great distinction. You can say my destiny led me to *Nuevo Méjico*, where I married and settled down. But at that time, as you probably recall, the Spaniards established restrictive tariffs and forbade *gringos* to trade in Santa Fe and Taos. It was for that reason I moved to Texas."

"Yes, but in so doing, you did not exactly escape what you wished to, is that not so, Señor Baines?" Santa Anna's smile was bland and humorless. "In fact, perhaps the only difference is that the Spaniards ruled in *Nuevo Méjico*, and we Mexicans now rule in Texas."

"No, *excelencia*, that was not the only difference," John Cooper gently pointed out. "The *americanos* who came to settle in Texas did so with the full permission of your government, through the application of the Austins. They were not restricted and harassed as the *gringos* were in *Nuevo Méjico*."

Santa Anna's face retained the bland, meaningless smile, but his eyes narrowed as, leaning slightly forward, he declared, "At the time of the Austin grants, there were valid reasons for my government to do what might now be considered foolish. For one, the *tejanos* were needed to help quell the Indian uprisings. Understand me, Señor Baines—in all sincerity, I am not overly fond of *gringos*. They defy our laws, they flout our traditions, and they have their own selfish purposes. And what concerns us most in Mexico City is that they may foment revolt. To have an enemy so close to our border, even within our country, is not a good thing. I am sure that, although you are not a military man, you would admit this."

"But these settlers were carefully investigated, and only

those with families, who wished to farm or raise cattle, were granted permission to live on Texas soil, *excelencia*," John Cooper replied.

Santa Anna smiled. "Truly, Señor Baines, you should have been a lawyer. You ignore my arguments, and instead you wish to teach me a history lesson."

"That's unfair, *excelencia*." John Cooper was nettled, though he tried to show a pleasant expression to the man across the table from him. "Do you object to the fact that we are armed? But what settler on any new frontier would not bring weapons with him to protect himself against hostiles, or to hunt for the provender he needs for his family?"

Santa Anna shook his head ruefully. "Señor Baines, we in Mexico are a peaceful people, and we do not like all these guns. I tell you in all frankness, señor, that those in power in Mexico City are thinking of preventing any more *americanos* from coming to live on Texas soil. They are afraid, as I myself must be, that this increasing population of *gringos* could easily form the nucleus of an army that would seek to take away Mexican territory, given the opportunity."

"May I remind Your Excellency that, in your letter to me, you promised we could come to an arrangement that would be satisfactory to both of us. Speaking for the *americanos,* I tell you that we want no war with you, that we will not encroach upon your territory, and that we wish only peace for our families and for our children who will come after us. I don't think this in any way interferes with the plans of your government."

"And I am to take your word for that?" Santa Anna waved an impatient hand and scowled. Then, leaning back, he suddenly burst into laughter, startling John Cooper. "*Caramba,* Señor Baines, I like you! You speak your mind, and you're not afraid of me. *Bueno.* Now, let's begin all over again. We are not sitting in the legislature trying to pass a law. You and I—I representing my country, you the *tejanos* —meet as friends for the first time. And yes, I am sure that we can come to terms. I told you in my letter that I am willing to halt the policing of the settlements of your *gringo* people. But in return I require an act of trust from you, which will prove that you are willing to make concessions to obtain this peace you say you want. You know that the *peones* are very poor in my country, and since I am not yet *el presidente,* I can do nothing to relieve their poverty. Money can, *mi amigo.*"

"Yes, if it is justly and fairly distributed to those who have nothing." John Cooper was relieved that Santa Anna had finally gotten around to the heart of the matter—the silver.

But, disarmingly, the general made no further reference to the hinted topic, and instead cajolingly remarked, "I wish you, yes, and your men also, Señor Baines, to be my guests this afternoon and evening. In the other two tents I have food and wine, tequila, rum, and brandy, and also many lovely ladies of the village. I will tell you a secret in confidence, since we are both men of the world—" He leaned across the table with a broad wink, as if to intimate that he and John Cooper were cronies. "Some of these *mujeres,* when I told them I was to meet face to face at last with the famous *el Halcón,* pleaded with me to introduce you to them." He winked again. "Choose whomever you wish, and she will be your companion during your sojourn here with me, *mi amigo.*"

"I thank you for your gracious hospitality, *excelencia,*" John Cooper said, "but I did not come here to enjoy food and drink and women. To begin with, I am married to a very beautiful and loving young woman whom I cherish, and I would not be guilty of an act of infidelity against her."

Santa Anna chuckled. "Now, that is surprising, coming from a man who has lived so richly and fully, so adventurously. Do you not understand that women are distractions, and that even a married man may take his pleasure where he finds it, without in the least losing his love for his true *esposa*?"

"I've heard that said, yes, *excelencia,* but I don't regard marriage quite that way."

"It saddens me to think that you will not partake of my hospitality, *mi amigo.*" Santa Anna shrugged philosophically. "But I will not force you to it. I wish our meeting to be harmonious and fruitful—and I believe you have the same desire."

"You know that's true, or I wouldn't have come."

"But at least you will allow me to offer you and your men a little repast. It is nearly noon, and I confess that I was so eager to meet you for the first time that I scarcely breakfasted."

"Very well, if Your Excellency wishes."

Santa Anna chuckled once more and nodded as he rose from the table and came around to John Cooper's chair. Again, he extended his hand. "You will see that I have called you *mi amigo*, Señor Baines. It is because I sincerely wish you to be my friend and to understand me. When friends talk of important matters, there are no falsehoods between them, and things can be achieved in good order."

"Let us hope so," John Cooper adroitly responded, all the while thinking that he would never, in a thousand years, consider this treacherous fiend his friend.

"That, at least, is a good start," Santa Anna purred. "Come now, let us see what delectable viands we can find for ourselves in the first tent. In the other, I tell you frankly, the lovely ladies fervently hope that you will change your mind about not wishing to meet them."

"I'm afraid you'll have to convey my apologies to them, *excelencia*." John Cooper followed the bemedaled general to the tent at the left and behind the central tent. The sergeant standing guard there stiffened to attention and smartly saluted.

Santa Anna turned to John Cooper. "Bid your *vaqueros* join us."

John Cooper gestured to the five men to follow him, as Santa Anna led the way into the large tent, where a magnificent buffet table stood, piled with many tempting dishes. There was one sideboard on which reposed decanters of wines and various-colored liquors, and another arrayed with plates of the finest imported chinaware and monogrammed silver. Two pretty peasant girls, who could not have been more than eighteen, stood ready to serve the food. They were dressed in colorful shawls, low-necked blouses with short sleeves that bared their olive-sheened arms, and flouncy skirts that fell only to midcalf.

Don Pablo de Vasconcellos had already seated himself on one of the ottomans at the far end of the tent, and as Santa Anna entered, the old *hidalgo* respectfully inclined his head.

Seeing him, the bemedaled general took John Cooper by the elbow and whispered, "It is frequently the case, Señor Baines, that when a man becomes a leader and stands out from the crowd, envious enemies attack him, wishing to detract from his achievements. It has been said of me, for instance, that I am against the *ricos*, the *hacendados*, and all the old traditions that made Spain great through the time of that mighty king, Philip, who launched the Armada upon England. Yet the very presence of my aide, the most honorable and estimable Don Pablo de Vasconcellos, disproves that slanderous accusation. Indeed, there is much to be admired about the institutions of the monarchy and nobility. You see, Señor Baines, you will find, if you study history, that when the world was young, the rulers of most nations came to their thrones through military skill or their ability to unite rival factions. And once having achieved power, they bestowed upon their most capable allies titles of nobility, both to reward their past services and to ensure their future loyalty. This, in my humble way, I seek to do by empowering Don Pablo as my aide and emissary."

"I follow your reasoning, *excelencia*," John Cooper noncommittally replied. As he spoke, he covertly glanced at the old *hidalgo*, and it seemed to him that the latter's eyes brightened, and that there was an almost perceptible bond between them—a bond that went beyond the purely political loyalty envisioned by Santa Anna in his self-laudatory speech.

"But come now, *amigo*—let me continue to call you this, for I am certain that we shall be friends henceforth," Santa Anna unctuously resumed. "Let the *criadas* serve you and your men, and let us be at our ease here. Then, when we have finished our repast, you and I will go back to plan how we may best serve our peoples."

John Cooper did his best to show no aversion to these blandishments, but his distrust of the man who uttered them grew apace. The effusive praise, the self-justifying explanations Santa Anna used to excuse his shameless manipulation of others, revealed only too well to the candid Texan the dangers of trusting such a man. Still, John Cooper forced himself to smile as he sat down and let one of the *criadas* serve him with a plate of food and a glass of Canary wine. He gestured to his *vaqueros* that they imitate him, all the while listening to Santa Anna's continued avowals of friendship. The brigadier general seated himself beside John Cooper and now, in a confidential tone, commenced to relate the history of his military career, detailing how he had risen from the humble rank of cadet to his present lofty post.

Even though he suspected much of the story was fabricated, John Cooper could not help but admire the masterly craftiness of this man who sat beside him, the beguiling, if overflorid, oratory, designed to convince his hearers that his dedication and honorable motives were without flaw. It was no wonder, John Cooper thought, that Santa Anna had won such popular acclaim; he knew how to appeal to the yearnings and dreams of a downtrodden and impoverished people, to fire their imagination with his own meteoric rise from obscurity. Such a man, John Cooper knew, was far more dangerous than an enemy who would bluntly declare his hatred. With the latter, one could always know what to expect; but with Santa Anna, one could never be certain what scheming course he was plotting, even while he spoke so ardently of friendship and understanding.

During the lengthy luncheon, John Cooper seemed to listen attentively. Occasionally he would nod or interject a word or two, which was all his garrulous host seemed to require of him. At last, Santa Anna exhaled a sigh of repletion.

"I am happy that we have had this brief and informal time together, *mi amigo*. I find you a man of great wisdom and understanding, such as I knew that you would be, when first I learned of your exploits. Now, at your pleasure, shall we resume our private discussion?"

"I am at your disposal, *excelencia*," John Cooper answered.

"Good!" Santa Anna rose from his seat, and John Cooper followed his example. "Why not allow your men to remain here, Señor Baines, to enjoy the attentions of the *criadas*?" Santa Anna put his arm around his guest's shoulders and led him toward the opening of the tent.

The five *vaqueros* rose, not certain of what was expected of them. John Cooper paused at the tent door and called back to them, "You may amuse yourselves as you see fit, *mis compañeros.*"

"*Gracias, patrón.*" Felipe Rogales grinned and touched his fingers to his forehead in grateful acknowledgment.

Don Pablo joined Santa Anna and John Cooper outside the tent. "Have you further need of me, *mi general?*" he asked.

"No, *gracias,* Don Pablo. Amuse yourself as you like. You may find it more comfortable in the other tent, and there are enough *criadas* to serve your needs, too," he bluntly replied.

"*Con su permiso, mi general,* I plead my burden of years and should like to take my siesta at the house in town."

"By all means, if you like, Don Pablo. You have served me well. If I have further need of you, I shall send a courier to summon you."

While the old *hidalgo* went off to retrieve his horse, Santa Anna and John Cooper repaired to the general's tent and resumed their former seats.

After shuffling a few papers around, Santa Anna leaned back and gave a contented sigh. "Yes, *mi amigo,* I like you very much indeed. You're a man who doesn't mince words. I confess that I am sometimes guilty of many verbal flourishes, but this is the language of diplomacy." He paused for a moment, as if gathering his thoughts, then announced, "Now, let us get down to the real reason for my sending for you. Some years ago, it came to my knowledge that you had stumbled upon a miraculous discovery in a place known as *la montaña de las pumas,* where you came upon many bars of pure silver. They had been mined by *los esclavos indios,* doubtless under the rule of the Spaniards."

"That is true, *general.*"

"I point out to you that *la montaña de las pumas* is on Mexican soil. And also, most recently, there came to my attention the news that you had apparently found another rich deposit, which you conveyed to a New Orleans bank, to add to the first discovery."

John Cooper did not blink, but he wondered how Santa Anna could have known this. Finally, he answered, "That is true also, *excelencia*. But it has long been accepted that treasure rightfully belongs to whoever is first to salvage it.''

Santa Anna's face darkened, and though he uttered a hollow little laugh, he leaned forward, his eyes dark and menacing. ''I think, señor, that even the most simpleminded lawyer could easily dispute such a claim in any court. Treasure that is found on land belonging to a nation, I am quite certain, cannot fall to the ownership of another.''

''I don't know what your laws are, *excelencia*, but I'd say it would be pretty difficult to produce proof that these mines even existed, and impossible to determine how much silver, if any, was removed from them. On that basis alone, I should think it would be very hard to win a legal claim.''

Santa Anna released a sigh, then decided to try another tack. ''For the sake of argument, Señor Baines, let us pretend that what you say is true—even though I do not admit this.'' Once again the general's face took on its ingratiating, smiling expression. ''As two men of honor who wish only the safety and the peace of their countries, might we not reach some sort of compromise? A settlement, *no es verdad*? Undoubtedly, if I were to ask our advocate general to undertake the pursuit of a legal case to recover the treasure, it might drag on for years. Rather than that unsatisfactory course, I propose the following: In return for an agreed portion of this treasure, to be contributed to the Mexican treasury, I will pledge you my word as military commander that our troops will not bother your settlers in the Texas Territory.''

''That sounds very much like a bribe, *general*,'' John Cooper stolidly responded.

Santa Anna bit his lip, then brought his open palm down hard on the desk with an unintelligible oath. ''*Gringo*, you make things needlessly difficult between us! I approach you in all friendship, and now you begin to offend me.''

''I have no intention of doing so, *excelencia*,'' John Cooper countered. ''But right is right. The Texas settlers in no way interfere with the operation of your government, nor pose a threat to your country. Both Eugene Fair and Stephen Austin are constantly vigilant to make sure that the families who come to Texas are honest, peaceful folks, without the least intention of forming any revolt or war against Mexico.''

"Come now, *mi amigo*—" Again Santa Anna's ingratiating smile curved his sensual lips, and his tone softened. "Let us not use harsh words that may be misinterpreted. Admit that the silver you took from those mines is far more than any one man could possibly use for all the rest of the long life that I fervently pray *el Señor Dios* will grant you. Consider my country, in its growing pains, with so many thousands of *peones* starving and dispossessed. Even a pittance of that fortune would ease their burdens."

"By enacting sensible laws, *mi general*, your government could do much toward correcting that situation" was John Cooper's answer.

Santa Anna's lips tightened, and he glared at the tall Texan. "Take care, Señor Baines, I do not wish to have any man flout me. Do not make me think you have come here with your mind obstinately set against an amicable agreement, as I had hoped for."

"I don't wish to offend you, *general*, but when you propose that I turn over some of this silver to you in return for your not molesting the *tejanos*, I get the impression that you intend to do everything short of war against them if I don't agree with you."

"*¡Por los cojones del diablo!*" Again Santa Anna lifted his right hand and brought it down on the top of the desk. "You try my patience, *gringo*! You wish everything, yet you will yield nothing. From the military viewpoint, you are not in a position to bargain. You see, I know much more about the *tejanos* than you think. There is an adventurer named Jim Bowie who has formed a corps of men he calls Texas Rangers, but their number is insignificant compared with the troops at my command. The *tejanos* could not hope to stand against my forces, if it came to that, Señor Baines. Be reasonable, therefore, for what we speak of here today concerns the future well-being of your settlers."

"That sounds like a threat, *general*." John Cooper's voice was steady. "I'm willing to bargain, but not out of fear."

Brusquely Santa Anna rose from the table. With a visible effort he controlled his temper, as finally he declared, "We can go no further this first day. Let us sleep on this matter, and perhaps tomorrow we can meet again, with more enthusiasm and understanding, to effect the pact that each of us seeks.''

"Very well, *excelencia*." John Cooper rose. "Perhaps that would be the wisest course to take. We seem to be at odds today.''

"Not a situation of my choosing, Señor Baines," Santa Anna tartly replied. Then, with an obsequious smile, he approached the blond Texan and, again putting an arm around his shoulders, gently added, "It is impossible for a man to know everything about another on the basis of a single meeting. You will learn that I am a man of my word, señor, but also that I am sworn and dedicated to uphold the welfare of Mexico, my beloved country. It is this dedication that makes me speak as I do. Understand this, and you will know what is in my heart. Until *mañana*, then! I will send Don Pablo to bring you to the meeting tomorrow.''

Twenty-eight

When John Cooper returned to the house of the *alcalde*, the five *vaqueros* hung back somewhat sheepishly. After having left Santa Anna's tent, the blond Texan had gone to collect his companions; two of them, he found, had succumbed to the enticements of the pretty young *criadas* and were engrossed in fondling and kissing them as he entered.

He could not prevent a wry smile at the thought that they, at least, had profited far more than he in this first encounter with *el libertador*, and quickly he had bidden them to mount their horses and ride back with him. Now, as they prepared to enter the house, Felipe Rogales blurted, "Forgive us, *patrón*—you didn't say anything, and there was nothing else to do, and the *muchachitas* flirted with us. After all, we have no *novias*—"

"You needn't apologize, Felipe," John Cooper replied. "I'm certain that you had a far better time than I did."

The *vaquero*'s expression was sober, and in a serious tone he inquired, "Were you able to come to terms with him, *patrón*?"

"No. We'll have to meet again tomorrow; maybe by then he'll realize that bluffing and threatening won't work with me, Felipe. But we'll see. Meanwhile, you men may as well catch up on your *siestas*. Once we get back to the ranch, there'll be work for everyone to do. I hope to sell a lot more cattle, and there'll be the drive to Corpus Christi, which will certainly be more entertaining for you than coming to this dusty little town. As for me, I'm going to stretch out on a bed and catch up on my sleep."

* * *

John Cooper wakened to feel a hand grasping and shaking his shoulder. When he opened his eyes, he saw Andy Worringer standing over him. Quickly he sprang to his feet. "What are you doing here, Andy?"

"Looking for you, Mr. Baines," was the Texas Ranger captain's answer. "My men and I got to your ranch the day after you'd left, and old Miguel Sandarbal told us you'd headed for Piedras Negras to meet up with that high and mighty General Santa Anna. After what's happened, I thought I'd take a chance and ride here with my men to be of service to you. But I came into town alone, in case anyone was watching."

"What do you mean, Andy, 'after what's happened'?" John Cooper shook off his somnolence; now wide awake, he saw that the captain's face was taut and grim.

"Just that we helped fight off another attack at the Brazos settlement, Mr. Baines. And it wasn't Indians this time. There were about seventy-five soldiers—Mexicans, commanded by a young major—and they sent a man in under a flag of truce, to demand that the settlers leave Texas. When Simon Brown sent him packing, this major took a notion to do the job then and there by force of arms."

"My God, that's an overt act of war!" John Cooper gasped. "Santa Anna *must* have known about it—and all the while he's been . . ." A look of sudden realization swept over John Cooper's face. "He must have been intending all along to use that attack to raise the ante—to get me to give up the silver. He doesn't care a whit for the safety of the hostage he sent—"

"I'm of the same opinion, Mr. Baines, if you want to know the truth," Andy Worringer retorted. "You brought twenty-five men here, didn't you? And you're like sitting ducks in this house. Look, I've got another twenty-five, including a half-breed Kiowa scout by the name of Poromanti, who's the best there is. And we've got plenty of arms and ammunition to raise a little Cain of our own."

"A Kiowa, you say? I'd like to do some scouting myself right now, to see what Santa Anna is really up to," John Cooper mused aloud.

"You're probably wanting to know how I found you here in this house. When we got to the edge of town, Poromanti dressed up like a *peón* and just walked right in. He found an old woman carrying water from the well and asked her if she'd seen any *gringos*. She told him that you and your men were holed up here, and that you were having a big powwow with Santa Anna."

"Tell me about that attack on the Brazos, Andy."

Quickly the Ranger related what had happened, how Simon Brown had been wounded in the arm but still had managed to pick off the Mexican major, and how the alert settlers had dispatched over thirty of the enemy before the remainder finally galloped off. Only three of the settlers had been killed, and three more wounded.

"Thank God it wasn't more serious!"

"Amen to that, Mr. Baines. What do you say we send Poromanti out to do some scouting later tonight? Maybe he can get over to Santa Anna's camp and find out what's going on. He speaks Spanish like a native, and he's got good ears, like any Injun."

"I'd be grateful for that, Andy." John Cooper seemed to come to a decision. He went to the corner where "Long Girl" was leaning and picked up and checked his rifle. "Like you say, Andy, we're sitting ducks here, if Santa Anna really wants to do something nasty. Maybe it would be a smart idea for us to pull up stakes. I'll tell our host here that we've decided to pitch camp outside of town, because we prefer to live outdoors. They can make of it what they want. We'll light some campfires to assure Santa Anna we're not running off. Then we can join your men, and if *el libertador* has any skullduggery in mind, we'll be more than ready for him."

"Now you're talking my language, Mr. Baines." Andy Worringer took a seat as John Cooper stepped into the hall and gave a series of quick orders to his men to pack up their gear quietly and prepare to leave.

"We took the same trail you did to come here, Mr. Baines," Andy said as John Cooper returned to ready his own gear. "About ten miles east of town we caught sight of a small troop of Mexican cavalry riding southward. They didn't see us, and we didn't bother with them, because I wanted to get to you as quickly as I could with news of the attack. By the way, Simon Brown says to wish you lots of luck."

"I'll need all of it. I'm indebted to you, Andy."

Ten minutes later, Andy Worringer slipped out of Piedras Negras to rejoin his men and send out the Kiowa scout. John Cooper gave him a half-hour head start, and then, after speaking to the majordomo—who seemed somewhat offended that his guests were deserting him for the dubious comfort of a campfire—the tall Texan led his *vaqueros* out the front door. They walked directly to the stables, and after quickly emptying the remaining provisions from the supply wagon, rode about two miles south of Piedras Negras. There they made camp, lighted fires, and hobbled their horses. John Cooper himself stood guard, holding "Long Girl" at the ready.

The night was still and silent, the heat lingering from the day. Only a few night birds chirped in the distant bushes, and then they, too, were quiet. John Cooper heard the sound of approaching footsteps and leveled his rifle in that direction.

"*Amigo*, it's Andy," came a low call.

"Good! I've been waiting for you."

The Texas Ranger captain approached, with the tall half-breed scout beside him. The brave wore only trousers and moccasins, and to blend in with the night he had rubbed mud onto his naked upper body. Now he turned toward the darkness from which the two of them had emerged and made the call of a coyote. Within a minute, two dozen men on horseback rode up, to be greeted cheerfully by John Cooper's *vaqueros*, many of whom had friends among these Rangers.

"Poromanti has just come back from his scout, Mr. Baines," Andy Worringer said without further ado. "I'll let him tell you what he saw."

"Poromanti, I await your words with eagerness." John Cooper made the universal sign of brotherhood, and the Kiowa *mestizo* answered it by holding up his right hand, palm forward.

"*Wasichu*, there are at least two Mexican camps—the one near the boulders, where I am told you met the general, and another, much bigger camp on the Texas side of the river. This second camp was not there when we arrived, and there are many, many horses.''

John Cooper exchanged a troubled look with the Ranger. ''What else did you learn, Poromanti?'' he asked.

''*Wasichu,* I did not go too near to the large camp, but at the small camp I crept up and listened from atop a large boulder. There was a fire lit, with a *sargento* and a *soldado* standing over it. And the *sargento* said, '*El generalísimo* is too smart for that *yanqui.* He will rid him of his silver, never fear. And if the *gringo* is stubborn, he will never return to his *estancia.*' After I heard that, *wasichu,* I hurried back to my *capitán* to tell him, and now you know.''

''I am in your debt, Poromanti.'' John Cooper made a sign of thanks with his hands, and the Kiowa *mestizo* nodded once and made the reciprocal gesture.

''Andy, it sounds worse than I thought. That sergeant might have been exaggerating a bit, but a campful of cavalry troopers between us and home doesn't leave much room for error. I think I'm going to forget all about that meeting tomorrow.''

''I think you're wise.''

''I would have been wiser never to come'' was John Cooper's blunt reply. ''Looks to me as if Santa Anna had a trap in mind all along, his hostage be damned. Well, at least you've confirmed what I suspected from the beginning. We'd better be getting out of here.''

He turned to issue orders to his men, when the sound of a horse's hooves came suddenly to his ear. ''Now, who's that?'' Instinctively he brought his rifle to bear, and Andy Worringer and Poromanti followed suit. A brown mare and black-clad rider came into the light of the campfire, and John Cooper told the others to hold their fire. It was Don Pablo de Vasconcellos.

''My thanks to *el Señor Dios* that I found you, Señor Baines!'' the old *hidalgo* gasped. ''I had the feeling you might not wish to stay another day in the vicinity of Piedras Negras. Santa Anna has been informed of your absence and has sent for a troop of cavalry to bring you back. They will surely be here within a half hour. And another large body of troops is stationed across the Rio Grande, I have just learned.''

"So have I, señor," John Cooper said. "But I thank you for your warning." Knowing there was no time to waste, John Cooper called out for his men to remount immediately.

Andy Worringer looked concerned. "According to Poromanti here, the Mexican cavalry camp is blocking our escape route."

The white-haired *hidalgo* now interposed: "Señor Baines, I cannot countenance Santa Anna's treachery, especially since you came here under a flag of truce. I know a trail that will take you across the river and around both forces, a trail used by *los indios*. It will at least give you a head start."

"Then you must show us," John Cooper told him. "And you must escape with us, or Santa Anna will punish you severely when he learns what you have done. Unlike you, Don Pablo, he is not a man of honor."

"I will come with you, and willingly." The *hidalgo* frowned. "One day, I am afraid, Señor Baines, that that man will plunge all Mexico into terrible violence and bloodshed. Perhaps my hopes for my country's future have made me blind to this until now."

Felipe Rogales rode up on his pinto. "We are ready, *patrón*."

"Good. We shall follow Don Pablo; he will show us the way." John Cooper turned to the old man, who nodded and spurred his mare onward, heading northeast toward the moon-lit hills.

"*¡Adelante, mis compañeros!*" John Cooper called to his *vaqueros*. "We go home now!"

The fifty-odd horsemen crossed the shallow river without incident, but the Mexican cavalry camp still lay between them and home. Andy Worringer and his Texas Rangers had dropped back to act as a rearguard, and as he and his companions neared the crest of a ridge on the hilly trail, Poromanti pulled his gelding up beside the captain's horse and pointed down to the right, where the campfires of the Mexican camp glowed in the distance. The two men conversed briefly, then Andy, after calling softly to his new sergeant, Moses Wilson, to assume temporary command, spurred his horse up the line, passing the *vaqueros* and reining in beside John Cooper and Don Pablo.

"Anything the matter, Andy?" John Cooper asked. "It still looks pretty quiet down there to me."

"That's just what Poromanti and I were discussing, Mr. Baines," Worringer replied. "It's quiet now, but by morning they'll be able to track us down, and then they'll be on our tail until God knows when. But maybe we can give them something of a good-bye present to slow them up a bit."

John Cooper smiled at the man's audacity. "Thinking of bearding the lion in his own den?"

"Exactly. And if we hit them hard enough, maybe even scatter their horses, they won't be able to follow at all. But this is a job for my Rangers, Mr. Baines, and we wouldn't want to endanger any of the *vaqueros*. Besides, after the attack on the Brazos, we figure it's our turn now."

"Fair enough," John Cooper replied after some hesitation. "If you think your men can handle it alone, that is. I wouldn't want to jeopardize Don Pablo's safety, in any case."

"Nor would I," Andy replied, doffing his hat respectfully to the old *hidalgo*.

"But will you be able to find this trail again?" Don Pablo asked the Ranger. "It is easy to get lost in these hills."

"Poromanti said it will be no trouble, and with luck we'll catch up with the rest of you by daybreak."

After another minute of discussion, the question was settled, and Andy Worringer dropped back in line and directed his Rangers away from the main trail and down a gentle slope toward the Mexican campfires. When the hillside became too steep for the horses to proceed any farther, they were hobbled and left with two of the Rangers, and the rest of the men continued on foot.

As he advanced in a crouch, Andy whispered to Moses Wilson, "We'll spread out along the hill. That way they'll think our force is greater than it is. Pass the word along to the men, and tell them to wait until I open fire."

"Yes, sir, Cap'n!" Moses saluted, then moved down the line, whispering orders and motioning for the others to spread out. In the meantime, Andy and Poromanti crawled within thirty yards of the edge of the camp. There were a score of tents and a few dimming campfires, around which uniformed soldiers sprawled, joking and swigging tequila. Apparently their leaders had not yet been informed of John Cooper's escape.

In front of the nearest tent, a stocky, black-bearded major was talking to a young lieutenant, who saluted and hurried off toward the campfires, while the major went back into the tent, puffing at a cigar he had just lighted.

But Andy's attention was elsewhere. He gazed down at the improvised remuda the soldiers had roped together to herd the horses safely for the night. Motioning with his rifle, he whispered to the Kiowa scout: "If you could get down there without being seen and cut the ropes, Poromanti, they'd be at our mercy."

That was all the instruction the Kiowa needed. "*Sí, capitán*," he said, and then was off, moving as silently as a shadow.

Andy rechecked the priming of his rifle and pistols and took up position behind a pile of small boulders. He watched Poromanti until the brave slipped into a clump of scrubby mesquite and disappeared from sight.

As the minutes passed, the soldiers at the campfire, rousted by the officious young lieutenant, grumblingly gave up their swilling of tequila and went back into their tents. Meanwhile, Poromanti, his knife between his teeth, had reached level, open ground some twenty feet from the remuda. As the horses nickered softly, he flattened himself on his belly and looked carefully this way and that. A fat *soldado* suddenly emerged from the darkness to the right of the rope corral, his porcine figure silhouetted by the flickering embers of a distant campfire. He yawned, and then, glancing furtively behind him, pulled a flask of tequila from inside his tunic.

"*Bueno*, Rinaldo," the soldier said to himself after he had taken a swig; then, because of the harshness of the liquor, he began coughing.

As he did so, Poromanti sprang to his feet and, moving as swiftly and silently as a cat, clamped his left hand over the *soldado*'s mouth, then plunged his knife twice into the man's chest. The soldier slumped without a sound, and Poromanti lowered the lifeless body to the ground. Then, resuming his crouch, he cut the ropes of the corral, slapped the nearest horse on the rump, and uttered the cry of a hoot owl.

The mare lifted its head and galloped out of the enclosure, the other horses following. At that moment, Andy Worringer, squinting down the barrel of his rifle, pulled the trigger and felled a sentry on the opposite side of the remuda. All at once, the other Rangers opened fire, and cries of alarm rose from the camp as half-dressed soldiers rushed out of the tents, carrying sabers and carbines. The major, in his underwear, a half-smoked cigar between his teeth, emerged with a pistol in his right hand. Moses Wilson took careful aim and pulled the trigger; the major spun around, the cigar dropping from his gaping mouth, then sprawled to the ground and lay still.

The young *teniente* whom the major had ordered to dispel the tippling soldiers came out of his tent, eyes wide with shock at the unexpected attack. One of the Rangers aimed and fired, and the ball took the officer in the fleshy part of his right arm. Undaunted, the lieutenant transferred his pistol to his other hand and began running through the line of tents, bidding his men to flatten themselves onto the ground and take aim at the flash of the enemy's firearms. Meanwhile, a gray-haired *capitán*, who in the opening volley had been wounded in the left calf, saw that the major was dead, and quickly took command. He called out orders to a burly *sargento* to lead the men by way of the now-empty remuda and scale the hills to carry the battle to the unknown enemy.

The Mexicans were just starting to rally when Poromanti, bullets hitting the ground nearby, leaped astride the last fleeing horse and, crouching low on its bare back, urged it up the hill.

By now the night was filled with the noise of rifle, musket, and pistol fire, the hoarse shouts of the Mexican officers, and the frantic orders of corporals and sergeants who sought to rally their hesitant men. But it was evident that the troops held back for good reason, because the rifle fire from the Rangers above was murderously accurate. Already at least seven Mexican soldiers had been killed and three others wounded. Nevertheless, the gray-haired *capitán*, cursing as he hobbled forward, managed to urge some three dozen troopers up the base of the hill.

They had scarcely advanced twenty yards, however, when Andy Worringer, Moses Wilson, and six other Rangers rose from cover and, shouting "*A free Texas!*" unleashed a volley of rifle and pistol fire at close range. Several of the Mexicans fell dead or wounded, and others, frightened witless by these ghostlike raiders materializing from nowhere, turned tail and stumbled back down the hill.

The *capitán* and nearly a dozen others still came on, however, and Andy and Moses, each with a brace of pistols, killed two more and wounded a third. But the Rangers on either side of them had been wounded in the return fire, and the valiant *capitán*, heartened by this, brandished his saber and urged his remaining men forward as the Rangers wisely began to fall back. Near him, a private aimed a pistol at Andy and pulled the trigger; in his haste the shot was low and only grazed the Ranger's leg, but it was enough to send him to the ground.

At last seeing his chance for revenge, the Mexican captain snarled, "Now you die, *gringo!*" and pulling back his saber, aimed a thrust at Andy's belly. Moses Wilson had triggered his remaining pistol, only to have it misfire, and with a frantic oath he flung himself at the enemy captain, knocking him over as the point of the saber dug harmlessly into the earth only inches from Andy's midsection. Using the butt of his pistol, the freed black struck again and again until the Mexican captain lay inert.

"C'mon, Cap'n, let's get the hell out of here!" Moses panted, reaching down to help Andy to his feet. Behind them, a grim-faced Mexican corporal raised a saber, but a Ranger farther up the hill saw this and quickly aimed his rifle. The shot rang out and the corporal stiffened, eyes enormous as he dropped dead.

Glancing behind him, Moses quickly sized up the situation and hoarsely said, "Guess we're even, Cap'n. C'mon, now, let's get back to the horses. . . ."

A few minutes later, all the Rangers, including the wounded, who had been dragged back, mounted their horses and, after getting off a last few rifle shots at their demoralized pursuers, set off uphill for the trail. It would take the Mexican cavalry troop the better part of the next day to round up their scattered horses and attend to their wounded, and despite his own flesh wound, Andy Worringer could not keep from smiling with deep satisfaction as he took his place at the head of his Texas Rangers.

Santa Anna paced back and forth outside his tent, his face twisted in a furious scowl. He looked up to see a young bearded lieutenant hurrying toward him and only grudgingly returned the officer's enthusiastic salute. "What is it, *Teniente* Morabito?" he growled.

"The *gringo* has escaped, *excelencia!*"

"But how is that possible? *Estúpido,* tell me how! Did I not have troops to the northeast of Piedras Negras, by which way he would have had to go to return to his accursed *estancia*?"

"*Sí, mi general,* but the *gringo* must have taken another trail of which we know nothing. There is no sign of him anywhere."

"You bring me the worst of news! Quickly, I order that you immediately ride to the cavalry camp and send them after the *gringos* tonight. They must not be allowed to escape!"

The *teniente* looked as white as death. "I am afraid that is impossible, *excelencia.* There was a raid on the camp this very evening, and . . . and the horses were scattered. They will not be able to find them until—"

Santa Anna spoke between clenched teeth. "Do you mean to tell me that we cannot give chase to the *gringo*?"

"I fear that is the case, *excelencia;* but when the morning comes—"

Santa Anna could stand no more. "Out of my sight!" he shouted. "Before I demote you to corporal! All of my officers will answer for this tomorrow!"

As the *teniente* hurried off, Santa Anna turned in the direction of the little town and, clenching his fists, shook them at the skies. "May all the devils in hell take that accursed *yanqui* and all the damned *tejanos*! He thinks he has tricked me—me, *el libertador, el generalísimo* Antonio López de Santa Anna! Surely, *el Diablo* must protect him!"

Suddenly a thought occurred to Santa Anna, and he shouted for one of his aides, a sallow-faced *capitán* by the name of Martin Perez.

"*Capitán* Perez," the general began, "I have reason to suspect the continued loyalty of one of my subordinates— Colonel Luis Dominguez, to be precise. I shall convene a summary court-martial this morning on the charges of . . . oh, say, traitorous activities, and I need you to see to the formalities of having his estate seized and his command reassigned. Oh—and you should also post guards on the road to San Antonio, just in case the traitor has the nerve to return from his secret rendezvous with the *tejanos*. Give them orders to shoot to kill. That will be all."

"*Sí, mi general.*" The loyal subaltern clicked his booted heels and left.

With that troublesome matter disposed of, Santa Anna returned to his previous thoughts of how best to seek revenge against the cursed *gringo*.

"*O Señor Dios,*" he muttered aloud as he recommenced his pacing, "I pray to you for vengeance! I won't cease until I have defeated this Yankee dog and all the *americanos*, driven them from the sacred soil of the motherland! This I swear to you by all I revere and by all my hopes of becoming the savior of my poor, oppressed people!"

Galloping through the night, John Cooper and his *vaqueros*, reunited with Andy Worringer's Texas Rangers, put distance between themselves and the little town of Piedras Negras, which had been meant to be their death trap. At dawn on Monday, May 26, in the year of 1828, they rode under the archway of the Double H Ranch. And when Miguel Sandarbal and Raoul Maldones hurried out to welcome him home, John Cooper dismounted and said, "I don't think I've ever felt better about coming home, Miguel, Raoul! Santa Anna had a little trap prepared for us, but thanks to God and the help of Don Pablo de Vasconcellos here, we escaped without any serious casualties. And I guess I should also thank Andy Worringer and his Rangers."

"But you met Santa Anna? And you heard what he had to propose?" Raoul anxiously asked.

"As he said in the letter, he proposed to take the silver in return for letting the settlers alone. But with a troop of cavalry at our backs, we weren't given much room to bargain! If I'd known that when I started out, I'd have sent his precious colonel back to him and saved everybody a lot of time," John Cooper declared.

Miguel and Raoul exchanged a worried look, and the tall buckskin-clad Texan, seeing this, frowned and demanded, "What are you keeping from me?"

"It's just that . . . well," Miguel hesitantly began, glancing again at Raoul, "Colonel Dominguez tried to escape one night—probably the night that you arrived in Piedras Negras. Maybe that's what he was counting on. At any rate, Ramón found him trying to get a horse out of the stable, and the colonel must have stolen a kitchen knife, and he tried to kill Ramón. By the grace of God, Ramón escaped with a few bruises and a bad gash, but—well, he had to kill the colonel."

"That is certain to bring reprisal upon us, do you not think so, *mi yerno*?" Raoul worriedly asked.

"I think we're going to be the object of Santa Anna's wrath, no matter what happened here, *mi suegro*" was John Cooper's thoughtful answer. "I think that Santa Anna washed his hands of Colonel Dominguez when he sent him here—the main purpose being to get me to Piedras Negras so he could get the silver. Dominguez might have suspected that, but whatever the case, I'm sure Ramón did what he had to do."

"He acted in self-defense, of that there is no doubt," Miguel declared.

"Ramón's a good man," John Cooper said, "and we're going to need more like him, for it looks to me that every settler in this entire territory of Texas is going to have to strengthen himself against what I believe to be an inevitable war."

"A gloomy prospect, indeed," Miguel sighed.

"Pray God I'm wrong, Miguel. And pray to God that, one day soon, this territory will become part of the United States, for that's what it will take to hold off a vulture like Santa Anna. Until then, every man who loves freedom, like

Andy Worringer and his Rangers, and like you, Miguel, and you, Raoul—until then, we will fight, if we must, to defend our right to live here in freedom and decency, in the sight of Him Who made us all.''

★ WAGONS WEST ★

A series of unforgettable books that trace the lives of a dauntless band of pioneering men, women, and children as they brave the hazards of an untamed land in their trek across America. This legendary caravan of people forge a new link in the wilderness. They are Americans from the North and the South, alongside immigrants, Blacks, and Indians, who wage fierce daily battles for survival on this uncompromising journey—each to their private destinies as they fulfill their greatest dreams.

☐	24408	INDEPENDENCE! #1	$3.95
☐	24651	NEBRASKA! #2	$3.95
☐	24229	WYOMING! #3	$3.95
☐	24088	OREGON! #4	$3.95
☐	24848	TEXAS! #5	$3.95
☐	24655	CALIFORNIA! #6	$3.95
☐	24694	COLORADO! #7	$3.95
☐	25091	NEVADA! #8	$3.95
☐	25010	WASHINGTON! #9	$3.95
☐	22925	MONTANA! #10	$3.95
☐	23572	DAKOTA! #11	$3.95
☐	23921	UTAH! #12	$3.95
☐	24256	IDAHO! #13	$3.95
☐	24584	MISSOURI! #14	$3.95
☐	24976	MISSISSIPPI! #15	$3.95

Prices and availability subject to change without notice.

Buy them at your local bookstore or use this handy coupon: